# Foreign & Domestic

## *Part II*

## *Hannibal is at the Gates*

# Foreign & Domestic

## *Part II*

## *Hannibal is at the Gates*

*By: David J. Kershner*

# Character List – Part II
## (alphabetical by last name/maiden name)

*Adar* – Iranian terrorist, follower of Suhrab Esfahani

*Alysin Baker* – Pathologist, member of the Tin Foil Hat Club

*Mimi Bessum* – Proprietor of Mama Renie's Restaurant

*Bryan Billson* – former neighbor to Josh and Amanda Simmons, friend of the Simmons family

*Emily Calhoun Chastain* – Doctor, researcher, wife to Gregg Chastain

*Gregg 'Longbow' Chastain* –US Army Operator, husband to Emily Chastain

*Chester Daniels* – Nuclear Engineer, member of the Tin Foil Hat Club

*Kristen Delgado* – Sister of Amanda Simmons (deceased), former sister-in law to Josh Simmons, aunt to Layla and Katherine Simmons

*Javy Dolbrow* – Drug dealer, rapist

*Abbas Esfahani* – Iranian terrorist, brother to Suhrab Esfahani

*Suhrab Esfahani* – Iranian terrorist, leader of jihadi cell, brother to Abbas Esfahani

*Lawrence (Larry) Fielding* – Secretary of Defense

*Harold Goodspeed* – Prime Minister of United Kingdom

*Victor Henry* – Portland (Oregon) Police Officer

*Brent Howard* – Chairman of Joint Chiefs, General in USMC, Josh Simmons' former CO, father to Jessica Howard (deceased), grandfather to Heather Howard

*Heather Howard* – Actress, stage name Heather White, daughter to Jessica Howard (deceased) and Josh Simmons, grand-daughter to Brent Howard

*Jessica Howard (deceased)* – Actress, stage name Jessica White, daughter to Brent Howard, mother to Heather Howard

*Wilson James* – Colonel in the US Army, Doctor of Psychology

*Samantha (Sam) Jameson* – Retired USAF Colonel, Hyloset CEO (a GMO corporation)

*Navid Kashani* – Iranian terrorist, follower of Suhrab Esfahani

*Mahtab* – Iranian terrorist, follower of Suhrab Esfahani

*Abelardo Martinez* – Assistant Farm Manager, son of Juan and Basilia Martinez, brother to Jesus Martinez, friend to Simmons family

*Basilia Martinez* – Doctor, wife to Juan Martinez, mother to Jesus and Abelardo Martinez

*Jesus Martinez* – Tracker, son of Juan and Basilia Martinez, brother to Abelardo Martinez, friend of Simmons family

*Juan Martinez* – Manager of Josh's farm, husband to Basilia Martinez, father to Jesus and Abelardo Martinez

*Elias McInerney* – USDA Secretary, granduncle to Mara McInerney

*Mara McInerney* – Exec assistant to USDA Secretary, grandniece to Elias McInerney

*Dallas McKutcheon* – Childhood friend of Josh Simmons, friend to Simmons family

*Edward Monahan* – Secret Service Agent, currently assigned to former President James Sarkes

*Evan Noosman* – Unofficial protection detail to Layla and Katherine Simmons, friend to the Simmons family

*James (Jim) Rayburn* – President of the United States (current)

*Carlos 'Hoplite' Rayna* – Captain in the US Army, former CO to Gregg Chastain

*James Rooney* – Retired USMC Sergeant, former NCO to Josh Simmons, friend to Simmons family

*Thomas Sarkes* –President of the United States (former)

*Amanda Simmons (deceased)* – VA nurse, ex-wife to Josh Simmons, mother to Layla Simmons and Katherine Simmons

*Josiah (Josh) Grant Simmons* – Farmer, Retired USMC Lt. Colonel, former POW, ex-husband to Amanda Simmons (deceased), father to Layla Simmons, Katherine Simmons, and Heather Howard

*Katherine Simmons* – College student, former kidnapping victim, daughter of Josh and Amanda Simmons (deceased), sister to Layla Simmons

*Layla Simmons* – College student, former kidnapping victim, daughter of Josh and Amanda Simmons (deceased), sister to Katherine Simmons

*Eustace Stokes* – Lieutenant in the US Army, Combat Engineering platoon CO

*Anna Sullivan* – Sister to Airmen Cecil Sullivan

*Cecil Sullivan* – Airmen in USAF, brother to Anna Sullivan

*Lily Summers* – Biochemist, member of the Tin Foil Hat Club

*Taj* – Iranian terrorist, follower of Suhrab Esfahani

*James (Jim) Watson* – Sheriff of McArthur, Ohio, friend to Josh Simmons

*Declan Edward Wrigley* – Orphaned child

# Chapter 1

Former President Tom Sarkes exited the armored limousine with his usual compliment of Secret Service Agents in front of The Hague's United Nations Complex. Given his previous position and title, he was quickly spirited around the assorted security measures and went straight to the U.S. Ambassador's office.

Without so much as a 'Hello', Tom threw his overcoat and briefcase in a leather upholstered chair, and emphatically questioned, "What the hell have you done?"

"Me?" the Ambassador replied with equal emphasis. "Correct me if I'm wrong, but weren't *you* the President when we forfeited our Permanent Seat on the Security Council? Wasn't it *you* that took a more isolationist stance toward foreign policy? My predecessors and I have been trying to clean up *your* mess ever since."

Sensing where and how this conversation was going to go, the Secret Service Agents quietly backed out of the Ambassadors office and discreetly closed the door as they departed. The five Agents then took their standard defensive positions.

"That's bull and you know it! You and *your* predecessors have been asleep at the wheel," Tom shot back. "Bunch of idiots. While you and your wives were off rubbing elbows at every banquet and ball, the British Prime Minister and his cronies have been busy re-writing international finance law. I've just spent a week in a dank NSA basement culling over every piece of intercepted communication between that conniving jackass and the heads of every country that owns our debt. Hell, I've even read through all of the data provided by the

French. It seems that there's still an ember of hatred for the English, turns out empires never really die."

Tom paused for a moment to assess the diplomat's body language. It was clear that he was unaware of any of what Tom had just said.

"You haven't got a clue, do you?"

"President Rayburn just called me and informed me of our predicament," the man replied with pride.

"Did you know what I was talking about before then?"

"Well, no," he answered haltingly. "We aren't privy to secure NSA intercepts. The only intel we receive is filtered through the State Department after it's been scrubbed," the Ambassador replied in defense.

"Open your eyes man! How is this country even moving forward with you morons running the show?" Tom said more to the empty room than to the Ambassador.

Having been in politics long enough to know when to keep his mouth shut, the UN Ambassador stood stoically until President Sarkes engaged him in the conversation once more.

After spending days on end at the NSA, and another seven hours in solitude on the flight, Tom had formulated a plan to try and head off the Prime Minister.

"I want you to call the French Ambassador and set up a meeting for tomorrow morning. Tell them that we need to have a face-to-face," Tom instructed.

"What makes you think they'll agree, or even show up?" the Ambassador questioned.

"Because, you're gonna say it's *me* that's requesting the sit down," Tom replied.

"Why don't you call them yourself?" the Ambassador answered incredulously. "I'm not your secretary!"

The two paused to take stock of one another before the diplomat continued. "Why don't you fill me in on whatever is going on... maybe I can be of assistance. I've only had a five-minute conversation with President Rayburn. He had enough time to hit the highlights and to inform me that you had just landed at Schiphol airport."

Exhaling loudly, Tom turned to the Ambassador and said, "Take a seat."

\* \* \*

The French Ambassador to the UN glanced down at the screen on his smart phone. The device had vibrated in his pocket to alert him to the incoming call. With the display lit up, the caller ID read: U.S. Ambassador.

*Well, that didn't take long*, he thought as he pressed the 'Decline' button. Former President Sarkes had been in the country barely two hours. The diplomat accessed the text message app on his phone. He quickly typed: *Finishing up with PM Windbag. Meet ur office in 30. Bringing friend. Adieu.*

The information was relayed to Sarkes and both men sighed in relief that the French were expecting the call.

Thirty-five minutes later the Frenchman walked in with the Director of their Foreign Intelligence Service (DGSE). The head of the DGSE looked like a character right out of a 1940's film noir spy caper, complete with tan trench coat. The two bypassed the American Diplomat and went straight to Tom. They exchanged handshakes and began a conversation. As they conversed and renewed their friendship, they completely ignored the U.S. Ambassador. The trio and their friendship went back over a decade, all the way to the early years of Sarkes' presidency. It was with the heavy heart, and the best wishes of the French, that he planned and executed the United States exit from the Security Council.

The three promptly raided the U.S. diplomat's liquor cabinet for the scotch and took seats around a circular table in the Ambassador's office. When the pleasantries were out of the way, President Sarkes said bluntly, "So what's the word?"

"Monsieur President, if you and your countrymen were not on the wrong side of this, I would actually admire the work he has put forth. The Prime Minister has managed to cobble together just about every nation holding U.S. debt."

"But to what end, Gabe?" Tom said, referring to the Ambassador informally.

"Monsieur, based on the briefing we just sat through, it is his intention to incite a financial coup d'état. They have written and revised so many international finance laws that the United States might as well declare bankruptcy."

"What does that even mean? We'd never do that."

"Thomas, if I may," the Ambassador began. "If every nation holding U.S. debt were to try and collect all at once, could it be paid?"

"Hell no. That's over thirty trillion dollars. We've been off the gold standard for nearly a century and using fiat money ever since. Given the current levels of U.S. debt, no, we couldn't even come close to paying that. No nation could do that," Tom answered with his usual candor.

Prior to absolving itself from the gold standard, the United States Treasury functioned similarly to a casino. They had to 'guarantee every chip on the floor'. When the United States walked away from the long held global system two years after the British in 1933, it essentially stopped guaranteeing the dollar domestically. It wasn't until 1971 that the U.S. stopped the practice internationally. Complicating matters for the United States was the involvement of the International Monetary Fund (IMF). The institution had been entrenched in international finance and currency exchange since WWII. Every dirty little secret the United States had regarding its debts was known to the powers that be in the IMF. If this organization were assisting the English, there wasn't any path that would allow the U.S. to force or bluff its way out of any international financial obligations.

"Monsieur, I would start preparing for that eventuality," Gabriel replied just as candidly. "According to the latest plan from the British, austerity sanctions will take immediate effect if it cannot pay. The interest rates for any 'assistance' in the form of multiple bailout loans would be exorbitant and extremely painful. If the United States doesn't 'voluntarily' shrink its expenditures to less than 20% of its Gross Domestic Product, then a provisional international board is convened to 'assist' the government."

"Holy shit," Tom muttered.

"Exactement," the French Ambassador replied.

Pausing to let the weight of the information sink in, President Sarkes asked the obligatory question, "And if we refuse?"

Gabriel clicked his tongue rapidly before saying, "No, no, no, Monsieur. You do not want to do that."

"Why not?"

"If the United States refuses, the UN has authorized the use of force to collect as much hard currency as possible."

"WHAT!" Tom exclaimed.

"Oui," Gabriel replied.

"No foreign army has stepped foot on American soil in over two hundred years! There are over 350 million firearms in the United States right now... probably more. Hell, there's almost twenty million registered hunters. That doesn't even account for the highly trained veterans that'll stand up and lead and teach tactics. This is absurd! They better bring a healthy supply of body bags because there's gonna be a lot of blood spilled! What are they gonna do... raid Fort Knox!?"

"Oui, and how ever many Treasury banks, branches, mints, foreign accounts, and bank vaults it takes until they have their trillions," the Ambassador replied knowingly.

President Sarkes slumped back in his chair, sighed, and said, "Complete madness... Hannibal ad portas."

"Oui, Monsieur," Gabriel replied.

"What's that?" the American Ambassador asked.

"It's Latin," Sarkes replied, crestfallen that he had to even explain it. "It means 'Hannibal is at the gates'. The Romans used to teach it their children," the former President answered with his head leaned back and his eyes closed. He concluded, "The spoils of war then. But why do this?"

Looking up at the French Ambassador, he added, "They have their own financial problems. Invading us won't absolve them of their own obligations. They'll spend billions trying to take ours. It doesn't make any sense."

Gabriel glanced over at the Minister Pinault, "Monsieur."

The Head of the DGSE cleared his throat and said in heavily accented English, "A few months ago, Prime Minister Goodspeed flew covertly on a commercial airliner to meet your President Rayburn. He also met with heads of the Federal Reserve and the Treasury. At that time, he attempted to broker a back door deal for several hundred billion dollars that the U.K. owned of U.S. debt."

"I know. Rayburn told him to take a hike," Sarkes stated.

"Oui," Minister Pinault replied. "This situation is not all that dissimilar to the Iraqi's and Kuwaiti's."

The U.S. Ambassador was thoroughly confused. "What does the freeing of Kuwait have to do with England thinking about invading the United States?"

"My God man! How did you even get this job?" Sarkes exhorted. "The Iraqi's invaded the country over an insult. They were negotiating oil rights in the region and the little nation didn't like being bullied by its big brother. When the delegation stormed out, the Kuwaiti Ambassador spat on his counterpart. That's a huge deal, a major insult over there. King George is feeling just as aggrieved."

"He wants you... oh, merde. What's the translation for 'sur les genoux'?" Minister Pinault asked.

"On our knees?" Sarkes asked.

"Oui, Monsieur. On bended knee begging for mercy."

"Well, they're in for one hell of a shock when they get to Kentucky," Tom inserted.

"Why's that? How much is there?" the U.S. Ambassador asked.

"Next to nothing now," Tom replied. "We've already started relocating a great deal of our assets."

"Monsieur," the Minister said. "Forgive me, but you are in checkmate."

"Sir, shouldn't we call President Rayburn!" the inexperienced diplomat proclaimed in a panic. "Tell him what's going on and that we need to go faster! We –,"

The former President rolled his eyes and calmly responded, "Relax, relax. 'Operation Delta' started weeks ago. In a month or so, all of the vaults will be empty and the resources safely hidden away. Screw the British. If they want another Revolution under the auspices of the UN flag, there's not much we can do to stop it now."

# Chapter 2

The three women cautiously approached Javy with their weapons drawn. Once they were satisfied that he was alive, but unconscious, they removed the noose and tied him to the oak tree with a series of constrictor knots.

While Layla was finishing her knot, she asked, "So the photographer thing, you knew who we were the whole time?"

"Pretty much," Heather answered as she watched the two check the horses. "Are you guys headed back to your farm?"

"Yeah. We need to call the Sheriff," Katherine answered then asked, "You wanna ride?"

"Can I? I'm pretty exhausted," Heather replied matter of factly.

Smiling, Katherine replied, "Hop on."

Satisfied with Javy tied to the tree, the three mounted the two horses and rode the remaining distance back to the farm. On the way, Heather detailed their fathers visit to California and the conversation they had. She explained how she had tracked him down only to be turned away by their mother. Javy hadn't lied about any of it. Layla and Katherine just listened. Once inside the barn, they quickly unsaddled the horses, brushed out their coats, and placed them in their stalls with water and feed.

"You ready to meet your father? Officially?" Katherine asked.

"You don't think he'll be mad? Me just showing up like this?" Heather asked, starting to second-guess her decision.

"Seriously? He basically told you to come find him. Besides, he has a lot of explaining to do," Layla answered.

The three headed to the front porch and entered the house expecting to see an irate Evan. What they didn't expect to find was their father's employee, the Martinez family, the Sheriff, *and* their father examining a relief map of the Hocking Hills region over the dining room table.

"What took you guys so long," Evan demanded to know.

"We were waylaid," Layla answered. She then turned her head and said, "Come on in."

Heather crossed the threshold and in to view of the others.

"Heather? What happened?" Josh said as he went to her and surveyed her battered face.

"Hi, Dad."

Josh smiled at her softly.

Basilia walked over and immediately began examining Heather's injuries. As she looked her over, she said aloud, "This swelling will go down in a couple days, but these cuts and abrasions need cleaning. Josh, where's your med kit?"

"Upstairs. I'll show you," he replied and escorted the pair to the medical supplies stowed in the bathroom cupboard. When he started to make his way back toward the group in the living room, he heard Layla explaining what had happened.

"Javy followed her from the movie set – ,"

All heads immediately snapped in her direction.

"WHAT!" her father said forcefully from the top of the stairs. "Where is he?!"

"Calm down, Dad. We took care of him," she said as she casually walked over to the map sprawled out on the table. She reviewed it, collected her bearing, and pointed to a spot. "He's tied up to that big white oak right about here. He's got a rope burn around his neck and a few extra holes though."

"You hung him *and* shot him?" the Sheriff said incredulously.

"Well, yeah. He was beating the crap out of her when we came up on them, so Katherine put a round in his shoulder to get his attention. Then he held a knife to her throat, so I hit him again in the other one. After what he did to me as a child, and what he attempted to do to my new sister, the least we could do was give him a dose of his own medicine. Besides," she concluded, "he deserved it."

Behind them the front door slammed shut.

Josh was gone.

He had heard Layla's description and seen where she had pointed on the map. That was all he needed. If he had his way, the last living cretin that had stolen his daughter's innocent youth wasn't going to see the next sunrise.

Startled by the slamming door, Katherine ran over and yanked on the handle. "Daddy, NO!" she screamed into the evening air.

With the exception of Heather and Basilia, the house immediately emptied and went in pursuit of Josh. On his way out, Evan checked for his boss's Beretta.

It was gone.

As the search party began exiting, the barn doors burst open. Josh and his Rhino quickly filled the void. He turned the wheel hard over to start heading toward the forest trail. The abrupt command put the vehicle up on two wheels. He deftly regained control and in a flash, before most were off the porch, the tail lights disappeared into the wilderness.

The group scrambled into the Sheriff's Blazer and Juan's truck and went in pursuit of their father, friend, and employer. The four-wheel drives made quick work of the gap in distance and arrived at Javy's location just as Josh was exiting his ATV.

Josh began marching steadfastly toward the semi-conscious Javy. His daughters watched in horror as he drew his weapon level. Before the Blazer came to a complete stop, Evan jumped out and sprinted towards Josh.

Continuing to close the distance between the two, Josh flicked the safety off and started directing it at his target. Tunnel vision was forming as he zeroed in on the pronounced welt from Layla's pistol whipping.

*Die you little son-of-a* –...

Just as the powder in the cartridge was being ignited, Evan slammed into his employer and disrupted Josh's careful aim. The bark above Javy's head exploded from the impact of the discharged round as the two tumbled to the ground. The crack of the weapon echoing through the forest made the girls scream in protest.

Josh actively resisted being restrained and continued to do so until the Sheriff cuffed him. Through it all, Josh could hear the bound man taunting him.

Javy was inciting the rage of his executioner, "I can't believe you missed! Some Carlos Hathcock you are! If they had sent you instead of Lee Harvey, JFK would still be bangin' movie stars and cocktail waitresses. Maybe it would be easier for you if I was hanging in a warehouse!"

No sooner had Josh been brought to his feet as he took off running toward Javy. He managed to get a boot to the side of the taunting man's head before he was dragged down by Evan again.

Josh screamed out in anger and pleaded to be un-cuffed. The Sheriff drove his knee into Josh's spine until he relaxed.

When Javy caught sight of the Jim in his uniform, he upped his ante. "You sissy bitch! You brought the 'man' with you? What's the matter Mr. Macho-Marine, you afraid to go mano-a-mano with me?" the scrawny malnourish addict asked. Then he started singing, "Bad boys, bad boys..."

Once calm, Josh was helped to his feet and dragged back to his Rhino, Javy just kept singing. The prisoner bound to the tree couldn't resist and switched his tune, "Na-na-nah-na, na-na-nah-na, hey, hey, hey, goodbye..." as his would-be killer was removed.

Unable to bear her father's agony, Katherine walked over to Javy and provocatively straddled his immobilized legs. She had experienced enough of life at this point to know what made men tick. Javy lost interest in his taunts as she slowly and seductively lowered herself down to just above his groin. She could tell he was becoming excited by their proximity.

In a low sultry whisper she said, "Hey, Javy."

The man that had haunted their restless nights for over a decade became very still. His singular focus now was to satisfy his urges. Katherine was batting them around like a kitten with a ball of string.

"When you're sitting in your jail cell, I want you to think about only one thing," she began as she drew closer to his ear.

"Ooo, I'm gonna enjoy this. What should I dream of, sweet little Katherine?" he cooed. "Tell me. Tell me, tell me," he begged.

"He may have missed you, but I sure as hell didn't," she said as she jammed her thumb in one of his bullet wounds. Javy howled in agony. When she stood up, she forcefully added, "Now shut up!"

The lawman and Evan placed Josh in the passenger seat of the Rhino as Heather and Basilia arrived in Josh's truck.

"Take him back to the house, Juan," Sheriff Watson commanded. "And make sure he stays there."

He then turned and looked at his friend. "That was stupid, Josh," he said as he exhaled. To ensure that he was paying attention, and to let Josh know he was serious, he said, "This isn't a warehouse. You catch my meaning?"

Josh shot back a glare that screamed murderous intent.

"If you leave the house, I will arrest you. There is no double jeopardy law to save you. Am I clear?" the Sheriff asked.

"Crystal," Josh growled in reply.

\* \* \*

After Juan returned Josh to the cabin and uncuffed him, the protective father was unable to just sit idle and simply wait for them to return. Josh spent the next hours cooking in an effort to divert his aggression and anger. The two men barely said a word.

With all of the cars, trucks, and ambulances coming and going up and down the driveway, the wired alarm system was constantly chiming and dinging. In a fit of madness and frustration, Josh had ripped the device from the wall.

Once the girls had given their statements to the Sheriff, and Javy had been unceremoniously shoved into the ambulance under heavy guard, they were returned to their father. Heather was gratefully relieved to hear that her manager was still alive. Her friend was bruised and battered, but conscious and en route to the hospital.

After being released by the Sheriff, the three girls, without so much as a peep, walked through the front door and immediately headed upstairs to find warm dry clothes. The girls were cold and wet from the rain, but no one was tired. The adrenaline was keeping them going for the time being. Basilia started a fire in an attempt to take the chill off of the girls and the cool fall air. The Martinez family took their leave for the evening when it became apparent that Josh needed to be alone with his daughters.

Josh asked the trio downstairs. They came when called, but rebuffed his enticements of food. After enough glares had been flashed his way, he asked the three to take a seat on the couch. Without uttering a word, Josh produced Amanda's letter.

For Josh, trying to find the right words would have only generated a long drawn out debate. The letter would explain their intertwined histories far better than he could. The only person that could provide the answers that they each were seeking was his ex-wife.

He handed the letter to Layla, walked to the kitchen, and began fixing a plate of food. His girls sat huddled, with a fire crackling in the fireplace, and read word for word, how the events and their lives had been thrust together by time and circumstance.

*My Dearest Josh,*

*Hi, my name is Amanda and... I am an addict. I guess the secret's out on that one. I've said that to absolute strangers in a hundred AA and NA meetings, but I never said it to the one person that I should have... you.*

*FACT: If you are reading this, I am dead. Doesn't much matter why or how, dead is dead.*

Layla and Katherine flipped page after page and read as their mother detailed the path and life choices that led to her dark addictions. Most of it was already known to them from their aunt. Amanda's next item of business was to explain why she had regressed back into her dependencies.

*I cleaned myself up and became a nurse, your nurse actually. Remember how we met at the VA? We were happy with two beautiful daughters living the American dream. Then the cards came crashing down when Jessica's daughter appeared on our doorstep. Decades of sobriety went out the window in an instant.*

*She said her name was Heather, and she seemed like a very nice young lady. I'm sure she meant well. After all, she just wanted to meet her father. Unfortunately, what she didn't know was that I was sworn to secrecy by her grandfather. He came to visit you in the hospital when you were in the coma. Brent took one look at you and all of those tubes and machines, read the doctor's prognosis, and he knew. Well, I should say he figured you'd never be the same man he had entrusted with his daughter.*

"What a cruel bastard," Katherine said under her breathe. "No offense, Heather."

"None taken, I have my own issues with that man. Don't worry, we'll be talking."

*He never lost hope in your recovery though. You may not have known this, but he was the anonymous source that provided your military records to Giuseppe during the trial... not that he'd ever admit it of course. In the end, it looks like he saved you as much as you did Jessica.*

"Well at least he redeemed himself by keeping Dad off death row," Heather offered.

"I wouldn't be so quick to sing his praises just yet. Wait til you need the next paragraph," Layla replied.

*Unfortunately, for my side of the bargain, he asked me to do whatever it took to prevent any of the media coverage from reaching you. He didn't want you to hear a single mention of Jessica or the child you two had created. So, I did as promised. I broke TV's, abruptly changed channels, and cancelled subscriptions. I did everything I could in order to keep my promise.*

"That son of a bitch," Heather said incredulously.

*I didn't do it for him though. I did it for me. I thought that if I kept you from all of that then I could keep you for myself. I thought I could hide you away from the rest of the world. You were, and are, a good man who would do anything for his family, and I blew it. When Heather showed up, I felt everything crashing down around me. I was convinced if you ever knew that she existed you'd leave me and the girls to fend for ourselves.*

"Hey, Dad?" Layla called out to her father.

"Yeah?" he replied eagerly as he poked his head out of the kitchen doorway.

"You wouldn't have left us if you knew, would you?"

"No sweetie. I took a vow. It would have been difficult, but I would have done everything in my power to make it work so we all knew Heather and Jessica. I –," he said as he tried to provide a thorough answer.

While he was answering, she continued to read. "Never mind, mom answered it," she said cutting him off.

Undeterred, Josh lingered in the doorway. He knew more questions were coming his way.

*In hindsight, you'd have never done that, but how was I going to compete with a movie star? The simple answer was that I couldn't, or, at least I didn't think I could. So I had a drink. That led to another, and another, and another, and that's when I met Emil Bedford. He eventually reintroduced me to an old friend, heroin.*

"Holy crap!" Katherine exclaimed. "That *was* mom in the warehouse!"

*Once I started using again, the affair started and it all went sideways. I told him about your uncle's wealth and we hatched the plan. I swear, the girls were never supposed to be hurt. The ransom would be paid, the girls would be released, and Emil and I would split the money. I was convinced you were going to leave me and I didn't want to be left with nothing. I thought I could control the addiction. I was a misguided fool, but the heroin took me further down the rabbit hole. I couldn't get out. Those two lecherous bastards in the warehouse deserved everything they got from you and then some. I wanted you to know that. Unfortunately, one got away. I wish I could tell you who he was, but I honestly don't remember.*

"That dirty bitch sold us to feed her addictions because she was afraid of being alone? What kind of mother does that?" Katherine said to no one.

*I know you knew. I think I told you when you were in jail, but I can recall so very little about those days, weeks, and months. Even if you did manage to make sense of what I'm sure was incoherent drug induced babble, you never told the girls, and for that I am grateful.*

"So all this time, when one of us would mention trying to forgive her, you would always say you could never do that. Her confession in the jailhouse, is that why?" Layla asked her father.

"Something like that," he said briefly so as to not be cut off again.

"It either is or it isn't. It is *not* 'something like that'," she scolded.

"You want full disclosure?" he asked, annoyed at her tone.

"I think we are entitled to it now, don't you think!" she shot back.

"Yes, she confessed in the jailhouse, but it was damn near incoherent, like she said. As a result, I never knew if it was her or the heroin doing the talking. When I got this letter from Kristin at the funeral, I lost it all right," he answered.

"So this is what sent you on a bender? Why didn't you just tell us?" Katherine asked.

"Because you guys had just lost your mother. As screwed up as she was, I didn't know how you two were going to handle that," he replied.

"So drinking yourself silly was your answer," his youngest replied flatly.

"Seemed like a good idea at the time," her father answered sheepishly.

"And your clandestine trip to California?" Heather asked.

"When the booze ran out, I finally realized what she had written and why she went back to the drugs. She had been successful at keeping Jessica's pregnancy from me. I didn't know a thing about you other than what was in the letter. Then when I saw your mother had been killed in a car crash, I knew I had to try and find you. When I got there though, I chickened out. You had just lost *your* mother and I wasn't entirely sure how the whole 'Hi, I'm your long lost Dad' thing was going to go. On top of that, Brent had successfully lied to you for your entire life. He was there too and I wasn't prepared to deal with him, so I dropped some subtle clues and came back home praying you understood."

Satisfied with his answers, the girls returned their attention to the letter and dismissed their father back to the kitchen.

*I understand that in the end, the girls have witnessed far too much of my addiction for there to ever be a substantial relationship between us. I am responsible for that.*

*I am so very sorry for everything. Please tell them I love them with all my heart. Each of you deserved better. I stole you for myself when I know with every fiber of my being that all three of those girls should have been Jessica's children to bear.*

*For what it's worth, Brent was wrong by the way. You did make it back. Watching you with the girls and listening to the never-ending JD stories tells me you did.*

*If you do ever meet Heather, please tell her I am sorry for keeping her father from her all these years. I don't need a blood test to know she's your daughter, Josh. You can see it in her eyes. Big and hazel and just like yours.*

*Promise that you'll remember me for the good things I did. Layla and Katherine were the greatest gift I could have ever received. They deserved a better mother, but they at least got the father they needed.*

*Amanda*

As each of the girls completed the letter, they tearfully removed themselves from the couch and made their way to the kitchen and their father. Heather was the last to join her new family.

When she reached the kitchen she handed the letter back to her father and said, "I'm so sorry."

Before Josh had a chance to reply, Layla said, "Sorry for what? You didn't do anything wrong."

"I destroyed your entire family. You two were kidnapped and abused by that lunatic and his brother as a result," Heather continued.

"You didn't have anything to do with that, Heather," Katherine intoned. "Our mother was an addict. It could have been anything that sent her back down that path. Her own secrets and demons and paranoia did all of this. You didn't do anything either one of us wouldn't have done." Then she turned toward her father and said, "You still should have told us about this."

"I wanted to tell you guys a million times. Every time I was about to, there was always a reason not to," he answered.

Heather wandered toward the stove and began investigating the various offerings.

"Hungry?" her father asked.

"Starving! What have you got?"

"Pork tenderloin stuffed with spinach and cheese, sautéed grape tomatoes, and homemade red skinned mashed potatoes," Josh said as he ticked off the menu items.

Her sisters quickly jumped in to explain her father's coping mechanism.

"This is completely normal. Dad cooks when he's working things out or becomes agitated. It's really good. You should have some," Layla said.

"Heather," Josh started to say as he fixed her a plate. "I have to ask, how did you find out I was still alive? When we met in California, you said your grandmother told you?"

"Yeah. Papaw and Nana attended some military ball or function and he had a few drinks. She says she made a comment about how sad my mom still seemed. It was like she never got over you or lack of closure or something. According to her, Papaw simply replied, 'He's not dead'. No preamble, just bam. There it is."

"Nice," Josh said sarcastically then added, "That sounds like Brent."

"Nana asked him for details and he told her what happened when you were abducted. He described all of the wounds and the doctor's reports and declared that you'd never be the same Marine or man he knew. He was trying to spare my mom a lifetime of dealing with the recovery."

"And what did she tell you about my time as a POW?"

"I was sixteen and touring the country for my music at the time, but all of them always babied and protected me. She kept the details PG and omitted what I'm sure were the more graphic things."

After a brief pause, all Josh could think to say was, "I see."

Josh and his daughters continued with their meal for a few minutes in silence when Heather couldn't resist any more.

"Dad?" she asked.

"Yeah, hun," he answered reflexively.

"What do I call you?"

Laughing, Josh answered with, "Dad, Josh, either is fine."

"Okay," she replied and then asked the question that had been haunting her since the day she found out about her father. "What did they do to you over there? What made Papaw decide you were too broken to be with my mom?"

Josh thought for a moment and looked at Layla and Katherine.

"Show her," Katherine said.

He glanced over for agreement from Layla. She nodded and added, "She'll never understand it until she she's it."

Josh proceeded to stand up and began unbuttoning his worn flannel shirt. Once all of the buttons were undone, he removed it to reveal the systematic scarring that adorned his body.

Heather covered her mouth as she gasped, "Oh my God! Why would they do that?"

"Well, not all of this was done by them. Some of it is from the doctors trying to address the injuries from a horribly executed rescue attempt. The long scars on my chest and back were the result of torture and interrogation. These here, here, and here," he said as he began to point to different locations on his chest and shoulders. "The ones that look like stars, those are bullet wounds." Next he held out his arms and explained, "These on my forearms are from surgery where they repaired tendon and ligament damage."

Heather stood up and walked timidly toward him. As she approached, she reached out her hand and began to run her fingers over the raised scars and burn marks on his chest and back. After a few moments of silence, she asked, "What caused these?"

"A whip mostly. Some of it was red hot steel being pressed against my flesh," he answered matter of factly.

Josh had been through this routine before with Layla and Katherine when they were children. As parents, he and Amanda decided that they needed to teach the girls not to be afraid of their father's scars. As a result, they youngsters examined their father's chest and back, much like Heather was doing now, and were told to ask whatever questions they wanted.

Katherine interjected and said, "He's got a real nasty one on his thigh too. The idiots crashed the helicopter on the way to the field hospital. It was the crash that broke his arms and leg and put him in a coma."

"To be fair, it was hit by an RPG," her father corrected.

"How did you get shot then?" Heather asked.

"Have you ever heard the story of William Tell?" Josh answered.

"The guy with the apples?" Heather answered.

"Exactly, but they tried it with a can of beans and a pistol. The shooter was another prisoner with a broken arm. She couldn't properly grip the weapon or deal with the weight so..."

"So you got hit," Heather said and finished his sentence.

"Four times actually, but one bullet just grazed me here," Josh said as he pointed to his 'USMC' tattoo on the outside of his left bicep and the scar that bisected it.

"Why were they doing this?"

"The Serbs were convinced that one of the soldiers under my command had raped a local village girl. When the Marine Corps, or more specifically your grandfather, wouldn't turn the guy over, they kidnapped eight of us in the middle of the night."

"That's when you stuffed mom in a wall locker?"

"Yeah, I heard the commotion. Jessica snuck into my quarters a few hours earlier and the only thing I could think to do was stick her in the cabinet. No sooner had I closed the door as they burst into the room and dragged me off. That was the last time I saw her."

"And the woman you were kissing this morning on TV? Who's that?" his daughter asked with a sly smile.

# Chapter 3

After recuperating at the house of Berwari for several weeks, Gregg was transported to the U.S. outpost on the outskirts of Mosul. While the roads near Chammah were passable, they were a far cry from the interstates that crisscrossed America. The thirty-kilometers jolted and jarred his body the entire way.

Unaware of Emily's involvement in the committee meetings, Gregg tried numerous times to reach his wife. At every turn he was thwarted. Her cell was no longer in service, there was no house line to speak of, and her work number went straight to voicemail.

Once his identity was confirmed at the U.S. controlled checkpoint, Gregg was spirited to the infirmary. He was hooked up to numerous solutions to rehydrate and nourish his ravaged body. While he lay there, he was scanned for tracking devices. The debriefings began immediately from his hospital bed. The former POW recounted everything he could remember about his captivity. As soon as the nuclear launch vehicles were mentioned, he was put on the first transport and shipped to Germany.

Colonel Wilson James, head of the PSY/OPS division, aggressively tried to reconstruct Gregg's disjointed memories. The doctor was able to confirm Gregg's suspicions that he had been drugged in preparation for his transport. He stated that it wasn't uncommon and that this was a known insurgent countermeasure against an attempted escape.

Couch therapy and panel discussions revealed additional insight, but everyone was becoming frustrated. The man's mind was severely damaged. In the end, it was determined that the key to unlocking the entire ordeal was going to require unorthodox techniques. As a result,

Gregg was asked to agree to hypnosis. The prevailing thought was that the method might allow him to better recall the events in more detail. Reluctantly, Gregg agreed.

The doctor and his patient watched the playback of the session recording together as it was sometimes deemed helpful in these situations. It wasn't. The hypnosis procedure itself was somewhat successful in that it provided a clearer picture. However, the doctors were convinced there was more to be gained. There were still too many pieces missing.

All Gregg wanted to do was give them what they wanted so he could get home and find his wife. At this point, he was willing to agree to just about every test they had.

When he mentioned this, Col. James presented him with an option called Recovered Memory Therapy (RMT). The premise behind RMT was relatively straightforward and was not all that dissimilar to hypnosis. As an example, the doctor explained in lay terms that, "When someone drinks too much, they forget things. In order to remember them, they need to drink again. The idea is to recreate the conditions that a person was experiencing at the time of that memory's loss."

"You want me to go back under the scopolamine?" Gregg replied astounded. "Go down that road again?" he concluded hesitantly.

"Exactly," the Colonel answered.

Gregg reluctantly nodded his agreement.

"If I do this though, no matter what I say, I want to be discharged from the Army and have transport back to the States. I need to find my wife," he pleaded.

"I can't agree to that, Gregg," he replied. "I have no idea what you told them. However," the doctor started to continue, but stopped when he saw Gregg starting to perk up. He concluded with, "You have my word that the minute we feel we have extracted all available actionable intel from your damaged mind, you're on the first transport off this rock."

He then picked up Gregg's service record file and said, "You, young man, have done enough for your country."

Shortly thereafter, with video and audio rolling, Gregg was administered the scopolamine.

While under the effects of the drug, answers with more specifics about the launch vehicles, details about the cave structure, and the rooms and people he had seen came freely. They asked him seven ways from Sunday about the other prisoner, but all Gregg could remember were his screams. He had a faint recollection about Mahtab or Taj referring to him as 'Airman'.

Over the course of the dozen years that the war in the Middle East had raged, numerous sides had captured prisoners. The coalition forces were holding hundreds of thousands of enemy combatants. The insurgents used the scant few they had, mostly civilian contractors, as pawns in various ransom schemes. A few were even beheaded live on the web. Only a handful of the POW's, like Gregg, were active duty servicemen. The addition of the 'Airman' reference immediately narrowed the pool to three.

The doctors and Gregg poured over the service records of the three Airman, only one stood out. Airman Cecil Sullivan had accompanied a shipment of B2 mounted nuclear tipped missiles to Bagram. He was the odds on favorite as the anonymous cellmate. He had only been on base a few weeks before his bunkmate was found with his throat cut and he went missing.

However, since all three Airmen had been POWs, they were removed from the active theatre of operations and returned to the States for debriefing and therapy. Gregg was to accompany his doctor to Walter Reed to see two of the former captives. Once that task was complete, they would pay a visit to Cecil in Albany, New York. Given Gregg's revelations, they needed to identify the Airman and take him into custody quickly.

The first of the three 'Airman' was in fact a Captain in the Air Force. His service record indicated that his jet had been shot out from under him by a surface-to-air missile (SAM) as he patrolled the skies above southern Iraq and Iran. The detailed account of his captivity put him in an insurgent camp near the Iranian city of Ahvaz. Gregg and the Colonel attempted to get the pilot to contradict himself and reveal himself as the person in the other cell, but to no avail.

The second Airman contained even less information. The man had been horribly disfigured and was left unable to speak due to the loss of his tongue. Through written word, the patient was cleared as well. As expected, only Cecil remained.

Although he had been on the receiving end of hot meals, showers, and warm beds, Gregg still wasn't back to full strength. The interrogation of the Captain, combined with the two days of non-stop travel, had taxed him in ways he wasn't familiar. He needed rest. Colonel James agreed and admitted him to Walter Reed for recuperation and observation. All Gregg cared about at this point was that he was back on his native soil.

That was halfway home to Emily.

* * *

Chairman of the Joint Chiefs of Staff, General Brent Howard, stood ramrod straight as units of men paraded past the podium. The former Camp Lejeune Base Commander had been invited to oversee maneuvers and inspect the military installation as part of the yearly base inspection and readiness tour.

The man had served his country for over four decades and answered the call whenever the nation had a need for him and the Marines under his charge. Brent had survived numerous wars, battles, and skirmishes, but sadly he had also outlived both his wife and his daughter. If the losses were wearing on him, the casual observer wouldn't have known. To those around him he seemed just a stoic and squared away as ever.

Just when he thought his career was beginning to reach its waning years, his division was deployed following 9/11. The man had practically done it all militarily, but he was growing old, tired. Mandatory retirement age was fast approaching and he was grateful.

General Howard was introduced with the usual pomp and circumstance befitting his rank and position as Chairman of the Joint Chiefs. As he took the podium, and surveyed the hardened faces of the Marines making up the latest incarnation of Lejeune's II Marine Expeditionary Force, he softly smiled to himself. He then proceeded to fold his speech back up and replaced it in his breast pocket. He then launched into a speech derived from experience, from memories.

"Stand at ease," he started. "I have proudly worn this uniform for a shade over forty years. As a child, I remember reading about the glorious history of the Marine Corps in WWII, Korea, and Vietnam. My brothers and I would run around the country side in our fatigues scaring the holy hell out of neighbors as we would pop-up from behind cover and yell 'Bam bam bam, I got you!'," he said excitedly to laughter from those assembled. "But playtime ended when I received my commission. In my forty plus years, I've seen my share of war. In my career I've been involved in wars and conflicts in Panama, the first gulf War, Somalia, Bosnia and Kosovo, Afghanistan, the second Gulf War, and Uganda. In that time, I've lost over seventeen hundred men under my various commands. It's a staggering number, all dead." Then he woefully concluded, "I've also buried my wife and my only child, Jessica. As many of you are aware, the call to serve can exact a heavy toll."

Clearing his throat and refocusing, he continued.

"Fortunately, medical and technological advances throughout my career have drastically reduced the casualty numbers we see during firefights and in the written after-action reports."

The General paused and looked out among the assembled, trying to gauge the audience. After a few quiet moments of continued reflection, he continued.

"You wonder sometimes why we train, teach, instruct, scold, and harangue you day and night. We do these things so that when the situation arises, you will know *exactly* what to do at all times. War causes chaos, gentlemen," he said and then added, "and ladies. Chains of command are broken. Communications go down. We train for every possible situation and conceivable scenario so that I don't see that number reach eighteen-hundred. Technology and advanced weaponry help, but the greatest attribute a Marine has is six inches above his neck."

As he looked over the ranks again he saw that some of them shifting. "I can see from some of your faces, you've lost men too. Some were friends. All were Marines." He then proceeded to engage his audience,

"How many officers here today have served as enlisted? How many Mustangs are present?"

Several hands were hesitantly raised.

"NCO's, how many of your commanding officers came to you, on day one of their assignment, and asked for a status of the men? How many asked what their needs were? How many asked your opinion?"

An equal amount went up.

"Those of you with your hands up, how many of your CO's raised theirs?"

None went down.

"I see," said the wizened warrior. General Howard then changed his tone and demeanor and barked an order, "I want all officers' front and center right now!"

When the senior staff and dignitaries seated on the stage didn't budge, General Howard turned, glared at the assembly, and said, "That means you gentlemen. Move your ass and toe the line!"

The men hastily exited their seats, quickly went single file down the stairs, and stood at attention with their officer corps.

The Chairman of the Joint Chiefs of Staff became more reflective and he started describing the man that he thought would have been his heir.

"Thirty years ago," he began. "I had a soldier under my command that took everything I knew about the Marine Corps and threw it out the window. Gone are the days when you taught and administered out of fear or an iron fist. I watched this man lead troops through Khafji while coordinating a multinational multi-branch assault on that city. He did all of this *while* directing air assets overhead. He took over three hundred men through the gates of hell and he brought every one of them home, save six. Then he endured weeks of torture as a prisoner of war. This officer was beaten, shot, whipped, and branded to within an inch of his life. Yesterday, I saw this same man tell a joint Congressional body that he doesn't acknowledge a promotion to Lieutenant Colonel because he didn't feel that he had *earned* it. Can you even fathom that? Unbelievable."

The General became quiet. He wasn't sure where he wanted to go with his speech. Then he remembered Josh's playful banter with him the night he was abducted.

"What I learned from this man was that, as officers, your sole responsibility is simply to address the needs of the men and adapt to the situation given the task at hand. If your soldiers are lacking equipment, training, anything, you improvise. You overcome. You beg, borrow, and steal whatever you have to until they have what they need to get the job done. Your comfort is always secondary. If your men are sleeping in the mud, you are too. Am I clear?"

"Sir, yes, sir!" erupted from the officers.

"The Mustangs seem to have their heads screwed on straight. The rest of you commissioned officers might learn a thing or two from them. Ask your NCO's a million and one questions about their Marines and then shut up for a couple of minutes while they answer. Believe or not, Officers don't always know best or have all the answers."

Wry smiles began to form on the faces of more than few platoon First Sergeants.

Out of the corner of his eye, General Howard saw an aide sprinting towards the stage. He stopped his speech and turned to watch the man bound the stairs two at a time, stop several feet shy, and immediately snap a salute.

"What is it, Corporal?"

"Sir, you need to see this," the enlisted man replied and handed the General the hand held electronic device.

The General quickly glanced down to read the headline of the article: *Serial Rapist Accosts Actress*. He only made it as far as the first paragraph before turning to the microphone, "Colonel, I need to borrow one of your choppers!"

General Howard pushed his way past the young man and started heading to the stairs and his waiting Humvee. The Base Commander and Deputy Commander were right behind him. Before entering the military vehicle, the Chairman turned and said, "Dismiss the troops, Sergeant Major," and flashed a quick salute.

The General took his seat and tersely said, "To the flight line, double time it, son."

The driver slapped a devilish grin on his face, jammed the pedal on the floor, and tore across the parade ground. General Howard used the minutes of the drive to finish reading the article on the aide's smart phone.

To his astonishment, not only had his granddaughter been accosted by a drug addled lunatic, but she had also managed to find her father. The author didn't state this detail per se. The text simply stated that 'Layla and Katherine Simmons happened upon serial rapist Javy Dolbrow assaulting actress Heather White while out on horseback. The three women then restrained him until authorities arrived. The wanted fugitive was currently in surgery under heavy guard'.

Josh was the son he never had. As a result, he didn't think twice about tasking him as his daughters chaperone. The young Major had accomplished his mission and saved his daughter from herself by giving her a renewed purpose in motherhood. That one act brought Jessica back from the precipice she was fast approaching. Brent was able to return the favor by providing Josh's military records to his lawyer, Giuseppe Rossi, during his double murder trial. All the while, he had always kept a watchful eye on his pupil and his family. He knew exactly where he had relocated and why.

The General pulled a small leather bound black notebook from his inside breast pocket. He quickly turned pages to find what he was looking for and then handed it to the Base Commander. The page was blank with the exception of a set of coordinates for Josh's farm.

Over the droning of the loud military tires on the pavement, the General commanded, "I need to get here, ASAP!"

The driver, under General Howard's direction, brought the Humvee to a screeching halt in front of one of the dozen CH-53E Super Stallions parked on the tarmac. Next to the line of massive choppers were dozens of aging UH-1Y Huey Venoms. General Howard always prided himself on knowing the machinery being utilized by his men and knew that the workhorse choppers didn't have the range to get him where he needed to go. He would have gladly hitched a ride in a Harrier, but all were either in various states of repair or were deployed on maneuvers elsewhere.

The Base Commander exited the now parked Humvee, followed closely by General Howard, and handed the coordinates to the Chief Warrant Officer that would be piloting the Super Stallion flight. The man promptly punched them into the computer. As the Base Commander and Brent looked over his shoulder, the distance came back on the flight system screen.

The pilot whistled and turned to the base CO and said, "Sir, that's over five hundred nautical miles from here. It'll be tight, but we can make the destination. We will need fuel to get back though. Where do we get that?"

General Howard answered by saying, "Rickenbacker Air Force Base is forty clicks northwest of there. Get refueled there, son."

"That's still cutting it close, sir."

"Lose some weight by ditching the combat crew and remove the guns. Turn this thing into a flying gas can. Get on it, Chief," the General ordered.

Having received a satisfactory answer from the Four Star General, the pilot took his seat, began flipping switches, and started spinning up the machines seven massive rotor blades. The gunners exited the chopper grabbing the .50 cal's and accompanying ammo on their way out. Ten minutes later the General was airborne and headed to see Josh for the first time in decades.

The Super Stallion typically has a range of five hundred and forty nautical miles. By ditching the extra weight, the General provided more than enough fuel savings to make the trip.

Throughout the flight, Brent goaded and cajoled the pilots to push the aircraft to its max speed of two hundred miles per hour. As a result, the flight took just under three hours.

# Chapter 4

Josh had awoken to his customary 4:45 AM alarm. He showered and quietly opened Layla's door and quickly peeked inside. All three girls were asleep. There were mattresses on the floor and clothes strewn everywhere. Granted, his room at the Academy was never allowed to look a shambles, but what he saw before him is what he had always envisioned college to resemble.

The new blended family of four had stayed up close to midnight talking. Heather had regaled them with stories of Hollywood, movie premieres, and her life with Jessica. In kind, Josh supplied her with all of the pertinent background information on himself, his parents, and his time in the military. He also told her everything he remembered about her mother. He even managed a fairly decent impression of her grandfather when he was trying to give Josh orders to essentially babysit the budding actress.

In response, Heather had confided, "You guys want to know a secret I've never said out loud to anyone?"

"Sure," her sisters replied eagerly.

"The top five biggest hits for me as a singer were written by my mother. The song writing credit was officially listed as me, but they were all penned by her."

Heather went on to explain that all were ballads dealing with heartache, lost love, and bad breakups. Given the information being provided by her father, she was confident now that they were all about their time together, as brief as it was. The three of them thought she was joking until she pulled up the lyrics to her songs on Josh's computer.

Layla and Katherine then used the opportunity to brag about their father's musical talents by pulling up video of him from the Vinton County Harvest Festival. The song and the dedication to Samantha made her cry. She proclaimed her father to be hopeless romantic.

Josh strode back into the cabin by 7:45 to find his three daughters and Basilia chattering away like a bunch of little old ladies in the kitchen. Josh took one look at the assembled estrogen-fest and headed back out the way he came. The interaction was good for all of his daughters nonetheless; he just didn't need to be there for the gabbing. As a result, he hopped back in his Rhino and went to Juan's for breakfast.

When he knocked on Juan's door, Juan and his sons immediately began raucously laughing. Jesus opened the door and said confidently, "Thanks, Patrón! I just won twenty dollars!"

"How do you figure that?" Josh replied.

"We had a bet to see how long you'd stay in a cabin full of women. I figured you'd be back here in less than ten minutes. Abelardo said fifteen, but Dad said you'd gut it out."

"Nice vote of confidence guys," Josh sheepishly replied.

The four men ate and then resumed their normal daily tasks around the farm. Josh and Juan reviewed the next weeks produce orders while his Juan's sons moved the grazing animals to the north paddock. In all, Josh's farm held a small twelve head herd of Randall cattle, seven Corriedale sheep, three Morgan horses, and, although it took some research, two Gypsy Horses.

Josh had chosen this breed of bovine because they fulfilled three purposes: beef, milk, and draft. The Morgan's were for riding and the lamb used for wool and meat. The Gypsy's were powerful and were meant as replacements to the tractors and machinery if the need ever arose. If the Tin Foil Hat Club could be believed, it wasn't a matter of if they'd be needed, but rather when.

The farm also held an assortment of dove, quail, duck, and pheasant, but they were content to roam and inhabit the hedgerows and underbrush. There were also a dozen chickens and one annoying rooster kicking around the farm. Josh thought that he might have to kill that thing if it didn't learn to shut up.

By early afternoon, the four men were hungry and headed into the cabin for lunch. Once inside, they found that the women had moved a grand total of twenty feet. The distance needed to get from the breakfast table to the family room. A fire was going, but the kitchen was immaculate. Basilia had left a loaf of bread, a side of smoked ham, lettuce, tomato, and condiments on the counter for them.

The four men were summarily scolded for wearing their boots in the house and then again when it was discovered that they had destroyed the previously spotless room. They had just finished cleaning up their mess and were about to take their seats when Josh heard the distinctive thwack, thwack, thwack.

He put down his sandwich and walked silently into the family room. The four women stopped their conversation and stared at him. As the thumping of the rotor blades grew louder, Josh audibly sighed.

Layla was about to ask what the sound was when her father, whose eyes and total concentration were locked at the ceiling, said, "Ah, shit."

When he headed to the door, the whole of the cabin followed suit. Josh unassumingly put his boots back on and went silently out on the front porch as the sound grew more intense. With his daughters on either side of him, Heather asked, "What is that?"

"That is a Marine Corps Super Stallion," he replied.

"The Marines don't have a base anywhere near here," Katherine interjected. "They must be lost. What's it doing here?"

"It's here for Heather," Josh answered.

"Me? What did I do?" Heather questioned.

"You didn't do anything. It's your grandfather," he offered.

Josh's youngest daughter could feel herself filling with rage. It had been less than twenty-four hours since she'd learned the truth from Amanda's letter.

"I'm sorry, Heather, but this has to be done," Katherine said as she stepped off of the porch and started walking toward the descending chopper.

The enormous bird touched down and the rear door slid open to reveal General Brent Howard in full regalia. He shut the door, snapped a quick salute to the pilots, and the helo immediately dusted off. As they were ascending to begin the quick flight to Rickenbacker for fuel, the pilot glanced down in time to see Katherine sucker punch the Four Star and knock him on his butt.

Once the dust and debris churned up by the massive rotor blades stopped flying, the rest of the group stepped off of the porch. Josh was in no particular hurry and stayed on the porch. *He's earned every bit of that ass kicking*, Josh thought as he smirked and lit his pipe.

\* \* \*

"Dr. Chastain is here to see you," Mara said into the speaker phone, startling her uncle.

"Send her in," Elias announced.

Emily walked through the door as the Secretary was coming out from behind his desk to greet her.

"Dr. Chastain, what brings you to D.C?"

"Please don't call me that."

Taken aback, he changed the greeting, "Oh, okay. Mrs. Chastain?"

"Don't call me that either."

"Then I'm at a loss," the confused man replied.

"Emily will be fine," she corrected as she took her seat.

Bewildered, Elias returned to his seat. As he sat, he asked, "So what can I do for you... Emily?"

"I need you to give me a job," she responded flatly.

Chuckling, he replied, "I'm sorry?"

Without realizing what she was saying, she hit him with a flood of personal information. "I gave Bathemore my resignation yesterday. I had to disconnect my cell phone because the press wants every piece of me. My husband successfully lied to me about his career in the Army. He's currently listed as 'missing in action'. Presumably, he's dead. As if that weren't enough, the doctors have added insult to injury by removing my ability to have a child." She waved her hand in the air dismissively and said, "You already knew most of that."

Elias looked as if he were about to say something when she preempted him.

"I'm trying to move on and I need you to give me a purpose. I've sold the house and I have some money to travel if I want, but I don't want to leave my field of study. All I *do* know is that I can't work at Bathemore anymore, not right now anyway."

"Why did you resign?" he asked clearly wanting to stay as far away from the husband and medical topics.

"I guess I should correct that. I tried to, but they talked me into a sabbatical instead. I have one year to recharge my batteries they said," she answered.

Elias leaned back in his chair and contemplated the request. After a few silent moments of thought he proposed, "I think a change of scenery might be what you need. You said you're open to travel, so would you be willing to collect data? In the field, I mean."

"Really?" she questioned quickly. "Absolutely!"

"Well, all right then, it's settled," the old man replied. "Give me a day or two to work it out?"

"That'll be fine," she replied.

"Great. In the meantime, go see the sights, take in some monuments, and do a historical tour. Do you have a place to stay while you're in town? If not, you can stay with me or Mara."

"I think I'd prefer to be alone at this point. I'll find something. Maybe a nice B&B, I don't know," Emily answered.

"Suit yourself. Anything else?"

"Actually, yes. There was a man, a farmer," she corrected. "The one that saved Samantha," she began. "Do you know where I might be able to find him?"

* * *

Suhrab, Mahtab, and Taj stepped aboard the Puerto Penasco, Mexico bound freighter and bid farewell to the Middle East with a quick prayer. For them, it was Allah's will to strike at the heart of the infidel once more. The West had dominated the world and perverted it until it was nothing more than a decaying carcass. Neither Suhrab, nor any of his followers, concerned themselves with the headline making issues associated with women's rights and the terroristic nature of Islamists. They didn't adhere to those interpretations of the Koran. However, what they did concern themselves with was the warring between the tribes and the general decline of civilization as a whole. Their beliefs aligned more with the actual teachings of the Prophet.

The three quickly reached their quarters inside the ventilated cargo container. Even with the cover of night, the dock lights illuminated much of the ship's deck. Once they were in the belly of the ship, they relaxed a little.

Eventually, they were joined in their compartment by five additional followers that comprised the team's total complement. As they prepared their beds and stowed their effects, Suhrab turned and saw the trepidation on his men's faces.

Suhrab stopped what he was doing and said, "I know you are fearful. We are headed into the lion's den. Just remember that every issue and problem we see today started with the West and its decadence. Throughout time, there have been monarchies with their empires and dynasties. Just about every country in recorded history has taken their turn at trying to rule the world. The Persians, English, Spanish, French, and Germans all failed. Some were more successful than others and some tried more than once. There were also the Romans, Incas, Aztecs, Ottomans, Mongols, and Russians. These civilizations all faded too. There is only one true empire left, the United States.

"This journey is wrought with danger and peril. Remember your training. Maintain the communication silence. Keep your head down and wait for the appointed time."

Suhrab continued to misdirect and distract them from dwelling on the mission. The men needed to take their mind off of their future tasks. It was going to be a long ocean crossing.

"Mahtab, tell me about the religions. What do you recall of the Imam's teachings from the mountains?"

The man quickly and nervously reiterated what he had been taught. "All three of the dominant religions of the world, Judaism, Christianity, and Islam, believe in one true God and that it is the same God. We have different names for our God, but it is the same God. The earliest teachings of the Prophet acknowledged that life began with Adam. When Muhammad retook Mecca, he did it to unite the feuding tribes. He even removed all of the false god idols from the square surrounding the Kaaba, just like Jesus in the Temple."

"Excellent, Mahtab," he replied. He then turned and said, "Taj, what happened after the Prophet won Mecca?"

"The unification only lasted a generation beyond the Prophet's death. The Sunni's and Shiite's began warring again and they have been at each other's throats ever since."

"That is correct. Thank you, brothers," Suhrab replied before continuing. "The tribes have been feuding non-stop for hundreds of years. Every time a global power intervened, the pendulum swung the other way. The Russians in Afghanistan and the United States response brought Bin Laden, the rigidity of the Taliban, and strict adherence to Sharia Law. The English and their oil exploration gave us the Saudi Royal Family and those little fiefdoms in Kuwait, the UAE, Bahrain, and Qatar. All of this meddling in Islamic affairs, coupled with the 'Arab Spring's' and the Zionist State's attacks have only served to heighten the conflict between the tribes.

"The last empire will be the resurgence of the Muslim world and a return to the Prophets teachings. There is going to be peace in our lifetime, I swear it! We will shun the Islamists and their radicalized hooligan death squads. When we are done, the West will have been fully punished for their wickedness. Only then can the true unification of the tribes begin anew."

Suhrab and his intelligence network had been scheming for years just waiting for an opening. When the British PM approached all of the former oil producing nations, the situation was too perfect to let pass by.

The more and more he thought about the reports that had been ferried to him from diplomats, the more ironic it was. The United States, with their greed, zeal, and worship of money were about to be undone by a bunch of debt collectors that had helped to create and fuel the machine. The least they could do was aid in its demise.

"Does everyone know their assignments? Navid, where will you be heading?" Suhrab asked to keep lowering their tensions.

"If Mexicans and the whole of Latin America can seemingly jump fences and rivers into the United States, we shall do the same. Their politicians in Washington have thundered on for years about the need for immigration reform and greater border security. Luckily, all they accomplished was division between their political parties. We will take advantage of these deficiencies.

"We are to cross the boundary individually and maintain communication silence. I am to secure residence in the Mid-Atlantic region, acquire a P.O. Box, and begin resourcing the parts necessary for my device. Once assembled, I am to exert my training and the technology and perform a test fire at a target visible enough to make the news and alert all of you that I am online. Each of you will go to separate regions of the country and do the same."

The handheld RF tech had been born out when they took Gregg's transport out of the sky. They had used the weapon to blast the low-flying aircraft with a directional EMP and disable all of the on-board electronics. Once they heard the engines shut down, they fired an RPG at the plane to disguise the use of the technology.

The RF device was relatively simple in its design. Just about everything they needed could be bought in specialty stores. Some of the team members may get lucky and find the key component in an electronics store, but the members had to reconcile themselves with the fact that they may have to order the high-voltage pulse capacitor online. Thus the mailing addresses.

"And how will we go undetected in the lion's den?" Suhrab asked the assembled group.

From the shadows of the container, a lone voice responded.

"Every failed attack on the decadent homeland has been thwarted because of increased communication among the combatants. The NSA, FBI, and CIA and their snooping whisper programs can't and won't detect even a hint of us because we will be dark. No telephones, cell phones, or email allowed."

"Excellent, Adar! Spoken like a true warrior!" their leader replied emphatically.

Suhrab always smiled and praised Allah every time a disillusioned and naïve whistleblower went running to the press or posted 'Top Secret' program initiative documents to internet sites. It may have eased their conscience, but all it really did was tell everyone wanting to do harm to the United States how to subvert the spy programs.

The divulging of the software and tactics eventually derived the team of eight that Suhrab had assembled. At the appointed date and time, the group would go active and create chaos, panic, and mayhem. While they were busy shutting down key pieces of the U.S. infrastructure, Suhrab's brother, Abbas, was to use the intel garnered from Gregg to complete his mission.

As an act of compassion, or faith, Suhrab had released Gregg after they had everything they needed. He could read the displeasure on his men's faces, but he had convinced himself that he wasn't a monster. He didn't kill for pleasure. He only did so when necessary as a means to an end. He killed to prove a point when someone needed convincing. The torment his prisoner would have to live with would last the rest of his life; that coupled with the scarring was punishment enough.

Their timing couldn't have been more perfect. That was, assuming the United Nations and their posturing could be taken as fact. If the PM and the rest of the assembled core that owned U.S. debt had the stomach for an actual invasion, then Suhrab and his men would make their job all that much easier. He relished the thought of the Americans in the streets throwing rocks at tanks.

# Chapter 5

General Brent Howard sat on the front porch of the cabin licking his wounds. Josh exited and handed him a bag of ice and a glass of bourbon, neat. He would need both to assuage the shame in having being beaten on by Katherine.

"Your daughter has one hell of a right hook, Josh," the General said in an attempt to break the ice.

"Yeah well, she's got a lot of pent up anger towards her mother. Thanks for not fighting back though."

"Fight back hell! It was all I could do to keep my head covered! That girl's a fighter."

Josh chuckled at the comment, sat down, and said, "The three of them just learned the truth about Amanda and her treachery. You dropping in out of the sky didn't help," Josh replied.

"Me? What the hell did I do?"

Josh leaned forward to retrieve Amanda's confession from his back pocket. He had placed it there knowing full well that the General was going to need to read it. Brent Howard was the lone remaining person that needed to understand. When he was done, Josh was set to burn it. All of the vile truths contained in step nine of Amanda's AA derived letter had harmed enough people.

"You read that and then we'll talk some more," Josh said as he got up and re-entered the cabin.

While the General read, Josh returned to the task of reassembling the relay for the driveway alarm system. After a few minutes of tinkering, reconnecting, and soldering wires, the device began chiming anew. Josh thought he had misconnected some of the wiring when the thing kept going off. When a realtor with a 'Mossy Oak Properties' magnet on his door swung down out of the woods, he realized his mistake.

Josh had used the land company to help locate the farm property in the rural southeastern region of the state. He hadn't chosen the area or the location at random though. Of the eighty-eight counties comprising the state of Ohio, the barely four hundred square miles encompassing Vinton County was the most heavily forested and least populated in the entire state. If you were looking for a life outdoors and away from people, there was no better place.

Brent knocked on the cabin wall and yelled to Josh, "You have a visitor," but his host had already seen the man approaching.

Josh put down the soldering gun, walked through the threshold of the cabin's front door, and saw a familiar face exiting his SUV. The realtor was a bit taken aback to see a Marine Corps General in full dress uniform sitting on Josh's porch, but progressed toward his potential client all the same.

"Hey Scott, what brings you out this way?" Josh asked.

Surprised, the man said, "Hi, Josh, I didn't think you'd remember me."

"Of course. What can I do for you?" Josh inquired.

"I don't know if you are aware of it, but your neighbor recently passed on."

Josh nodded that he knew.

"Well, seeing how you have right at a hundred and fifty acres here and she has another fifty adjoining. Long story short, her kids want to sell. I thought I'd check with you and see if you were interested."

"What's she got over there?" Josh asked feigning indifference.

"Other than the acreage, it's got a farm house, four hundred foot well, a couple of out buildings, some older machinery, and a good sized barn."

"Is her well pump in good order?"

"Seems to be working. The inspector will be by in the next day or so to let me know for sure."

"She had about half and half, timber and field?" Josh asked already knowing the answer.

"Yeah, that sounds about right," the rep replied.

"Why come to me? Why don't they keep it in the family? That land has been paid off for some time now, right?" he asked inquisitively.

"It has, but her husband passed some time ago and their children aren't interested in the land, timber or gas rights, or the prospect of being farmers. They'd prefer to stay near the city in the suburbs."

"Seriously, with all of this going on, they are gonna sell their birth right?" Josh asked amazed at Scott's answer.

"Yup, damn fools if you ask me, but," he said with a sigh. "I do what the client wants," he replied.

"What are they asking?" Josh offered.

"We've got it priced at $199,900 right now."

"And the mineral rights?"

"Transfer with the property," the realtor answered.

Josh had been thinking about the influx of visitors to the farm and this would be a perfect way to start letting his daughters spread their wings. He looked down at Brent with a smirk and said, "Tell them I'll offer $175 cash. Offer's good 'til sundown."

Scott smiled at the answer and pressed 'Send' on his cell phone. He had already dialed the number while they were talking. He knew full well that Josh wouldn't pass up on a large piece of adjoining property. Once the sellers were on the line, he proposed Josh's offer. The realtor gave him the thumbs down.

Josh replied with, "$180, as is."

He relayed the raised bid and listened intently. He frowned and mouthed the words 'eighty-five'? Josh nodded his agreement. In truth, given the infusion of Amanda's life insurance funds, Josh would have paid the full asking price. If they were foolish enough to accept a lower offer then they deserved it. Josh smiled inwardly. *Spend it on the girls Sam said.*

The pair filled out paperwork for the next twenty minutes and then Josh cut him a check for the agreed upon amount to put into escrow until the closing. The two shook hands and the realtor headed back to his office with the promise to stop by tomorrow with the finalized dates and details.

"What the hell, Josh," Brent said as Josh took the seat next to him on the porch.

"What?" Josh replied.

"You just bought fifty acres sight unseen and stroked a check for $185,000. Is this normal for you?" Brent asked, amazed at the speed of the process and the amount involved.

"That wasn't *my* money! I don't have that kind of dough just laying around," his old friend replied incredulously. "Amanda left my name on a life insurance policy. What I did do, however, was ensure that my girls would be close by when it all goes sideways. Plus, I wouldn't say it was sight unseen either. I've been surveying her land since we got here. Now we have almost thirty acres of free hay fields for my animals and another twenty wooded acres for hunting and trapping. Besides, that old 'nosey

Nelly' was practically giving the stuff away some years. That and she's got the deepest well in these parts. The well pump fills a five hundred gallon cistern. The farmhouse is in good shape and the concrete storage tank uses a gravity feed to supply the house. These foothills are good for something if you've got a mind to plan accordingly.

"That old lady may have been a certifiable pain in my ass, but her husband was a genius. The man had homesteader in his genes. To be honest though, I needed to get some of these people out of my cabin," he finished with a laugh. "If I'm reading the signs right, I think I might be getting remarried."

"Seriously? Who's the lucky girl? More importantly, is she sane?" Brent questioned as he handed the letter back to his friend.

"More so than me and the woman that wrote that at this point," he replied with a smile. "I haven't asked her yet though. I need to talk to the girls first."

"Well good luck. Nobody deserves to be happy more than you. As for that," the General replied as he motioned toward the letter. "I don't know what to say. As a father, I think we can both attest to the fact that I did what I thought was best for my child. You have children of your own now. I don't think there's any argument there."

Sighing, Josh flatly said, "Agreed."

"I'm telling you now, as God is my witness, I had no idea Amanda had so many issues. When I asked her to hide things about Jessica from you I meant while you were in the hospital. I never intended for her to continue the charade through a marriage."

"She had a number of skeletons in her closet that I wasn't aware of, I'll grant you that. Here's the problem though, and the reason why Katherine just went after you. The girls, Heather included, have read this letter. All three are feeling different things right now. I'm pretty sure Layla is still processing it so you might get another beating once she's done. Your granddaughter's is guilt. She believes that she was the reason Amanda snapped and fell off the wagon. My youngest on the other hand..." Josh said before his voice trailed off.

"She is one angry young lady who thinks I poisoned her mother against her and her sister before she was even born," Brent said with great empathy.

"Unfortunately, yes. That is exactly what she's feeling," Josh replied in earnest.

"Where are they?" Brent asked.

"The girls? They are all up in Layla's room. Why?"

"Because I need to set this right, that's why," the General answered determined.

"Have fun with that," Josh said sarcastically. "When you're done, I might as well talk to them about Samantha and see if I can get their blessing."

Brent stood and started to enter the house.

"Which room?"

"Top of the stairs, first door on the left," Josh replied casually as he began packing his pipe.

Mumbling more to himself, the General added, "Wish me luck."

"You're gonna need it," Josh muttered back at him.

A minute later, Brent swallowed hard and knocked quietly on Layla's door.

"Girls? Are you decent?"

After several silent seconds, Katherine replied, "Enter at your own risk, *General*."

Brent slowly turned the knob and entered the room.

"What can we do for you, General Howard?" Layla asked.

"I think we need to have a conversation about your mother," he stated bluntly.

"Tread carefully, *Brent*," Katherine quickly retorted.

The General glanced over at her and gave the slightest of nods.

"There are several things that I believe are pertinent to understanding exactly what took place. First, neither I, nor your father, was privy to her past substance abuse issues until she fell off the wagon when Heather tracked down her father. Had I known, I would have had her removed from his medical team. Second, none of you were alive when I made the decision to keep my daughter separated from your father, Heather. I will *not* be second guessed in this regard."

Katherine began to flash boiling hot.

"To his credit, your father managed to survive some of the most inhumane unfathomable shit that man has perpetrated on another human being. What the Serbs did to him was right up there with what the Viet Cong and the Japanese did to our troops. He was touch and go for over a month as he lay there in that coma. Breathing tubes, feeding tubes, ventilators, blood and plasma infusions... more surgeries than I care to remember. I personally witnessed him code twice. All I knew was that there was no way in hell I was going to subject my only daughter to any of it. Not his incapacity in that hospital bed and definitely not the months and potentially years of his recovery."

"So are you gonna tell us anything substantive or are you just going to lecture us?" Katherine asked snarkily.

Brent cast her the sternest look in his arsenal and held it for far longer than the uncomfortable silence should have dictated. When she eventually relented and cast her eyes downward to acknowledge the intent of his hardened glare, the General cleared his throat and continued.

"What your mother wrote is one-hundred percent factually true. I did ask her to hide any news of Jessica from your father. What I didn't realize at the time was that I should have been clearer in my request. My intent was to limit his exposure to news of her while he was recovering. I had no way of knowing that she'd interpreted this to mean for life.

"For that, I do offer my most sincere apology. That being said, I do know that she loved you both, fiercely."

Slowly, the three young women began looking up at him.

"Unfortunately, and you've likely seen this first-hand, when you're dealing with addictions like that and holding on so tightly it doesn't take much to unravel and destroy what you covet the most. In my estimation, As God is my witness, I do not believe that a single person in this cabin can be blamed for any of the events that transpired. Every single ounce of the blame should, and does, fall squarely on the person that wrote the confessions contained in that letter."

"Then why continue the lie? It's obvious you knew where he was after all this time because you flew straight here. Why did you let mom believe he was dead all these years," his grand-daughter asked.

"I felt it was better to let sleeping dogs lie. I didn't see either of you pining your days away. Both you and your mother had become highly successful all on your own and by all accounts everyone concerned had moved on with their lives. Adding Josh and his family into the mix would have turned all of you into fodder for the tabloids. You and Jessica may have become accustomed to that life but your father and his family didn't sign up for the chaos. I thought I was doing the right thing by keeping everyone oblivious and that obliviousness was keeping everybody safe."

"Well, that didn't quite work out like you had hoped, did it General Howard," Layla stated.

Sighing heavily, Brent answered.

"No, it sure didn't. If I could change it or fix it, I would. No one could have ever imagined how badly this whole situation spiraled out of control."

Layla glanced left and right at her two sisters who were both gently sighing and subtlety shaking their heads in agreement.

"We hear your words and thank you for coming today to check on Heather. We appreciate your explanation of the role you played as well as your candor."

Brent slowly nodded at her.

"Now," she added. "If you don't mind, we were in the middle of something… sooooo… you're dismissed."

Heather's grandfather audibly guffawed at the dismissal, but managed a, "Yes, ma'am," through his chuckling.

He was still chuckling as he existed the cabin through the open front door. Once he was on the porch, he caught the sight of the last remnants of the letter burning in Josh's finger tips then wafting to the ground in flames.

Turning, Josh asked, "So how'd that go?"

"They appreciated my insight and frankness and then I was dismissed," he stated bluntly in response.

His friend started chuckling too.

Brent stayed for two nights then Josh drove him to Columbus to catch a train and head back to D.C.

\* \* \*

Airman Hector Ortiz awoke with a start when the pounding on his door began. The male voice on the other side was speaking rapidly in Spanish. They were asking for help. Their wife was in labor and the subfreezing temperatures had killed his car battery. Hector understood the man's pleas. He threw off the covers and quickly went to the door to offer assistance.

Hector hastily unlocked it, turned the knob, and yanked it open. In front of him was a man so similar in stature and appearance that he could have been looking in a mirror. Without warning, the man raised a suppressed weapon, aimed it at Hector's forehead, and pulled the trigger. With a 'thwack' from of pistol, the assailant was in the room before Hector's body barely had time to hit the floor.

He quickly shut the door to the motel room and began the search for the dead man's transfer order. Hector had just completed his technical training for Missile and Space Systems Maintenance, and was scheduled to report for duty at 9:00 AM that morning. As the assailant searched the room, he saw that all of Hector's Air Force issued possessions were still neatly folded in his duffle, or on top of the dresser. This made searching for the assignment orders all that much easier. It took him less than a minute to find what he was looking for carefully placed in the nightstand drawer.

Once found, he threw it on the bed and walked over to Hector's body. He grabbed the deceased under the arms and dragged the leaking corpse to the bathroom. After placing him in the bathtub, he caught his reflection in the mirror as he exited. He saw blood splatter from the kill shot adorning his face. He quickly turned on the faucet and began washing it off. As he stood, the assassin stopped and starred at himself.

*You're a bad man. A very bad man.*

His mother had said that to him numerous times throughout his youth. Usually after he had been picking on his sister or fighting with his older brother.

He dried his face with the hanging towel and headed to the bed to review the orders. He had four hours to memorize the contents, make the latex fingerprint overlays, brush up on anything he might not have already known about the Airman, and report for duty. On top of that, he also needed to dispose of the body. The gunmen already knew a great deal about his counterpart though.

The man had been under observation for some time. As a result, the dossier was quite extensive. Spending habits, family contact frequency, likes, dislikes, tastes, and female companionship preferences littered the documentation. Unfortunately for the deceased, he had no enemies and therefore had no reason to survey his surroundings. The Airman had failed to notice the tail following him all the way from Texas.

As he read the packet, he was struck by the thought that his Oxford education had cost about fifty thousand pounds while the late Hector Ortiz had received comparable training for free from the U.S. military. Had he been born in the States, instead of the U.K., he too would have probably taken that path.

Three and half-hours later, he completed his tasks at the motel and was just about to finish the thirteen mile trip. The murderous doppelganger turned off of Route 83 on to Missile Avenue and approached the main gate of Minot Air Force Base. The remote northern North Dakota airbase was home to the 5th Bomb Wing, and its aging B-

52 Stratofortress', as well as the 91st Missile Wing. Hector Ortiz, or rather, the man wearing Hector Ortiz's uniform and carrying the dead man's orders, was about to report for duty and start working on the hundred and fifty Minuteman III guided nuclear missiles currently residing on station. Hector's body, on the other hand, was spread all over the little town in every available dumpster he could find, carefully placed in double layered black trash bags.

While he waited in line to be checked through the gate in the Airman's car, he began scanning and memorizing the locations of all sentries, guards, and patrols. *Relax. Just relax, Abbas. You are Airman Hector Ortiz from Tuscan, Arizona.*

\* \* \*

Colonel James and Gregg Chastain exited their rental sedan in the parking lot of the Bear Claw Saloon in Crestline, California and stretched. After spending a day observing the home in Albany, New York, they saw no sign of Cecil Sullivan's presence. The pair decided enough was enough and Colonel James approached the house. As he approached, Gregg went and stood concealed by the back door.

When he knocked on the front door, Cecil's sister, Anna, greeted him warmly.

"Hello, you must be looking for Cecil," she said as she opened the door and observed his military uniform.

"Well, yes, actually. I'm Dr. James. I'm a psychiatrist from Walter Reed. I'm trying to follow-up with Cecil," he answered. It wasn't a complete lie. He was a shrink after all.

"Oh, thank God," Anna said relieved. "Please come in."

The two took seats on the couch in her living room. Colonel James then asked her to explain her relief.

"Cecil has been having a rough go of it," she started.

"How so?"

"Well, most nights he wakes up screaming covered in sweat. When I would run into his room he'd bark at me and send me away. He always said it was a bad dream."

Colonel James didn't offer any commentary. She noticed.

"Look, you don't have to treat me with kid gloves. I know he was a POW for almost a year. I was briefed about the torture when I signed him out. The doctors told me all about it and I've seen the scars. I didn't want to push him by asking him to talk about his experience, but I knew he was in pain," Anna concluded.

Colonel James did reply this time. As gently as he could, he explained aspects of the 'bad dream'. He described the torture techniques, the beatings, the sleep deprivation, and the mental and physical toll it all took. Anna began to weep.

Through her tears, Anna said, "He's been drinking heavily since he arrived two months ago. I think he's trying to drown out the voices."

"It's very important that I speak with him, Anna. Where is he? When will he be back?" the Colonel asked.

Anna discreetly removed a tissue from the box and cleared her sinus. When she finished, she said, "He took the train to JFK and caught a flight to Los Angeles a few days ago. One of his friends called a week or so ago while Cecil was out. He asked how he was doing and we got to talking."

"And how did that go? The conversation I mean. How did the friend react to what you told him?" the Colonel asked.

"He seemed concerned for Cecil. He wanted to help. He phoned again later that night and they spoke. He convinced him to go backpacking near Big Bear Lake in the San Bernardino National Forest. That's good, right? That he got out into open air, out of the house, out of the bar, right?"

Colonel James quickly answered, "Yes, yes. That's very good. He's recognizing that a change is needed."

The doctor thanked her for the information and said his goodbyes with the promise to help Cecil as much as he could. Gregg and the Colonel caught the first flight they could get from JFK to LAX the following morning. Between the airtime, time zone changes, car rental delays, and traffic, the pair didn't reach Crestline, California until just before sundown. The pair were starving.

Crestline, California is the last town of note between San Bernardino and the village of Big Bear Lake. The car needed to be topped off after the drive up the mountain as much as they did. The thirty-mile stretch along the Rim of the World Highway from Crestline to Big Bear was going to take over an hour.

Before heading up to Crestline, the pair stopped at the Forest Headquarters station in San Bernardino. They had no record of Cecil pulling a permit for a campsite. They told Colonel James it was entirely possible that they were renting a cabin or staying in a motel in Crestline or in Big Bear Lake.

As they entered the restaurant, the patrons of the local watering hole turned and gave the pair a discerning eye. The two took a seat at the nearest booth and waited for the waitress. An older woman approached and sat next to Gregg in the booth.

"Welcome to the Bear Claw Saloon, gentlemen. I'm Tammy and my husband and I own this establishment," she said.

Gregg slid over to accommodate her girth when Colonel James answered, "Nice to meet you, Tammy. What's good here?"

"The burgers are top rate, but before I decide whether or not to serve you, you two need to answer some questions."

*This ought to be good*, Gregg thought to say, but opted to keep his mouth shut.

Colonel James, ever the psychiatrist, replied, "Well, since this is your establishment, by all means, ask away."

She smiled a demure, but flirtatious, smile and asked, "Question one. Are either of you boys revenuers?"

"Like tax collectors?" Colonel James asked.

Tammy sighed, "A revenuer can be anyone who works for the government. Like DHS or BLM. You boys work for any of those?"

"In a manner of speaking," the Colonel started to say as Tammy's eyebrows went up. "We are in the Army."

"Well, why aren't you fellas in uniform?" Tammy asked.

Throwing a little caution to the wind, Colonel James said, "We are trying to locate someone that might not appreciate it."

"Is this person a criminal?"

"No ma'am. He has a severe case of PTSD and is a danger to himself and possibly others. He needs help and we need to find him. He may have been in here just a few days ago with a buddy."

Colonel James reached into the inside pocket of his coat and removed Cecil's service record photo and placed it on the table. "They were headed over to Big Bear Lake to do some hiking. Maybe some camping too."

Tammy picked up the picture and said, "Hey, George. Can you come over her a sec, hun?"

A burly thirty something man stepped out from behind the bar and started heading over to the booth. Gregg took one look at the tank and reflexively began sliding his hand toward his concealed Glock. The last time he saw a man that big, the man was slumped on the floor with screwdriver thrust into his skull.

Tammy handed the bartender the picture and asked, "Is this the young man you boys had problems with the other night?"

George was an observant man and had seen Gregg moving his hand inside his unzipped coat. As he took the picture from Tammy, he said, "Sir, I can appreciate the fact that you are carrying, but you are in no danger here. Please leave it in its holster."

Gregg laughed off the comment and feigned ignorance. When he removed it, he was holding his wallet.

"Just reaching for this is all," Gregg replied.

Not taking his eyes off of the picture, the man replied with a grunt and said, "Sure you were."

He studied the picture for a few more seconds. "Yeah, this could be him. It's hard to tell though. The drunk we threw out of here hadn't cut his hair or shaven in a few months."

George handed the picture back to Tammy and returned to the bar after looking Gregg over one more time.

Colonel James asked, "Did you guys happen to recognize who he was with?"

"Oh," Tammy started to reply. "He's a flatlander that comes up here every couple of weeks. I think he has a cabin somewhere west of Big Bear Lake."

Without looking at Tammy, Gregg provided, "Beggin' your pardon ma'am, but that's a lot of ground to cover. Could you be a little more specific?"

Tammy turned in her seat to look at Gregg and quickly noticed the scars on his exposed wrists and the branded welts on the side of his neck. As she motioned to his hands she said, "That why you where that coat, son? To hide those?"

Still continuing to stare at the table, Gregg self-consciously pulled the sleeves down farther.

"My Lord," she said as she leaned a little closer to examine the branding. "Did they brand a star and crescent into your neck?"

Not surprised by question, Gregg said, "Yes, ma'am."

"Please tell me you killed the guy that did that."

Gregg nodded.

"Good. Bastard deserved it for doing that to one of our boys. How'd you do it?"

"Screwdriver."

"Well done," she said with a hint of pride in her voice. "The man he was with is named Travis Smalls. Damn flatlander. He has a cabin three miles west of Big Bear. Always bragging about his money and his possessions. Won't do him a hill of beans without some common sense when it hits the fan." Tammy sighed a little sigh and finished with, "The folks in Big Bear should be able to help you with a property search."

Colonel James wrote the information down on a pocket sized notepad and said, "Thank you, Tammy. You've been more than helpful."

"Not a problem, anything for our boys in uniform. Now let me get those burgers on for you."

Tammy started to slide her way out of the booth when she suddenly turned to Gregg.

"Son?" she said.

Gregg stopped staring at the hole he had drilled into the table with his eyes and looked over at Tammy.

"Ma'am?"

Tammy leaned over and softly kissed him on the lips and said, "Welcome home. You don't have anything to be ashamed of. You boys are free to dine here anytime."

"Thank you," Gregg replied.

Tammy exited the booth and called out, "George, call your cousin over at the Sleepy Hollow Cabins and get these gentlemen a room for the night. They don't need to be on the 'Rim' after dark."

# Chapter 6

Evan and several of the men from the greenhouse nervously approached Josh as he neared the structure. None of the assembled men wanted to hear that their services were no longer needed, but they needed to know where they stood.

"Sir?" Evan said hesitantly.

"What's up, guys?" Josh answered.

"We were wondering what we're supposed to do," Evan offered.

"About?" Josh asked curiously.

"Our employment status, sir. Do we need to turn in our weapons now that Javy has been caught?" Evan replied.

Josh knew this day was coming and, frankly, was a bit surprised the topic hadn't already come up.

"I see," Josh said as he stopped walking just in front of the men.

"Well, sir, we're not sure what we are supposed to be doing. Javy's under heavy guard and headed to death row. Given that, we were wondering what we were supposed to do since the security aspect of our employment isn't needed anymore."

"Is Javy dead?" Josh asked.

"No, sir," Evan answered.

"Then you can keep your side arms," Josh said flatly. "Anything else?"

The men looked at each other and back at Josh. No one spoke.

"Look guys, for twelve years I've asked you to help me protect my daughters from that lunatic. Until they strap that idiot into the chair and light him up, I don't consider the mission accomplished. As far as I'm concerned, there's nothing to talk about. This is still a working farm and we have contract orders to fulfill. We have fruits and vegetables to harvest and deliver. Nothing's changed.

"However, given Javy's current location, we might be able to relax some of the more stringent procedures. Regardless, until that execution day comes, I'd like all of you to continue working with the girls and Heather. The Martinez's included. I need everyone fluent in our commands and signals."

"But why?" Evan asked quickly. "The country is back on the straight and narrow and the hearings are almost over.

"I've had my suspicions about a number of things for some time. I figured I was just being paranoid. I know you guys thought so after I shared a few of them with you individually," Josh began.

Smiles and chuckles permeated the group.

"Yeah, yeah. Laugh it up. I wish I could say it was paranoia at this point. However, over these last couple of days, I've had several interesting conversations with the Chairman of the Joint Chiefs. Suffice it to say, this nation is far from being out of the woods politically, financially, or internationally. Things are coming. We are isolated out here and we know how to take care of our own, so we should be safe. That being said, use whatever free time you have and get your family's prepared for a tough road ahead," Josh answered cryptically.

"What does that even mean, sir? Prepare them for what?" Evan replied for the group as the smiles disappeared.

Josh was about to divulge further information so his employees would have a fighting chance when Katherine drove up.

"Dad! Dad! Dad!" she exclaimed as she brought the vehicle to an abrupt stop.

Josh spun around to witness the last of her reckless driving.

"Rayburn, Elias, and some of those Congressional guys are holding a press conference thingy!" she decreed as she turned the radio up.

The men rushed the cab of the truck and listened.

"Today marks a landmark day for our nation," the President began. "After scores of witnesses and weeks of debate and testimony, several bills have been placed before me that I am fully prepared to sign. Combined, these three key pieces of legislation will be known as the Safe Food Act. From this day forward, once signed, this law will provide safety and peace of mind for all Americans.

"To summarize, Senate Bill 3853 bans the development and planting of genetically engineered crops designed for human or livestock consumption. House Bills 8702 and 8703 places restrictions on, and severely limits, the scope, use, and toxicity of synthetic pesticides, fertilizers, and insecticides, as well as the use of cloud seeding and disbursing agents respectively."

Wide smiles and pats on the back went through the group huddled around the truck.

"You and Sam did it, Dad!" Katherine exclaimed as she leapt in to her father's arms. "I'm so proud of you," she said. Then she leaned in close to his ear and whispered, "We've talked it over and, yes, you have our blessing to marry Samantha."

\* \* \*

Suhrab and his men waited until the cover of night to slip off of the larger cargo ship and into the streets of Puerto Penasco. Once his group of eight was safely into the underbelly of the city, each would procure their own transportation and disburse throughout the country. After dropping Gregg in Chammah, the eight men had endured a treacherous journey south through Iran, across the Strait of Hormuz, and into the UAE. Once there, they traversed the western coastline down to the port of Dubai. The rolling seas encountered during the crossing around the Horn of Africa had them chucking their guts out.

Suhrab had chosen the southwest region for himself because its terrain and climate were comparable to his homeland. These states were comprised of high deserts in California, Arizona, Nevada, and Utah. That appealed to him. He knew what to expect and how to operate in the obsessively dry heat and could handle the wild swings in temperature between day and night. These issues were less of a factor now that winter was approaching.

The contingent had contemplated trying to work their way up to northern Europe, but even with the 'open borders' mindset of the EU, the prospect of attempting to cross into and out of that many countries was a deterrent in and of it itself. As a result, the longer, more arduous journey was chosen. Now that they had arrived in Mexico via cargo ship, each of the men were to use the next several weeks to successfully cross the border and arrive in their assigned region within the U.S.

Suhrab and his men were convinced that, with eight men running around with small portable RF devices, functioning independently, there was no way they would all be caught. Even if the U.S. authorities grabbed one or two men, that still left the bulk of the operation to accomplish the mission. Needle in a haystack didn't begin to describe it. Since they weren't communicating or procuring large quantities of explosives, chemicals, or fertilizers, there wouldn't be anything to trigger the government software programs.

After meeting up at a seedy dockside cantina one last time, the men split up and began their solitary journey to the border towns of Nogales, Naco, and Agua Prieta. Less than two weeks after reaching Puerto Penasco, all of the group members were in the United States and working their way through the heartland to their destinations. In a few short months, all hell was going to break loose.

\* \* \*

Evan turned the corner, with bags in hand, and headed down the stairs of the Martinez's farmhouse. To his astonishment, Josh and his family, as well as Juan, Basilia, and their sons, were standing in the living room waiting for him.

"What's all this about? I'm just going on vacation for a few weeks. I'm coming back," Evan said clearly surprised at the gesture.

In truth, the man was headed to collect his young wife from her parents. Josh's voracious reading habits and spatial ability connected a great number of dots on the political, financial, and military landscape. Some were debunked by the General. However, Josh's remote location and the pair's friendship allowed Brent to confirm others. He'd wind up in Leavenworth if any of it ever reached the light of day.

"I've got a surprise for all of you," Josh said. "So I asked everyone to get together to send you off and see the surprise."

Layla nudged Heather and whispered, "This oughta be good. Dad's presents are always over the top."

Josh motioned for the assembled to take a seat. He produced a legal sized manila envelope and a cardboard tube. He handed the documents to Katherine and the tube to Juan.

"OK girls. Open it," Josh said.

Katherine did so with relish and removed the paperwork.

"What is it?" Heather asked.

"Yeah, come on... spill it," Layla intoned.

"It's a deed to fifty acres called the 'Three Sisters Farm'? I don't know what I'm looking at. I don't understand," Katherine said.

"Here, let me see," Heather said as she turned the documents toward her.

"Oh my God, Dad. This is too much. We can't accept this," his daughter stated in shock.

"It's already done," Josh replied smiling.

"Too much what?" Layla asked.

"These are the closing docs from a land deal. It says Dad bought the neighbors farm. He registered the property as farmland under the name 'Three Sisters Farm'."

Katherine squealed at the pronouncement, jumped up, and ran to her father. Basilia quickly dodged the onrushing woman. Josh caught her and returned the hug.

"You're kicking us out?" Layla asked.

"Oh, honey. No, I'm not doing anything of the sort," Josh said as he put Katherine down. "With Javy rotting in jail, I think it's about time you spread your own wings and see what's out there. Besides, my cabin isn't big enough for everyone. It's time for you guys to find your own path."

The fear in Layla's eyes was palpable and the group saw it. Heather placed an arm around her sister and said, "It's gonna be great, just the three of us, working the land... bossing Jesus and Abelardo around."

"Hey!" the Martinez boys said in unison to which she winked in response.

"Besides," Katherine said continuing the thought, "He won't be hundreds of miles away. He's right on the other side of the hedgerow."

Not fully buying into the concept, Layla said, "Well, where will we live?"

Her sister answered the question as she had continued reviewing the documents.

"It says here that the fifty acre property comes with a three bedroom, two and half bath farmhouse as well as assorted barns and outbuildings." Jokingly, Heather looked at her father and said, "Only two full baths? That'll never work. Don't you know a girl needs her own space? Geez, Dad."

Not wanting to fully interrupt the banter, but curious as to what he was holding, Juan said, "So what's this?"

"Open it," Josh replied.

The farm manager slipped the white plastic end cap off and upended the cardboard tube. A rolled up set of blueprints slid out and into to his open hand. He unfurled the document and spread the bound renderings out on the table for all to see.

He took one look at the front elevation rendering and said, "Señor! This *is* too much!"

The girls extracted themselves from the couch and came around to look over his shoulder.

"It's already done," Josh said. "They start construction next week. You guys can stay here until it's finished."

Turning the pages, the blended families scanned the documents together. There were a couple of 'oh's' and 'ah's' as each of the blueprints was revealed.

After buying the property with Amanda's money and fixing the things that needed attention, there was enough left for Josh to provide a modest remodel of the Martinez farmhouse as well. All of the money was now officially gone, the weight lifted. Aside from the expense of travelling to California to find Heather, Josh had spent the bulk of the life insurance money to take care of his daughters and extended family.

"Oh my," Basilia exclaimed as she continued reviewing the blueprints. "You would do this for us?"

"Señora, you and your family are as much a part of our family as we are of yours. You helped me raise these girls and provided them with a constant, stable, and sane female presence. I could never begin to repay you for that kindness. This is the least I could do. Besides, being paid in chickens won't provide you something you've most definitely earned."

Juan stood, walked to Josh, and extended his hand as he said, "Gracias, Señor."

Shaking Juan's hand, Josh replied, "You're most welcome, my old friend."

Shortly thereafter, hugs and handshakes were exchanged as Evan headed to the SUV. Josh would drive him to Columbus to catch the train to his destination.

As he was searching for the key fob, Heather pulled her father aside and quietly asked, "Are you dying?"

Laughing out loud, Josh said, "No. Why would you ask me that?"

"Because you just blew a quarter mil, that's why," she answered. "People don't do that unless they're doctor tells them they're terminal or they found religion."

"The money wasn't even mine," Josh replied. "It was from the life insurance policy paid to me from my ex-wife's estate. Samantha suggested that I spend it on you girls and that's what I've done. To a farmer, that was easily three years' worth of revenue, but it was tainted. It needed to be used for good."

Josh stopped and surveyed Heather's confused face. "Why don't you ride along with me to take Evan to the train station?"

* * *

Cecil Sullivan sat on the edge of the bed sobbing uncontrollably. From where he was seated, he could see his friend Travis lying in a heap on the floor. The pool of blood was slowly spreading its way across the floor.

He didn't know what to think or do. All he had were questions. Why was his friend bleeding? Why were his own hands covered in blood? Had he tried to help? Everything was blank. It was like someone had erased his mind.

If Cecil could have remembered, he would have known that his Air Force buddy had rushed to comfort him when he heard Cecil screaming in his sleep. Unfortunately, the man had not put the knife down that he had been using to prepare breakfast. When Cecil opened his eyes and caught sight of the implement, his mind's eye saw Aban about to torture him again.

The two had wrestled to the ground and Cecil had taken the sharp blade away from his friend. He then repeatedly thrust it into his torso. Travis Smalls was dead and he had absolutely no recollection of the entire ordeal.

Not knowing what to do, and not wanting to be seen standing over a dead body that he couldn't explain, Cecil quickly transitioned from sobbing to panic. The man abruptly stood and ran into his bathroom. He hastily turned on the faucet and instinctively tried to wash the blood from his hands. Once he hands were sufficiently clean, he wiped down the sink, discarded the towel, and sprinted toward the door. As he ripped it open, two men were walking up the front steps onto the porch. He ran over the first one, but was promptly tackled by the younger man. Cecil was quickly subdued and a knee was placed in his spine effectively immobilizing him. He stopped thrashing when he felt the muzzle of a gun being forcefully pressed against the back of his head. Once Cecil was sufficiently restrained, the two gentlemen stood him up.

As the pair helped him to his feet, they caught sight of his blood caked clothing. The older man spoke first.

"Airman Sullivan? My name is Colonel James. I'm a psychiatrist with the U.S. Army. Are you hurt? Where are you bleeding?"

The man said nothing.

"Let's get him inside," Colonel James said to Gregg as he began scanning the woods for witnesses and passers-by.

Cecil began leaning back against Gregg's pressure, resisting his efforts to force him back into the house. The pistol was once again pressed against the back of his skull.

"Don't make me shoot you, Airmen," Gregg threatened.

Cecil's resistance waned and he was eventually placed in one of the armchairs in the living room.

"I'm gonna have a look around and see where that blood came from," Gregg said as he started heading to the kitchen. He could see breakfast ingredients piled up on the cutting board and the eggs had already been scrambled in a bowl. Not finding any signs of foul play he went toward the bedrooms.

Colonel James stood in front of Cecil and, in calm soothing tones, said, "Airman Sullivan, can you hear me? My name is Colonel James. I am a psychiatrist. I would very much like to help you. You are safe here."

No response. All Cecil was capable of doing at this point was rocking in his armchair and humming to himself.

Gregg looked in the bedroom off of the kitchen and found no signs of a disturbance. Whoever's room it was kept it clean. The bed was made and the clothes were in the dresser. Everything in the bathroom was in its place as well. Gregg started to head into the second, but stopped when he saw a pair of hiking boots lying sideways on the floor.

Gregg snapped his fingers at the Colonel in order to gain his attention. When the man turned his head, Gregg drew his Glock and slowly worked his way up to the opening of the room. In a flash, Gregg was in the doorway with his arms partially extended like he had done hundreds of times on house-to-house searches in the sandbox. He was ready to fire in a moment's notice. Lying on the floor beneath him was Travis. The blood was fresh, no coagulation. Gregg knelt and felt for a pulse. There was none. The man was still warm, but he was dead. Gregg holstered his weapon and grabbed one of the disheveled sheets off of the bed. As he placed the sheet over the body, the Colonel came through the doorway.

In an understatement, the Colonel said, "Well, I guess that answers that."

Gregg nodded in agreement and said, "How's Cecil?"

"Not talking. He's in shock," the Colonel replied.

"I'll get him to talk," Gregg replied as he started to push his way past Col. James in the doorway.

The Colonel quickly grabbed his arm and just as forcefully said, "You will not lay a hand on that man. Do I make myself clear?"

Gregg stopped and took in the man's comment. He glanced down at the hand clutching on to him and said, "Who said anything about touching him? Just watch. If he was held by the same people, he'll talk to me."

The Colonel slowly released his grip and Gregg made his way into the living room and Cecil. The former Special Ops soldier walked around the humming man a number of times taking in his disheveled state, his stale beer smell, his breathing, the subtle rocking. When he was standing directly behind Cecil for the third time, Gregg stopped. The pair had read Cecil's service record forward and backward. He knew his propensity for the military. The Airman had wanted to make a career out of it. His parents were dead and his sister, with the exception of the late Travis Smalls, was probably the only living soul that cared if he were alive or dead.

Knowing this, Gregg leaned over the back of the armchair and screamed in his ear, "Attention! Officer on deck!"

Cecil shot out of the chair as if he had just been electrocuted and stood at attention.

Gregg slowing came around the chair until he was in front of Cecil.

"What's you name, Airman?" Gregg said in an authoritative tact.

"Senior Airman Cecil Sullivan!" he answered in like voice.

"Where you from soldier?" he was asked in a softer, but still voluminous tone.

"Albany, New York, sir!" was the reply.

Gregg looked at the Colonel, who was standing with his mouth agape, and said, "This is Colonel James. He's going to ask you a few questions... and you *will* answer him. Is that understood?"

"Yes, sir!" the man yelled in response.

The Colonel cleared his throat and began stepping toward Cecil. As he neared he said, "Stand easy, Airman."

Cecil immediately complied.

Col. James had never seen this before. It was like he was in a hypnotic state. When this was all over he was curious as to whether or not the man would remember any of the questions.

Following Gregg's lead, but more gently, the Colonel said, "Were you ever a prisoner of war?"

"Yes, sir," Cecil said.

"Were you tortured?"

"Yes, sir."

"Can you name any of your captors?"

"Aban, Mahtab, Taj, and Abbas, sir."

Gregg's eyes drew large as he didn't hear Suhrab's name mentioned.

Colonel James followed the reply with another question. "Is that all? Were there any others?"

"No, sir. Just those four plus two nurses and a doctor."

"No other tormentors?"

"No, sir," Cecil answered immediately.

"Can you describe Abbas?"

"Soulless jet black eyes. Tanned skin, not as dark as a Middle Easterner, almost Latin. Spoke English with a British accent. Was always practicing Spanish."

Gregg stepped forward and asked, "Did Abbas have a last name."

"Yes, sir. Esfahani. He was very proud of it, sir."

*Damn it*, Gregg thought. *Suhrab had a brother. Son of a bitch!*

"Were there any other prisoners?" Colonel James asked.

"Yes, sir. They brought in another prisoner two months after I was snatched out of my quarters at Bagram."

"Can you describe them?"

"No, sir. We were kept in separate cells, sir. I could identify his screams though."

"Did you break, son?"

"I held out as long as I could, sir."

"There's no shame in it, son. How long did you last?"

"Seven months, twenty-seven days, sir."

"What broke you?"

"My sister, sir."

"How's that? Your sister was in Albany."

"They showed me a video taken from a sniper's scope. They were going to kill her, sir."

The interrogation went on for another ten minutes as Cecil answered each question posed by Gregg and Colonel James. When Cecil's memory had been sufficiently taxed, Gregg motioned for Colonel James to end the Q&A and the doctor agreed.

"Thank you, Airman. You've been most helpful. Please, have a seat," he said.

Cecil complied with the order just as efficiently as he had to the line of questioning. The entire time he had answered their questions, he had been completely oblivious to the fact that his hands were tied behind his back.

Gregg went and stood next to the Colonel and said, "Now what?"

"I have no idea. I've never seen anything like this before in my life. He's definitely conditioned to the military or else he wouldn't have reflexively stood at attention. It's like he's in a trance, or hypnotized or something."

"Well, how would you wake someone up from hypnosis?" Gregg offered as a suggestion.

The Colonel shrugged, "Worth a shot."

Colonel James stepped toward the seated Airman and said, "Cecil, I want you to close your eyes."

He did as he was instructed.

"Now take three deep breaths."

He complied again.

"I'm going to count backward from three to one. When I snap my fingers, open them, and you'll be awake. Do you understand?"

"Yes, sir," Cecil replied drearily.

"OK. Three... two... one," the Colonel slowly counted and then snapped his fingers. Cecil opened his eyes and saw Colonel James and Gregg standing in front of him.

"Who are you guys? What are you doing in Travis's cabin?" Cecil asked in a demanding tone.

"You don't remember what just happened here, Airman?" Colonel James asked compassionately.

"Remember? What are you talking about? Why are my hands tied!" he demanded.

# Chapter 7

General Howard stood up, as did all of the other Joint Chiefs, when the President rose and exited the Briefing Room. Rayburn, his advisors, and the head of the FBI, CIA, and Homeland Security had been meeting several times a week with the Joint Chiefs for months to plan for an attempted occupying force on American soil. It took the better part of three meetings to get everyone fully onboard with the very real possibility that a conflict with a foreign army was brewing.

The reports coming from former President Sarkes and the U.S. Ambassador at The Hague were not encouraging. The English were rebuffing every effort toward diplomacy and détente. They wanted their pound of flesh and, come hell or high water, they were going to do everything in their power to get it.

Once everyone realized the seriousness of the situation, upper echelon military leaders, and their assorted advisors, began reviewing their 'worst case scenario' invasion plans. They'd even gone so far as to dust off ancient WWII and Cold War era contingency plans. Every conceivable scenario was explored ad nauseum. Updates included details regarding current force/strength levels for all five branches, deployments, system and technological advancements for everything from weapons platforms to satellites, as well as current and predictive signals analysis based on intercepted secure communications. Even with former President Sarkes' insight regarding the sheer volume of firearms in the hands of the citizenry, the outlook was still scary as hell.

One of the few details they all *did* agree on was that, given the number of firearms and the total volume of ammunition currently in the hands of over twelve million register hunters in the U.S., things were going to get messy in a hurry if UN troops arrived on American shores.

One planner surmised that, "The United States has 5,000 miles of coastline in CONUS, thousands of airports, not to mention the thousands of government and military installations. This is too much to possibly defend. Trying to fortify the coastline is analogous to Rommel defending the Atlantic Wall. If Hitler could have mustered a large enough force and invaded CONUS, he would have been hundreds of miles inland before being contained."

It seemed as if history were repeating itself when another planner proposed the marshaling of forces on the east coast since the aggressors were in Europe. The Pacific was too vast to cross by an armada without detection. General Howard had to intervene several times to remind the planners that, while the threat initiated in the EU, it was the UN and their collective global body that would be sending 'Peace Keepers' onto American soil. A modern day military aircraft could easily traverse that distance and drop three hundred men right on top of a city and no one would know a thing about until it was all over.

Since the creditors were after the United States financial resources, the Federal Reserve along with its two dozen banks and branches were on the top of the list for defense. These locations were closely followed by the U.S. Mint facilities. West Point and Fort Knox were military installations; therefore, they had their own battalions. Although, the cadets would need reinforcing at West Point. That left the facilities in Philadelphia, Denver, and San Francisco to be defended.

All three were heavily populated cities and two could be quickly reached from the coast. Just about every potential security protocol suggested, if implemented, would draw attention and possibly incite a panic. There was no way to fortify these facilities with much in the way of tech given the timetable provided by Sarkes and the Ambassador. As a result, weapons vaults were installed and troops were ordered into street clothes while being discreetly housed in every available apartment and loft within ten blocks of each facility. If the UN troops got through the secreted troops, only concrete Jersey barriers would stand in their way as an impediment to their heavy equipment and eventual looting.

By and large, security at these locations had been upgraded after 9/11, but most of those improvements were electronic. Cameras, screening equipment, metal detectors, and facial recognition software had been the preferred choices. They were less visible, but extremely effective. Unfortunately, the people that were looking to get into these facilities were not going to concern themselves with those mechanisms or placards decreeing that personal firearms and weapons were prohibited.

As a country, the United States had stockpiled the Federal Reserve and U.S. Mint locations with tangible goods. These were items like precious metals in the form of gold, silver, platinum, and palladium bars and coins that could be pilfered, looted, and loaded on to trucks, planes, and boats. Once plans were in place for the fortification and defense of these, the focus then shifted to the electronic currency located in the hundreds of Federal Treasury accounts worldwide. These held the funds for the publicly traded securities and could be accessed by only a handful of government employees with clearance. Hackers had been trying for decades, since the advent of computers it seemed, to access these financial records and cause havoc on the federal monetary system. As a result, the highest levels of security protocols, encryption, and algorithms had been employed to thwart such advances.

President Rayburn waded into the fray when he declared, "The intel and spy satellites will give us all of the advanced notice we need. As soon as we see them loading up, we got 'em."

That statement was quickly debunked by all of the planners and Joint Chiefs. Several counter scenarios were immediately provided as examples as to why the man was misguided.

"Sir," the Chairman offered. "Planes could be loaded with personnel while still in the hangar. Satellites could be avoided simply by loading when they weren't in range. I can give you a hundred different ways where our ability to see can be thwarted."

Rayburn listened attentively to their points and conceded, "Perhaps my statement was ill advised."

However, all agreed that a fairly predictable sign of the coming advance would be the departure of the foreign Ambassadors from their embassies in the U.S.

General Howard made his way through the Pentagon corridor thinking about all that was going on. If he were being honest with himself, he never would have given up his control of the Southern Command (USSOUTHCOM). The title 'Chairman of the Joint Chiefs of Staff' was impressive to anyone that didn't know that they held zero authority. If former President Sarkes and his reports could be believed, it appeared more and more likely that both the Northern and Southern Commands would be needed to fend off Hannibal and his ocean going horde.

When the Chairman turned the corner into his office and found Heather surrounded by staffers posing for pictures and signing autographs, he boomed, "What the hell is this?"

His staff members immediately stood at attention and Heather squealed, "Papaw!"

The two embraced and the General said, "Finish up out here and then come in to my office," as he kissed her on top of her head.

Heather posed for a few more pictures, signed the last of the autographs, and then made her way into her grandfather's office.

"How'd you get in here? I wasn't notified," Brent said.

"Security called your office and one of your staffers came and got me. I hope you don't mind," she answered.

"No, not at all. I thought you'd be in Ohio with your Dad and sisters. What brings you by?" he asked.

Heather looked around the office like she trying to spot someone eavesdropping when she noticed the office door was still open. She promptly walked back and quietly closed it. She stood there for a few moments and then placed her hand on the frame for balance.

Without facing her grandfather she blurted, "The man is crazy."

Chuckling, Brent said, "And why do you say that?"

"He says there's going to be war, a UN invasion on U.S. soil. That there'll be famine, depravity... all of it, you name it. They're all nuts. They've all been drinking his Kool-Aid."

Brent and Josh had similar conversations during his time on the farm visiting Heather. Brent tried to BS his way out of it, but then Josh plunked down a file folder full of printed online financial news articles, newspaper, and magazine clippings. Josh might be an eccentric now, but he wasn't wrong. As a result, Brent had been sending coded missives back to Josh through Samantha ever since his return to the Capital.

Josh had tried to have a similar conversation with Heather when she bolted from the SUV screaming that they were all insane. Evan had discreetly followed her and confirmed that she bought a ticket and boarded the train for D.C. Brent had known she was coming long before she showed up. He expected to see her sitting on the steps of his Georgetown brownstone though, not in his office posing for pictures.

When Brent didn't answer, Heather finally turned around and he could see the wetness from the tears on her cheeks.

"Have a seat, sweetie," the grandfather said compassionately.

Heather walked over, sat in one of the upholstered chairs, and stared at the hands folded in her lap.

Weeping, she said, "I looked for him for so long. I thought if only I could find him he would make me whole. Then Mom would be happy and everything would be great. All I managed to do though was destroy his family. A decade later, mom's dead, and he tracked *me* down. I had this idea that if I ever found him again there would be this fantastic reunion, but he's certifiable and it's all one big fat… Charlie Foxtrot."

Brent smiled at her use of military jargon, leaned back in his chair, and closed his eyes. He began to think that the world would be a much better place if everyone went back to being oblivious.

Heather looked up and saw him deep in thought when she asked, "You knew he was a crack pot, didn't you? You left me there to discover for myself that the man I searched close to fifteen years for was clinically insane."

Brent could feel her piercing eyes shooting daggers into his heart when he said quietly, "He's not crazy. He's actually telling you the truth."

"Did you not just hear a word I said? War, famine, depravity… he went on and on about how screwed up everything is going to be. I couldn't run fast enough away from that car when we got to the train station! What do you mean it's true? How can you even say that?"

Brent opened his eyes and leaned forward in his chair.

"Fuck it," he muttered to himself.

He picked up the black leather briefcase that he'd brought back from the Briefing Room and placed it on the table. Brent entered the combination for the two locks and they snapped open. Her grandfather removed a thick folder from the briefcase, closed the lid, and placed it back on the floor.

He set it down in front of her and said, "How fast can you read?"

* * *

Dallas answered his phone in the usual manner, "Go for Dallas."

A smart sounding woman replied, "Please hold for the Chairman of the Joint Chiefs."

"Whoa," Dallas said aloud as the Pentagon switchboard Muzak kicked on. *This oughta be good.*

After a few seconds, the droning noise clicked off and a commanding voice said, "Dallas McKutcheon, this is General Brent Howard and I need a favor."

"OK. And a good afternoon to you too, sir," Dallas replied sarcastically.

"I don't have time for niceties. Can you to come up here to D.C. and pick up my granddaughter and return to her to her father's farm," the General said coldly and abruptly.

"I see. And who would that be exactly?" Dallas asked.

"Heather Simmons. I believe you are good friends with her father, Josh. He gave me your number."

Dallas couldn't resist the opportunity to continue playing the smartass and said, "Maybe you should lead with that next time."

Exhaling loudly though the phone's receiver, the General said, "I'm sorry, son. I'd take her myself, but I can't get away. Josh specifically asked me to call you."

"Why didn't Josh call me?" Dallas asked.

"I don't know that answer, but the last encounter between those two didn't go so well. If I had to guess, I think he feels that she needs to hear a few things. She's not exactly receptive to hearing from him right now. Do you understand my meaning?"

"Yes, sir, I do. What's the address?"

General Howard gave him directions to his brownstone and Dallas said, "I'll be there in about five hours," and disconnected the call.

*Huh, I just hung up on the Chairman of the Joint Chiefs of Staff. I wonder how he feels about that nicety?*

Dallas quickly showered, shaved, and packed an overnight bag. He thought about hopping in the farm truck he typically used, but thought better of it once he figured it'd be a nineteen hour round trip. Instead, he jumped in the Gator and went to the barn next to James' house. James was working in there with the acetylene torch when Dallas pulled up.

"Hey, you up for a road trip?" Dallas asked the large man.

James stood up, cut off the flame, and placed his hand on his lower back and stretched.

"Where we going?"

"D.C. to pick up a package," Dallas said cryptically.

The big man removed his protective shield and placed it on the workbench. He thought about the prospect of getting away from the monotony of the mountain retreat as he turned the dials on the cylinders to shut off the gas.

"No Congress this time?" he asked.

"Nope," Dallas replied.

"Is this package something I might enjoy?" James asked.

"I think so, yes."

"Is it live like ammo or people?"

"Will you stop with the twenty questions already? Do you want to come or not?" Dallas answered.

James loved toying with Dallas' impatient nature. He paused again and feigned the contemplation of the road trip once more, just to irritate him.

"Oh my word!" Dallas bemoaned at his indecision. "I'm leaving."

Dallas then turned and started heading toward a sedan that was under a canvas cover in the corner of the barn, tucked out of the way.

"You didn't say you were breaking out your Lexus!" James decried.

"Does that mean you're comin'?" Dallas shot back.

"Hell yes, I'm comin'! This should be good. Gimme five minutes to clean up," James responded.

"Clocks tickin', jarhead! Trying movin' with some purpose for a change!" Dallas barked at him like a drill instructor.

Half an hour later, after James showered, packed a bag, and fixed some sandwiches, the pair was on the road. As the clock struck 10:00 PM, they were parked in front of the General's brownstone.

Dallas and James approached the building, but before they could knock the General opened the door.

"Come on in, gentlemen," the General said without any fanfare. "You boys are gonna have to rack here tonight. My granddaughter's fast asleep."

"What's he talkin' about? You didn't say anything about –," James started to whisper to Dallas before his friend interrupted him.

"Classified, need to know," Dallas sarcastically answered in a hushed tone.

When they got to the back of the house, the General reached into the refrigerator and handed each a beer. "How was the drive?" he asked the pair.

"Uneventful," Dallas answered.

"Good. I'm guessing you're Dallas?" the General asked.

"I am, sir," he answered as he stepped forward.

The two men exchanged handshakes. Brent turned and said, "That means you're James."

"Pleasure to meet you, sir," he said and they too shook hands.

"The pleasures all mine, son. Josh used to tell me about you and another non-com he had when he first graduated the Academy. You guys made a hell of an impression on him."

"Yes, sir. Thank you, sir. And he us, sir," James replied.

"Whoa," the General exclaimed. "That's a lot of sirs. Just call me Brent," he added.

"Roger that, sir," James said reflexively. "The other NCO was First Sergeant Ernesto Mattone. He was killed in Anbar Province during the surge," James offered.

"Sorry to hear that," Brent answered reflectively.

After letting the awkward pause linger for a few moments, Dallas cleared his throat and said, "So what is going on? Why are we being tasked with transport duty?"

"Right," Brent said abruptly. As they stood in the kitchen sipping their beers, Brent proceeded to tell Dallas and James about the conversation he and Josh had on the farm, albeit abbreviated. It was the same one that Josh had tried to have with Heather when she bolted from his car and hopped the first train to D.C.

When he finished, Dallas said, "That's great and all, but that doesn't explain how she's his kid. Does she even want to go back?"

Brent slumped down in one of the chairs at the kitchen table and exhaled loudly and slowly. He took another sip of his beer and said, "I entrusted my daughter, Jessica, to Josh when she came to visit me as part of a USO trip in Bosnia. She was starting to show signs of falling in with the wrong crowd out in LA. She had lost a lot of weight and you could tell she was into some things that were more than highly questionable, legally and morally. There were whispers in the papers and magazines and stuff that her mother and I tried to ignore, but when she showed up," and his voice trailed off.

He cleared his throat and continued, "I could see that she wasn't taking care of herself. The bags under the eyes, the weariness, and the temperamental behavior; all of it pointed to Jessica turning into all of the things we feared when she first decided to become an actress. I figured if she was exposed to men of character and principle she would see the error of her ways and realize that the path she was headed down only led to tragedy. What I didn't figure on were those two becoming lovers. The fleeting romance produced Heather."

He sat more upright and concluded with, "Josh somehow cleaned her up and the pair was inseparable. She had a light in her eyes when she was just near him. He gave her that. I don't know what he did, but he managed to relight that spark. She was more determined, focused, and energized. It amazes me still to this day because she was only there, in and out of the region doing shows, for about three or four weeks. The night he was abducted, and dragged off in to that hellish nightmare, she snuck into his quarters and that was that. Heather arrived nine months later."

"I've never heard you tell that story before, Papaw," Heather said as she stood in the doorway behind him.

Dallas and James had seen her approaching, but held their interest on Brent when she held a finger to her lips to silence them.

Brent turned in his seat and said, "How long have you been standing there?"

"Long enough," she replied.

Brent stood up and wrapped her in an embrace as only a grandfather could do. He held her silently for a few moments before saying, "I'd like to introduce you to some friends of your father's."

He motioned toward the pair still seated at the table and said, "This is Dallas McKutcheon and James Rooney. Dallas grew up with your father and knows more about him than anyone alive. James was one of your father's NCO's in the Marine Corps. If there's anything you ever wanted to know about Josh, these two men have the answers."

James stood up and walked to Heather. When she held out her hand, he brushed it aside. "Come here, girl! Handshakes are for strangers. You can call me Uncle James," he said as he wrapped her in a giant bear hug.

After he broke the embrace, he could see she was a little embarrassed by the gesture. "Oh, don't be shy," James said. "That man over there," he began as he motioned to Dallas. "He and I helped raise your sisters and we're gonna teach you everything we taught them. You might have heard them refer to us as JD."

Heather sprung to life and replied excitedly, "Yes! They mentioned you guys all the time!"

"Excellent!" James said. "Don't worry. We'll take the training nice and slow. We don't want you jumping out of any more cars and hopping the first train you see," he finished as he smiled down at her.

Heather's eyes grew wide and Dallas, having witnessed what he perceived to be fear, said, "It'll be all right. We've got plenty of time."

"No. No we don't," Heather answered.

Brent began shaking his head as a sign to not say anymore, but Heather ignored him. "Enough is enough. I'm tired of the secrets."

James spun on his heel to face Brent and said, "What secrets?"

"There aren't any. Josh already knows. He'll tell you when you get there," Brent quickly spouted. "Heather, I can't. It's classified."

Ignoring his pleas, Heather replied sternly, "One of two things is going to happen here. You can choose Option A, where I tell them. Or Option B, where you unlock that little leather briefcase of yours and show them the report."

"Report?" Dallas asked.

"I vote for Option B," James said and then added, "Sir."

# Chapter 8

Prime Minister Goodspeed entered his office on Downing Street to find the head of MI-6 and the Chief of the General Staff from Army Headquarters sitting across from his desk sipping tea.

"Good morning, Sir William... Field Marshal. Thank you for coming on such short notice," the PM said as he extended his hand.

"Not at all," they said returning the greeting.

"Welcome back," the Field Marshal replied.

The three shook hands and all took their seats.

Once seated, the Prime Minister began, "I've got a busy schedule this morning so I'll be brief. We've completed all of the various tasks that King George has charged us with at the UN. How are we coming on the deployment of the Watchers?"

The British SAS units had been nicknamed the 'Apostles' during the Second Gulf War and were their elite Special Forces. They were comparable to others employed in various nation states throughout the world. Each unit had their own specialty as well. The espionage group, known as the 'Watchers', were on standby in Aldershot, southwest of London.

"They are prepped, orders in hand, and awaiting your word, Prime Minister," the Field Marshal replied.

"And your agents, Sir William?" the PM asked.

"They have already been deployed and are currently observing the Federal Treasury and U.S. Mint locations. We've been receiving reports of activity at some of the installations," the MI-6 man replied.

"What kind? There not stupid enough to try and relocate all of those resources, are they?" the PM inquired.

"Not at the present. They *are* adding security, though. For the time being, it doesn't appear that they have attempted to move any of the bullion, copper, nickel, or silver at any of the facilities... as far as we can tell," Sir William answered

"What does *that* mean?" said the Field Marshal.

"You know those Yanks, always building tunnels and passageways. We need to get your men on the ground," he said referring to the Watchers. "We have to penetrate those structures so we'll have some eyes in there is all I meant to say. Our assets can cover the outside perimeter and observe, but it's just too much to ask of our contingent to do that *and* infiltrate."

The two men turned to look at the PM and awaited a response.

"If you were given a green light, how quickly could you get men inside?" the PM asked the Field Marshal.

"We have three units of ten men prepared to be split into two-man teams. Each team, under the watchful eye of MI-6, will access the Treasury and Mint facilities. If they departed within the hour, nightfall tomorrow," the Field Marshal answered as if knew the question was coming.

The PM picked up his secure phone and its counterpart rang in the private residence of King George in Kensington Palace.

The sovereign answered after two rings.

Sir William and the Field Marshal couldn't hear the King's side of the conversation, but the PM answered him with, "Nightfall tomorrow."

The Prime Minister listened intently for a few seconds more and then replied, "Very good, your Majesty. We'll get it done," and hung up the phone.

"It's a go. Don't let us down."

\* \* \*

Dallas and James had already showered and dressed. They were making breakfast when Heather staggered into the kitchen at 9:30. General Howard, in an effort to keep up appearances, had departed for the Pentagon at 6:00 AM, per his usual routine, but not before he awoke Heather to say goodbye. He had stayed up most of the night contemplating many things, but mostly his retirement. In the end, he had made his decision and decided to tell Heather that today was the day that he would file his paperwork. Given everything he knew about the UN build-up, Josh's invitation to retire to the farm was too good to pass up. By the end of the year, he and his granddaughter would be living in the most desolate piece of forested landscape imaginable. After forty-two and half years of service to his country, he would officially be retired from the United States Marine Corps.

He had also poked his head in to say goodbye to Dallas and James, and to thank them for coming to get Heather. The pair was already stirring when he opened their door. Before he departed, he asked them to give Josh a message. It was cryptic, but they said they would pass it along.

"Don't people ever sleep in this house," Heather said sleepily as she entered the kitchen.

"Sweet!" Dallas said. "She's up. Can we go now?"

"Hold on a minute Dallas. Let the girl get some coffee and some breakfast... maybe a shower. What's wrong with you? Geez," James said before Heather had a chance to reply.

"I'm with James," she added.

"Dude, you've got to learn to relax. The road ain't going nowhere," James concluded.

"And neither are we if you two don't get your butts in gear. It's an eight hour drive and, if you don't mind, I'd like to get there in time for dinner," Dallas intoned.

"Always thinking with your stomach."

The two carried on with their banter while Heather got her coffee and sat patiently at the table dunking her bagel. Before it was all over, the two were stuck on a debate regarding who was the better cook, Josh or Basilia. When she left the kitchen for the shower, they were contemplating whether or not they should call and ask who was cooking and what was for dinner.

The three were on the road by 11:00 AM and the first hour passed in relative silence. When Heather asked for a potty break at 12:30, Dallas guffawed and started a debate over who had a smaller bladder among their adopted nieces. James, always looking to save a couple dollars, had again packed snacks and sandwiches so they would not have to buy 'crap food' along the highway. He didn't care that his argument over processed laden foods didn't hold water anymore given the removal of the GMO's. He had his routines.

By the third hour, Heather was fully engaged in the discussions and holding her own. When she grew tired of the debates, she'd ask a question about her father.

Dallas and James were eager participants when it came to playfully throwing their friend, and her father, under the bus. When she asked how he became a Marine, Dallas regaled her with an overly dramatic interpretation of the events that led to Josh's enlistment.

"Before I tell you what *really* happened, why don't you tell me what he *thinks* happened," Dallas said before he began his story.

"He said he graduated from high school and you two went down to Myrtle Beach for 'Beach Week'. When you arrived, his girlfriend was on some guys lap. The two of them got into it and when it was all done he was sitting in front of the Marine Corps Recruiters office. That was it," Heather answered nonchalantly.

"That's it? That's all he said?" Dallas said incredulously.

"Pretty much," Heather replied.

"Well, sit back and relax 'cause Uncle Dallas is about to tell you what really happened. The girl on that dude's lap was Josh's high school girlfriend and they had been dating since 9th grade. When that boy mates, it's for life… let me tell you," Dallas started.

Half an hour later, he finished his story.

"So he did join because of a woman," she said more to herself than Dallas or James.

"What do you mean," James asked.

"When he came to California for mom's funeral, the concierge was so enamored with my mother and me that he had Josh pose as a security guard and we met. He didn't tell me who he was at the time, but when I asked why he joined he said 'a woman'. He got out because of 'a different woman'. Which motel did they stay at?" Heather asked.

"The Blockade Runner, why?" Dallas wondered.

"Because when my girlfriends and I went to Myrtle for *our* Beach Week, we stayed there once or twice."

"What! Where did you grow up?" Dallas said shocked.

"When mom flew back to the States, she was hidden away at my grandparents house in Carthage, North Carolina."

"Ho-ly crap!" James exclaimed. "You, your dad, and mother grew up forty-five minutes apart? That is amazing."

"Not only that, but my friends and I used to go up to the other side of Troy, to Lake Tillery, and go water skiing in the summer as well," Heather added.

"I remember the first time I went there actually," she continued. "I was ten, I think. My grandparents took me up there for a picnic and Papaw let me drive his boat. He seemed distant, though. It was like he wanted to be there for some other reason. He drove us down to the south end of the lake, near the eastern shore. The boathouses were built into the cliff walls, which completely fascinated me. The tiny railroad tracks leading from the docks and the water to these massive doors were amazing to me.

"When we reached this little bluff, he stopped the boat and dropped the anchor. There was a cabin and these men in uniform up top and a handful of men at the water's edge below. I think it was a funeral."

Dallas and James glanced at each other, but neither offered any commentary on her story. They just nodded to each other knowingly.

"It was a military funeral, I know that. This guy came out with a bugle and played taps and then the men in uniform fired their rifles. One of the men looked like he was spreading ashes into the lake. Seems like it was only yesterday," she said wistfully.

"I remember feeling very sad, but calm at the same time. It was weird though. There was a woman dressed in black at the top of the bluff and she was holding her two young daughters hands. They were cute as could be with these blonde curls and little white dresses. I waved to them and the mother looked like she was pointing out at our boat. Then Papaw stood up too. He just kind of stayed there, then he saluted the men on the shore. I'd never seen him do that before.

"As we were pulling up the anchor and starting to leave, one of the girls waved back. It was like a dream or something. We went back to the lake a few months later and there was a for sale sign in the yard on the bluff."

"And you remember all of that?" Dallas asked.

"Yeah, like it was yesterday, why?" Heather replied.

"And you have no idea why you were there? But you happened to come across this funeral?" James asked.

"Papaw and Nana just said we were going to go on a boat and have a picnic," Heather answered.

"That was your family, Heather," Dallas inserted. "That was us at the lake. Your father, me, James, and Ernesto. We were at the water's edge spreading your grandfather's ashes. The girls on the bluff were Amanda, Layla, and Katherine."

"You didn't wind up there by chance. Brent brought you to your grandfather's funeral," James added.

"I'm sorry. What?" Heather said, clearly stunned by the revelation.

Dallas and James said no more. Heather needed time to process this new information.

After a few minutes of silence, Dallas could see Heather weeping in the backseat. He elbowed James and motioned toward the back seat. James was always better with the emotional side of things and said, "Did Josh tell you he was from Troy?" James asked.

"Yeah, before he started with all his crazy talk," she replied.

"After reading that report, he doesn't seem too insane, now does he?" James said gently.

"Nope. Not anymore. Wanna hear something interesting?" Heather asked slowly.

James nodded and Heather said, "Last night, when I came into the kitchen, I didn't say anything because I thought I was imagining things. When I turned the corner and saw you, I could have sworn I'd seen the two of you before. I couldn't remember where though."

"Small world," James replied.

Dallas offered to change the subject when he said, "What other questions do you have? I have lots of stories about your dad."

He then spent the rest of the trip telling Heather all about Amanda, her step sisters, Josh's upbringing, and assorted adventures they'd experienced as kids. As they pulled up to the cabin, Layla and Katherine squealed with delight and ran to greet Heather and their adopted uncles.

When their friend asked how the ride went, Dallas replied, "It was fine. I think that little girl is sufficiently up to speed on the Simmons family history now. She had an interesting bombshell of her own."

"Oh. How so?" Josh asked.

"Remember those boaters at your dad's funeral?" Dallas asked.

"Vaguely. Why?"

"That was Brent, his wife, and Heather. The General brought your daughter to her grandfather's funeral," Dallas answered.

"Seriously?" he replied shocked at the news.

James added, "Not only that, but one of them waved to her."

The man was truly at a loss for words.

Observing their stunned friend, Dallas said, "He asked James and me to give you a message though. He said to tell you 'twelve twenty four and the Ides of March'. Any idea what that means?"

# Chapter 9

Navid Kashani sat in his little cramped Herndon, Virginia apartment just staring at what he had built. His fully assembled RF device was beaconing to him. *It doesn't look like much. Damn thing looks more like an old radio than a sophisticated mechanism for mayhem and chaos.*

The insurgent fighter had been an ardent follower of Suhrab's from the earliest days of the movement. It was time to announce to the rest of members that he, and the mission, was ready to take the next step.

*Time for the test fire, but on what?*

Per Suhrab's instructions, the initial target was supposed to be large enough to make a headline and be recognized, but not kill anyone. Under no circumstances were they to draw attention to the group or the device. Therefore, no military targets and no electrical grid substations. At least, not yet.

While he sat there wondering how and where to test the contraption, the Metro line became a flurry of activity outside his apartment complex as two trains passed one another. One was leaving Dulles and the other headed to it.

*Why not? What better way to cause a stink than by disabling a Metro train full of weary infidels during their Christmas travels.*

He got up and retrieved the D.C. Metro map he had procured at Union Station. As Navid sat and studied it, his eyes kept wandering back to the open briefcase on the table. Unable to fully focus, and with commuter traffic rumbling by outside, he opted to disable the new public transportation line connecting the capital to the Dulles Airport. The power failure would most likely be blamed on shoddy union mandated electrical work so there was no need to worry about the FBI or DHS banging on his door.

The man put on his winter coat and hat, grabbed his miniature pocket scope, and closed the lid on his briefcase. Before exiting the room, he turned and surveyed the little apartment one last time. He wondered if he would ever see it again, but he was confident that he would. Unlike conventional weapons, the device left no residue for some government agency to analyze. It didn't explode and cause collateral damage. It would simply look like some sort of electrical problem had shorted out the system and melted relays and wiring in the process.

Navid exited the tiny studio, locked the door, and made his way toward the back of the complex. He paused for a few moments to check if anyone was about. With no signs of other tenants, he quickly headed in to the woods that served as a buffer between the apartments and the Dulles Toll Road. The Metro line that was to be his target ran parallel to the roadway on a raised rail bed. Since the tracks were elevated, there was no place for the passengers to exit if the train became disabled. *Even better*.

As he approached his position, he used the pocket scope to scan for any of the hundreds of thousands of video cameras that blanketed the D.C. Metropolitan area. There were several at the toll entrance, of course, but they were pointed downward for facial recognition software and to capture license plates. He didn't see any mounted on the light poles like they were all over downtown.

Navid smiled as he began to setup and prime the device. The only thing left to do was to wait for the next passing train. All of the members had been trained and drilled extensively in the caves of Iran. Every single member could activate and fire the weapon in less than ten seconds if the need ever arose. He anxiously consulted the Metro timetable one last time before folding it and tucking it into his coat pocket, then nervously checked his watch. *Shouldn't be long.* A few minutes later, he heard the rumble approaching with the typical click-clack of the steel wheels on the rail.

When it came into sight a half mile down the line, Navid prepared to fire. Before doing so, he placed his hand over his genitals as a precaution. *You never know.*

With a flick of his wrist, the device activated. There was no 'boom', just silence. No recoil, combustion, or muzzle flash. It was like turning on a TV, radio, or microwave. The invisible waves bombarded the on-board electrical systems until it slowly came to a stop a quarter mile in front of him. His tunnel vision hadn't accounted for the cars coming to and from Dulles on the toll road though. Below the stopped train, the roadway filled with dozens of disabled cars as well.

Land Rovers, BMW's, beat up Chevy's, it didn't matter. Anything relying on electrical circuitry and computer chips was affected. Calmly and quietly, Navid turned off the device, closed the briefcase, and walked back to his apartment. *I'd say that was successful.*

Throughout the night, he watched the news and could see, both from the reporting and from his balcony, that the VDOT had transported cherry pickers and boom trucks to remove the passengers from the motionless tram. Over the course of the next few weeks he kept a close eye on the news. One by one, other members came online.

A streetcar went careening through the streets of San Francisco. It would have plunged into the Bay had it not been for a crafty bus driver. New York City's famed Madison Square Garden mysteriously became dark during a basketball game. The ski lifts in Telluride, Colorado ground to a halt, stranding hundreds of vacationers aloft. An Air Asia flight on approach to Sea-Tac Airport in Seattle, Washington had to abort its landing when the control tower lost power. The Metrodome in Minneapolis blacked out and thousands of cars parked in a lot at Dallas Fort Worth International wouldn't start.

That accounted for all but one of the team members. After that, everyone would be online. From there on out, all any of the group would have to do was monitor the New York Times classifieds for communication from Suhrab.

\* \* \*

"Mayday! Mayday! Mayday! This is 'Charlie-Lima-six-three-nine-heavy and we are declaring an emergency! Mayday! Mayday! Mayday!'"

"Any response?" the co-pilot asked.

"Nothing," the pilot replied as he ripped the headset off. "Ever seen a two hundred and twenty-five ton glider?"

Both men had their hands wrapped around the controls in a death grip as the Captain continued to give commands.

"How far are we from Port Columbus," the man grunted as he tried to keep the beast aloft.

"Twelve miles," his friend replied.

"Altitude?"

"Eight thousand and we're losing that rapidly, sir. What the hell happened?"

"No idea," the pilot groaned as tried keeping control. "That Cessna passed us on the port side as we were turning to line up the runway and then everything went tits up."

"I don't think we have enough to get there. Can we put down on that four lane road down there?" the co-pilot questioned.

"In the middle of all those Christmas shoppers! Are you serious!" the pilot shot back. "I'm aiming for that golf course!" the man declared, but with no flight computer he couldn't use the rudder. Everything was electronic, they didn't have the ability to fly by wire.

"Oh crap!" the Captain exclaimed as a strong crosswind began pushing them further north. Without warning, a blast of wind shear violently thrust them toward the ground.

"Mayday! Mayday! Mayday! This is 'Charlie-Lima-six-three-nine-heavy! We are going down! Mayday! Mayday! Mayday!" the co-pilot screamed into his headset as the plane slammed into the frozen earth below.

Given the cargo haulers massive bulk, the wings and tail section tore away when the machine pancaked the first house. What remained of the fuel from their cross-country flight began spewing across vast tracts of land. With its landing gear down and locked, the plane skipped left and right as each rear assembly touched down, until they too eventually snapped off. The violent impact sheared the reinforced hinges that attached the retractable cabin from the main body of the fuselage. Once freed from the rest of the structure, the projectile proceeded to skip and bounce as if it were a cartoon character smashing anything in its path on its way through the neighborhood.

After the cockpit separated, the exposed fuselage of the cargo hold worked like a shovel digging its way into the manicured lawns full of

Christmas lights. The momentum brought the tubular section vertical and flipped it over and over until it came to rest on a gas station. Pallets of packages were strewn across a half-mile of chewed up earth through the affluent suburb.

The destruction and debris left by the wayward aircraft was coated in jet fuel. The most insignificant little spark turned the formerly plush landscape into a wall of fire igniting everything in its wake. Propane cylinders on back yard grills started flying through the air as they erupted into fireballs. The crushed and burning cars were smoldering at first, but once the fires reached the gas tanks, they too were turned into firebombs and thick black smoke. The gas station resting under the main body of the fuselage began spraying and leaking fuel from its half dozen pumps. When the flames came into contact with vapor, the magnitude of the shockwave from the explosion blew out windows for blocks. The destructive force with which the plane hit left a debris field that could only be compared to a war zone or a tornado.

Amanda's sister, Kristen, was in the basement finalizing the last of the buyer requested fixes when she heard the pronounced 'boom'. To her, through the insulation and framing, it sounded like thunder.

*A thunderstorm?* she thought. *It's the middle of December.* She wiped away a layer of dinge and cobwebs to have a look at the horizon when she saw the massive brown tinted fuselage and fireball headed right at her seemingly in slow motion.

Instinctively, she shrieked in horror, ran back to the washer and dryer, and dove between them to take cover.

The earth shook as the remnants of the plane approached. Suddenly, with a horrendous crash, the entire back of the home exploded into oblivion. The breaking of glass, twisting of metal, and the snapping of lumber were deafening. Kristin covered her ears while she continued to scream in protest. The stairwell quickly filled with debris. Her only means of escape blocked.

Then, as quickly as it had started, it was over.

* * *

Josh's former neighbor, Bryan, watched in horror. The concussive explosion had brought him to his front door. As he opened the solid wood door and peered through the glass storm door, he found himself frozen in place. His legs wouldn't obey his brains' command to flee as the cockpit section came barreling toward him through his old friend's home.

As soon as the cabin came to a full stop in the street between the two homes his legs finally kicked into gear. Like a gazelle, he sprang from his front door and darted across the street to find Kristin. He knew she was there. He had seen the taxi drop her off.

As Bryan climbed atop the remains, he scanned west toward the carnage left in the planes vicious wake. In the distance, he saw the chewed up path for as far as the eye could see. The horizon appeared to contain miles of billowing black acrid smoke in the doomed airliners wake. Bryan cautiously waded through the remnants of Josh's former home. His attention was temporarily stolen away when secondary explosions began violently announcing themselves.

As for the home Josh and Amanda had once shared, the fuselage barreled directly through the center of the house as it was rapidly decelerating. When it tore its way through, all of the debris had been thrown outward against neighbor's homes making them lean like the tower of Pisa. There were almost no walls to speak of, and the second story and roof were scattered to the winds. All that remained on the main level were thousands of shards of broken glass and the hardwood flooring. Water pipes sprayed their contents several feet in the air. If Bryan hadn't seen it disintegrate right in front of him, he'd have thought someone was actually building a home.

Kristin had been fortunate. The nearly eighty year old home had been sturdily built with an I-beam running through the center of the basement. When she took cover between the washer and dryer, she was protected further by one of the three steel posts anchored into the concrete.

The low profile of the foundation pushed the cockpit of the destroyed craft up onto the main floor of the house. From there, the hardwood acted as a slip-n-slide for the cabin. Other than some dust being knocked free by the collision, nothing else was disturbed in the unfinished basement.

As Bryan leapt on to the remaining structure, he began searching for her.

"Kristin!" he called. "Are you in here!?"

She heard the repeated calls loud and clear. Meekly she answered, "I'm down here. I'm in the basement."

The muffled sounds were slight, but intelligible. He quickly went to where the stairwell had been and began heaving and tossing debris in an effort to uncover the opening.

Bryan tried to calm her, but the frantic pitch of his own voice betrayed him. "Hold tight! I'm gonna get you outta there!"

Kristin, far calmer than he, extricated herself from her hiding place, walked to the bottom of the stairs, and awaited her resurrection. She patiently listened as he kept digging. When she saw the water from the severed lines pouring down the cinderblock wall, she casually shut off the water main to the house.

"How's it coming," she asked nonchalantly.

"Just about there," he grunted as he heaved another section away from the stairwell opening.

A small ray of sunlight began peeking through and she reached her hand through.

"I'm right here, Bryan," she said calmly.

He knelt down and grabbed ahold.

"Are you okay?" he asked her out of breath.

"Everything's fine down here. I turned off the water. The pipes should empty in a minute or two. What happened?" she asked.

"Looks like one of the cargo planes from Port Columbus just freight trained about nine city blocks. Amanda's was the last one. What's left of the cabin is parked out in the street," he answered.

"Josh is gonna laugh his ass off when he sees this," she said candidly.

Bryan let go of her hand and said, "Yeah well, he always did hate this house. Now let's see about getting you out of there first."

"There's a chainsaw in the garage," she offered and he began laughing.

"What's so funny?" she asked.

"You'll get the joke once I get you out," he answered.

A few minutes later the two were standing and staring at what remained of Amanda's home. There was no garage. Kristin finally got the unintentional joke.

The pair worked their way up the debris field getting as close as they dared to the burning rubble. The plane took out several dozen homes in the tightly packed community before coming to rest in the front yard. The house behind Amanda's had been rented to students attending Ohio State. The only way anyone would have known that there was a home there previously was by the foundation of the now fully exposed basement.

An hour or more passed before fire crews and medics arrived at the remains of the cockpit. They quickly removed the dead Captain and co-pilot from their seats. Their necks had snapped in the impact. It wouldn't be long before the news crews descended on the scene. While there, the EMS squad gave Kristin a once over and declared that she had to be the luckiest person in this whole disaster. She didn't have a scratch. The first responders hastily returned to where they were needed, but decreed that they would keep an eye on what was left of the house in case floating embers reached the potential tinderbox.

Barricades of yellow 'Caution' tape were erected, but given the size and amount of devastation, the perimeter couldn't be held, not yet at any rate. News crews simply lifted the flimsy plastic tape and drove under.

Once they found the cockpit and Kristin, she quickly became inundated with requests for an interview. While she was dealing with that, Bryan attempted to call Josh.

It didn't take long for him to discover the futility of the endeavor. The disintegrating plane had just severed all of the aerial phone lines as it tore its way through the hundred-year-old neighborhood. Once realized, he reached for his cell. There, he discovered jammed towers and the pre-recorded message stating that 'all circuits are currently busy'. He hung up and tried again, and again, and again. Giving up, he retreated to his basement and the Ham radio. It had been years since the pair had spoken on the device, but maybe Josh would hear his pleas.

\* \* \*

Gregg had had enough of Col. James' delays and Cecil Sullivan's incessant whining and weeping. Unfortunately, when he reached his breaking point, it was in the middle of a therapy session between the three of them. Cecil had yet to divulge much about his experience and wouldn't consent to hypnosis, or Gregg's more radical suggestion of scopolamine. Every time the sessions began heading toward the torture, Abbas, or Aban, Cecil would shut down.

Gregg couldn't take it anymore. When he snapped, he had screamed at Cecil, "Hey buddy! Quit your friggin' whining! I was held in that same hellhole too. I killed that SOB, all right! Get over it! You're about as useful as a flaccid penis!"

Cecil just began crying harder and louder.

Col. James attempted to intervene, but Gregg kept at it.

Gregg was thrown out of the session when he shot out of his seat and whispered in Cecil's ear, "I'm curious, Cecil. What wakes you up first... the sound of your screams or the smell of your own urine?"

The next day, the Colonel ordered Gregg to apologize. He did so, but only half-heartedly.

Each day, after making a comment to Cecil, and the subsequent removal from the session, Cecil would open up just a little further. What Cecil didn't know was that it was planned. On some level, it was sick and twisted what they were doing to the former Airman, but it was working. As they found out at the cabin, Cecil was conditioned to the military, but he was no longer in shock. In fact, he had no memory of killing his friend or of answering Gregg and Col. James' questions afterward. They needed another way in to the vault of Cecil's mind.

The pair was making progress however. The Colonel and Gregg were convinced that it would only be a few more days before Cecil finally spilled everything. Every time Gregg was removed from the session, he watched the remainder of the session from behind the two-way glass. When he noticed something change or shift in Cecil's demeanor or posture, he'd alert Col. James through his ear piece to stay with a topic or move on and go another direction.

After a week of being thrown out of the sessions, Gregg finally found Cecil's button. His sister, Anna.

Gregg made a comment about how they had met her while searching for him and Cecil visibly stiffened. Gregg backed off immediately, but mentioned it to Col. James afterward. He had seen it too. The next day Gregg brought her up again, but proceeded to break into a full sprint right over the lines of decorum and taste.

"Hey, Cecil," Gregg started. "You think your sister would want to go out with me some time? She sure was pretty. Nice rack too. Do you know if she does it on the first date?"

That was all it took.

Cecil bolted out of his seat and lunged across the table at Gregg. Both the Colonel and Gregg knew that Cecil was no match for Gregg's advanced skill set in hand-to-hand combat. However, when they hatched their plan, the therapist stipulated that under no circumstances was Gregg to go on the offensive and neutralize Cecil's attack. He would was only permitted to take defensive postures. He could not fight back and strike Cecil.

When Airman Sullivan snapped, Col. James quickly left his chair and backed away. The man was like a rabid animal. He hit Gregg with knees, haymakers, and forearms for about a minute before the Colonel decided it was probably enough and needed to break it up. When Cecil tried stomping on Gregg's head with his boot, he quickly interceded. Gregg kept his word and merely protected himself. There were dozens of opportunities where Gregg could have reversed the tables and probably killed Cecil with a few quick moves and the snapping of his neck, but he let the process run its course. Cecil needed to get this out of system.

For effect, Gregg played up the moaning and agony while being escorted from the session to the infirmary on a gurney. That, once again, left only Colonel James and Cecil in the room.

Cecil gleefully broke open like a cofferdam. He provided a flood of information so quickly that Col. James stopped taking notes. It was all being recorded anyway. Cecil was able to give a description of Abbas, his mannerisms, things that seemed to intrigue him during the interrogations, what set him off, and the man's insatiable need to study and practice his Spanish. All the while, Cecil basked in the knowledge that Gregg had killed Aban and now he had been strong enough to take out Gregg.

When Cecil divulged what Abbas had been after during his yearlong captivity, the Colonel jumped out of his seat like he had been shot out of a gun. He went running toward the door and the nearest phone. As he exited the room, he and Gregg nearly ran each other over.

The United States maintained an arsenal of over four hundred land based nuclear missiles. All were located within the continental U.S. at either Malmstrom Air Force Base (AFB) in Montana, Minot AFB in North Dakota, and F.E. Warren AFB in Wyoming.

Cecil had been stationed at two of them and Abbas had a several month head start.

# Chapter 10

The PM and the head of MI-6 stood as the Iranian Foreign Minister entered the PM's office.

"Good Morning Prime Minister, Sir William. This was a most unexpected call," the man said as he extended his hand.

Immediately after escorting the diplomat into the office on Downing Street, the agent exited and closed the door. Even though he was standing just outside, the room was sound proof, he heard nothing of their conversation.

"Good morning," the PM said in a clipped tone. "Please, do have a seat."

The Foreign Minister, sensing the urgency and thinly veiled anger replied, "Is there a problem? Has our nation not done everything you have requested of it?"

"Minister Nafisi, perhaps you could explain what the bloody hell one of your jihadists is doing on American soil," the PM said tersely.

"I'm sure I have no idea what you're speaking of, Mr. Goodspeed," the diplomat replied coolly.

"Really?" the PM said with mock surprise. "Care to explain this," he said as he spun his computer monitor around for the Foreign Minister to see. The PM pressed a key on his keyboard and a video began to play.

The video clearly showed a man open a briefcase on a park bench in front of the U.S. Mint facility in San Francisco. As the video played, Sir William narrated.

"What you are seeing here is an Iranian jihadist, or citizen if you prefer, enabling what is commonly referred to as a suitcase EMP device. This man has chosen a trolley as his target. The Americans like to call them streetcars. Please observe what happens after he closes the briefcase."

Minister Nafisi watched, not in horror, but with pride and complete fascination. The famed San Francisco streetcar began rolling down the street, picking up speed as it did so. It smashed in to a car as it careened through an intersection. The steel wheeled behemoth collided and bounced off anything it came into contact with as it made its way down the steep incline of the area streets. As the video neared its conclusion, the Iranian diplomat watched as a quick thinking city bus driver prevented it from splashing into the Bay by allowing it to rear end the larger vehicle and bring it to a stop.

The PM spun his monitor back toward himself and said, "Well?"

Wiping the slight grin off of his face, Minister Nafisi replied, "While this is a most tragic event, I fail to see how the briefcase or we, as a nation, had anything to do with this."

The PM and Sir William said nothing. The PM swung his screen back and hit the key on his keyboard again. A second video began.

"We have agents observing the U.S. Mint and Treasury buildings," the head of MI-6 said as he continued his narration. "One of our teams observed and followed your man back to his apartment. This is a recording of his capture and interrogation."

The video started with a close up of a door. Suddenly, a leg came flying in to view and kicked it open. Three men quickly entered with weapons drawn. They were closely trailed by the fourth man holding the camera. By the time the cameraman was in the room, the suspect was already on the floor speaking a hundred miles an hour in Spanish.

"See!" the Foreign Minister exclaimed. "How many Persians speak *that* language? Not many! He's probably a tourist or some Mexican that jumped the border."

"Please keep watching Minister Nafisi," the PM said tersely.

The monitor went black for a few seconds and then resumed playing. The backdrop of the apartment was replaced by a derelict warehouse. The Foreign Minster watched as the bound man was dunked repeatedly into a tank of water, beaten unmercifully, and asked scores of questions in numerous languages. As the agents worked their way through the numerous Middle Eastern languages, the man's expression changed. When they reached Farsi, the man cracked.

The detainee began begging for mercy in his native tongue. 'No more, no more,' the man kept calling out. For the next twenty-seven minutes of raw video, the man answered every question put to him while the Foreign Minister sat stoically silent. The man divulged every operational detail he knew; how many men, the training in the caves, what the device was, how it worked, how they were transported to the Mexican port, how they crossed the border, mission objectives, everything.

Minister Nafisi had to contain the smile that was building. The captured man knew nothing of Abbas.

When the video ended, the PM slowly turned the monitor back. In a softer, more diplomatic tone, said, "Now, shall we begin anew?"

* * *

Layla stealthily crept through the cabin and disconnected the power supply to the driveway chime mechanism. Once that task was complete, she motioned for her sisters to enter the room.

"Hey Dad?" she called for her father.

"In here," he replied from his office as he quickly began covering un-wrapped Christmas presents. "Okay, you can come in."

All three girls entered smiling.

"What's up," he said nonchalantly.

"We have a present for you," Layla answered for them.

"Great! Put it under the tree," he declared.

"Can't," Heather said. "It's too big. We need you to go to your room so we can bring it in."

"I guess that answers the 'bigger than a bread box' question," he replied with a sly smile and began complying with their request.

Josh entered his room and waited for the door to close. As soon as it clicked shut, he opened the top drawer of the dresser and removed the ring he had bought for Sam.

"Silly girls," he said to himself. "Nothing happens on this farm that I don't know about."

For days the girls had been whispering and scheming. He knew something was up. When he tried to reach Samantha in DC, Secretary McInerney's niece had let the cat out of the bag. She was on her way to see him for Christmas. He could hear hushed conversations and giggling.

With his daughter's blessing, and trying to be as romantic as possible given the circumstance, he got down on one knee just inside his bedroom. He had the ring box open and presented in his hand.

"Okay, you can come out," the girls decreed in unison.

*Dang*, he thought dejectedly. *Maybe she's not here yet. Must be something else.* He closed the lid, shoved it in his back pocket, and went to the door.

When he opened it, there was Samantha in a skinny black dress and pearls down on one knee.

"Josiah Grant Simmons, will you do me the honor of being my husband?" Sam asked.

Josh smiled at the gesture, but said nothing. He calmly reached back and removed the ring box. He opened it as he went down to his knee to join her.

"Only if you'll do me the honor or being my wife first, Samantha Marie Jameson," he replied as he presented the diamond.

She eagerly nodded her approval as Josh slid the ring on her finger. Weeping tears of joy for their father, the three girls then rushed over and wrapped them in hugs.

"You guys set us up," Samantha said from middle of the smothering embrace.

"Funny story," Layla started to say.

"You two asked for our blessing only days apart," Heather added.

"It was the least we could do," Katherine concluded.

The blissful exchange was interrupted when Josh heard the Ham radio crackling to life in his office.

"Raven calling Mother Hubbard. Come in Mother Hubbard. Raven calling Mother Hubbard. Come in," the call repeated frantically.

The group broke the embrace and went to the sound of the distress call.

"I thought you said you came up with that name on the fly," Sam said as the entered the office. "Who's Raven?"

"It's my old neighbor. We gave each other those names as a joke. I asked him to keep an eye on the girls when they went to visit their mother. I wasn't allowed within five hundred yards of the house. He's an electrical engineer with a penchant for Greek mythology. The raven was the messenger of the gods. So he took the call sign 'Raven' and I became the over bearing, over protective 'Mother Hubbard'. I guess I just reverted to that when I tried to reach Elias."

Josh picked up the handset and queued the mic. "This is Mother Hubbard. Go ahead Raven," Josh replied into the handset.

"You need to get up here ASAP!" came the harried reply.

* * *

Two hours after Bryan made his transmission, Josh and his caravan were parked only a few blocks from his former home. With more police on scene, the perimeter was no longer porous. During the brief radio exchange it had been explained that Kristin was unharmed, but the house was obliterated. As far as Bryan could tell, there was nothing to salvage except whatever was in the basement.

Josh contemplated bringing one of the big farm trucks in his haste to get to Columbus, but opted to leave it at the cabin. Neither he nor his girls needed anything from their former home.

The group quickly exited their vehicles and bypassed the assembled law enforcement detachments by hopping fences and cutting through backyards. Within minutes, they were approaching Bryan's driveway. As they neared, they could see the pair standing in the front yard. When Layla and Katherine caught sight of them, they broke into a sprint yelling, 'Aunt Kristin!' The three embraced and the girls acknowledged Bryan by saying 'Hi, Mr. Billson'.

"Your girls sure have grown," he said to Josh as the old friends shook hands.

Josh introduced the rest of his merry gang and Bryan's eyes nearly popped out of his head when he heard the words, 'Heather is my daughter' and 'Samantha is my fiancée', exit Josh's mouth.

The group walked across the street and surveyed the damage. Bryan showed them all of the lumber and material he had to remove from the opening and relayed Kristin's comment about the chainsaw to several chuckles.

The girls climbed up on what was left of the first floor decking and could see the water stains in the hardwood where they had repeatedly stomped their snow boots as children and began to cry. The house represented the last symbol of their tormented youth and they couldn't hold in the hate and anger anymore, not after they had read their mother's confession. The brave faces and years of therapy melted away at the sight of the destroyed home.

Kristin tried to take their minds off of the subject of their mother and the kidnapping by taking them to the basement to show them all that remained. The plan backfired. In the basement they found the dance recital outfits Amanda had saved. Right next to them, on another clear plastic covered rack, they saw their mother's dresses from various high school dances, proms, and weddings that they had used when they played dress-up as children. Layla began crying and Katherine became physically sick. The two ran haphazardly through the shell of the structure back into their fathers arms.

"Mind if they sit in the house while we have a look around?" Josh asked as he rubbed their backs to warm them.

Without hesitating, Bryan replied, "Since when do they need permission? Go on in girls, the candy is in the cabinet as usual."

Samantha suggested that she stay with the girls, but when she entered Bryan's home the girls were nowhere to be found. Eventually, she discovered them upstairs in one of his son's old bedrooms. The two were lying on the floor playing with Lego's.

"Mind if I join you?" Samantha asked.

Sniffling, Katherine said, "Sure, but you have to get your own."

Samantha looked around and hastily grabbed a half completed set on top of the dresser.

Without prompting, Layla said, "We used to spend hours over here. The five of us were inseparable. We did everything together."

"Where are they now?" Samantha asked as she snapped pieces into place and began building the toy structure.

"The twins just graduated from OSU. One moved to Texas for his first job, a bank, or something. The other one went to Europe to find himself. The youngest one is in school at Juilliard," Layla replied.

"You guys stay in touch then?" Sam asked.

"We exchange email once in a while. Mom used to get so mad at us when we came for our supervised visits. Every time we were up here all we wanted to do was go outside and play with the boys. She yelled at them pretty good one time and scared them off. I always hated her for that. Bitch," Katherine answered.

"Katherine!" Sam exclaimed.

"Well, she was," she replied calmly. "She turned Heather away when she came looking for Dad and then she ruined our lives by using drugs and getting involved with that psychopath and his brother. She deserved everything she got."

Samantha thought for a moment and said, "That's one way of looking at it."

"How else would you look at it? Javy was right. The woman turned into a greedy drug addicted whore," Layla said.

"That's it!" Samantha exclaimed. "No more 'bitch' or 'whore' talk. Understand?" she decreed.

The girls jerked their heads up and glared at her. After a few seconds, when Samantha's stern look didn't disappear, the pair nodded their agreement.

"What I meant was, yes, you two went through hell, but you came through it stronger, more independent, and self-reliant. You have your father to thank for that. He moved mountains to ensure your safety and provided as much of a normal life as was humanly possible. Yeah, he goes a little overboard sometimes, but that man's world would end if something happened to either of you."

"A little?" Katherine said with a smirk.

Samantha exhaled loudly and said, "All right, a lot overboard, but you're missing the point. There aren't many fathers that would have gone to the lengths that your father did. Most would have shut down, built up walls, and let you to sink or swim on your own. He could have stopped caring, but he didn't. He stood up and declared that no one was ever going to hurt you like that again. Even his friends all treat you two like you are their own. That's a rare thing in this world. There isn't a person standing outside this house that wouldn't go to the ends of the Earth to help the two of you."

"Three of us, actually," Heather said tearfully. "Sorry, I didn't mean to eavesdrop, but I was wondering where you guys went." She surveyed the room and said, "Can I play too?" as she swiped another half completed set from the dresser.

"I've seen the lengths to which our father is willing to go," she added as she took her position on the floor. "I may have only met him, but I do know one thing. Your mom was wrong. Had he known about me, he'd have figured a way to make it work. He never would have left you guys, or your mother. He would have been as involved as was humanly possible. I know that now." Then, as an afterthought, she added, "People do some really stupid things for money."

\* \* \*

Dallas and James stood in the street looking at the fuselage talking when Josh, Kristin, and Bryan came walking back from the destruction of the house.

"Hey, Bryan," James called out. "Have any of those NTSB boys checked this out yet?" he asked while pointing up at the wreckage.

"The fire and EMS crews were here for about twenty minutes or so. Just long enough to remove the bodies. I imagine they are back there somewhere," Bryan answered as he pointed west behind the house. "They're probably looking for the black box."

Without asking or receiving permission, Dallas jumped into the open end of the fuselage and started climbing up toward the cockpit. The other men followed suit, leaving Kristin standing guard outside.

"What are you doing," Josh said as he trailed Dallas.

"I'm looking to see if there are any clues as to why this thing fell out of the sky," Dallas answered as he moved dangling wires and debris out of his path.

Bryan started to climb up as well when something caught his eye and he stopped. He reached out and grabbed a burned wiring harness that was hanging from the exposed ceiling and rotated it in his hands, inspecting it. As he looked closer, he saw other harnesses and relay switches, all fried.

"I think I found what you're looking for," he called out, as he peered at the sheathing on the wires.

"Son of a gun," he exclaimed.

Dallas and the others stopped climbing and started heading back toward Bryan.

"What have you got there," Josh said as his old friend yanked some of the wiring free.

"At first, I thought this melting and burning was a result of the fireball when it crashed, but look at the interior. There's hardly any fire damage. And look at these," he said as he handed Josh a relay. "What do you see?"

"It looks like it was burned," Josh said as he looked it over and gave it to James. "All of the circuits are toast."

"And this?" Bryan said handing over a harness.

"Fried too," Josh answered.

"Now look at the wires," he continued as he began providing wire after wire. "The plastic sheathing is melted."

"Yeah, but you said there was a pretty big explosion and fireball. This stuff could have shorted when it crashed," Dallas said.

"Look a little closer. See how it's bubbled like that?" Bryan explained. "That came from the inside out. Fire damage doesn't do that."

"So what did it?" Dallas asked impatiently.

"Lightning could this, right?" James asked.

"Yeah, it could, but I don't see any storm clouds. If I had to make an educated guess, based on the damage I see to all of the on-board electronics, I think this sucker got hit by an EMP."

# Chapter 11

Brent Howard pulled up to Josh's cabin to find it deserted. He knocked on the front door, rang the doorbell, and tried the handle. Nothing. *He knew I was coming.* The man took a seat on the front porch and decided to wait. *Some grand welcome.*

The sound of a distant hum piqued his interest though. Since no one was home at Josh's cabin, he thought he'd take a look. He didn't have anything else to do.

When he cleared the hedgerow, he saw the speck of a quad copter drone hovering high in the sky. *What the hell?*

Without warning, the reconnaissance vehicle began rapidly descending. As it approached the ground, it abruptly slowed back to a hover in front of him at eye level. As he stared at it in disbelief, the camera mount rotated to face him. The General reached out to touch it and it quickly backed up.

Brent cocked his head at the hovering device. In response, the machine seemed to dip left and right and waggle at him, like it was laughing. As he stepped closer to it again, the copter turned around and started leading him toward the Martinez farmhouse. The retired General followed it like a child being enticed by a stranger with candy.

The home started to come into view around the last of the hedge and he could see Basilia standing on the front porch with the remote in her hands. She calmly directed the flying ROV and landed it gently next to her.

"What is that?" Brent called out.

She shushed him and motioned for him to approach quietly.

"I couldn't resist," she whispered sheepishly.

"Resist what?"

"I bought this for the boys for Christmas so they could survey the farm remotely. I couldn't help myself and had to try it out."

"Speaking of that, where is everyone?"

"You haven't heard the news?"

"No," Brent replied confused. "What am I missing?"

"Come on in. I'll fix us some coffee and bring you up to speed."

\* \* \*

Former President Sarkes exited the armored car in front of the main house at Camp David and began walking steadfastly toward the front door. His body was drained physically and mentally from the months of travel and non-stop negotiations. He needed to rest. Impulsively, he saluted the Marines standing guard outside as President James Rayburn opened the door and welcomed him in.

The two Presidents had been in constant contact with each other as Tom attempted to do President Rayburn's bidding across the Atlantic at The Hague. During his time overseas, he had managed to negotiate four backdoor deals with France, Spain, the Netherlands, and India. The former History major enjoyed the irony. All had a built-in deep seated disdain for the English as either former colonies or colonial rivals, but billions were owed to each by the U.S.

Even with the Keystone pipeline online, reduction in entitlement spending during the Sarkes administration, and copious amounts of natural gas exports, the U.S. was still burning through cash. All told, over one hundred billion needed to be distributed to these nations in order to garner their support, albeit subversive.

The DGSE had informed Sarkes that the English had dispatched MI-6 and several 'Watcher' teams from the Apostles to infiltrate as many facilities as possible. When Tom asked how they knew all of this information, the Minister answered slyly, "No man can resist the allure of a French maidens pout."

In response, the U.S. employed its own covert forces. The spies were now spying on the spies.

With the Treasury and Mint buildings being watched, it would be near impossible to sneak out the millions of gold bars needed to repay each of the countries in bullion. With the assistance of the Federal Reserve and the Treasury Department, they began draining discretionary and slush funds, as well as black accounts from hundreds of banks worldwide.

Before Sarkes stepped foot in the Camp David compound, they had cobbled together the hundred billion dollars owed to the four nations. The United States now had some allies.

"You look like hell, Tom," Jim Rayburn said.

"Oh yeah? What's your point? You look like crap all the time," he retorted.

The two chuckled as Jim took Tom's bags and handed them to the porter. A raging fire was going in the oversized fireplace and two drinks were waiting on the bar.

"Veronica preferred this place at Christmas," Tom said referring to his late wife. "The staff always goes all out for the holidays. Why aren't you at the White House?"

"Probably for the same reason she liked it here so much, I guess," the POTUS replied.

"Avoiding the Press Corps too?" he said with a laugh.

"Exactly," Jim replied. "Listen, Tom, I need you to take one last trip. I'd like you to accompany the 'Delta One' shipment out of Denver. The Commander up there is a jumpy little bugger. I'm afraid he's gonna make a wrong move and get some people killed."

"Why not," Sarkes replied with shrug. "It's not like I have anything else to do. This international business is as far as I can take it."

"Excellent!" Rayburn responded.

The POTUS looked as if had more he wanted to say, but stopped.

"And?" Tom prodded as he started heading toward the two glasses at the bar.

"We need to discuss a few things. Issues other than the Hague."

Tom slowed his walk and sighed, "What now?"

"We've managed to keep a lid on it for now, but Homeland and the FBI are investigating a series of 'electrical disturbances' throughout the country," Jim said in a slightly annoyed tone.

"What are we talking about here?" the former leader asked.

"For about a month, power surges and shorts caused all sorts of problems. Sea-Tac is operating on VFR only, the DC Metro stopped working out at Dulles, sporting events went dark, street cars, ski lifts, parking lots... you name it. But today," he started to say.

"What, Jim?"

"A plane was brought down over a suburb."

"Casualties?"

"Thankfully, it was a cargo plane so only the pilot and co-pilot were onboard. Latest reports have it north of fifty dead on the ground. Double that wounded," the President responded.

Sarkes thought about the man's comments before he asked, "You know what this sounds like?"

Jim exhaled loudly as he said, "Yeah, unfortunately, I think I do."

"Is the NSA still keeping tabs on the fringe tech folks?" Sarkes questioned.

"Yup, and this has 'he who shall not be named' written all over it," Rayburn began.

"Don't say it, Jim," Tom said cutting him off. "We had that guy committed when he went off the rails. He doesn't exist."

"Then you do remember him," Jim said.

"Of course I do, I was the one that signed the commitment order. Reginald Lee. That little bastard escaped the psych ward and disappeared. He warned us about these types of devices; small, portable, and concealable. He was brilliant and designed some of the NSA's more advanced systems and programs."

"If I recall," the POTUS interjected. "He started doing experiments with EMP's for us with that Chester Daniels fellow when he went off the deep end and gave that interview. You had him committed in the interest of National Security. I agreed with that decision. Think someone else figured out the tech and is using it on U.S. soil?" Jim asked.

"Sure as hell sounds like it. We never found Reggie though. Just up and disappeared. Please tell me you guys found him," Tom inquired.

The President responded candidly. "We went looking for him when it first started. According to the report I was given, he's been living the quiet life off the grid with some other conspiracy theorists he met in the mental ward, including Chester. We had the NSA use their facial rec software and track him down. It took some doing, but they found him out near Portland."

"Any chatter from the usual suspects?" Sarkes questioned.

"Unfortunately, no. We're not hearing anything out of the Middle or Far East, or the former Eastern Bloc. It's a complete global radio silence," Jim answered, clearly puzzled.

"Brits?"

"We don't think so, but we haven't ruled them out. Whatever it is, it's lightweight and portable."

Tom thought for a few moments as he walked over to the bar and retrieved the drinks.

"How many occurrences," Tom asked

"Just the eight," Jim said half under his breath.

Tom spat his drink back into his glass and said, "Holy crap, Jim! Homeland and the FBI have nothing to go on?"

"I didn't say that, Tom," Jim replied. President Rayburn then stood and turned toward one of his Agents, "You can show Col. James and our guests in now please."

"What's going on, Rayburn?" the former President asked.

A side door opened and Sarkes could see a full bird Colonel enter. He was followed closely by two additional men.

"Tom, I'd like to introduce you to Col. Wilson James. He's the head of the PSY/OPS group out of Germany. He's been following some intel for us."

Col. James quickly stopped, came to attention, and saluted.

The former President gave an abrupt return salute and asked, "His shadows are?"

The Colonel stepped to his right to reveal a young man in an Air Force uniform, who said, "Senior Airman Cecil Sullivan, sir," as he saluted.

President Sarkes returned the gesture again, and said, "Next?"

"Weapons Sergeant Gregg Chastain," the third man answered.

"Okay, we have a Colonel, an Airman, and a special forces operator. *All* of these things are not like the other," Tom quipped. "What are we into gentlemen?"

The next hours were spent bringing the former leader up to speed as he sat in disbelief. No detail was spared. When they were finished, President Rayburn had four rooms made available for the guests. At Col. James' request, a guard was posted outside of Cecil's room.

At 6:00 AM Christmas morning, Tom Sarkes exited his bedroom to find Gregg rummaging around in the kitchen.

"Can I help you find something, son," Tom said from behind Gregg startling him.

Once he recognized the voice, he relaxed. "I'm just looking for some coffee grounds, sir."

"Did you get any sleep?" Tom asked gently.

"It was fitful. You'd think Camp David would have more comfortable beds," he replied and the man laughed.

"Next cupboard over, top shelf," Tom replied.

The two made coffee in silence and then took seats on the leather couch situated in front of the still glowing embers from the previous night. Gregg sat his mug down on the coffee table and tended to the fire. Once it was ablaze again, he retook his seat. Behind them they heard the shuffling of slippers across the hardwood floor.

"I thought I smelled coffee," said a voice from the shadows.

The two men quickly stood and turned around. The First Lady was staring back at them.

"Glad to see some men still have manners," she said with a sly smile on her face.

"Yes, ma'am," Gregg answered. "Coffee, ma'am?" he asked.

"Have a seat young man. I can get it myself," she replied as she shuffled off to the kitchen.

The two men sat in silence staring at the fire until Tom said, "So *Weapons Sergeant* Chastain, what was your specialty, if you don't mind my asking."

Without looking up, he answered, "Shooter."

"I see," the former President said knowing exactly what that meant. "What was your call sign... or handle, or whatever?"

Gregg smiled at the man's attempt.

"Did you know they gave me the moniker 'Ironside'? Like I'm some sort of slow moving ship. The nerve of those kids in the Secret Service sometimes. You'd think they'd let me pick it," he concluded incredulously.

"Longbow," Gregg said softly.

"Like the Europeans of old?" Tom asked.

"Yeah, our unit derived its names from the Greek and Roman militaries," Gregg answered matter-of-factly.

The First Lady returned and interrupted the stilted conversation. The pair stood again.

"Oh, sit down. I was just playing with you boys," she said as she took a seat in the arm chair next to the couch.

Once she was seated, she looked at Gregg and said, "So, how's the recovery going young man?"

"Ma'am?" Gregg asked.

"Please don't presume that I have no idea what goes on in this house, Sergeant Chastain. You've been through hell and back. Now, how are you doing? Are you able to sleep through the night yet? Was your bed comfortable?" she asked.

Gregg thought for a few moments before answering. When he did, he just said, "Not especially, ma'am."

"Sorry to hear that. I'll have someone look into that. And you can dispense with the formalities and call me Evelyn," she said with a warm smile.

"Okay," Gregg replied.

"What's on your mind, Sergeant?" the First Lady asked.

The two men sat there staring at her before Gregg answered. "My wife," he began. "She doesn't know I'm alive. The minute I mentioned the nukes they shipped me straight to Colonel James in Germany. All I want to do is get back to her," he concluded.

"I thought as much. Hold on," she said as she excused herself again. A few minutes later she returned with paperwork in hand. She placed the stack in Gregg's lap as she retook her seat.

"What's this?" he asked.

"That is everything my aides could find on your wife. I had them start looking after Jim told me about you and Cecil. As far as I can tell, it looks like she took a sabbatical from Bathemore."

"I tried to reach her when I was dumped in northern Iraq, but her cell was disconnected and her work phone went straight to voicemail," Gregg added.

"If I'm not mistaken, I believe Secretary McInerney over at the USDA hired her as a consultant and he put her out in the field running tests on-site," Sarkes interjected. "Last I heard she was trying to track down one of the other witnesses from the hearings. That big fella that saved the whistleblower."

"Simmons?" the first lady offered.

"Yeah, that's it. He's a farmer somewhere in Ohio."

"What farm? Where? What's his name!" Gregg hissed.

# Chapter 12

Lily Summers and Chester Daniels stood staring at the two mounds of fresh dirt. In turn, each walked toward the new graves and placed a rose on the makeshift crosses. The bitter January air in the Pacific Northwest was piercing through their tattered dirt covered clothing. Behind them, Alysin Baker was fashioning little hats from several pieces of tin foil.

"What now?" Lily asked of Chester.

Chester looked up from the gravesite and stared out on the Portland skyline spreading out below the wooded knoll. The Rose City was still weird, but now it was out of control, violent, and chaotic. In the distance, Chester and Lily could see the remains of several charred blocks where a number of breweries and micro distilleries once stood. The flames, smoke, and ash from the latest clash with National Guard troops could be seen rising toward the horizon as well.

"I don't know. It might be time to head somewhere else, Lily. We need protection and sanctuary from this. We're not cut out for this fighting in the streets stuff," Chester replied.

Alysin finished making her hats and walked between them as she made her way to the gravesite. She carefully placed each tin foil hat on the crosses and took up position between the two. The three stood silently for a few minutes and watched their adopted city burn.

"I think we need to go see Josh," Alysin said without pretext.

"Alysin, that's not even remotely possible. For starters, it's over two thousand miles away," Chester started to say.

"And lets' not forget its winter. I don't know about you, but I'm not prepared to cross the Rockies on foot," Lily added.

"We have no money, no food, and no transportation," Chester concluded the combined rebuttal.

"And, and, and. But, but, but," Alysin replied emphatically. "That's all I ever hear out of you two anymore. Whatever happened to can, can, can and do, do, do? Josh treated us right. He didn't call us nut jobs when everyone else did. He helped us get out here, away from that institution, and 'control our crazy' enough to get through Dr. Vandersal didn't he?" Alysin explained.

The five members comprising the 'Tin Foil Hat Club' had been institutionalized for one reason or another over the years. All had been highly educated and worked in respectable fields with nice salaries. Over time, though, each had slid further and further over the edge. As new discoveries were made, new conclusions drawn, their collective eyes were opened wider. Their group started on a lark at the institution when each shared why they had been committed.

"Or have you guys forgotten all about the Appalachian Behavioral Healthcare Hospital, because I still do. I remember the day Dr. Vandersal brought Josh in to meet us. Now *that* was a man in control of his crazy," Alysin added.

"Yeah," Lily said recalling the memory. "He took one look at our group with our little tin foil hats and said, 'What are ya in for'?" All three smiled fondly at the impersonation. "He sat with us for hours just talking about our various issues."

"He was the first person I'd met in years that didn't write me off as certifiable the minute he saw me," Chester added. "He asked questions like he was trying to solve problems of his own. Remember when he talked her into the field trip to his farm? I thought she'd pop a gasket. I would have put money that her response would have been 'you wanna let the patients run the asylum?' That man could talk anyone into just about anything."

"How do you imagine us getting there, Alysin?" Lily asked. "Winter is already here and we have nothing. Everything we owned went up in flames when the van exploded. I know you can't handle the bad and the negative in life, but those are the facts."

"It's not that I can't deal with it, Lily," Alysin started to say. "That was always everyone's mistake. It's that I simply choose to look at the bright side of a situation. Right now the only positive I can think of is getting back to Josh's farm. He said we were welcome there anytime, no matter what."

"You haven't answered the question, Alysin," Chester chimed. "Avoidance won't get you out of answering this."

Alysin knelt between the two mounds of dirt and began to pray. She fingered, twisted, and rotated her rosary for fifteen minutes before she answered. Lily and Chester stood silently and watched the city burn itself to the ground.

After her brief pause for introspection, Alysin answered with, "This is the left coast. People hitchhike all the time. We should hitch our way down into California and take the southern route. We can stow ourselves on a big rig or in the cargo hold of one of the Zephyr trains headed east if we can't find a ride."

Chester and Lily contemplated her response and conferred with one another for some time. They couldn't argue with her logic, aside from the obvious safety concerns.

"Say we do this and just start walking. We need food and shelter. Where do we get that if we don't have the kindness of strangers to rely on?" Chester replied.

"Churches," was all Alysin said.

"Your grand plan for hitchin' all the way back to Ohio is… churches?" Lily intoned.

"This could work," Chester interjected. "If we stick to secondary roads, we could conceivably ask for aid from our brethren. They'd assist us in our time of need."

"There are hundreds of thousands of people in need, Chester. People are already starting to migrate and double-up with family. Who knows how many are tryin' to hitch somewhere else too. Who's to say they haven't worn out any welcome or charity we might have received," Lily said exacerbated.

Behind them, a fallen branch cracked. The three turned quickly to see a Portland police officer standing by the graves.

"You guys do know that this isn't a cemetery, right?" the man asked.

The remaining members glanced down and the piles of dirt, but said nothing. The stranger crossed himself as he passed between the graves and stood in line with them looking out over the city.

"This use to be a beautiful city, albeit plenty weird." He exhaled loudly before concluding, "Sure went to hell in a hand basket quick enough though."

"You're not going to arrest us?" Chester said.

"Nah, there's no room in the jail and the courthouse is burning. There's no point in even citing you. I just came up here to say goodbye," he answered.

The three remaining members stole quick glances at one another before Lily asked, "Why are you leaving? Where are you headed?"

"I was gone at the end of the month anyway. I've still got family back in St. Louis so I got a new job back there to be closer to them," he replied. "I heard you guys say that you're in need of a ride. You're welcome to tag along as far as the Mississippi if you want. It's just me now so I have some extra food and supplies I can give you."

"You would do that for us?" Lily asked.

"Seems like the Christian thing to do. Besides, your friend seemed to be praying awful hard for a really long time," he answered and looked over at Alysin. "If I can be someone's answered prayer then my time here has been worth it."

"What's your name?" Chester asked.

"Officer Victor Henry. Everyone just calls me Vic," he replied in a melancholic tone.

"Did you lose someone close?" Lily asked curiously.

"My brother, Dominic," he said somberly. "We used to call ourselves the 'Vic and Nic Show' when we were together. He was standing next to some idiot's idea of an IED when it went off."

Alysin gasped and covered her mouth.

"That thing took out our van when it exploded," Chester started to say as he gestured toward the fresh graves. "These two were in it when the gas tank was pierced and it went up. They never even had a chance."

"I'm sorry. Who were they?" Vic asked.

"Reginald Lee and Algernon Brixton," Chester said stoically.

"No kidding? *The* Reginald Lee? I remember watching him implode on national TV. *60 Minutes* I think it was. He sure scared the hell out of some folks. Some compared his rant to the *War of the Worlds* broadcast in the 30's."

"He was a brilliant man," Lily said emphatically.

"I'm not saying he wasn't, ma'am. It's just that he could have found a better way to present his ideas that didn't freak people out is all. In truth, he's the reason I got rid of all my technology. I deactivated all of my online accounts, social media, cell, home phone, email, you name it. Starting getting paper statements for my banking and credit cards. The PD only does direct deposit so they forced me to reopen my checking account. I withdraw my paycheck the minute it hits the bank just in case. I use library computers to looks things up from time to time though. My house is devoid of tech. I wasn't going to take any chances if half of what he said was true. As a result, I learned how to use tools like the nocturnal, pelorus, and the sextant. Taught myself how to make my own sundial to replace an old ring dial I picked up," he stated proudly. "I owe that man a great deal for opening my eyes. If I can repay that by giving his friends a ride to St. Louis, then that's what I'm gonna do."

"Finally!" Lily said, "Some civilian understands!"

Shocked at her enthusiasm, Vic jumped a little.

"Oh, sorry," she said. "I just get excited when someone gets it."

Smiling at her pronouncement, Vic said, "I've heard the name Algernon before, but I'm not familiar with him. Who is he?"

Chester answered somberly, "Algernon Brixton was a 'Gentlemen Scientist'. He came from money back east so he never had to work. As a result, he spent his time learning and studying geology and volcanology."

"My God!" Vic proclaimed. "He's that guy? He had people so scared that housing prices along the Mississippi took decades to recover."

"That's the one," Alysin said proudly.

"I thought they locked him up. Dude was crazier than a –," he started to say and then stopped short when he saw Lily about to implode. "All of that Yellowstone caldera and New Madrid stuff really freaked some folks out," Vic concluded.

Chester quickly reached out and grabbed Lily.

"Control the crazy," he quietly whispered in her ear.

Lily spun away from the three to go and perform her breathing exercises. Josh had taught her this technique as a way to display improvement to Dr. Vandersal. She needed to do this every so often when she got worked up over a topic or had a disagreement.

"I'm sorry. Did I upset her?" Vic asked.

"She and Algernon were very close. She doesn't like it when people speak badly of him. He may have been wrong about New Madrid, but his instruments and inventions were quickly accepted by the USGS and employed in numerous active zones," Chester responded calmly.

Vic took in Chester's comments and loudly said over his shoulder, "I'm sorry..." and then turned to Chester and said, "What's her name?"

"Lily," he answered.

"I'm sorry, Lily. I didn't mean to offend you."

Realizing that they hadn't introduced themselves, Chester said, "Where are our manners? Victor Henry, this is Alysin Baker, that is Lily Summers, and I'm Chester Daniels."

Chester and Vic shook hands and Alysin curtsied. The gesture made Vic chuckle. Alysin stood there staring at Vic for a few moments before Chester noticed.

"If you have a question Alysin, just ask. You know people get uncomfortable when you just stand there and stare at them," Chester said gently.

Vic shifted his gaze away from the burning city to Alysin and said, "Yes?"

"I was wondering what happened? There were minor food riots all summer, but nothing like this. Nobody ever got hurt before. Where's the press? Where are the circling news helicopters? The National Guard showed up and boom!" she said with emphasis. "All hell breaks out all over town."

"One of the kids in the Guard discharged his weapon. It was an accident, but it went off while the food was being distributed. It caused a panic and the mob lost it. The delivery was trampled, shops were looted, and people died. The government didn't want another Kent State story so they shut down everything. All roads in and out of Portland for a twenty-mile radius have been closed. No news and no people are getting in or out. Companies that wouldn't willingly comply with the order had their power cut. Portland is one big media black hole."

"So we are all on our own," Lily said rejoining the group. "How can they do that? What about freedom of the press?"

"What does it matter, Lily? You and I both know they only report what Washington tells them," Alysin shot back.

"Provided it's one of their guys in the White House!" Lily added as the two high-fived each other.

In an attempt to bring some sanity back to the discussion, Chester asked, "What are they telling people on the highways and interstates that approach the city? They have to be asking questions, don't they? Folks are smarter than that, right?"

"A person is smart. People are sheep and when they get spooked they turn into dumb panicky mobs," Vic replied to nods from the other three. The officer smiled in return.

"Last I heard they are employing the fine art of misdirection. Seems like everyone is being told something different," he added.

"Like what?" Alysin asked.

"Oh, things like hazardous waste spill, train derailment, toxic fumes, automobile pile-up, plane crash... stuff like that," he replied.

"And people are buying that BS?" Lily intoned.

"So far. They won't for long, though," Vic answered.

"Are there other cities as bad off as Portland?" Chester asked.

"As far as I know, Portland is the only city with National Guard troops. The Governor is about to declare martial law. There have been issues in some of the larger ones for the last six months though. If it wasn't the produce truck hijackings it was ration book forgeries. Winter's here and the people that didn't store enough food are starting to take it from those that did. That doesn't even begin to account for the dealers, pimps, working girls, and addicts that sold their allotment on the black market. We need to get moving before the authorities widen their perimeter around Portland though. We can talk more on the ride. You guys ready here?" Vic answered and asked.

"I need to deliver my eulogy," Alysin answered.

"Make it a quick one, hun. We gotta go," Vic said.

Alysin smiled and curtsied once more. She then took position behind the two crosses and recited two verses from memory.

"My first reading is John 6:35-40. It's a message about eternal life," she said and then quoted the bible verse. "My second is from 1 Kings 13:2."

Chester and Lily, who had been standing with eyes closed and heads bowed, quickly looked up at her. One of Alysin's favorite pastimes on their homestead was to read her Bible to the other four by the light of the fire in the evenings. As a result, even though they weren't the most religious bunch, they all knew what was coming.

*"And he cried against the altar in the word of the LORD, and said, O altar, altar, thus saith the LORD; Behold, a child shall be born unto the house of David, Josiah by name; and upon thee shall he offer the priests of the high places that burn incense upon thee, and men's bones shall be burnt upon thee."*

She finished with the Lord's Prayer.

"Nice touch, Alysin," Lily said as the four made their way to Vic's truck. "You just had to recite a passage with Josh's given name in it."

"I thought it was fitting... considering our destination. I wanted their spirit to know where we went," Alysin replied with a smile.

# Chapter 13

Suhrab picked up the latest edition of the *New York Times* and began perusing the classified section. The Ayatollah's network of handlers had worked with Suhrab and Foreign Minister Nafisi to devise a means of communication that wasn't electronic, but still secure. The communication needed to be coded to the point where only Suhrab would know what it meant. Suhrab couldn't reply back, but they could feed him intel and planning information as new details became available.

As he read, he quickly found what he was looking for.

*Are you displaced?*

*Does your luck need to change?*

*Then try these lucky numbers:*

*27, 12, 20, 22, 5*

Suhrab saw the string of digits and immediately retrieved the *New York Times* for the 27th of December from the stack of papers he kept. He unfolded the paper and turned to the fifth page. He then began feverishly searching the remainder of the classifieds for similarly worded ads. He found two.

*Change your stars with these numbers:*

*11, 3, 7, 15, 45*

*16, 1, 9, 30, 32*


*Guaranteed Inner Peace*

*Your Weekly Numbers Are:*

*21, 4, 14, 23, 47*

*35, 12, 17, 18, 26*

The order in which they appeared in the paper didn't matter, that couldn't be controlled. The one line advertisement was the master key and only told him where to start. Once he knew the specific date for the periodical, the rest was fairly straight forward. The lowest numeral from each ad determined the message. Once that was established, each row held the location for the decode. The '11' was actually a two single digits. They indicated column 1, paragraph 1, and the same were true for the others. The other values comprised the text of the communication.

Suhrab began talking out loud as he began piecing the puzzle together.

"Column one... paragraph one... third, seventh, fifteenth, and forty-fifth word. That translates to... 'British', 'know', 'operation', and 'detail'.

*What! How?* Suhrab's mind was racing. *What else do they know?*

"Same column, paragraph six... first, ninth, thirtieth, and thirty-second. 'Watch', 'reserves', 'witness', and 'test'.

*By Allah!*

When Suhrab finished translating everything, the message read:

*British know operation detail*
*Watch reserves witness test*
*Good speed wants cooperation*
*Target list amended soon*

\* \* \*

Navid approached the gift shop at the Dulles Metro terminal and began scanning though the stacks of available newspapers. Every day he made the same trip, bought the *New York Times,* and a pack of unfiltered cigarettes. For three weeks, he was met with disappointment. *Will today be any different?*

He paid his money and headed back to his apartment. As he sat and ate his flat bread and jam, he perused the classified ads in the *Times* looking for some sort of message.

Earlier in the year, the U.S. had been divided into sectors for the distribution of food and ration books. Suhrab read all about it. Consequently, when the topic of communication came up during the planning phases, Suhrab dispersed his team members according to Secretary McInerney's conveniently advertised sectors.

Navid had been assigned to a city in the Mid-Atlantic sector. Suhrab would use the placement of ads to direct one, two, or all members. When Suhrab needed to make a broadcast announcement to all sectors, the ad would be placed and contain the phrase 'Brothers in Allah'. When the ad was directed at a particular sector, the sector's name would be used.

Navid methodically read through the pages of classifieds in the hopes that the green light had been given. On page seventeen, he found what he was looking for.

*ATTN:*

*Brothers in Allah*

*National Meeting*

*April 5th, 2023*

*Locations: TBD*

*Finally!* Navid was so excited to see the headline that it didn't immediately register that the location was undetermined. Once it became clear that it was only half a message, as only the date had been set, his mind began to race. *This can't be right! What are the targets?!*

Then he began doubting and second guessing leadership. *Was a believer discovered? Was someone caught? Why the delay? They know we are all online and ready!*

Navid had espoused a simultaneous nationwide attack throughout their training. His entire family had been wiped out in one fell swoop by a drone strike years earlier. He wanted his pound of flesh, sooner rather than later. His impatience and boldness was a constant conversation within the leadership hierarchy. He had been cautioned several times not to deviate from the plan. He reminded himself of those conversations with Suhrab and resisted the impulse to go and test fire the weapon again. *Be patient. Suhrab knows what he's doing.*

Navid walked over and retrieved the small 2023 calendar he had placed on the refrigerator. As he retook his seat in the lone upholstered chair adorning his apartment, he began counting down to his retribution.

*Today is January 12th. That's eighty-two days.* Then it hit him. *What am I going to do for three months? What are the targets?*

The temptation was too great. *Let's have a little fun and see what this thing can do.*

He sat and re-read all of the articles he had torn from the papers covering the incidents, all safe and highly visible. Then he struck upon a thought. *No one had tried this against a military target.*

Navid had been collecting all of the various branch periodicals in addition to his daily quota of the *New York Times* just in case. He quickly went over to the stack and started looking for a suitable objective. In the third magazine from the top was a copy of the *Navy Times* with a front cover depicting a destroyer leaving port. The heading read: U.S.S. Gravely Sea Trials Commencing.

Navid flipped to the article and read that the ship had recently been retrofitted in dry dock to accommodate the latest generation of nuclear propulsion. The conversion from four GE gas turbines to the lone reactor was heralded by the Westinghouse designers as a successful coup for naval engineering. The nuclear powered vessel would spend a week at sea testing its new propulsion system, fire control systems, and sensor arrays. The ship was due back in Norfolk around sunset.

*Perfect! Let's see how hardened their Navy really is.*

With a network of Muslim contacts at their disposal, it took less than a thirty minute cab ride to get to the car rental agency. For three hundred dollars, the man now had a fuel efficient and unassuming vehicle for the day. Four hours later he was sitting huddled at the top of the Old Point Comfort Lighthouse overlooking Hampton Roads. He was directly across the mouth of the James River from the Sewells Point docks.

Navid went back down to the second floor, removed one of the panes of glass from the stairwell window unit, and then glanced at his watch. It was almost 2:00 pm. *Three hours to sunset.*

As he started to head back up to the top and make himself comfortable, and possibly take a nap, the shipping lane came alive with the repeated celebratory blaring of a horn. The man went back to the landing and discreetly peered out with his pocket scope. Navid quickly identified the offending racket. The *Gravely* was early and had just cleared the Fort Story peninsula. It had a broom strapped to its mast.

*Wonderful! A clean sweep at sea trials. Let's see you fix this.*

The device powered on quietly and efficiently began charging, same as before. He didn't want to take any chances with the armor plating so he waited until the ship was passing between himself and Rip Raps Island in the middle of the bay.

Navid pointed the wand out the window at the massive steel hulk and flicked the switch. He left the device on for twice as long as he had with the commuter train. The *Gravely* was bombarded with repeated waves of electromagnetic energy until its propellers stopped churning the brackish sea.

With a devilish grin, Navid replaced the glass and watched as the *Gravely* floated dead stick into the mouth of the James River. Eventually, the current stalled the vessels momentum. With all of the on-board circuitry fried, the crew was unable to reach the shore via comms. With no other options available to him, the Captain of the *Gravely* ordered the manual release of the anchor and the firing of emergency flares. Two hours later, the *U.S.S. Gravely* was towed by tugboat back to its mooring at Norfolk Naval Station.

Navid observed the entire ordeal giddily. Once the tug had secured the ship and began the arduous task of dragging it back to the pier, the man picked up the suitcase containing his device and nonchalantly walked to his car. Several hours later, as he sat in his apartment flipping through one news show after another, there was no mention of the *U.S.S. Gravely* going dead in the water within sight of its mooring.

* * *

"Sir! Sir! Sir!" the young assistant exclaimed as he burst through the meeting room door. "Sir, you need to read these!" he said as he thrust the handful of decoded messages into Sir William's calmly outstretched grasp.

"Thank you, Nigel. That will be all," Sir William replied coolly and unemotionally.

Recognizing his bosses displeasure regarding his outwardly emotional display, the young aide composed himself and said, "Yes, sir. Thank you, sir."

Once the doors were closed, the Field Marshal and Prime Minister Goodspeed had a laugh at the man's expense. The head of MI-6 quickly scanned through each decoded report.

"Bloody hell!" the normally unemotional man exclaimed as he thrust the paper stack across the table.

The PM perused the text and proclaimed, "Those damn jihadists took out an American destroyer!"

"Keep reading," Sir William ordered tersely.

"Ah, those crafty Americans," he replied with pride as he read on. Once he finished his review, he handed the mass of papers off to the Field Marshal.

The Army practitioner groaned, guffawed, or mumbled something under his breath as he made his way through the pile.

"You guys actually got a guy inside the vaults at Fort Knox?" the Field Marshal said more as a compliment than with surprise.

"We certainly did. Unfortunately, those scheming buggers moved the contents," Sir William replied. "They've called our bluff, Prime Minister. You probably should call the King and have our boys stand down."

"Who said we were bluffing," the PM retorted.

"What is the King looking to accomplish? There's nothing there. Begging your pardon sir, but it's a big damn colony and the Americans are damn crafty. Those resources could be anywhere by now. Why are we even contemplating this?" the Field Marshal asked.

"The country is bankrupt, Winston!" the Prime Minister exclaimed as her referred to the Field Marshal informally. "The monarchy is broke. Can you imagine the chaos and panic that would descend on the streets of London if this ever became public knowledge? The EU monetary system is already crumbling under the weight of social programs… taxed even further by the opening of the borders. If we don't follow through on this and receive a serious infusion of funds, the EU and the whole of Western Europe will disintegrate. There'd be anarchy, plain and simple," the PM answered.

"If there's no money, how do we pay for this excursion?" Sir William asked.

"The same way the Germans did. Stockpile petrol then unleash hell and take it," the Prime Minister replied cooly.

"And our time table?" the head of MI-6 asked. "Some of the other reports show the Americans are forming up a good bit of resistance along their sea lanes. Air, artillery, and missile units are being repositioned and deployed to a number of bases, active and decommissioned, on both coasts. By the looks of things, it appears we are headed straight into another Atlantic Wall. The more time that passes the more difficult it will be breach their defenses."

"I have an idea on how to thwart those. As for our landing craft, we will continue our planning for the St. Lawrence waterway as a flanking maneuver. The Canadians are still on relatively good terms with the Yanks so we'll stay in their territorial waters as best we can and quickly subdue the northeast and their financial center in New York. Actually, the states comprising the Northeastern region of the country have done us a huge service. They disarmed their people for us. There should be little to no resistance in the that sector, let alone New York."

"And how do you plan on getting our aircraft through the wall of lead and missiles they are sure to put up?" the Field Marshal asked. "We really ought to bring in the Air Chief Marshal for that discussion."

"That won't be necessary," the Prime Minister replied as he pushed the 'Call' button on the intercom.

"Yes, sir," quickly came over the device.

"Alister, this is Prime Minister Goodspeed."

"How may I be of service?"

"Be a good lad and contact Foreign Minister Nafisi in the Iranian Consulate. Please ask him to come to Downing Street at his earliest convenience."

Turning his attention back to Sir William and the Field Marshal, the Prime Minister concluded their conversation by adding, "Across the Atlantic lays a colony that was once ours. Its government is rife with corruption and ripe for manipulation. Their economy is a house of cards teetering precariously on the brink of ruin, and its foreign policy is ineffectual and laughable. Our King has given us the key to the front door and provided an opportunity to retake it... and that, gentlemen, is what we intend to do."

* * *

Emily's USDA issued cell phone chirped in her backpack. She quickly used a bottle of water to wash off as much of the caked on mud as possible, dried them absentmindedly on her pants, and then went digging for the device.

"This is Emily," she said as she answered.

"Hey, Em. It's Elias. How are things in sunny Southern California?" his asked jovially.

"It's nice. The weather's beautiful and the views are breathtaking. I'm just about done here so I'll be sending my samples in a couple of days," she replied.

"Perfect. It sounds like the travelling is doing you some good. You seem happier. Where are you off to next?"

"It seems kind of silly to fly over Texas and go to the east coast only to turn around and come back. So I've reorg'd my itinerary to handle north Texas first then wrap things up in the Florida. Okay?"

"Good. Keep me posted," he said as he was about to disconnect the call and hang up.

"Elias?" Emily said quickly.

"Yeah, I'm here," he replied putting the receiver back against his ear. "What's up?"

"Have you had any luck finding Mr. Simmons? I gathered a wealth of information and I think his operation might be one of the final pieces I'm looking for," she stated quickly.

"Sorry, hun. That guy doesn't want to be found. Best I've come up with is a phone number. No one ever answers the damn thing though. How'd that be?" he asked.

"It's a start. Text it to me?" she inquired.

"Oh, Lord. More technology hoo-ha," he said as he sighed. "I'll get Mara to do it, okay?"

"Thanks, Elias. I appreciate it," Emily replied.

The tireless researcher hunkered down in the shade of an almond tree and waited for the message to arrive while she nibbled on a snack. A few minutes later, it chimed.

She pressed on the hyperlink number and the phone automatically dialed Josh. After three rings, it was answered.

"Simmons residence, bride-to-be Samantha speaking," echoed in her ear.

"Sam! Is that you?" Emily said excitedly into the cell.

"One in the same. Who may I ask is calling?"

"It's me! Emily," she replied enthusiastically.

"Emily Chastain! Where have you been? I tried reaching you at Bathemore and they said you were on sabbatical! Wait. How did you get this number?" her friend inquired.

Emily quickly explained the circumstances of her employment, as well as how she came into possession of Josh's home phone. The two had become friends while they worked together with Elias during the hearings. They were both gratefully relieved when Congress enacted several new laws governing the U.S. food system. Then Emily's mood turned more sorrowful.

"Still miss your husband?" Sam asked.

"Honestly, yes, but it's waning. The Army has him listed as missing, but it's been almost a year. I don't think he's coming home. I'm out here doing all of this just hoping I can fill the void and eventually move on," she concluded regrettably.

"Don't give up yet, Emily. Until they tell you they found him, don't ever lose hope. Josh survived hell on earth and Gregg will too," her friend remarked.

"I think it's a little different. Josh's daughters were abducted. He got to get his closure. Where's mine?" Emily asked.

"Actually, what I was referring to was his time in Bosnia."

The two spent the next half hour conversing and talking about what a person is capable of surviving. Sam made her queasy when she described Josh's adorned torso. The call ended with Samantha asking if she wanted to be a bridesmaid and an invitation to the farm once she concluded her research in Texas and Florida.

Emily's mood was now sufficiently improved.

# Chapter 14

"Josh?" Samantha called out as she exited the basement stairwell dripping with perspiration.

"Kitchen," Josh answered.

He caught a glimpse of her as she entered in a sweat soaked jog bra and shorts and decried, "What are you guys doing down there? How did you get so sweaty?"

"Never mind that," she answered. "You owe me a date."

"Not like that I don't," Josh said chuckling.

In rebuttal, she stepped in and wrapped her arms around him pressing their bodies together. She then proceeded to use him to towel herself off. Josh groaned and pushed her away.

Samantha placed a demure smile on her face and struck a pose. "Better?" she asked.

"Nice. Thanks for that," Josh bemoaned.

"Now, about my date," she began.

"Oh, I think you've lost your shot at that," he replied playfully.

"The girls and I were talking and we've determined that you and I have never had a proper date. We spent month's together hold up here before the hearings and we have the letter writing, but we never left the farm for anything more than supplies."

"I'm not dancing," Josh said flatly. "If that word was about to come out of your mouth you can forget it," he concluded with a degree of finality.

"Not even for a slow dance," she replied seductively as she provocatively sauntered her way back toward him.

Josh starred at her, taking in her grace. The effortless manner in which she came to him was reason enough to reconsider.

"What if the music were nice and low?" she asked as she methodically wrapped her arms around his neck and began humming a tune. Ever so slightly, she began to sway back and forth.

Josh instinctively wrapped his arms around her and pulled her toward him in response. The two began a slow turn as if they were on the dance floor. Sam's gentle humming was the only thing needed for the pair to keep time.

"And the lights were really dim?" she practically whispered as she titled her face up to meet his.

Josh leaned in to her.

As their lips were about to touch, she broke the embrace and pushed him away.

"I'll be ready in an hour and I don't want to see any flannel," she ordered as she exited the kitchen. Josh trailed out after her, but stopped and propped himself against the doorjamb as his eyes followed her. He watched as she swished and sashayed her way up the stairs.

When she made it to the top, she bent herself over the banister and provided him with a gratuitous cleavage shot. "Oh, and tell Dallas we are taking his car and not some dusty farm truck."

Ninety minutes later, Samantha came down carrying a bag and wearing an outfit Josh had never seen before. She had on knee high black leather boots, tights, and a skirt that said she was a lady, but short enough to still be playful. She wore a silk top with a scarf and a matching tailored jacket.

When she visually inspected Josh, who was grinning ear to ear, she nodded her approval. He had dug out a pair of khaki's, a classic white dress shirt, and ironed both. *The sport coat and wing tips are a nice touch*, she thought.

"So where are we headed?" he asked. "I'm one hundred percent at your disposal."

"First, we are heading to Columbus. I want to do some shopping in an actual store, not online. Somewhere in there will be a long lunch and maybe a glass of wine followed by some more shopping and dinner."

"Uh, Sam? What's with the bag?" Josh asked.

"Oh, I called my aunt Jenny over in Springfield. We'll be staying the night with her and attending church with her in the morning. On our way home we'll stop and do some antiquing," she replied. "It's non-negotiable, Josh. Go fill a bag with some extra clothes and a dopp kit. Something appropriate for services and the car ride back."

"But tomorrow's Saturday," he replied.

"Josh, she's eighty-four years old. Every day is Sunday to her. She goes whenever she wants."

Josh's two friends were sitting on the couch observing the entire exchange. They watched as he offered no rebuttal, hung his head in mock disdain, and returned to his room to pack the requested overnight bag. Dallas couldn't resist the temptation. As Josh neared the doorway, his old friend made a whipping sound. The childish gesture was heard, but not immediately acknowledged. When he was about to enter his room, he flipped Dallas the bird. The room erupted with laughter.

While Josh was off packing, Samantha checked her hair and make-up in the mirror one last time before walking over to Dallas. She held out her hand, but said nothing. Dallas looked up at her and scowled. She simply snapped her fingers at him and continued to leave it extended.

Begrudgingly, he reached into his pocket and removed the key fob. Dallas hesitated a moment before giving it to her.

When Josh exited his room a few minutes later, Dallas and James were nowhere to be found. Samantha, however, was sitting at the kitchen table reading a magazine.

"Where did they go?" Josh asked.

"I told them they needed to take the girls camping," she replied without looking up.

"It's the middle of January!" They've got no business going out in this," Josh replied emphatically.

"It's time to cut the cord, Josh. We both survived cold weather training at their age and they can too. What good is all the training you guys have provided if it's never tested? They don't have any real world applicable or practical knowledge? If they don't know what to expect or how to handle different scenarios and situations in this environment then it's pretty much useless information, isn't it?" she replied.

Josh was speechless. What could he say?

"Oh, don't worry," she started to say to alleviate the dread written all over his face. "They've been trained well and they have all of the necessary tools, gear, and knowledge to survive." Samantha stood up and began ticking facts off on her fingers. "They know how to pack, track, snare, hunt, shelter, patrol, orient, and whole host of other extremely useful skills. Yet, none of these has been adequately tested. The glaring hole in their resume is necessity. One of you boys has always been with them. They've never had to do it for themselves. Besides, James, Dallas, and Juan will be observing from a distance to see how they do. They won't know they are there, but they'll be watched. Those three can intercede if things turn into the *Lord of the Flies*. Happy?"

Josh thought for a moment. After a while, he finally retorted, "Why didn't you just send them to Lake Hope and put them on a sugar cookie diet?"

"I'm sorry, the what?" Sam asked.

"When the 'squids' would screw up during basic, they'd be sent to run around and do PT with the SEALs. They dress them in full camouflage and have them run into the surf. Once they came out, they'd be ordered to roll in the sand. Then they'd have to get up and run whatever distance was deemed appropriate by the SEALs. When they were done rolling around all soaking wet in the sand, they'd look like sugar cookies. It's the only diet you were guaranteed to lose weight on," Josh concluded joyfully, but somewhat incredulously.

"Sounds like sadistic torture to me," she replied.

"Potato potah-to. So where are they taking them? For how long?"

"I have no idea where they are being taken and don't know when they'll be back. I would assume it'd be at least a week. Maybe more," she replied nonchalantly.

"What! Why? Why would you do that?" Josh exclaimed.

"Because, if I knew, you'd get it out of me and want to go observe, and that's not happening. Now get in the car," she answered as she threw Dallas' key fob to him. "We're on a date."

Josh groused for the first part of the ninety mile drive to Columbus. Samantha sat quietly and read her magazine, waiting for Josh to speak. *He's a stubborn as a mule.*

"So who's the Tin Foil Hat Club? Katherine mentioned them the other day," she offered, unable to bear the silence. "Why did they give themselves that moniker? It seems like that would be just another reason to keep them institutionalized."

"They *were* brilliant scientists, but their given fields of expertise made them privy to some less than savory information," Josh said.

"How did you come to know them?" Sam asked.

"Dr. Vandersal. When she was treating the three of us shortly after the trial I mentioned a few things in passing that resonated with her. She thought we might have some common ground," he started to say and then chuckled. "For a while there, I think she was planning on trying to commit me too."

"So who are they? Would I recognize their names?" Sam asked.

"Some of them, maybe. Algernon Brixton?" he asked.

"Absolutely. He helped reduce property values all throughout the Mississippi Valley. Land was so cheap for so long the farmers made a killing because they were paying so little in taxes. Why was he committed?"

"He had a rather out-sized fear of the New Madrid Fault. When he started shouting about it from the roof tops, his family had him committed," Josh replied.

"And the others? How many were there?"

"Let's see, the two that helped explain some of the tech concepts to me were Chester Daniels and Reginald Lee," Josh started to say before Samantha cut him off.

"Holy crap!" she exclaimed. "You met the infamous Reggie Lee? What was that like? I heard he was crazier than a bag full of cats!"

Josh laughed out loud at the description.

"He was actually very down to earth. That is, when he was on his meds. He just needed some help coping when he wasn't."

"You can't be serious. He went on *60 Minutes* and spewed some of the most inarticulate paranoid drivel ever produced on television. That guy couldn't stay with one subject for more than thirty seconds!" Samantha decried. "By the time the interview was over, I actually felt sorry for him."

Josh cocked his head toward her and grinned a little grin.

"Are ya done?" he asked.

Samantha exhaled loudly and said, "You were saying?"

"Reginald was a Computational Scientist that used to work for the government. Remember those TV shows about do-gooders utilizing mysterious AI machines to fight crime?"

"AI?" she asked.

"Artificial intelligence… machines that think, basically. These are machines the government actually utilizes but has convinced the public it's all science-fiction. Even when whistleblowers go running to the press, websites, blogs, and forums to divulge secret programs that spied and collected data… the public still thinks they are the stuff of legend."

"Why would they ever think that?"

"Because, the sheeple have been indoctrinated into believing, since kindergarten it seems, that the government knows best. Why would we or they ever need to fear our omnipotent overlords? Anyway, it wasn't fiction. Reginald built most of it. When he tried to tell everyone about it, it all came out as this giant blob of information."

"So the myth continued as a result of his delivery?" Sam inquired.

"Pretty much. The government had him committed for 'evaluation'. Then they basically forgot about him. He was left there to rot for about a decade," Josh concluded.

"Seriously? They can do that?" she asked.

"Absolutely," Josh answered. "Once you sign one of those little non-disclosure contracts, they're free to do pretty much whatever they want. Polygraphs... waiving of rights or due process... you name it. I helped him though."

"Oh," Samantha said with a raised eye brow. "How so?"

"I gave him a purpose," he said proudly. "Once Dr. Vandersal introduced us I got to know the five of them pretty well."

"Tell me about the others," Samantha said thoroughly intrigued.

"Oh, let's see," Josh started to say before he asked, "Do you just want their names, or what they used to do, or what made them take a break from reality?"

"All of it. We've got another hour until we reach Columbus," she answered."

"OK. There's Algernon, he was a volcanologist and geologist. He was afraid of the New Madrid Fault and the Yellowstone Caldera. He'd probably have a field day with the natural gas fracking going on around eastern Ohio and western Pennsylvania. Then there was Reginald and he was the tech guy. He learned so much about how the government used his technology that he was in constant fear of Orwell's 'big brother' type stuff. The others were Lily Summers, Chester Daniels, and Alysin Baker." Josh answered thoroughly.

"What were they in to?" Samantha asked.

"Why do you want to know this?" Josh asked.

"I'm curious," she answered. "That and it'll continue to take your mind off of the fact that you're mad at me for sending your daughters into the woods."

Josh grunted before answering, "Ms. Summers was a biochemist by trade. She was committed due to her paralyzing fear of viral pandemics.

Chester Daniels was a nuclear engineer with the Navy for a while and then went into the private sector. He and Reginald played off of each other with the tech stuff, but Chester's issues revolved around EMP's. Alysin Baker was a pathologist in a former life. She was horrified by the things she was finding in nature. She became convinced that man would find a way to wipe out the human race. She and Lily complemented each other. Those two hit it off immediately once she was committed."

"Sounds familiar," she replied with a smile.

"Yeah well, Alysin and I found common ground on that one," Josh answered.

"That's quite the collection of insanity though. How did you help Reginald, or all of them for that matter?" Samantha asked as she closed her magazine and sat more upright.

"To quote Dr. Vandersal, I shared some of my 'crazy' with them to provide an achievable goal."

"I'm sorry. Your what?" Sam questioned.

"That's a term that the five of them used because, while they were all institutionalized, nobody had the same problems. They used the phase to refer to their fears collectively. As for my part, I simply helped them realize that if they could show Dr. Vandersal that they could handle and channel their issues without the aid of heavy medication, then they could possibly be released. I'm sure you heard that when they were removing Javy from the woods, I spent the entire time in the kitchen."

"I did, but I didn't want to ask. What was that all about?" Samantha asked.

"That's my coping mechanism. When the world gets to be too much to take, the head shrinks came up with breathing exercises and meditation as a way to handle the PTSD issues. I prefer to use my hands though so I learned how to cook. It's procedural. First this, then that, add this, measure that, and so on. For some reason it helps calm my mind. I figured it would work for them too."

"So how did you help Reginald? Specifically," Samantha asked.

"Over time, the doc agreed to the discharge of four of the five 'tin hatters', but Reginald wasn't going to be getting out anytime soon. The other four refused to leave him behind though. They are extremely loyal to one another, like a family comprised of nothing but crazy aunts and uncles," Josh started to answer. He sheepishly added, "I might have had something to do with the insertion of useful tools in a 'Congrats on the Release' cake when Algernon was released."

"Josh! You helped a mental patient escape? Have *you* lost *your* mind," Samantha said astonished.

"He was better off with the other four," Josh answered defensively. "Dr. Vandersal didn't get it. He would have regressed if they were separated. So, I provided a means to an end. It took him about three days to saw through some bolts on the bars covering his window. Then he used the screw driver, foil gum wrappers, and some other stuff he collected to circumvent the alarm. He totally 'MacGyvered' his way out of there," he said with a hint of pride. "Anyway, once he was out, they came straight to the farm. The five of them stayed for a few weeks and then I sent them on their way."

"You kicked them out? After all that? You should be ashamed of yourself," Samantha said incredulously.

"No, no. I told them that they were welcome to stay as long as they wanted, but they said they needed a change of scenery. That and they figured my place was one of the first places they'd look."

"And did they?" she asked.

"Oh yeah!" Josh said emphatically. "They looked all right!"

"So where were they for those few weeks?" Samantha asked.

"I hid them in the root cellars behind a false wall. Once the hospital staff and authorities relaxed their search, they asked if they could borrow some money for a car and clothes and what not. I gladly gave them what I could and told them to come back anytime."

"Did they?" she asked"

"A few days later they showed up in VW van like a pack of roving hippies. I hadn't laughed that hard in a long time when they came driving up in that thing. They said their thank you's and goodbyes and started out on a cross country 'excursion', as they called it. Said they always wanted to see the northwest. Got a blank postcard from Portland a few years ago," he answered in reply.

# Chapter 15

Gregg thanked the nice little co-ed for the ride to McArthur and strode confidently into the diner like he knew *exactly* where he was and *exactly* what he was doing. He and Emily had passed through the berg numerous times when they came to the area for hiking and camping, but had never stopped. Hitch hiking in winter comes with its own challenges due to the weather. However, with fewer cars on the road, those that can afford the fuel are more inclined to give someone a lift than in years past.

The confidence Gregg was exuding once he entered the diner couldn't be further from the truth. Several days earlier he had caught the train from D.C. to Ohio. Once he was in Columbus, he went by his old house only to discover the place had been sold. Sullen and confused, he hailed a cab and made his way to the nearest library. He sat down at the first available computer terminal and typed in a simple search parameter, 'Josh Simmons'.

Links to every news article for the past decade and then some came back in his results. He found what he needed in the fourth one he read. It was a local piece in the *Vinton Courier* announcing Josh's release from the county jail. It detailed his exploits with regard to the double murder trial, the Congressional hearings, and the obstruction of justice charge he served time for. *Great, my wife has run off with a murderous ex-con. This oughta be fun.*

Now that he was in McArthur, he had no idea where to go. He decided to play the only card he had. Gregg placed a few dollars on the counter and played the 'down on my luck veteran' routine to the waitress. *People are so gullible.*

Within twenty minutes of starting up the conversation, he knew exactly where Josh's farm was. The afternoon was spent walking the last remaining distance between him and a perceived reunion with his wife.

* * *

Josh and Samantha entered the Martinez's home and Sam declared, "Got the note you left on the counter."

Jesus and Abelardo were sitting on the couch with Evan while Basilia and Evan's wife sat in recliners. Josh smiled a genuine smile at the pair. He was truly happy to see that they had returned. Their rapt attention was drawn towards the now retired General having a very loud and an extremely animated conversation on his cell phone.

"What do you mean the Ambassadors are leaving in droves?" Brent bellowed into the device. "That's months ahead of what we expected."

"Well just follow the contingency plans we devised," he replied to an unheard question.

Brent sighed and said, "Then you need to remind the POTUS that 'Operation Delta' was designed with this in mind."

Josh started to ask what was going on when Evan raised a finger to his lips to silence him.

Brent turned and saw Josh and Sam standing in the doorway. He covered the mouthpiece and offered, "My replacement is having difficulty reconciling himself with his new position as Chairman of the Joint Chiefs."

He then returned his attention back to the person on the other end of the line and answered, "Yes, I'm still here."

Brent listened intently and then concluded the call by saying, "That'll be fine. I'll look to hear from you at 08:00 tomorrow," and hung up.

He slid the phone into his pocket, and asked, "Who's hungry?"

"Nice try," Josh replied. "Out with it."

"Can I tell you while we eat? I'm starving," Brent practically whined.

Josh received a nod of approval from Basilia and replied, "Okay, but I want details."

No sooner had the group fixed their plates and said 'Amen", as Josh asked, "All right, let's have it."

"The Brits have advanced their timetable and started orchestrating the removal of diplomats from American soil. Rayburn started freaking out and my replacement still has an overgrown respect for the office."

"Meaning?" Josh asked.

"He's having issues being candid with the man."

"And this means what to us exactly," Evan asked.

"It's our turn to move a piece on the chessboard," Brent replied.

"What are the options?" Evan countered.

"Yeah, and what's Operation Delta and what's a 'POTUS'?" Basilia added.

"POTUS is just military jargon for the President. As for Operation Delta, before I retired we came up with several contingency plans. Operation Delta is where we thumb our nose at the Brits and begin moving resources. This option was designed to remove any conflict from the cities and localize it away from major population centers."

"Can someone please translate that," Basilia countered.

Josh interceded and said, "The U.K. and their allies want to be repaid for their portion of the U.S. debt. They want it in tangible goods like gold, silver, etcetera. All of those resources are housed in the Federal Reserve Banks and the United States Mint facilities.

"There are twelve primary Reserve Banks and Branches located around the country. All of which are essentially high population centers... big cities with major hubs for airfare, trains, and interstates. There are only five Mint locations. Those are in spots like San Francisco, Denver, and Philadelphia. The other two are Fort Knox and West Point. Both of those already have a military contingent attached to them. What the General is saying is that Operation Delta is consolidating the remaining assets in specific locations."

"That just about sums it up. President Rayburn doesn't want urban warfare in American streets, but he's also willing to fight," Brent added.

"So where's this fighting going to take place?" Evan asked.

"Well, that's the thing. We can't move all of it to one location. So, we looked at the geography of the country and made some decisions," the General began to answer. "The assets in the Reserve Banks and Branches were shipped to Omaha, Nebraska. Well, as much as we can quickly get there at any rate. It's in the middle of the U.S. and not easily accessible from either coast. It's open terrain out there and that equals tanks. We have a lot of those. So we moved some of the Armored Brigade Combat Teams from Fort Carson in Colorado to defend that facility."

"What happened to the divisions?" Josh asked.

"The face of war changed after 9/11, Josh. Those were appropriate organizational structures sixty years ago, but they became so massive it took months to deploy. You remember how long we had to wait to get all of our elements into Saudi Arabia for the first Gulf War. These smaller units are much more agile and more to scale for the types of engagements we are encountering today," Brent answered.

"And the Mint resources?" Samantha asked.

"That's where it got interesting. The material at West Point will stay where it is. Fort Knox is empty and functioning as a diversion. We've reinforced the New York based combat teams for a dug in defense of the site," Brent replied.

"You're stalling, General," Josh said. "Where are the rest of the materials headed?"

The former Chairman of the Joint Chiefs played with the food on his plate and didn't look up.

"Where's it going?" Basilia asked innocently.

"Well, we couldn't very well leave it in San Francisco or Philadelphia. And we definitely didn't want to draw any UN forces towards our NORAD facility in Colorado Springs by keeping anything in Denver," the General replied.

Josh slammed his fist on the table and growled, "Where is it headed, Brent! Stop dancin' and start talkin'!"

Josh's aggression startled the man and he quickly looked up.

He met his former pupils anger with his own and shot back, "Don't bark at me like some sort of junk yard dog, Josiah! I'm still your commanding officer!"

The student returned fire with, "Not out here you're not!"

Samantha interceded and calmly said, "General, what Josh is having difficulty articulating is that we would all very much like to know what the location is for the Mint resources. We are all adults here. Whatever you tell us will be handled maturely and rationally."

The two alpha males dialed down their intensity after hearing Sam's calm reassuring tone.

Brent looked around the room and saw anticipation and fear on the faces staring back at him.

"Fine. In addition to the Omaha location, Operation Delta calls for the repurposing of the reserve facilities in Cleveland. All available assets from the other three mint locations are currently en route. President Sarkes is managing the effort."

"Why there?" Juan asked.

"We picked that location because we didn't feel that the probability of an invasion force heading up the St Lawrence was a viable threat. Happy? Can I eat in peace now?" Brent responded.

Josh sat back in his chair in stunned silence.

After a few long moments, Abelardo asked, "What's wrong with that, Patrón? It's not anywhere near us."

The group began looking around the table. Each person was wondering who was going to answer the question. Most were thinking the same thing. *What's the big deal.*

After regaining his composure, Josh said, "Omaha and West Point aren't an issue for us here. Cleveland and Fort Knox, are however. In order to get from one to another, which the British and their UN lackeys are sure to do, they have to come awfully close to us."

"I'm no geography major here, Josh," Evan's wife started to reply. "But McArthur, Ohio isn't exactly on the beaten path. They have to go through Louisville, Cincinnati, and Columbus to get to Cleveland. We are almost two hours from the capital. What do we care if they have stashed the stuff in Cleveland?"

"It's a problem when the standard operating procedure, which the good General here left out, dictates that military forces stay off the main road and out of the major cities. When conflicts have arisen in other nations the world over, most assets will bypass urban centers unless their mission calls for it. There are too many places for ambushes and insurgents to hide, so they are avoided."

"When they sidestep these three populated areas, you're saying it could possibly bring them to our doorstep?" Basilia asked.

"Well, that depends," Josh replied.

"On what," Basilia quickly asked truly disturbed by the conversation.

"It –," Josh started to answer when Samantha cut him off.

"What he means, guys," Sam interjected, "Is that if their forces swing south of these larger cities, McArthur isn't off the beaten path anymore. Route 93 goes right through McArthur and takes them well clear of Columbus. Compounding this is President Sarkes' movement with said resources. Sarkes is the rabbit that the hounds will be chasing to Cleveland."

"Won't he be on-site before they arrive on our shores?" Evan asked. "How do they even know where he is?"

Then it dawned on the group. They were all being watched.

* * *


Layla and her sister were sleeping soundly in their tent when Heather quietly shook them awake.

"What? What is it?" Katherine replied groggily.

"I spotted something and I think you guys should take a look," she whispered in reply.

"This better be good," Layla added as she unzipped her bag and began searching for her boots.

Several minutes later the three were dressed and standing outside their tent in the frigid winter air. Once their eyes had adjusted to the lack of light in the night sky, they saw why their sister had awakened them. Off in the distance there was a glow emanating from the other side of the ridge. It was faint, but it could be seen.

"What is that?"

"That, ladies, is our ticket out of here," Heather replied. "I betcha."

When the three women were unceremoniously kicked out of the vehicles with their gear into the rugged wilderness of the mountains of West Virginia, they were given two instructions. The first was, 'find your own food'.

They had successfully accomplished that when Heather and Katherine tracked and killed a deer. She taught Heather where to aim and she had done the rest. Layla went foraging and brought back plenty of edible greens. The pair watched as Katherine field dressed and butchered it right on the side of the mountain. With each delicate movement of the blade, Katherine explained what she was doing and why. Heather vomited.

Juan had observed the entire lesson from a distance with a set of binoculars and radioed it back to the others.

The second instruction was, 'successfully raid our camp and we go home'.

"This smells like a trap and it has Uncle Dallas written all over it," Katherine said flatly. "There is no way in this world that any of those three would allow that much light pollution. They would have to make a giant bonfire for us to see it from here. That, ladies, is a homing beacon for disaster. You two can do what you want, but I'm out."

Katherine started heading back to the tent when Heather said, "What about some recon? We could just go up and scout it out. It would be like tracking, right?"

Katherine stopped and turned toward her sisters. She didn't say anything. She was standing there and thinking.

After a few moments of awkward silence, Heather leaned toward Layla and whispered, "What's she doing?"

She stepped closer to hear Layla's response when a large smile appeared on Layla's face.

"What is it?" Heather asked.

"That my dear sister, is what it looks like right before we win this thing and get the hell off this mountain," she answered quietly.

Dallas took the binoculars down and queued his headset. "It worked," he said into the mic.

He knew his niece well. If a spark of imagination entered Katherine's mind, she would work her way through every feasible scenario and permutation until she settled on a plan of action. He couldn't hear what Heather said to provide that motivation, but it was clear Heather was the muse to whatever Katherine concocted.

The youngest of the group was a natural leader, always had been. Heather lacked the experience and Layla required determination. However, the deficiencies in both were rapidly changing. Katherine was her father's daughter. She asked for input effectively, knew what resources were available to her, was decisive, and was willing to take the calculated risk. Her uncle's had quickly recognized this skill set. The 'camping trip' only confirmed their suspicions.

Through his binoculars, he saw Katherine say something to the other two and then they all returned to the tent. Dallas continued to observe.

Inside the tent, Katherine began breaking down packs looking intently for a specific item. Heather and Layla sat on their sleeping bags, saying nothing. Suddenly she stopped and held something up in each hand to show them.

"Where did you get those?" Layla whispered.

"Christmas present from Sam," Katherine replied.

"What are they," Heather asked.

Her sisters grinned at each other. Katherine handed her one and said, "Put it on and find out."

Heather inspected the weird device, but did as instructed.

"Now move the toggle forward. It's between the two eyepieces."

The world went from dark to light inside Heather's retina. She could clearly see her sister sitting in front of her making faces at her.

"Whoa!" she exclaimed.

Her siblings quickly shushed her.

"Push the button on the right hand side," Katherine instructed.

Heather complied and what was once green, was now shades of red. "What is this thing?" she asked in amazement.

"It's a night vision headset. Complete with thermal imaging," Katherine replied proudly in a faint whisper. "Okay, here's the plan. Two of us are going to cut a hole in the back of the tent and sneak out. One of you has to stay here and keep up appearances. Act like nothing is out of the ordinary. Stoke the fire, make rounds, all of it. So who's it gonna be?

"Heather's the better tracker, take her," Layla determined.

"You go next time?" Heather asked.

"Sure," her sister replied with a smile.

"Now that that's settled, here's how we get off this mountain," she began as she unfolded her makeshift map.

"Where did you get that?" her sisters wondered aloud.

"I've been constructing this since they booted us from the SUV's a couple days ago. Every patrol and each hunting expedition provided more and more intelligence. I think we should take the western route toward the location because it's the least passable. We could use the cut-through to the east, but it's too obvious. If we know it's there, they probably do too. If that's the case, they're watching it. That leaves only west.

"Why not go straight over the top to the north? The shortest distance between two points," Heather stated.

"They are probably expecting us to come straight over the ridge. They will have directed their defenses in that direction with a back-up toward the cut through. I think we should swing west of their little bonfire and flank them. One of them has to be observing us so that leaves only two at the camp. We'll use the night vision to approach in stealth until we see where they are hiding."

"Then what?" Heather asked her new leader.

"Once we pinpoint their locations, we'll divide our force and capture their camp from opposing sides."

"Like the raptors in that *Jurassic Park* movie?"

"Huh?" Katherine asked.

"That's how Papaw described a flanking maneuver. One person may be seen, but the others are concealed until it's too late."

Katherine shook her head at the analogy and replied, "Something like that. Layla, just stay here and act normally. Got it?"

"Roger," Layla replied.

"We are going to head out in five minutes. In four minutes," she said looking at Layla, "I want you to get up, put a log on the fire, and make your rounds. That will give whoever is watching us something to look at besides the tent."

"How will I know if it worked?" Layla said excitedly, but quietly.

Heather pulled a flare gun out her bag and handed it to Katherine. She held it up to show Layla.

"We'll fire this thing off."

"Got it. Good luck guys," Layla replied and then glanced down at her watch. "Four minutes and counting starting... now," she said as she exited the tent.

The two snuck out of the tent unseen and began working their way toward the ridge from the west. The rocky vertical landscape made the journey strenuous, but the pair worked cohesively and most obstacles were cleared in short order. The glow in the distance grew brighter as they neared. The bonfire that was once ablaze had subsided. The embers that remained provided enough of a signal to find though.

The sisters sat huddled together several hundred yards away. They used their collective body heat to help keep each other warm while they rested and observed. Several hours had passed since they had seen the initial glow. The sun would be up in a little over ninety minutes. They needed to get the scene scouted and then determine the course of action.

The duo started at the fire and then visually inspected the surrounding area with the night vision equipment. Heather took the sector north of the fire, toward the ridgeline, and Katherine the southern toward the valley below.

"Got one!" Heather exclaimed in a whisper. "Go three hundred yards north of the fire toward the ridge. See that rocky outcropping?" she instructed.

"Yeah," Katherine replied.

"Now switch on the thermal imager."

"Tsk, tsk, tsk. Oh, Uncle James just poked his head out. He sure is a sneaky one. That little cave he's in is lit up like a Christmas tree. What's he got in there putting off so much heat?" Katherine asked.

"Could be a solar blanket," her sister replied.

With the lull in their conversation Heather added, "Does this terrain look familiar to you? If I didn't know better, I'd say we came through here two days ago while we were tracking that buck. I don't think their camp is here. You were right. This was just a diversion. A trap."

In the excitement of the excursion and finding Uncle James, neither of them had noticed that there was no camp near the fire. Katherine zeroed in on the remnants of the inferno that had drawn their attention and began visually inspecting the area again. She started searching beyond the fire pit toward the east. Over another ridge was a smoke line stretching toward the heavens.

"I think we've been looking in the wrong place, Heather. Come back to the embers and go straight over the rise. What do you see," Katherine said.

She followed her sister's instruction until they were both scanning the ridge.

"Bingo."

"Let's go handle Uncle James and remove him from this equation," Katherine directed.

The two approached his position from behind, spread twenty yards apart. Before heading towards the outcropping, Katherine scribbled something on a piece of paper and handed it to her sister with some fishing line. She smiled, folded it, and then stuffed it in her pocket for safe keeping.

Heather casually walked on top of the rocky outcropping and lowered the note in front of the opening as her sister closed in from the side. There was a tug on her thin filament as James snatched the message from it. The two giggled once they heard him read it aloud.

"Bang! You're dead!"

Just before sunrise, Layla saw the flare emerge from behind the eastern ridgeline. "Way to go, sis," she said as she smiled and calmly began striking the camp site.

# Chapter 16

*Mama Renie's Pizzeria and Restaurant* sits at the corner of the main crossroads in downtown McArthur and has been the central hub for activity for over fifty years. The matriarch namesake had long since passed, but the family owned operation was a mainstay in the small town. The locals always seemed to congregate there to either celebrate or commiserate with the players and their families after games at the small rural high school.

Things were relatively quiet on this cold dreary winter day, but the dinner rush was approaching. Prep work was taking place, dough being kneaded, and dressings mixed. At ten 'til five the bell on the door rang. All of the workers understood it as a signal that the crush of hungry patrons was beginning. Mama Renie's grandaughter, which the town had nicknamed Mimi, was working behind the bar when Layla and the rest of the entourage entered.

The woman looked up and barely recognized Katherine and her sister.

"Oh my word! Katherine? Layla? Is that you?" Mimi announced. "Where have you girls been?"

The two quickly glanced over and saw her, stepped toward the bar, and leaned over the lacquered mahogany impediment squealing 'Mimi' in unison.

The three exchanged hugs as Mimi inspected their smudged faces and matted hair.

"I haven't seen you girls since the Harvest Festival! What in the world have you girls gotten into? Why are you so dirty? Wait. What's changed?" she asked alarmed.

The bell on the door rang again and James ducked as he entered. What remaining light there was outside was blocked by his imposing frame.

"Lord have mercy! That answers that question. Who's that tall drink of water?" Mimi whispered to the girls.

They looked over their shoulder and saw James, Dallas, and Juan entering with Heather not far behind.

"Oh, that's Uncle James," Layla said nonchalantly.

"Uncle? You girls do know you're white, right?"

Katherine laughed at the comment. "That's just what we call him. He and Dallas helped raise us. He was one of dad's Marine buddies."

"Hmmm," she purred. "I do love a man in uniform. Let me come out from behind this bar and you can introduce me to your friends," Mimi replied as she started working her way out.

The group stood in a semi-circle waiting as she approached.

"Guys, this is Mimi. She and her family own this restaurant," Layla started to say and then turned to the owner. "You already know Juan.

"Hola," Juan offered.

"Next to him is our sister, Heather."

"I'm sorry. Your what?" Mimi said shocked.

"It's a long story. We'll tell you later. The skinny one is Dallas McKutcheon. He grew up with Dad down in North Carolina. This big fella is James Rooney. He was one of Dad's NCO's."

Mimi walked straight over to James and offered her hand, palm down. James, ever the gentlemen obliged her unusual handshake.

"Pleasure to meet you, ma'am," James said in his baritone voice.

Mimi purred flirtatiously and replied, "Welcome to Mama Renie's, James. Please have a seat anywhere you like."

The group dispersed into two separate booths while Mimi retrieved her notepad. She pulled up a chair from a nearby table and parked it next to the girl's booth. "So who's drinking what?" she asked.

Layla and Katherine both ordered their usual water with lemon. Heather shocked Mimi when she said "Seven and seven."

"Doesn't she know about –," Mimi started to say in reference to their mother's addiction problems when Layla provided her with the answer.

"Different mother."

"Ah, okay. I can't wait to hear *that* story."

James piped up and said, "We'll have three of the same over here and the brunette with the deer blood on her cheeks is buying."

Katherine had marked Heather with her kill. Her father had done the same to her so she figured she'd carry on the tradition. Heather was proud of the mark and was avoiding its removal until Josh saw it.

Mimi cocked an eyebrow at the girls table and said, "Y'all went hunting in this weather?"

"More like survival training," Heather provided.

"And who's idea was that?" she asked.

"Our step mother's," Layla said casually. "Well, soon to be," she corrected.

Mimi laughed and said, "What, there were no boarding schools to ship you girls off to?"

The group chuckled at the comment, but all were careful not to say much more. So far, only the people at the farm had an inkling about the UN plans.

"Why are you buying for them, Heather was it? Since when does the lady pay?" Mimi said as she directed the questions.

In a heavily accented French voice, complete with pouty face, Heather replied, "They're brooding because we won their little war game." Then just as effortlessly, she switched to her usual tone. "I told them the first round would be on me if they'd quite their whining about losing to a bunch of girls."

Mimi laughed at the comments. "That's pretty good. You should be an actress. Are they crying foul?" Mimi asked.

Katherine smiled and sheepishly said, "They never said we couldn't use night vision."

"Way to go, kiddo," Mimi replied and the two high fived.

The group's collective attention was drawn toward the back of the restaurant when raucous laughter rang out. As the seven turned to see what was causing the commotion, a young man was being thrust forward and evicted from the herd. He slowly and cautiously began approaching Mimi and her patrons.

As he neared, James stood and dwarfed the teenager. "Can I help you, son?" he said in his deep menacing voice.

The lone brave soul slowly turned his gaze upward until he was looking James in the eye.

The lad stammered, but managed to eke out, "My name's S-s-scott. Scott Watson. My friends and I were just wondering if that was Heather White with you. If it's not too much trouble, would it be okay if we asked her to take some pictures with us?"

Dallas nudged James' arm and handed him a spoon. Recognizing the boys fear and Dallas's propensity for a joke, James took the implement. He griped the cutlery so hard his knuckles turned white.

"Do you have any idea how many ways I could kill you with this, kid," he taunted as he showed him the instrument to his demise, then bent it half for effect.

Scott swallowed hard. James could see that he was either about to speak or cry and decided to end the rouse, "I'm just messing with you," he said as Dallas and Juan started laughing. "Go on over and say 'hi' if you dare."

The boy exhaled deeply and said, "Thank you, sir."

The young man took a few steps further and said, "Ma'am, we were wondering," he started to say and then glimpsed the faces of the rest of the women in the booth. "Katherine is that you?"

"Scooter!" she squealed as she leapt out of the booth and wrapped her arms around his neck. Before either knew what happened, Katherine pressed their lips together in an awkward and public first kiss.

Dallas nudged James and said, "Uh oh."

"Katherine!" Layla exclaimed.

The two quickly broke their impromptu embrace. "I'm sorry. I don't know why I did that," Katherine said embarrassed.

"Nice to see you too, Katie," he replied in taunting jest for her having called him Scooter.

Katherine blushed and giggled at the childish reference to their school days.

"What are you doing here? I thought you were back at OU?" Scott asked her completely forgetting about Heather. Not waiting for her to answer, he turned his attention to the back of the restaurant and excitedly said, "Guys, guys, guys! Katherine and Layla are here!"

The group of young men stampeded toward the front and swarmed the girl's booth. To James and Dallas, it appeared as if a reunion of sorts was underway. The three moved to another booth further away and casually observed the interaction.

The men watched and sipped their Seagram's as they admired the girls having normal interactions with friends. It was interesting to see them without the omnipresence of the fear that had once weighed them down. The boys dragged a table over and abutted it to the booth. The girls introduced everyone to one another and a never ending stream of questions and answers ensued, albeit reserved replies from the girls.

Mimi extricated Heather from the mix by saying, "Come on darlin', let's you and I head over to grown-ups table."

The two joined the men in the other booth. The two groups sat and ate for the next few hours. From their uncle's vantage point, it appeared that the 'kids' table did nothing but talk, laugh, whisper, and giggle. From Layla and Katherine's perspective, it was probably one of the first times they'd done something normal without looking over their shoulders in more than a decade.

Heather noted that it had been a very long time since she hadn't been the focus of attention when a group of people formed. She decreed that their collective adventures in the woods, and now again in the restaurant, was very cathartic and humbling.

The group watched as Scott and Katherine seemed to shift closer to each other as the night went on. Before departing, as the groups were saying the collective goodbyes, he pulled Katherine aside.

"Uh, Katherine, I was, ah, I was wondering if you –," he stammered before she cut him off.

"Yes!" she said excitedly. "Whatever it is, yes!"

"Well, all right. I was thinking that we could –," he started more confidently, but she interrupted him again.

"Anything you want to do is fine. Surprise me, okay?" she quickly added.

"I think I can do that," he said halfheartedly. "I may not come from much, but I'm pretty sure I could manage that. Will tomorrow work? Around 7:00?" he asked.

"You know I don't care about that stuff. If it helps, we can go Dutch," she offered compassionately. "Come early though, around 6:45. We aren't going anywhere until my dad has a crack at you," she said playfully.

The boy swallowed hard again. *Fathers*.

"Oh, don't worry. If you can stand eye to eye with this big lug," Katherine said as she motioned to James who was holding another spoon menacingly. "You can get my dad's approval."

Scott leaned in close and whispered, "What if I want to steal another one of those kisses?"

Katherine blushed and said, "Well then you better make a good impression," and then quickly kissed him on the cheek.

They dropped Juan at his house, and the gear on their own new front porch at Three Sisters. Josh's daughters then strode triumphantly into their father's home like conquering heroes. Their uncles came sulking in behind them like the defeated adversaries that they were.

* * *

As evening fell, Gregg was exhausted from his hike, but scouted around the outskirts of the Simmons farm all the same. As chance would have it, Gregg found one of James' observation posts overlooking the main field and the cabin. *How convenient.*

He unpacked a sleeping bag from his duffle and settled in. After the last light was extinguished in the cabin, Gregg opted to explore the land under the cover of night. He poked his head in each structure and assessed its usefulness. Greenhouses, root cellars, smokehouses, and storage buildings full of machinery held nothing of interest. As he worked his way by the cabin on his way to the barn, he leered in a few of the windows. Nobody was stirring.

Once inside the structure, he began a thorough and meaningful search. In the tack room, he found a stand of Baofeng walkies charging in their respective bases. The row of green lights told him they were all fully charged. Next to the neat row of charged devices sat a cheap plastic basket containing a variety of accessories. He shuffled through the assortment of spare batteries, extra antennas, belt clips, and pocket sized manuals until his found an unused earphone mic set.

Shoving the wired mic set in his bag, Gregg quickly removed one of the walkies and briefly turned it over in his hand to inspect it more methodically. Realizing he was holding a mini ham radio, he briefly turned it on and made a mental note of the frequency. He quickly checked a second hand-held and threw both in his pack.

Before leaving the room, he quietly opened each of the cupboard doors on the hodge-podge collection of mismatched cabinets mounted on the wall. In one cabinet, Gregg found a collection of 10, 12, and 20-gauge boxes and cases. Next to it was a collection of full and partially used boxes of .22, .9mm, 380 ACP, 40 S&W, and 45 ACP caliber pistol rounds. The third cabinet held dozens of boxes of .223 and .308 rifle rounds. He was about to close the cabinet when he caught a glimpse of a box at the back of the cupboard partially obscured by an old plastic grocery bag.

Reflexively, he reached in and moved the bag. Staring in disbelief, he read the label on the box. Gregg audibly 'ooh'd' as he pulled the box from the cabinet. He shook the box and 'ooo'd' again when he discovered that it was full.

"Now we're getting somewhere," he muttered under his breath as he tossed the box in his bag and renewed his search of the barn.

Behind a partially closed door stood a knee-high stack of empty burlap feed sacks. He grabbed a half dozen or so, rolled them up, and stuffed them in his backpack as well.

Gregg searched high and low for the rifle that went with the 10-round box he'd found in the cupboard but to no avail. Since he didn't find any weapons that went with any of the ammo he'd located he had to assume that all of the rifles and pistols were safely secured in the cabin.

On his way out, he decided to perform a cursory search of the hi-rail truck parked just inside the closed barn doors. As he approached it, he noted the railroad axles protruding from the front and rear of the vehicle. Peering in through the open windows he saw nothing of merit. Besides, what he was looking for would barely fit in the cab. Gregg stood on his tip toes as he tried to peak in the bed of the truck. Unfortunately, the build-in tool box bed prohibited that. Once he reached the rear of the truck, he slowly removed the 'S' hooks and chains holding the tailgate shut and started to climb up.

When he looked inside the bed, he didn't bother climbing in. He just reached in and slid the hard sided pelican case out and placed it on the dusty floor of the barn. As quietly as possible, he slowly unsnapped the six buckles. When Gregg lifted the lid, he realized he'd been holding his breath. Exhaling slowly through his pursed lips, Gregg began sweet-talking the rifle.

"Well, hello gorgeous," he said as hefted the thirty pound Bushmaster 50 cal from the padded case. "Where have you been all my life?"

He ejected the 10-round magazine, checking to see if it was loaded. It was. Gregg then partially worked the bolt back to see if a round was chambered. It was.

"Oh my," he whispered to himself then grinned.

Closing the bolt and re-inserting the magazine, he noted the two 10-round magazines still in the case. He checked them as well and unsurprisingly, they were fully loaded too.

At the end of the vented forend halfway up the 30" barrel, he grabbed the legs of the bipod and swung them down into position with a 'click'. Adjusting the weight of the weapon in his hands, he slowly brought the rifle up to his shoulder and peered through the scope.

Gregg's mind groaned at the memories where he'd had to hump a thirty pound beast like this through forests, deserts, and up and down mountain sides when deployed. Thankfully, the hide he was headed to wasn't multiple kilometers away over nearly insurmountable terrain in a foreign country but rather just a few hundred yards across a field in rural Ohio, U.S.A.

Before stowing the weapon back in its case, he inspected the rifles optics. He let out a low, slow whistle when he was able to make out the branding on the side of the Bushnell 6-24x50-mm reticle riflescope.

"This man isn't messing around," he lamented as he placed the Bushmaster back in the padding.

Carefully, he snapped the buckles closed, shut and secured the tailgate, and exited the barn. Once he was back out in the open air, the coldness of the near constant winter breeze sent a chill up his spine

Gregg stealthily walked to the front of the cabin and tried to visually imagine the line of sight from the front door to the approximate location of the hide he'd discovered. He sniffed from the cold and then pulled his coat sleeve back to check his watch.

It was 4:45am. Quickly he recalled his time living in the Columbus suburbs with Emily. It didn't take much for him to remember that in the dead of winter in central Ohio, or thereabouts, twilight was around 7:15am. Sunrise generally followed thirty minutes later. Satisfied with his line of approximation between the house and hide, he retrieved one of the walkies from his backpack and placed it on top of a fence post between the cabin and the barn and waited for his opportunity.

Gregg was in the hide by 5:00am. On his way back, he'd collected an assortment of grasses, leaves, vine, and fallen sticks. As he sat in his sleeping bag, he took the burlap sacks out of his backpack and began weaving and sticking the collected materials into the coarse fabric haphazardly. As he finished each, he laid them across his sleeping bag like a makeshift ghillie cover of sorts. Once satisfied with his handiwork, he removed the Bushmaster from its case and sat it down next to him. Gregg then carefully slid the pelican case down into the dugout spider hole along the length of his body.

Exhausted, he slowly turned and placed the rifle up on its bi-pod legs and covered it with the last of his ghillie burlap sacks. He checked his watch one last time. It was 5:45am. He sighed at the realization that he'd only get an hour or two of rest before the residents on the farm started stirring or the sun came up.

At 7:30am, Gregg was awakened by the sound of machinery and the farm coming to life. Engines were turned over and revved then left to warm under idle. He quickly picked up the rifle and peered through the scope. Gregg continued his over watch as Josh started his morning routine with Juan. He observed as the pair inspected the property. They came and went several times from the fields, pens, and barns all morning long.

Since he'd begun his observations of the farm the previous evening, he'd witnessed over a dozen people come and go. *He's probably starting a cult*, he thought wryly.

For Josh and the rest of the group that had just returned from the mountains, the need to get back to some semblance of normalcy was paramount. Gregg watched as two men, a big one and a skinny one, emerged from the cabin and climbed into a well-worn farm truck. The pair turned around in the field, eventually exiting the farm gates and disappearing down the main road headed toward McArthur. *They are probably running errands.*

Gregg did the mental math.

*Twenty minutes to town, another twenty to thirty minutes of bullshitting, then another twenty minutes back. Those two will be gone for at least an hour.*

Returning his attention back to the cabin, Gregg saw no sign of what he assumed were the man's daughters. He was watching as they excitedly entered the cabin the night before. Unfortunately, he had left his nest to relieve himself and didn't see the girls depart on foot toward their farmhouse through the hedgerow. By Gregg's accounting, there were four women still inside the cabin. None of which was his wife. In truth, Josh's three daughters were all asleep in their new home at Three

Sisters. Eventually though, even they couldn't ignore the massive fireball building in the morning sky. Gregg knew he was a lot of things, and regardless of whether his wife was present or not, he'd never direct his rage at a woman. Then he caught himself thinking more and more about the tangent concept and amended his original assessment to include the words 'innocent' and 'civilian'. The bitch wearing the suicide vest under her burka back in Afghanistan deserved every grain of the powder used to deliver that bullet in her head.

Gregg watched the comings and goings all morning with great interest through the Bushnell. Hours went by and no one went near the post balancing the walkie. He knew that, eventually, someone would venture near it and the opportunity would present itself. Through all of the observation though, whispers of doubt began creeping into his head.

Emily was nowhere to be seen as of yet, but he waived off his doubts given President Sarkes description of Josh. Given the news articles he'd read, and the grainy black and white images the articles contained, he knew he was in the right place. She had to be here. If he didn't know better, he swore he could even smell her sweet perfume wafting through the whispering pines. By the time lunch rolled around, everyone was either still off running errands or completing assorted tasks around the farm. All except for the man that stole her from him. He was casually fixing a sandwich.

He watched while Josh leisurely ate, read the local paper, and sorted mail. Eventually, his prey exited the cabin. His path was going to take him right past the post holding the walkie.

*Finally!*

As Josh neared the comms unit, Gregg peered through the Bushnell scope and squeezed the trigger.

*Time to dance!*

The beast in his grasp awoke with a thunderous boom. The fence post he'd been aiming at exploded as it was cut in half by the massive 50-caliber round.

Reflexively, Josh hit the ground and began scrambling for cover. He quickly crawled behind the nearest car he could find. He peered around the fender of Dallas' sedan at the remains of the fencing.

"What the hell!?" Josh exclaimed.

A second round echoed through the valley as Gregg put another round into the broken off chunk of wood in front of Josh. It seemed to exploded in to a hundred little punji projectiles. Turf, dirt, and snow were sent hurtling through the air.

"Come on out. Can you see it yet," the sniper muttered.

Gregg waited a while in order for the man to see what was on the ground. Josh was more concerned with staying behind cover. He was just about to squeeze off another round to direct Josh to the walkie when a truck hurriedly emerged from the woods carrying Juan and his sons.

"Where did you little fence jumpers come from?"

He quickly switched targets. The passenger side tire on the pickup shredded as the large caliber round tunneled its way through. The vehicle made a hard right and came to an abrupt stop just shy of the eviscerated fence post.

The three hastily exited the driver's door and took cover. Juan lay under the truck with his .308 and powerful scope scanning the hill. Jesus did the same from behind the bed of the truck. Abelardo felt useless. When they heard the shots, he had only grabbed the 1911 Josh had given him on his twenty-first birthday.

"These boys came to play. Let's see what we have," he stated to no one. He then used the scope of the rifle to scan over his three new targets. "Two .308's and one guy hiding behind the wheel well. This is doable."

Josh knew what a .50 sounded like from just about any distance. As soon as Juan and his sons hit the dirt, he immediately began using hand signals to alert Juan that whoever it was had most likely found the Bushmaster in the barn.

Abelardo peered around the front of the truck and thought he saw something lying near the shattered post as the ground exploded once more. He quickly ducked back behind cover and looked over at his friend and employer. Josh immediately signaled that the shot had been the fourth from the ten-round magazine.

"Come on. Take the hint buddy," Gregg pleaded.

The fifth round kicked up more debris. Abelardo poked his head around the front fender once more as Gregg swapped magazines. He wasn't imagining things, there was a walkie on the ground. He motioned to Josh that he was going to go and retrieve it. His boss quickly shook his head 'No'.

Abelardo stood with his hands outstretched and slowly placed his .45 on the hood of the truck.

"What have we got here? Does he see it?"

Gregg watched through his scope as the young man cautiously ebbed his way forward. The walkie was carefully picked up.

"Can we help you, Señor?" Abelardo said haltingly into the device and stood stock still waiting for a reply. A few moments later he received one.

"Give that to Josh," Gregg growled into the mic.

Abelardo slowly turned to Josh and said, "He wants to speak with you, Patrón."

"Tell him I'm coming out and to stop shooting," Josh answered back.

Abelardo relayed the message and placed the radio back on the ground. He then sprinted back behind the relative safety of the truck.

Josh slowly emerged from behind the sedan with his hands up to show he was unarmed. Before he was able to reach the walkie, Josh saw Evan's suburban passing the greenhouses and heading for the cabin.

"Juan! The girls are coming. Run out there and stop them! He won't shoot you. He wants me for some reason. Go. Now!"

His friend extricated himself from under the carriage of his damaged vehicle. He too placed his weapon slowly on the hood of the truck.

Gregg watched as he ran up the driveway with his hands raised to stop the inbound SUV. He already knew who was in that rig.

Josh bent down and queued the mic, "Can I help you with something?"

Gregg opted to start off with some flattery.

"I've got to hand it to you, this is a pretty nice rifle. You should think about upgrading though. The newer models are several pounds lighter than this and have more padding."

Then Gregg chose to insult him.

"Oh, and maybe consider locking it up, idiot."

The comment rattled Josh. "Um, okay," was all he could think of. "That was top of the line in my day."

"Try the L115 which chambers a .338 Lapua Magnum or the McMillian Tac 50," Gregg said.

"I'll have to look into those, thanks," Josh said quizzically.

"You serve?" Gregg asked.

"Marines. Why do you ask?" Josh asked.

"Because you didn't bat an eye when I rattled off manufacturers and ammo specs," Gregg answered.

Josh shrugged. "How about you?"

"Army," Gregg responded. "Where did you do your tours?"

"I made a trip through Saudi Arabia and Iraq in the first Gulf fiasco and then got shipped to Bosnia."

"Haven't been through there, but I've seen enough of the Middle East to know that I'd trade a hardwood forest over an oasis in the desert any day. I don't care how majestic the Bedouins say it is at sunset."

Josh actually laughed at the comment.

"You and I might have a lot in common. Why don't you come on down and we can talk about it," Josh said sincerely.

"The only way I'm coming down without putting a few holes in you is if you can magically present my wife."

"Okay. Who's your wife?" Josh asked.

The ground erupted in the wake of a fresh round.

"Don't play dumb with me! I know she's here!" Gregg screamed into the mic. "Now where is she?!"

Josh didn't flinch. It was clear to Josh that whoever was in the woods had no intention of killing anyone. He trusted this feeling so much that he turned and started walking toward the porch.

"Hey! Where are you going? Get back here!"

When he didn't stop his progression, Gregg sent another in to the steps. Josh calmly stepped over the shattered step and picked up a wooden chair. He nonchalantly carried it back to the area of chewed up earth and placed it right in the middle of it.

"What the hell are you doing? I could kill you at any minute," Gregg said incredulously into the handset.

"No you won't. If you truly wanted me dead you'd have done it already," Josh responded. There was silence on the other end. Josh took the lull as an opportunity to stuff his pipe and relax. He just sat there, reclined in the rustic log chair with the sun on his face, and calmly smoked his pipe.

"You smug son-of-a-bitch," Gregg started to say before he pulled the trigger and shredded what was left of the fence post.

\* \* \*

"Go for –," Dallas began before being cut off.

Juan, winded, interrupted him and quickly asked, "How far away are you from the farm?"

"Were about five minutes out, why? What's going on?" Dallas answered.

"Someone found the big gun in the barn and is currently taking pot shots at our friend. I think he's in Señor James' nest. Can you come over the top of the ridge on that location from behind?" Juan said hurriedly.

"On it," Dallas proclaimed then disconnected the call. Turning to James, he stated, "We got a big problem."

\* \* \*

Josh knew exactly what Juan would do. While he waited for the Cavalry, he decided to waste as much time as possible. He queued the handset and said, "Well, if you're not in the mood to talk, then I guess I'll tell you all about the British designs for our great nation."

Before Josh even got started with his winding tale, Gregg answered, "You don't know the half of it, buddy."

"Oh," he said surprised. "Then how about you enlighten me," Josh replied.

"I'm not here for that. All I want is my wife," Gregg shot back.

"And who is she exactly? I only ask because the woman I intend to marry is named Samantha. I don't know who you are referring to. Why don't you tell me her name and I'll see if I can rustle her up," Josh said calmly and reassuringly.

As silence permeated the farm land, a bird call rang out.

"Uh oh," Josh spoke into the mic.

"What are you going on about now?" Gregg demanded.

"Can you do me a favor?" Josh asked.

"Sure, why not," Gregg answered sarcastically. "What can *I* do for *you*?"

"How about you stop looking through that scope for... I don't know, just a few seconds... and look behind you. Tell me what you see."

Gregg was about to answer and tell Josh to go to hell when the distinctive click-click of a hammer being cocked resonated in his ears.

"Don't make us shoot you, son," James said as he drew down on the man hiding in his snipers nest.

Gregg slowly removed his hand from the pistol grip then calmly put his hands behind his head. To his right he saw the skinny one closing in as well.

"You sure are quiet for a big fella," Gregg said complimenting his captors. "Of course, the last time I had a run in with a guy your size I stuck a screwdriver in his head."

"Shut up and put these on," Dallas said as he threw zip ties at him.

"It's your world boss," Gregg answered and did as instructed. "Front or back?" he asked.

"Cuff yourself in the front, if you don't mind," James growled but answered as politely as possible.

The three emerged from the woods and began walking towards Josh reclining in his chair. The large sparsely snow covered field took some time to cross on foot. As they neared, he tapped out the burnt contents of his pipe and stood.

Off in the distance, the whine of a remote controlled plane taking flight could be heard. The low altitude buzzing sounded like a swarm of angry bees.

"Oh good," Josh stated as he heard the machine take to the air. "Do you hear that?" he asked the prisoner as they approached.

"Yeah, so," Gregg answered.

"Uncuff him," Josh said to Dallas.

"But we –," Dallas began to answer.

"It's okay. Please."

Dallas produced a large knife from his belt and cut the zip ties. Gregg began rubbing the scars on his wrists.

"See that little quad-copter way up in the sky?" Josh asked.

Squinting up into the noon day sun, Gregg proclaimed, "Yes, I see it… I even hear the damnable device. I don't give two shits about that damn thing!" Gregg snapped. "I just want my wife!"

"Young man," Josh started. "We have been more than polite... even when you were shooting at us. As such, I will ask you only one time to watch your tone with me. Do I make myself clear?"

Gregg was a trained operator. Everything about his being was forged in countless crucibles the world over. They had made him hard, cold to his surroundings, especially to his wife. What he thought was a protective shielding only served to push her away. He wasn't there for her when she needed him the most. When he was given a job, it was executed with military precision and to the best of his ability at all times. The man before him though, whether through the tone of his voice or through the ease and directness with which he carried himself, tore down the walls. He felt like he was a child being scolded by his father all over again. He was ashamed.

Josh could see the man shrinking in front of him.

"Son, look at me," Josh said.

Gregg slowly turned his gaze upward from the ground when Josh concluded, "I am only directing your attention to the copter because it is being flown by your wife, Emily. That is her name, isn't it? Gregg."

The man's mouth opened slightly.

Josh smiled at him.

"She just arrived this morning."

# Chapter 17

Secret Service Agent Edward Monahan ended the call and nudged his new partner and fellow Agent, "Start looking for exits."

He then turned and addressed the man half asleep in the backseat, "Sir, we have an issue," he said.

President Tom Sarkes arched his brow in response.

"Our airborne escort believes that they have identified a tail, sir."

Sarkes sat up and rubbed his eyes. He turned his head to look out the back window and began scanning for the offender. "Okay, Ed. Which one?"

The Agent sighed an exhale. "Sir, they're trailing almost a mile behind us. You can't see them."

"Oh," he said and turned back around sheepishly. "So who's spotting for them? We could turn anywhere and they'd never see us. Let's just get off the main road," Tom replied.

"Sir, we are the lead car in a twenty-eight vehicle convoy going sixty miles per hour in a seventy-five zone. We stick out like a sore thumb."

"Options, where are we?" Sarkes asked.

The driver turned his head and replied, "We just passed Richmond, Indiana. We are about to cross the state line into Ohio."

The armored sedan and the rest of the contingent had been on I-70 since departing the facility in Denver two days ago. The winter weather typically associated with the plain states was calm and allowed them to make good time. By mid-afternoon on the third day, the Delta One transport only had about three hundred miles to go to their destination in Cleveland, Ohio.

"Well this complicates things, doesn't it," the former President said rhetorically.

"Sir, I think that we should –," the Agent started to recommend some options when Sarkes' cell phone starting ringing. When it played the "Hail to the Chief" ring tone, they all knew who was calling.

"Hold that thought, Ed," Sarkes said to the Agent as he picked up his phone.

"How's it hangin', Jim?" Tom decreed as he answered the call. Seconds later the Agents heard Sarkes say, "Whoa, whoa, slow down. Hold on, let me put you on speaker so I don't have to relay this intel." He pushed the icon and then held the device aloft. "Okay, you're on speaker, go ahead."

"Who's on your end Tom?" the POTUS asked frantically.

"It's just me and two Agents, why?" Sarkes replied.

"Have they been read in?" Rayburn quickly asked.

"As much as they needed to be. What's going on?"

"Tom, do you recall our conversation at Camp David? The one regarding the electrical disturbances."

"Yes, why? Do you guys have more detail surrounding those incidences?" Tom asked.

"Well, it seems your trip to The Hague is panning out. Our French connection just called me. Those weren't random. Apparently there's an Iranian faction bent on bringing down the 'last empire', whatever the hell that means. The British were watching the facilities like we thought, and they caught one."

There was silence on the other end of the phone. Too much so for President Rayburn.

"Tom, are you still there?" he asked.

"Yeah, yes, we're still here. I'm just trying to process that information."

"Tom, those eight little bastards are running around our country with those devices," the POTUS added. "And they've linked up with the British. The Brits are now directing these jihadists to various targets around the U.S."

In the background, Tom and his security detail could hear a commotion in the Oval Office.

"Jim? What is that?" Tom asked in earnest.

"Hold on a sec. The Director of the Secret Service and the Secretary of Defense (SecDef) just walked in."

There were some muffled sounds like the mouth piece was trying to be covered and then President Rayburn came back on the line.

"Close that door, gentlemen," Jim said as he started to resume the conversation. "Tom, I have you on speaker with Director Anderson from Secret Service and SecDef Fielding."

"Secretary Fielding, Director, nice of you to join us. What's going on?" Sarkes asked.

"Hey, Tom, are your Agents on the line?" the Director asked.

"We are, sir," Agent Monahan said immediately.

"Who's 'we', son?"

"Special Agents Monahan and Smith, sir."

"Agent Monahan, secure that device please," the SecDef said.

Sarkes handed the phone to Ed who promptly took the phone off of speaker.

"Yes, sir. The phone is secured. How can I –," Agent Monahan started to say before his boss cut him off.

The Head of the Secret Service leaned on to the President's desk and spoke directly into the phone, "Agent Monahan, I want you to answer me with only 'yes, sir' or 'no, sir' is that understood?

"Yes, sir."

"Good. I am ordering you to secure that vehicle by any and all means necessary. Copy?"

"Yes, sir."

"Once the vehicle is secured, place Agent Smith under arrest. Is that understood?"

"Yes, sir."

Faintly, Agent Monahan heard, "Oh, would you cut the cloak and dagger crap. Just tell him he needs to shoot Smith in the head!"

"Hold one, Agent," the Director said as he pushed mute.

Not sure what to do at this point, Ed replied to no one when he said, "Yes, sir. I'll hold."

While he waited, he decided to start putting plans in motion, "Go ahead and take the next exit, Smith. They are telling us to get off the highway. I'm on hold while they finalize the route. We need to use the secondary roads."

"Roger that," Smith said casually.

Agent Smith turned on his blinker to alert the rest of the convoy and started heading down the off ramp. When the vehicle stopped at the end, Agent Monahan, dropped the cell phone on the seat, drew his service weapon, and pointed it at Smith's head.

"Put the car in park and turn off the engine," he said as he slowly reached over and removed Smith's service pistol from its shoulder holster.

"Sir, would you be so kind," he said as he handed the piece over the back of the seat to Sarkes.

The former President's eyes became as big as saucers.

Swallowing hard, Tom replied, "Oh, I'd rather not Agent Monahan. Perhaps you should just holster it and keep it up there with you."

"Whoa, what the hell, man! What are you doing?" Smith said as he reacted to the injustice.

Ed placed the driver's 9mm in his own holster and grabbed the cell phone. He checked if his boss was back on the line, but there was still silence. He flipped the phone to Sarkes who sat in the backset with his mouth agape. Agent Monahan toggled a switch in the dash and the bulletproof divider immediately went up between the front and rear seats.

"Car in park, engine off," he repeated. "Do it now or so help me," Ed growled.

"Okay, okay, relax man," Smith said as he pushed the handle up into park, turned the key, and complied.

With the car safely off, Ed ordered his detainee out of the car. Before exiting, the Special Agent in charge picked up his walkie and queued the other Secret Service vehicles, "Whiskey One, Whiskey One, Agent needs assistance."

Two trailing SUV's suddenly appeared from the middle and rear of the column in either side mirror. Each came to a screeching halt, one in front and one behind, prohibiting escape for the lead car. Both autos immediately emptied. Agents in bulletproof vests with weapons drawn littered the roadway. The business end of everything in their possession was now trained on Whiskey One.

"Okay, Smith, please exit the vehicle slowly."

Before putting the device in his coat pocket, Ed relayed his intent by saying, "We're coming out. Detain Agent Smith, driver-side."

The Agents outside the vehicle rotated their position accordingly.

The man was summarily manhandled and placed face down on the cold February pavement and cuffed. Once the prisoner was under control, President Sarkes began exiting the vehicle.

With half his body out of the 'beast', the former POTUS watched as the detainee was being stood up. Suddenly, a red mist exploded from his neck. His body went limp in his captor's hands. The muffled sound of a weapons report followed immediately thereafter.

"Sniper! Get down!" one of the Agents yelled.

Ed reflexively put himself between the President and their surroundings. In his ear he could hear the pilot above him in the air support chopper. Unfortunately, their altitude prevented them from ascertaining much detail on the ground. All they could see were people scattering and the tailing car stopped on the overpass.

As he shielded him, Agent Monahan grabbed Sarkes, pushed him back into the town car, and slammed the door. The remaining Agents scattered and took up defensive positions. The Secret Service agents had failed to notice that the tail previously identified by their air support was stopped on the overpass.

Their attention was only drawn to the bridge when the vehicle lost traction and squealed the tires as it accelerated.

Ed quickly spoke into his concealed mic and said, "Zulu-Tango-Two-Five-Eight, do you still have visual on the green sedan?"

"Roger that," the pilot answered back. "He's east bound on I-70 a half mile beyond your location."

"Pursue and keep eyes on that target!" Agent Monahan screamed into the device. "Radio updates as available." He then turned to the remaining Agents and said, "Whiskey Two and Three, chase that son-of-a-bitch down!"

The Team Leader from the other vehicles yelled over his shoulder, "How do you want him?"

"Alive if possible, dead if necessary!" Ed hollered in return.

The Special Agent in charge of the former Presidents security noticed the rear door start to open. He discreetly slid over and stood in front of it so it couldn't be opened further.

"Come on, Ed. Let me out of here. The threat has passed."

"Not a chance in hell, sir. Sit tight. We'll be moving again in a few minutes," he answered before gently closing it on Sarkes.

Agent Monahan removed the walkie from his coat.

"Damn it," he muttered to himself before bringing the comms unit up and queueing the device, "Alpha Team, presence requested. Column lead, ASAP."

Down the line, the whine of a diesel engine could be heard pulling out of formation. The initial dark plume exiting from the behemoths exhaust stack betrayed its position as the next to last vehicle. The convoy itself was a mix of heavy machinery. In addition to President Sarkes' armored sedan, there were two Secret Service Suburban's, two refuelers, three 'deuce and half's', and twenty tarp laden cargo haulers with material handling equipment.

Given the mission and the precious materials being transported, both President Sarkes and Rayburn insisted that all Operation Delta convoys carried armed escorts in the form of SpecOps teams. It was an extreme precaution that the Joint Chiefs eventually relented on. Also at the request of President Rayburn, Sarkes' convoy also came with added counter measures in the form of an armored box which had been placed inside one of the M35 deuce's.

As the truck slowed, Special Agent Monahan whisked the door open and grabbed the former President by the lapel.

"Come with me, sir," he said as he forcefully pulled the man from the vehicle.

Before the massive transport was even stopped, the tailgate was dropped and a ladder was extended.

"Get in!" Ed yelled over the sound of the rumbling diesel engine and tire noise.

Sarkes looked up and saw three heavily armed operators. One bent down to assist the President. Another turned and opened the vault like door. The third took a kneeling position covering the one hundred and eighty degree field of fire.

"You can't be serious!" Tom Sarkes said exacerbated.

"No choice, sir. I think you'll find the accommodations comfortable," the soldier replied as he half pushed half escorted the President inside.

Once he was in, the door was immediately shut and locked.

"Where to, sir?" the team lead asked Agent Monahan.

"Let me see your map," he replied.

President Sarkes began banging on the bulletproof window and held up the phone. Agent Monahan directed the President to a call button near the rear of the box.

Tom pushed it and said, "Would you like to know what I found out?"

The Agent pressed its counterpart on the outside to reply. "What's going on, sir? Where are we headed?"

"Two of the convoys making their way to Omaha were hit by a portable EMP. All personnel were lost," Sarkes answered.

The four men stood crestfallen by the news.

"Why did the Director order me to detain Agent Smith," Ed said through the device.

Sarkes replied in his usual candor, "That wasn't Agent Smith. They just pulled the real Alister Smith from the Potomac."

* * *

Airman Cecil Sullivan and Colonel Wilson James patiently stood and waited in the corner of the barracks with four MP's as the Master Chief performed a head count. When they received his confirmation, they began their inspection.

The pair had been on the ground only a few hours. In that time, they had managed to piss off a Major General, two full bird Colonels, and all of the personnel comprising their staffs. Calls were made, weight was thrown, but all requests for information were summarily denied. They met with the base commander and provided written authorization from the President to conduct house-to-house searches of the entire base. They were also to be presented with the service records of all personnel that had arrived in the last six months in addition to the addresses for those not residing on base.

Cecil led the procession through the ranks of men with the Colonel and MP's not far behind. Col. James had his hand on his side arm, ready to be drawn at a moment's notice.

On the flight in, the Airman had suggested that they winnow the number of troops to inspect by limiting the searches to male Spanish speakers and anyone looking remotely Latin or Arabic. The Colonel laughed and said, "Do you know how many laws that would violate?"

Airman Sullivan didn't much care about the civil liberties he stepped on, or over, as long as they found Abbas in time.

The former POW looked over each of the assembled in turn, drawing close enough to smell their breath on some. He recoiled from one and declared, "Drunk."

Out of the fifty service members standing at attention, no one stood out. When they group made the last turn and began inspecting the final row of soldiers, one of the recently rotated airman bolted for the door. Cecil stopped the Colonel from giving chase and pronounced, "Too young."

Col. James waved the MP's through the column and they apprehended the man not far from the barracks hiding under a car. When they searched him, all they found were four joints and a dime bag of weed. Dead end.

"You boys seen enough?" the base commander bellowed as he entered and announced himself.

"Not quite," Cecil shot back.

"Son, do you see the star I'm wearing?" the General replied.

"Do you see the uniform I'm *not* wearing?" the Airman retorted.

"How about I kick you and your shrink off my base, smartass."

Cecil spun abruptly, took the orders from Colonel James' breast pocket, and flashed them in front of his face.

"How about I raise you a Presidential Order, dipweed! I think I'd like to see the command bunkers for each set of silos now. We haven't inspected those yet. How would you feel about that?"

Taken aback by the civilian's candor, the General chose a different tact, "Young man –," he started to say.

"Sir, may I speak with you in private?" Colonel James asked.

The General unfroze the glare he was shooting in Cecil's direction long enough to acknowledge the Colonel's request.

"Absolutely," he replied with a smile.

The two aging warhorses excused themselves and entered a barracks anti-room. Col. James held the door for the General and then rolled his eyes at Cecil once the man had passed. Cecil snickered.

"How about you tell me what the hell –," the General began as he started in on the Colonel.

"Whoa, how about we dial it down a notch, sir. I asked you in here to explain a few things so this might go a little smoother."

"Great," he replied. "I'd love to hear this."

"So far you only have a name, Cecil Sullivan. What you don't have is a rank and a history. That man out there is Senior Airman Cecil Sullivan. He spent close to a year in an Iranian cave complex being beaten, whipped, branded, and all manner of torture I am not going to discuss right now. One minute he was asleep in his rack at Bagram and the next he was bound and in the back of a truck being kicked for a week before they made it to their camp in western Iran.

"For the first few months, he told them nothing. He took all of it for God and country. Then they showed him a video that had been taken from inside his sister's home in Albany, New York. He still didn't break... swore it was movie set or a sound stage and didn't believe them. A couple weeks later a second one arrived."

The General was completely enthralled with the story. "What was on that one?"

"It was his sister walking through a park with a sniper's scope trained on her."

"So why are you here?"

"We are here because of what he and another prisoner divulged once they *were* broken," the Colonel replied.

"And what was that?" the General asked with baited breathe.

"Cecil provided instruction on the U.S. nuclear arsenal. More specifically, he divulged information regarding the Minuteman III and its launch and navigation systems. He also provided a detailed layout for the service tunnels and the controls in the bunkers."

"And the other prisoner? What did he tell them?"

"He was a Special Forces operator," Col. James answered knowing it would be more than enough detail to get his point across.

The General slumped in his chair and sighed. "Oh, crap," was his response.

The man reflected on the ramifications for a few moments before the Colonel added, "In a nut shell, he basically told them how to bypass a number of our measures and systems and launch one."

"Great. Just so I understand you correctly, you're telling me that there is a lunatic running around my base with the knowledge and skills to sidestep all of our protocols and send up one of our birds?"

"That's about the long and short of it. But there's a catch."

"Of course there is," the General replied sarcastically. "Why wouldn't there be. What is it?"

"Airman Sullivan was stationed at two bases, F.E. Warren and Minot. If we don't find him here, we have to do the same thing all over again in North Dakota."

"If he's a missile systems operator, why was he even in the Gulf in the first place?"

"If there are nuclear weapons in country, someone trained in their maintenance tags along, you know that," the Colonel replied.

"They deployed nukes to that hotbed? Were they crazy?"

Col. James just shrugged.

"Nice. So what are we looking for? Specifics?" the General asked.

"That would be profiling, sir," came the immediate reply.

"I don't give a damn what you want to call it, Colonel. Gimme what I need!"

"Fine. We are searching for a male, approximately six feet in height, aged thirty to thirty five years, looks to be of Latin or Arabic descent and speaks fluent Spanish. We believe the person we are after managed to replace a service member and infiltrate one of those two bases. He's been embedded for months and the only person alive that can identify him is standing right out there."

# Chapter 18

Gregg watched Emily deftly work the controls of Jesus' new quadcopter. She didn't seem like she had a care in the world. Doubt crept into his mind. Doubts about him returning. Doubts about how she'd welcome him home. Doubts about their relationship.

*Has she moved on? Am I already just a faint memory?*

The radio controlled device swooped and soared across the fields. Emily maneuvered the toy with amateurish skill, but skill all the same. Gregg continued to observe from the safety of the hedgerow. Watching her fly the machine looked as if it was bringing her sheer delight. Emily practiced hovering the contraption above the brush, and then, without warning, she would suddenly pop it up and send it soaring several hundred feet into the air. On its descent, Emily would slow the quads rate of fall just before it crashed and then return it to a hover.

Gregg was astonished.

*Well I'll be. She could barely work her cell phone before I left.*

When the battery charge finally waned, the return to home feature slowly and softly landed the copter at her feet.

Gregg steeled himself to the reunion.

*Now or never.*

Gregg slowly emerged from the hedgerow, but only made it a few feet and froze.

*What am I afraid of? She's already been told the truth about my career.*

Then more doubt.

*Can she even begin to forgive me?*

Gregg quickly backed pedaled and returned to the cover.

"What do you think you're doing?" came a voice from behind him.

Gregg spun around and reflexively reached for his side arm. He groaned.

*Damn it. That skinny one took my weapon.*

Standing before him were Josh's three daughters.

"I said, what are you doin'?" Katherine asked, repeating the question.

"I… she," Gregg began to stammer. "Wait, you look familiar," he replied as he looked over the three. "Why do I know you?"

"Name's Heather White," she said as she extended her hand to Gregg. "These are my sisters, Katherine and Layla. You've already met our father, Josh."

"The actress?"

"One and the same," she answered.

"This day keeps getting weirder," Gregg said half under his breath.

"What's so weird? You've returned home and you haven't seen you wife in over a year. She misses you. You can see it on her face. You should go to her. The only thing that's out of place around here is you hiding among the brambles. Do you want us to take you over there?" Heather offered.

"No," Gregg said harshly, but quietly.

The girls were taken aback, but Layla would have none of it.

"Don't bark at us! From what we understand, she was a wreck after she lost another baby, her husband, and learning you lied all on the same day. Emily put herself back together and was one of the key scientific witnesses at the Congressional Hearings. According to our stepmother, Emily never gave up hope on a reunion with you. She knew you'd come home to her. Secretary McInerney took care of her until you returned.

So don't you *dare* take issue with us after what everyone has done for you, Sgt. Chastain."

Gregg swallowed hard and glanced longingly back at his wife.

The three women sensed something was off. The man hadn't reacted when told of his wife's experiences since he'd gotten on that fateful flight.

"Wait a minute," Heather said questioningly. "Why didn't you react when she said Emily knows about your career?"

Gregg returned his gaze back to the three interrogators, but said nothing.

"Answer me, Gregg," she demanded.

Softly, almost in a whisper, Gregg finally answered. "A couple months into my captivity, my Iranian 'hosts' showed me a video of Em being told that my transport had been shot down. I watched from the other side of the planet as my wife had yet another miscarriage. I continued to watch as the doctors said she had ovarian cancer. Do you have any idea what it's like to want to be somewhere, to help someone, to comfort and protect them, and not have the power to do anything about it?"

"I do," Katherine answered solemnly. "I know exactly what that's like."

"Look, soldier," Layla started. "She's either gonna hug you or hit you, or maybe both. It doesn't really matter though because, in the end, she's already forgiven you."

"Yeah, now move your ass!" Heather added. "Tell her that dinner's at six."

Gregg smiled at their candor. "Now or never then, I guess, right?"

"There is no 'never'. Only a 'now'," Layla said and shoved him out of the hedgerow.

Gregg crashed through the brush landing on his side and rolling on to his back. With the quadcopter off, Emily was able to hear the commotion and glanced over. Gregg didn't move.

Emily returned her focus to the device and started downloading the video the machine had taken. She quietly hummed to herself, lost in her own world, as she connected cables and scrolled through various prompts on her tablet. Gregg slowly rotated his head and began turning on to his stomach. He crawled on his belly toward the side of the cabin.

"What is he doing?" Heather asked.

"I have no idea. It looks like he's trying to sneak up on her," Layla answered.

"That'll never work," Katherine remarked.

"Let's wait and see how good this guy is. Sam said he was Special Forces for how long, twenty years?" she replied.

"Yeah, that sounds about right," her sister answered as the three watched him easily climb the side of the porch. "Oh, oh, he's up over the railing. Anndd there's the creek in the decking. Did she hear it?"

"Wait for it. Emily stopped whatever she was doing. She's looking around. He's totally busted," Katherine observed.

Gregg pressed his back against the structure and began slowly working his way toward the door and stairs. He froze and held his breath every time she looked up or turned her head slightly. He crept forward, slowly inching and progressing across the decking.

He was about to sit on the top step and announce himself when Emily said, "I heard you a mile away. What do you think you're doing?"

"She got him," Layla noted. "Let's give them some privacy. We'll see them at six for dinner."

Flustered, Gregg said the first thing that popped into his mind.

"Well, I thought I'd try and surprise my girl."

It was lame, but it was all he could think to say.

Emily's head jerked up. Tears began welling up in her eyes. After a few silent moments, she discreetly wiped them away.

"Well," she scoffed. "I don't know what you're talking about. I haven't been anyone's girl in a long time. I wouldn't even know what that feels like anymore."

Taking a seat on the steps behind her, Gregg replied and acknowledged his shortcomings, "Yeah, I know." He then added, "This DD 214 says that perhaps there's something I can do about that."

Emily quickly spun around to see her husband sitting casually on the stoop of the farmhouse. The tears she had tried to keep at bay began streaming down her cheeks. She watched as he removed the folded document from his cargo pants pocket and held it up.

"Sooo, whatdoya think? Is there room enough in this farmhouse for a… husband… and his wife?"

Emily quickly rushed him and grabbed the paperwork out of his hand. The pair fell back onto the decking of the porch wrapped in each other's arms. The two held on to one another for dear life and quietly wept together under a blanket swathed in the tribulations of a marriage. A marriage that was being given a second chance to find a faith and a hope and a love renewed.

* * *

At precisely 6:00 PM, Emily walked through the door with her husband in tow. All heads turned to see the couple entering the cabin. Gregg was now showered and clean-shaven. Emily had a glow about her that had not been present when she arrived earlier in the day. She pulled his hand to bring him forward and then glared at him.

"Go on," she admonished him. When he hesitated, she released her grip and smacked him on the butt. "Now," she quietly commanded.

Gregg cleared his throat and said, "Uh, Mr. Simmons?"

Josh beaconed, "Come in to the kitchen, Gregg."

Gregg did as he was asked. When he entered he saw Josh chopping vegetables, Dallas reading the paper, and the former Chairman of the Joint Chiefs basting chickens as soon as James had placed the pan on the stove top.

"What the hell? Is this the friggin' twilight zone or what?" Gregg said more to himself than anyone else.

"Got any cash on you, Gregg," Brent asked.

Shocked that the retired Four Star even knew who he was, Gregg answered, "Yes, sir. I have a few bucks. Why?"

"Put two of em' in the swear jar over there," Brent answered as he nodded at the container half full of dollar bills behind Gregg.

"You gotta be sh— ," Gregg started to say.

"Better just go ahead and throw in what you've got, son," Josh said as he cut him off.

The four men watched as he reached into his pocket and then threw in a wad. "That ought to cover me for the rest of the evening," he remarked.

"Now, what was it you needed?" Josh asked as he returned his attention to the vegetables.

"I just wanted to apologize for stealing your .50 and takin' potshots at ya'll. I'll replace the fence post in the morning, and I'll pay for a new tire and lumber for the porch," Gregg said as if he were reading from a sterile prepared script.

The four glanced at one another then Brent asked, "Emily put you up this?"

"Yes, sir," Gregg answered immediately.

The four men laughed at the response. When the laughter was heard in the other room, the women breathed a sigh of relief.

When Josh was finished chuckling, he asked, "Is there anything else?"

"I'd also like to thank you for your willingness to take on Emily. She tells me she's been moving around the country working with farmers and tracking... well, whatever she tracks for the USDA. I haven't wrapped my head around the science of it all." Gregg cleared his throat and continued in a more heartfelt tone.

"Anyway, I don't think I can ever repay that kindness, to you or to Secretary McInerney."

"Oh, there's plenty out here that needs to be done. You have an extraordinary skill set. I think we'll have to trade on that. How'd that be?" Josh replied.

"What did you have in mind?" Gregg asked inquisitively.

"We'll get to that, in time" Josh answered nonchalantly. "Those were some nice shots though. What's that distance, James?"

"Four eighty seven," the large man answered without batting an eye.

Josh whistled at the pronouncement, "Four hundred and eight seven yards with no spotter." Then he looked at Gregg and smiled. "That'll do just fine."

"Well, there was no wind to contend with and I found the bore sight in his pack," Dallas said clearly not ready to let Gregg off the hook just yet.

"Are you and I gonna have a problem?" Gregg said answering Dallas's challenge.

Never one to shy away from anything, Dallas answered him without taking his eyes off of his paper. "The only problem I have, *friend*, is with you taking potshots at my family and then being brow beaten by your wife to come in here and give an almost robotic apology. I would have thought that after being reunited with her and spending the last couple hours together you would have, at a minimum, displayed some contrition. Frankly, you strike me as unrepentant. That's what I have a problem with."

Emily and the rest of the assembled group heard Dallas' speech. A collective gasp went through the room. "Gregg?" she called out.

"Yeah, hon?" he answered without removing the imagined daggers from the man's lifeless torso.

"Gregg, honey," she started to say as sweetly and as melodically as she could. "If you can't do it right, your first night will be spent on the porch and not in my bed."

Gregg felt the flush of the heat starting to build in his face. He gritted his teeth and gutted out, "Mr. Simmons, I would like to apologize for my behavior. I misunderstood someone's comments and perceived them to indicate that you and my wife were an item. I didn't take it very well. My actions were unbecoming. I have no excuse."

Dallas shot out of his seat and extended his hand, "Now that's an apology! Welcome to the farm, kid."

As the two shook hands, Josh asked, "And who, exactly, gave you this impression?"

Before he realized what he was saying, Gregg offered, "President Sarkes implied that my wife had run off when I asked him –,"

"And how is old Ironsides these days?" Brent interrupted.

"He's good, sir," Gregg quickly answered.

"And where did you happen to meet the former President?" Josh pressed further.

Gregg explained, "We met at Camp David on another matter."

"Intrigue and mystery, I like this guy already. Can we keep him?" Dallas mocked.

* * *

A steady stream of people continued to enter the cabin for dinner. Gregg was formally introduced to Sam and Josh's daughters first. Then Evan arrived and the Martinez family followed him a few minutes later. Everyone wanted to speak with Gregg. They peppered him about his background and skill set. No one asked about his captivity.

After grace, the meal was served and the hard questions came at Gregg a mile a minute. The comment that immediately quieted the table was asked by Heather, "What did you mean when you said you watched a video from the cave?"

All eyes trained on Gregg as they awaited a response.

He eschewed the question when he responded, "I'm sorry. That's classified."

The former Chairman of the Joint Chiefs guffawed the answer, "Son, it's no more classified than the British designs for our nation around here. Now out with it."

"But sir, I – ," Gregg started to say when his wife cut him off.

"It's okay, honey. I think it's safe to say that we are among friends. By all accounts, it seems as if there are no secrets here."

"Or I could just tell you it's an order," the General interjected.

Gregg pondered the request for a few moments before speaking. "I'd like some answers first, if you don't mind," he directed at Josh.

"All right, fire away. What would you like to know?" his host answered as he leaned back in his chair.

"Well, on the surface, this looks like a normal farm. Last night I did some recon and this place is far from it."

"Oh, how so?" Josh asked as he leaned forward and confidently steepled his fingers and hands above his plate.

"To begin with, where did you people come from?"

Sam laughed, then added, "Sorry. That was my first question too. Please continue."

"As I was starting to say, there was the .50 cal in the barn and a sniper's nest overlooking the property. I found some spider holes spaced fifty yards apart along the driveway. I counted several hidden pumps that were fed by underground tanks. The other structures look like ordinary things. Greenhouse, smokehouses, root cellars, storage, etcetera."

"Fair enough," Josh said interrupting the man. "The .50 was for my daughter's protection. They were abducted some years ago and the lunatic was only recently caught," he said glossing over the details.

He continued by adding, "The pumps are attached to the underground fiberglass fuel tanks for the various machines and vehicles, but the heat oil tank feeds directly into the house. We have a three-thousand gallon tank for diesel, fifteen-hundred gallon tank for premium unleaded, and another one-thousand gallon tank for the heat oil. The diesel and unleaded tanks are stabilized.

"As for us, we are an assembled band of misfit toys. Let's see," he started to say as he directed Gregg's attention to the people around the table.

"I'm a retired Marine officer. Now I'm just a lowly farmer. Samantha is former pararescue and is soon to be my wife. Brent, you know as the former Chairman of the Joint Chiefs and once upon a time, my CO. Dallas and I grew up together. He's the outdoorsman, tracker, and hunter. James was a sergeant in my old unit who also happens to have made a rotation or two as a Recon sniper. Basilia is a doctor. Her husband, Juan, is my farm manager and his sons are mechanics, welders, and machinists respectively. My daughter Layla and your wife, for all intents and purposes, are herbalists or simply biologists if you prefer, Emily. Heather was an actress, but she's learning her way. My youngest, Katherine, is our resident butcher and quite the effective tactician."

Josh would have continued on, but was interrupted by the General's cell phone.

All focus immediately shifted to Brent.

The retired General embarrassingly answered the call, "We're in the middle of din—," he began when he abruptly stopped. When he spoke again he said, "Patch them through."

Brent listened as a series of dings and clicks chimed in his ear. He heard the caller say, "Hello?"

The former Joint Chief answered with, "This is General Brent Howard."

"Is that really you?" the voice said.

"Yes, it's *really* me. Who am I speaking with?" Brent answered as the collective group looked on with anticipation.

"This is President Thomas Sarkes and I'm afraid we are in a bit of a bind."

"President Sarkes, sir. It's a pleasure to hear from you. I'm not sure I can offer any assistance at this –," he started to answer before Gregg grabbed the phone out of his hand.

"This is 'Longbow'," Gregg said as he invoked his moniker from his former Special Operations team. "What do you need 'Ironside'?"

"It can't be," the President replied.

"It is, sir. If you'll forgive my candor, but you called us."

"Right, please hold for 'Hoplite'."

Gregg whistled at the pronouncement of his team commander's call sign.

"This is Hoplite, do you copy?"

"Loud and clear, it's good to hear your voice, sir," Gregg answered.

"You too, listen, we've got a big problem. Ironside is telling me you are familiar with our cargo, is that correct?"

"That's affirmative. I'm with the 'Old Grunt' and a number of others that appear to have been read in," Gregg replied. He then turned to Brent and said, "Sorry, sir. That was their codename for you when you were Chairman. It wasn't my idea. No offense."

Brent quickly replied, "None taken," and motioned for him to return to the call.

"Excellent," Hoplite answered. "What is your current location? We are en route."

Gregg turned to Josh. "My old commanding officer needs to know how to get to the farm," he said as he handed him the phone.

Emily had never been so happy to hear those words, 'my old commanding officer'. She smiled a genuine smile at him. *I didn't think I'd ever hear those words*, she thought. *He's truly home to stay.*

Josh hastily took the phone and asked, "Can you handle coordinates, or do you need an address?"

"Either is fine. Ready when you are," Hoplite replied.

Josh quickly and clearly recited the location of the farm. When he finished, they were read back to him as confirmation.

"What is your ETA?" Josh asked.

There was a pause and then, "One hour."

Josh hung up the phone and handed it back to Brent. "Young man, come with me," he directed at Gregg and started walking to his office.

Without being invited, Brent trailed and closed the door behind him as he entered. Josh turned and sat on the edge of the large oak desk, crossed his arms, and said, "All right, let's have it. What are we missing?"

"I'm not telling you sh—," Gregg started to say when Josh cocked his eye as a warning. "I don't know you people from Adam. It's National Security. That's all you need to know. Who the hell are you anyway?"

Brent was about to lay into Gregg for his insubordination and indignation when his friend held up his hand. "It's all right, Brent. Perhaps he needs some confirmation that we know a few things too."

Josh then directed his gaze at Gregg and said, "Let's review what we hicks out here in the boondocks do know."

Josh proceeded to tick off the list of items that had been confirmed. "We've got the British and the international finance law changes. The UN plans for an occupation if Rayburn tells the King to go spit and doesn't pay up. Then there's Operation Delta and the redistribution of the nation's hard assets to Omaha and Cleveland. Seeing how I just had a conversation with the Team Leader of a SpecOps group handling one of those convoys, I'd say they ran into to some trouble. Oh, and let's not forget about that portable EMP that brought down a cargo plane over a suburb seventy-files miles from here.

"From there it's just speculation. The Brits have probably planted some of their MI-6 rank and file personnel over here to keep an eye on our Federal Reserve and Mint facilities. Maybe some SAS teams too. Frankly, I wouldn't be overly surprised to hear that they linked up with assets from other countries. My guess is that somehow you're right in the middle of whatever hailstorm is heading our way. So I'll ask it again, what are we missing? Who's after them? I can help, but only if I know what I'm dealing with."

"That's an impressive bit of conjecture," Gregg answered. "You could have determined half of that by paying attention to the nightly news. The rest of it could have come from grandpa over here when he was talking in his sleep."

Emily, quietly listening on the other side of the closed double doors had heard enough.

Without warning, she burst through. "I've had it with you and your incessant need to mark your territory!" she decreed as she placed herself between Josh and her husband. Without skipping a beat, she continued to forcefully address Gregg as she turned to face him. "You've been here less than half a day and you're already alienating these people."

"But –," her husband started to say.

"But nothing. So help me, I love you, but you lied to me... for years you looked me in the eye and you lied. You will spend the rest of your life making that up to me. To that end, the first thing you're gonna do is trust me. Believe me when I say that they've been far more gracious then you've ever been!"

Gregg was stunned. He said nothing. He could *say* nothing. In just a few exacerbated sentences, his wife had unleashed every verbal missile in her arsenal and laid him bare. The Emily he remembered hated confrontation. She would have never done that before. His wife stared at him waiting for an answer or a reply. Still no response came.

"Fine," she said as walked to the door and closed it. She spun around and demanded, "You two need some common ground to get things started? Here ya go. Both of you, take off your shirts." She shifted her gaze briefly enough to command, "Brent, you're excused."

Brent started to say something, thought better of it, and quietly departed the office.

"What? Hell no. I'm not doing that," Gregg said indignantly as the General shut the door behind him.

Without warning Emily stepped toward her husband and slapped him as hard as she could in the face.

"Don't you dare tell me 'no' after what you did to me you son-of-a-bitch!" she hissed at him. "Do it now or you can pick your shit up off the front lawn on your way out!"

She hadn't realized it, but she was crying. Gregg wanted to grab her and hold her. He wished he could say the right thing, but the words were too far out of reach.

Realizing the gravity of the secret she had just blurted out in the tirade against her husband, Emily turned Josh's direction and said, "I'm sorry, Josh. Samantha told me about some things while I was working with the Secretary. I hope you don't mind."

Josh waved her off. "It's fine."

Emily slowly turned back and faced her husband. "Do it for me. Please," she whispered.

"I –. It took everything I had just to show you, Em," he said softly after absorbing her venomous rage.

"It's something you both have in common and need to see," she replied as she slowly began unbuttoning it for him.

Gregg was powerless. He never could refuse her. She was his kryptonite when she had a mind to get something from him when he was resistant.

His shirt silently fell to the floor and the pair turned to see that Josh had already removed his.

"I'll show you mine if you show me yours," Josh deadpanned.

The Chastain's chuckled. Emily snorted back snot and phlegm in a very unbecoming fashion as she laughed.

"Are those bullet wounds?" Gregg asked as he approached.

"Yeah," Josh answered as he glanced down at his chest. "What'd they use on you?"

"A branding iron, tasers, belts, and whips mostly... oh and a chair. Bare knuckles occasionally. You?"

The pair cathartically swapped the horror stories that comprised their captivity separated by twenty years of history. Somewhere in middle of it all, Emily slipped out of the office. Half an hour passed before they emerged. When it was said and done, Gregg had bared his soul about Suhrab, Abbas, Cecil, and the meeting with President Sarkes at Camp David.

"Evan, James, and Dallas," Josh barked as he flung the doors open and continued to button his shirt. "All essential electronic gear needs to be put in the back room of the barn, ASAP," he proclaimed as he threw James the keys. "Keep those doors shut and locked until further notice."

The trio started heading for the door as Josh continued.

"Girls," he said as he directed his attention to his daughters. "Take the Rhino and drag the sleds out to the well pumps here at the cabin and the Three Sisters," he commanded as he referred to their neighboring farm. "I want those shrouds clamped down tight."

"Jesus and Abelardo," he continued as he shifted his focus. "You boys handle to the greenhouse and your farmhouse."

The cabin emptied immediately and efficiently. Everyone knew their tasks. Only Josh, his bride to be, Brent, and the Chastain's remained.

"Uh," Brent started to say as he slowly raised his hand.

Josh looked at him quizzically. "What are you doing? This isn't school. You can put your hand down."

As it sheepishly came back down, the General asked, "What are we supposed to do?"

"Sam and I are gonna go oversee all of this activity and you, my old friend, are about to be briefed on one whopper of a tale. So hold on to your butt!" Then he glanced at Gregg and ordered, "Get to it, son."

# Chapter 19

At three in the morning, Chester Daniels stepped out of the muddy Toyota 4x4 truck in downtown McArthur. He walked over and looked at the sign that read; Hours 6:00 AM – 8:00 PM. He peaked in the truck to check on his travel companions. Alysin and Lily looked about as exhausted as he felt.

After relieving himself behind the service station, he climbed back into the cab and said, "We'll get some sleep here until they turn the pumps on. By dawn we'll be at Josh's farm," he said to his comatose passengers.

They grunted in reply.

In truth, he only knew how to get to the small town because they had a road atlas. It had been a decade since they had been to the cabin. He figured he would ask directions from the gas station attendant when it opened.

The trip from Portland to McArthur took close to four weeks instead of the one or two they had planned. After watching their adopted city burn, the three Tin Hatters and Officer Vic thought one last adventure was in order before they returned to reality. As a group, the four travelers opted for the warmer southern route and drove down the coast to LA.

Alysin was so overcome with emotion when Vic departed in the median outside the city limits of his hometown that she broke down in tears. Without telling Chester and Lily, she whispered their destination to him and told him to head there if things got too bad in St. Louis.

The three cracked the windows and settled in for some much needed rest. They were all asleep within minutes.

At 5:30, they were startled awake by the continued clanging on the glass. As they started to stir, the halogen beam of a flashlight illuminated the cabin.

"Step out of the truck, please," came the instruction.

Chester turned the key to begin drawing power from the battery and pressed the down button for the driver's side window.

"What?" he said drowsily. "What's going on?"

"Please exit the vehicle, sir," the unidentified voice said again.

"Why? We're just waiting for the gas station to open so we can be on our way," Chester replied.

"That's fine, sir. Please step out all the same."

Chester groaned, but complied.

"Do you have any weapons? Any paraphernalia on your person? Any needles?"

"What? No," Chester answered indignantly.

"Do I have your permission to search you and your vehicle, sir?"

"No, you certainly do not," he replied clearly annoyed. "We haven't done anything other than sleep. There's no probable cause."

"Oh, just let him get his jollies and look. We'll be on our way soon enough," Lily said as she started to climb out the passenger side.

"Ma'am, please exit slowly and come around the front of the vehicle."

Lily and Alysin complied with the order.

Once the three were assembled, the man identified himself. "My name is Sheriff Jim Watson. Would you guys like to explain why you're sleeping in a parking lot for a gas station that's been closed for four years?"

"Is that a crime?" Chester replied sarcastically.

"No, but this road here is a major thoroughfare for contraband headed to Columbus from Meigs County. Your Washington plates drew a red flag. I tapped on that window for over a minute before you showed any signs of movement."

The three looked around and realized the Sheriff had been correct. The stationhouse windows were boarded up.

Chester turned to Jim and sheepishly said, "Oops. It was a working gas station the last time we were here. I was so tired I didn't notice."

"We're exhausted, Sheriff. It took us almost a month to get here. All we want is some gas," Lily added.

"From Washington State to here? Where are ya'll headed," Jim asked quizzically.

"We are going to see our friend. He's got a farm not far from here," Alysin said.

Chester and Lily shushed her with their glares.

"I see. And who'd that be?"

"Josh Simmons. Do you know him? Chester doesn't know where it is since it's been so long. He thinks I don't know," Alysin offered innocently.

"I know Josh. Everyone knows Josh around here. Let's go over to the station and call him. He's not a huge fan of people just showing up and stopping by though."

"That'd be great!" Alysin answered. "When you reach him, tell him the Tin Foil Hat Club requests his assistance. I told him if we ever came back that would be our code word."

Jim laughed at the comment.

"Alysin, you're not supposed to tell them that. It defeats the whole purpose of the code," Lily said quietly to her friend, but not soft enough that the Sheriff didn't hear it.

Jim Watson looked over his charges with amazement. "The 'Tin Foil Hat Club'. You're serious?"

Chester just shrugged his response.

The four crossed the street and walked up the steps into the Sheriff's Office.

"Ya'll want some coffee or something?" Jim asked.

"That'd be great!" Alysin announced. "Do you have any brioche?"

"Fresh out," he said sarcastically. "Where did you guys find this one?" Jim said to her two companions.

"She's a little strange, but she's brilliant in a lab," Chester offered.

The man scoffed and replied under his breath, "By the looks of things, I wouldn't trust her with a butter knife."

"Hi, Uncle Jim," Scott Watson said as he entered Jim's office.

"Scooter, what are you doing here? It's not even six in the morning," the Sheriff said surprised to see his nephew.

"I'm an adult now," the young man replied incredulously. "Please stop calling me that."

"Right, sorry. I forgot. So why are you here? Why are you wearing your suit?"

"I've got a date," he answered. "With a girl," he added for clarity.

"Really?" Jim replied shocked. "Who's the lucky gal?"

"Katherine Simmons," Scott said matter of factly.

"Josh's daughter?" Alysin asked intrigued. "Not good. The girls don't like boys. They do bad things," she quietly said to herself.

Chester approached her quickly and whispered, "Sweetie, you should excuse yourself and try and hide the crazy."

"Where's the toilet? I need to pee," Alysin blurted out.

Lily groaned at her lack of social graces and etiquette.

"Down the hall, third door on the left," Jim replied oblivious to her societal misstep.

Chester waited until she was out of ear shot before asking, "If you're headed that way, would you mind if we followed you?"

"What's wrong with her?" Scott asked the pair without answering Chester's question.

"She has a touch of Asperser's Syndrome," Lily offered.

"Oh, like high functioning autism. My friend has that. Is she gonna be all right? She seemed kind of upset," he asked concerned.

"She'll be fine. She just needs a quiet place to relax for a few minutes," Chester replied.

Scott accepted the explanation and then turned to his uncle, "I can run them over there if you want."

If Sheriff Watson was anything, he was observant. It didn't take a PhD to know that this group of collected oddities clearly knew Josh and his daughters. At a minimum they were aware of the kidnapping.

He placed the phone back in the cradle and said, "It's about a fifteen mile drive. You guys have enough fuel for that?"

"Oh, yeah. We've got half a tank," Chester said confidently.

"Then why do you need gas?" the Sheriff asked.

"You should never let it get below half full. Everyone knows that, Sheriff," Chester answered with a wide beaming smile.

Jim just shook his head. *They're definitely Josh's kind of crazy.* "Go on, get out of here."

"Excellent!" Lily said emphatically. "Chester, go get the truck. I'll get Alysin." She then turned to Scott and said, "Where are you parked."

"Out back. Meet you there?" Scott answered.

"Excellent!" she replied again in a chipper tone.

The pair departed to collect their travel companion and vehicle. Before Scott exited his uncle's office, Jim pulled him aside.

"So you have a date with Katherine, do ya? Why are you in a suit at six in the morning?"

"She said surprise her," Scott replied proudly.

"At six in the morning?" the Sheriff said incredulously.

"I told her seven, but I didn't say AM or PM."

His uncle shook his head then reached in his back pocket and retrieved his wallet. He pulled a twenty and a ten-dollar bill from the billfold.

As he handed his nephew the cash, he said, "You're a little early. Take those three over to the diner and get 'em some breakfast before you head over. They don't look like they've eaten much lately."

\* \* \*

The driveway alarms chimed in succession as Scott and the Tin Hatters made their way down from the road. The inside of the cabin was a flurry of activity as men quickly awoke and scrambled over themselves and the gear strewn about on the floor.

"What the hell is that? Is that an alarm? Positions!" Hoplite barked out the command to the other two operators. The three had been given the couches and a cot in the living room after they arrived the night before.

Ed Monahan flew down the stairs and asked, "Sitrep?"

Hoplite worked his way to the front window and saw the two approaching vehicles.

"We got two inbound," he decreed. "Unknown number of occupants."

The two vehicles parked in front of the cabin.

"Positions," Hoplite said in a hushed tone.

The four travelers approached the front door. When Scott knocked, the door swung open, and Hoplite gave his booming command, "Go! Go! Go!"

The armed protectorate came flying out at Scott and the Tin Hatters with weapons drawn, safeties off.

"Get on your faces!" one of the men barked as he shoved him on to the porch decking.

Before the four knew what hit them, they were on their stomachs with a knee in their spine and a hand clamped down on the back of the neck.

Alysin was crying hysterically while Chester screamed, "Get off of me you steroid infused dirtbag!"

Scott called out, "This is a mistake! We can explain! We can explain!"

"Don't move, or we *will* shoot you," came the calm order from Agent Ed Monahan.

"Mister," Scott said. "There's been a misunderstanding. Call Mr. Simmons. He knows who we are."

"What's going on down here?" President Sarkes said as he wiped the sleep from his eyes.

Samantha pushed her way past him in her bathrobe and came through the front door. "What happened," she asked as she inspected the contorted faces pressed into the decking of the porch.

"We were asleep and then some alarm got tripped," Hoplite replied. "These two vehicles were approaching. We subdued the hostiles."

"We're no such thing you indifferent prick!" Lily shot at them.

Samantha stood up and looked at Ed. "I've never seen these people before. Better call Josh," she said as she reentered the cabin.

"Yes! Yes! Call him and tell him that the Tin Foil Hat Club has returned," Chester bemoaned under the pressure on his chest.

Sam stopped and turned.

"What did you say? Cap, stand him up, please."

Captain Carlos 'Hoplite' Rayna had successfully navigated the convoy to the farm the previous evening. Without warning, they found themselves in a firefight near the town of Chillicothe as they worked the back roads toward Josh's cabin. The wounded were being treated at the Martinez's home. In all, they lost two Secret Service Agents, four had minor flesh wounds, and the Whiskey Three SUV was disabled and left on the side of the road. President Sarkes' armored sedan had been jettisoned when the Agent Smith imposter had been assassinated. The remaining personnel were bivouacked with their haulers. Roving armed patrols had been circulating throughout the night.

Hoplite grabbed him by the back of his jacket and assisted Chester to his feet. The other three remained face down.

"Who are you," Samantha asked the man as he brushed himself off.

"My name is Chester Daniels. That's Lily Summers and the crying one is Alysin Baker. We are the Tin Foil Hat Club," he said proudly.

"Chester Daniels? Seriously? Is there anyone Mr. Simmons doesn't seem to know?" the President said incredulously as he turned and reentered the cabin.

"And the young man?" Sam said as she gestured toward Scott.

"I'm Scott Walker. I'm the Sheriff's nephew," he managed to say under the pressure on his spine.

"I didn't know Jim had one," she remarked.

"He does. I swear. I have a date with Katherine."

"Stand them up, please," Samantha ordered.

Once they were all standing, Sam looked at Scott and menacingly said, "I'll deal with you in a minute."

"Mr. Daniels," she started to say as she directed her full attention to the other three. "I was under the impression that there were five of you. Where are the other two?"

"They didn't make it," Lily answered for him.

"Oh," she answered in an apologetic tone. "I'm sorry to hear that. What happened?" Sam asked in a concerned tone.

"One of these trigger happy part time idiots fired his weapon while they were distributing food in Portland," she offered in disgust. "The city went mad after that. Damn near burned the whole thing to the ground."

"We haven't heard anything about that. If that were true it would be all over the news," Sam answered politely.

"I imagine you wouldn't. Not when the idiots in D.C. control the press," Lily replied indignantly in the former President's direction.

Chester could see that she was about to unleash her fury and turned to her, "Maybe you should sit in the truck and put the crazy back in the bottle."

The key to the Tin Foil Hat Club's survival off of heavy medication had been their unwavering and, sometimes, brutal honesty with each other. This served to keep each other in check. When one started to get amped up, one of the others would gently remind them to control it, like Josh had suggested. In truth, Dr. Vandersal had been preaching the same thing, but she wasn't able to speak their version of crazy.

Off in the distance, Samantha heard the Rhino approaching. "Speak of the devil, here he comes now."

The assembled mass on the front porch turned to see Josh round the cabin and park the ATV in front of the recently arrived vehicles in the drive.

Before anyone had a chance to tell him what had happened, Josh exclaimed, "Chester! Is that you?! Alysin, why are you crying, sweetie?"

Alysin extracted herself from her captors grip and ran to Josh. She leapt into his arms and began showering him with kisses. Samantha was shocked by the display. Lily slammed the truck door closed and approached as well. Chester stepped off the porch and worked his way over too.

Scott started to get up from the bench he had been placed in and was immediately halted by Sam, "I'm not finished with you, young man. You stay right there."

"Where's Reginald and Algernon?" Josh asked.

Alysin stopped her grateful child-like display and slid down his body. Her mood turned sorrowful.

"What is it? What happened to Reggie and Al?" he said again.

"They got blown up," Alysin replied mournfully.

"What! Where? What happened?" Josh exclaimed.

He looked over the faces of the newest arrivals for answers. They were dirty and gaunt. Lily's teeth were chattering in the cold February morning.

"All right, let's get inside," Josh decreed. "Showers and a change of clothes and then we'll debrief. Sound good?" he said as he rubbed his hands on Alysin's back to warm her up.

# Chapter 20

"By Allah!" Suhrab said as he took the binoculars down.

"What? What do you see?" his compatriot asked.

"I see an old friend," he said as he exhaled and handed the glasses to him.

Mahtab eagerly grabbed them and looked down across the field.

"You've got to be joking," the man replied. "Sir, if he's down there the element of surprise is lost. We should have killed him and left him to rot in those caves."

"It's too late now. We've come too far. We need to keep them busy until Abbas completes his mission."

"If they figure out what they have in their possession they can use it against us," Mahtab answered emphatically.

"Well then. Let's hope it doesn't come to that, shall we," his leader replied coolly.

With a hint of panic betraying the confidence he was trying to exude, Mahtab stated, "There are only a few of us left. We've been chasing this caravan for over a thousand miles. We can't just walk in there. He knows your face... and mine."

Suhrab thought for a few moments before responding. When he did, he replied to Mahtab's concern, "With our dwindling numbers, you're right, we can't go in there. Given that, we'll have to wait and see what they plan on doing and make a decision based on that."

He then turned to look at his comrade, "We have taken part in many battles. We've fought in many wars, side-by-side. You are one of my most trusted soldiers. Abbas and I have come to accept you as our brother. Collectively, we have lost numerous friends. If this is to be our last, then it is by Allah's will. Keep watching. I'm going to check on Navid and the Adar."

After spending half an hour working his way through the dense forest and underbrush around the farm, Suhrab made it to the second group. Only four remained from the original eight. The English, through their Iranian handlers, had signaled for them to all meet in Denver and track the convoys. They had been highly effective in crippling the machines so the British units could swoop in and clean up.

Unfortunately, one of the group members was snared by the FBI while exiting a mosque. Taj and two other insurgents had been killed in the shootout near Chillicothe.

Navid was the best marksmen in the group, but he was brash and prone to impulsive behavior. Without orders, he had disabled an Arleigh Burke class ship and taken the shot to eliminate the English Watcher that had infiltrated the Secret Service and impersonated Agent Alister Smith. The first act nearly got him executed for insubordination. The second almost saw them all captured.

Suhrab's close friend, Taj, went down while coming to Navid's aid during the fire fight. For reasons unknown, Navid had foolishly attempted a frontal assault. When he became pinned down, Taj was gunned down in the crossfire trying to assist his brother in arms. During the exchange, a member of Gregg's old unit had captured the directional EMP device that his compatriot had been carrying.

As Suhrab stealthily approached the second group, he heard the impetuous man flip the safety off.

"Don't you dare!" he said angrily in a hushed tone. "We're not ready for that. Any more stupid moves on your part and I won't hesitate to put a bullet in you myself!"

* * *

Josh was in the kitchen listening to the radio fixing President Sarkes some breakfast when the station began broadcasting an emergency message. Josh stopped what he was doing and began listening intently.

"What's this all about? There isn't any severe weather headed our way," he said to the President as he continued reading the paper.

"We interrupt this regularly scheduled broadcast for a brief statement from President Rayburn in the Oval Office..." the voice said over the airwaves.

"Turn that up!" Sarkes commanded from his chair.

Josh began bellowing names, "Sam! Brent! Gregg! Hoplite! Come quick! Hurry! Now!"

In seconds, the four were standing in the kitchen listening as he started his address.

"My fellow Americans," he began. "As many in the finance industry may already be aware, numerous countries currently holding our nation's debt are preparing for a run at our assets. While the debts are legitimate, the manner in which they intend to redeem that debt, is highly illegal."

"Oh, Lord. Here we go," Sarkes said under his breath.

"Several months ago, the British Prime Minister, a Mr. Harold Goodspeed," he said and paused for emphasis, "At the behest of King George, approached the Chairman of the Federal Reserve, the Secretary of the Treasury, and myself. At that time, a shady, backdoor, and highly unethical proposal was offered whereby the United Kingdom attempted to broker an exchange of our debt without utilizing the open market.

This was solely a political maneuver designed to keep panic off of the streets of London should that nation's citizens learn their country was on the verge of financial ruin.

"We respectfully declined the King's offer and urged them to engage the markets which they were legally and contractually obligated."

President Sarkes actually laughed at the statement, "Respectfully declined... that's rich."

Samantha turned and shushed him.

Rayburn continued his speech and explained, "In response to our refusal, the Prime Minister, again under the direction of King George, set himself to a singular purpose. That is, the ruination of their former colonies and these United States by any and all means.

"To begin, the British partnered with every nation holding even a dollar of our debt. Most of these are former oil producers in the Middle East, South America, and Africa. From there, this collection of countries rewrote and added dozens of international finance laws in closed-door meetings. They did so without the input or approval of the UN governing body. It is in this act alone that we have deemed any action taken by this group of rouge nations as illegal.

"Unfortunately, it didn't stop there. Many of you across this great nation's heartland have seen firsthand the depths with which the English and their consortium of terror exporters are willing to go. I have met with leadership of both Houses and explained the situation to them in full, sparing no detail. Then, just now, I have been presented with a Declaration. With this document in hand, I say to all of the citizenry watching or listening at home, or in their car, or at work... that it is my solemn duty as your President, to inform you that the United States of America is currently in a state of –"

The radio went silent.

Josh reached over and turned the volume up. Nothing. He changed the channel and found other stations still broadcasting.

"Where did he go?" Samantha asked.

"I have no idea," Josh replied frustrated. He moved the dial back. When he landed on the original frequency, the group heard, "There appears to be some technical difficulty in the Oval Office. Please stand by as we try and resolve the issue."

"State of war," Brent inserted. "Technical difficulties my ass. They know what he was about to say. They were given the text of the speech twenty minutes before he went on the air. That's what those talking heads don't want to say."

"Are you sure?" Sam asked.

Brent nodded. "Pretty sure. I wrote it as part of the contingency planning for Operation Delta."

"While we wait," Hoplite started to say, "Have you given any thought as to where we can stash this stuff? There's no way we are making it to Cleveland."

"Yup," Josh replied quickly. "I had Brent call his replacement in the Pentagon about an hour ago."

The man turned to the retired Four Star and said, "You did? What did you ask for?"

"I said we needed some engineers, their bridging equipment, and some bang," he replied nonchalantly.

"What are you guys planning on doing?" the Captain said directly.

The General shrugged and replied, "He told me to ask for that," and motioned toward Josh.

"Why on *earth* do we need bridging equipment?" Sam asked.

Josh put down the knife he had been holding with a death grip and flexed his hand. "I'll show you why. Come with me."

The group exited the kitchen and followed Josh to the dining room table. He opened a drawer on the hutch and removed a handful of maps for the local area. "Please, have a seat," he said as he slid copies of the map to different seats.

"Why would you –," Samantha began to say. "Never mind, I don't want to know."

As each was unfolded, Josh worked his way around and circled a spot on each map in pencil.

"What's a 'Moonville Tunnel' and why is my bridging equipment headed there?" Hoplite asked.

"That's an old railroad line about thirty minutes east of here, as the crow flies. The tracks were torn up decades ago, but the passageway is still there. We're gonna stick as much of that bullion in there as possible and then blow each end."

"If they only pulled the rails, then we can't just drive right up and unload? We shouldn't need bridging equipment for that?" the Captain said.

"I wish it were that simple," Josh started to reply. "If you'll consult the map, you'll see that Raccoon Creek runs just west of the tunnel. Unfortunately, the trestle washed out years ago. The stone pillars are there though."

"Can we come at it from the other side," Hoplite questioned as he reviewed the old DOT map in more detail.

"If we enter from the east, we need to cross Hewlett Fork Creek about a half dozen times as the tracks and waterway intersect continuously," Josh answered knowingly.

"What are we talking about," Juan said as he announced himself and Scott's presence upon entering the cabin. "Found this kid on the front porch. He yours?"

Before Josh could answer, Hoplite quickly exited his seat and responded, "Sir, this is a military matter. I'm going to have to ask you and your companion to leave the room."

Chester exited Josh's room showered and in a fresh pair of clothes. He glanced over and saw the suitcase sitting in a chair open. "Hey, where did you guys get the portable EMP?" he said as he removed the device and began inspecting it.

"Put that down!" he barked. "They're coming out of the woodwork around here," the man said as he looked at Josh exacerbated.

Scott turned and saw what Chester was fondling and said, "Shut up! No way! How'd you get this? Hey, I bet it was something like this that brought that plane down on Katherine's mom's house. Neato!"

"Scott? What are you doing here?" Josh said quizzically.

"I have a date with Katherine, or had, until the big one over there threw me on the porch and ruined my suit."

Josh's eyes just about popped out of his head.

Samantha grabbed his hand and mouthed the word 'breathe'.

Chester, always the inclusive type, motioned to Scott and said, "Come on over and have a look. You know about things like this?"

"Oh yeah," Scott answered excitedly. "I was President of the Science Club in high school. Our advisor had us do research projects as part of our graduation packet. I did mine on EMP style events. You know, solar flares, the Carrington Event, atmospheric detonation... stuff like that. I've read just about everything out there. The *Critical National Infrastructures Report* and its corresponding *Executive Report* where huge time savers in terms of generating a solid knowledge base. Of course, I dug into all of your papers too, Mr. Daniels, and by your friend Reginald Lee. I'm very sorry to hear he is no longer with us."

Chester nodded his acceptance of the young man's condolences.

"Can we stop for a minute, please. How can you possibly know anything about that plane in Columbus?" the President asked. "And how do you know about that device? That's classified," Tom replied as he turned back and glared at the former Chairman of the Joint Chiefs and the now retired SpecOps shooter.

"Don't look at us, sir," Gregg said quickly.

Brent added, "They had most of this stuff figured out before I even got here. And if you haven't noticed, 'Classified' doesn't seem to mean much to these people."

Scott and Chester examined the wiring and circuitry as the Tin Hatter provided his answer, "I think you know *exactly* how and why I'm familiar with this device, Tom. By the way, before Reggie exploded back in Portland, he did tell me that he always wanted to thank you for that one-way ticket to the looney bin. He truly appreciated those reflective years. Luckily, we met someone who shared our..."

"Panache?" Sam offered.

"What a perfect word. Thank you for that, Sam. Luckily we met someone who shared our panache for life. The hacksaw blade came in handy as well," he concluded with a beaming smile that exuded a big fat 'f' you to Sarkes and his administration.

"Ah, Chester. If you don't mind, can we get back to the planning piece of my spiel?" Josh intoned.

"Oh. Yes, yes. By all means my good man, by all means. Carry on," he replied with mock royal wave of his hand. "Come my young squire," Chester added as he placed a hand on Scott's shoulder. "There is a mystery afoot."

"You Tin Hatters are funny," Scott declared as he followed Chester back to the suitcase EMP.

Shaking his head, Josh returned to his explanation.

"Mr. President, it took about thirty seconds for my electrical engineering friend to figure it out once we climbed in what was left of the cockpit. Well, to be fair, he said it could have been two things. Lightning could have fried that much gear... maybe. Unfortunately, it was a clear day, no thunder snow, nothing. The only other explanation he could fathom was an EMP."

Sam added, "I'll bet this is what Rayburn was talking about during his speech."

"Presidential speech? What?" Chester asked.

Exacerbated, now it was Josh's turn to through his hands in the air.

"Everyone have a seat. It's time to put all of the cards on the table. Are Lily and Alysin ready?" Josh said as tried to restore some order to the discussion.

"Yeah, they'll be out in a few minutes," the Tin Hatter replied without taking his eyes off of the captured equipment.

"Scott," Josh called out and distracted him from his inspection. "Your 'date' with my daughter will have to wait. Use the wall phone in the kitchen and call your uncle. Tell him he is needed out here ASAP. Then I need you to go home. As fast as you can."

Dejected, the young man said, "Yes, sir."

"Sam, would you please head over and collect our daughters? Grab Evan, and his wife, as well as the remainder of the Martinez family. They need to be here," Josh asked.

Samantha beamed broadly at the proclamation of the girls being *their* daughters. As she stood, she kissed him on the cheek and collected her coat.

"Hoplite, Agent Monahan," Josh said as he turned to Captain Rayna and Ed. "We've got about half an hour until the Sheriff can get here. I'd like you and your men to head out to the haulers and make sure they are ready to roll at a moment's notice. We'll go scout out the creek bed and tunnel before the engineers arrive."

"That'd be fine, but this isn't your Op, buddy. Last time I checked this was still under Secret Service jurisdiction," Ed interjected. "We appreciate the accommodations, but if you don't mind, we can handle the strategic planning. You seem to have a rudimentary grasp of tactics, but I think it's best if we leave the rest of it to the professionals from here on out. Okay?"

Gregg laughed a quick, "Ha," but then opted to stay out of this fight.

"Uh, Agent Monahan," the President started to say.

"How old are you Agent?" Brent asked Ed tersely.

"I'm thirty one, sir. I don't see how that's relevant," he replied.

"Because, Lt. Col. Simmons here was leading troops through Khafji and coordinating a multinational multibranch assault on that city *while* directing air assets overhead before you were even friggin' born... so I'd say it's relevant! So how about you go out there and do what he says and keep the jurisdiction bullshit to yourself before I stomp a mud hole in your ass big enough to hide the fucking Titanic!" the retired General thundered.

As if flipping a switch back to calm and rational, Brent turned to Tom and said, "I'm sorry, Mr. President. You were saying?"

"Oh, nothing. I was going to say something similar... albeit a little more tactfully."

Bug-eyed and fuming, Agent Monahan began heading toward the door. Right behind him was a smirking Captain Rayna.

"Mr. Simmons," Scott said as he exited the kitchen.

Josh turned toward him.

"My uncle says he can't come right now."

"And why's that, son," the President asked.

"He's on crowd control. He says everyone's trying to break into the banks."

* * *

"What the hell just happened?" President Rayburn boomed through the darkened Oval Office.

The cameraman stooped down and began inspecting his gear wondering if it was his connection when the President's Secret Service detail hurriedly approached him.

"We need to move Mr. President, now," the Senior Agent said.

"Why? Where are we going? It's just a power outage. It'll be back on in a minute," Rayburn declared.

"No it wasn't and no it won't, sir. Let's go," the man replied as he started lifting the POTUS out of his seat.

"Be advised, we have 'Gardener'," another Agent reflexively stated into his comm unit referring to the President by his codename.

When no confirmation came back, he bemoaned the lack of communication. "Damn it! These things are fried too!"

The Senior Agent opened a concealed door along the wall and he and the President's team entered the private office.

When it was shut and locked behind them, Rayburn said, "Will someone tell me what the hell just happened, please."

"Sir, the 'Castle' is under attack from one of those directional EMP devices. We don't know if they targeted just this structure of any of the substations nearby as well. All backup generators, comms, and vehicles are neutralized. The sentries on the roof can't report in so we have no idea what is going on. We're blind and deaf."

"Call Marine I and let's get out of here," the man said not fully grasping the gravity of the situation.

"Mr. President, forgive me, but you're not getting it. There are no phone calls, emails, or texts. Anything with a chip in it is toast. Besides, flying wouldn't exactly be the brightest idea right now," the Agent replied.

Rayburn paused and thought for a moment before offering, "I need to get a message to the PEOC (Presidential Emergency Operation Center) in the bunker under the East Wing. I have to reset the DEFCON and Continuity of Government Condition levels. We need to get essential personnel out of D.C. and into their assigned alternative sites."

The Agent's contemplated the request for half a second and knew the man was right. The Senior Agent handed the President a notepad and said, "Write down your message."

When the runner departed, Jim Rayburn said, "What if we used Johnson's tunnels and just walked out and commandeered a vehicle? Hell, we could walk to the metro from here. We need to get to Andrews." Exacerbated, he then commanded, "Think gentlemen!"

# Chapter 21

Emily got up and placed another log on the dwindling fire as they waited for everyone else to arrive. Scott was sent on his way with a promise from Chester that they would examine the suitcase closely whenever he returned.

The Tin Hatters continued to tinker with the device and quietly wished their friends were still here to see the groups fears realized. Over the years, each of the five original Tin Hatters had warned their employers and bosses within the US government that something like this would happen. What they never could figure out was the order of things.

Algernon's New Madrid fault fears probably weren't going to come to pass, but Chester and Reginald's tech fears were staring back at them from the battered old suitcase in front of them. Alysin's suspicions regarding genetic modifications and the food chain had already come to fruition. Given the current information, if this business with the portable EMP's and Abbas trying to launch a Minuteman III missile continued, Lily's viral pandemic proclamations would wipe out a fair portion of the United States within just a few years due to the sudden evaporation of modern medicine.

"At least you and Reginald can take solace in knowing that you were right after all," Lily said as she placed the device back in the case.

Ed sat at the table with his arms crossed stewing over the tongue-lashing he received from Brent. Josh and Samantha were holding hands and reviewing various routes to the Moonville Tunnel when Brent approached.

James and Dallas entered with a racket and immediately took off their boots. Sawdust and woodchips flew everywhere. Samantha's dismay was written all over her face.

"Don't worry, Sam. We'll clean this up before we leave," Dallas said as he strode over to the table. "So what's up, chief," he said as he grabbed Samantha's other hand and began reviewing the map. "So why are we headed to the old Moonville Tunnel. Ya'll gonna bury those shiny baubles, or what?"

"Something like that," Josh answered as he stood up.

"Before we get to the execution of that though, I think it best if we have a quick debrief. Can everyone come to the table and have a seat."

Josh waited for the assembled group to find seats or stand nearby before beginning.

"Here's what we know. The British have used our agricultural misstep as a launching pad for their financial coup d'état. Foreign countries wagered big after President Sarkes authorized the Keystone Pipeline construction and now they want to collect when our country is at its weakest. The Brits have conspired with all of the major debt holders to make a run at our nation's tangible assets. By that, I am referring to materials in the form of gold, silver, nickel, platinum, and copper. If we refuse, UN forces will attempt to do something that hasn't occurred on American soil in over two hundred years, which is invade. Somewhere along the way, they linked up with Iranian jihadists who have managed to build and utilize portable EMP devices, like the one Chester's been examining. Extrapolating content from President Rayburn's truncated national address, it appears these terrorists have been wreaking havoc indiscriminately for several months.

"As a counter measure, President Rayburn authorized the movement and consolidation of our countries assets not currently on military bases to two key locations, Omaha and Cleveland. The Secret Service, President Sarkes, and some of Gregg's old unit were tasked with one of the last shipments from Denver. We know some of the convoys have been attacked by an unknown number of assailants toting these suitcase devices. Once immobilized, clandestine forces, likely with an assist from the British, then attack and loot the haulers. The cargo laden trucks parked in our west paddock were stalked and eventually ambushed about an hour from this location."

"Whoa!" Chester said breaking up Josh's monologue.

"Something to add, Chester," Josh said.

"Yeah, that explains why it took us a month to get here from Portland. We must have been right behind you guys the entire way. Every city we approached on I-70 was off limits. There were DHS personnel crawling everywhere redirecting traffic around the cities."

"That certainly fits within the timeline, but what do you mean? Alysin said Reggie and Al were blown up," Josh answered.

"The Governor called in the National Guard to assist in the distribution of food and for crowd control," Lily started. "According to the police officer that helped us get here, it seems one of the Guardsmen 'accidentally' fired his weapon while they were offloading the trucks. The city went nuts. Shops and stores were looted, people were mugged and beaten, and then the firebugs started doing their thing."

"I'm sorry? The what?" Hoplite asked.

"She means arsonists, Capt. Rayna," Chester offered as the conversation stole his attention away from the EMP device.

"Then the fourth angel poured out his bowl," Alysin mumbled to herself.

"Alysin, that's not helping, hun," Lily quietly admonished her.

Alysin sat more upright in her chair, collected herself, and said, "First they started with abandoned warehouses, but then they became brazen and started in on the housing and brewing districts. Next thing you know, idiots are chucking Molotov cocktails at the police and National Guard vehicles. That's when all hell broke loose. Think Kent State and the University of Texas with a factor of ten!"

Shaking his head in disbelief, Josh asked, "We haven't heard anything about this. How is that possible?"

The Tin Hatters turned their gaze upon President Sarkes. He offered a two word response.

"Media blackout."

"So how did our friends get 'blown up'?" Josh asked.

"Some jackass graduated from the firebombs to the pressure cooker variety," Lily answered. "They put one of those damn things under our gas tank. We were loading the last of our stuff to head back here when the timer hit zero. Reginald and Algernon were waiting in the van when it blew," she concluded.

Sam reached across the table and squeezed Lily's hand.

"I'm so sorry. We had no idea," Sam offered. "And your month long journey? What happened there?"

Alysin replied for the group.

"Officer Vic found us on the knoll overlooking the city after the burial service. He took pity on us and gave us a lift to St. Louis where he had family. He lost his brother in the explosion too."

Chester chimed in and said, "We decided to take the scenic route and hit Southern California, Vegas, and the Grand Canyon on the way. You know, to clear our heads and mourn our friends. They loved a good adventure. When we neared San Francisco, we were rerouted up to Sacramento. We eventually made it to the Pacific Coast Highway near Monterey."

"Of course, speculation and theory engulfed the vehicle as we tried to figure out why DHS officers sent us a hundred and fifty miles out of our way," Lily added.

"I can answer that," President Sarkes said. "You were routed away from the Bay area because of the U.S. Mint facility there."

"Figures," Lily said to Chester.

"We eventually made it over the San Gabriel mountain range and took in the sights and sounds of Las Vegas for a couple of days. When we tried to visit Hoover Dam, Homeland personnel thwarted us again. Needless to say we went round and round about the significance of the structure to the United States electrical grid. The North Rim of the Grand Canyon was accessible and awe inspiring though. We even stopped and went on that glass floored skywalk at West Rim. That'll make you puke."

Lily took over the conversation and interjected, "When we neared Grand Junction, Colorado there was signage stating that I-70 was closed due to an avalanche. This only incited our paranoia more. Vic thought we were funny as hell. We were on back roads from there until well into Kansas."

"But not long after we passed Lawrence and started approaching Kansas City, we started seeing smoke rising on the horizon," Chester said. "We never saw the city proper. We were routed north to St. Joseph when we hit the outer loop of I-435. The eastbound trip to Hannibal was uneventful."

"We made it as far as St. Charles before the gridlock on I-70 stopped our progress entirely. Victor got out in the median of the interstate. He strapped everything he could to his pack and then tossed the keys to Alysin. After that, we stuck to back roads and skipped Indy and Dayton," Lily concluded.

"That has to have been what Rayburn was talking about when he mentioned America's heartland feeling the repercussions. They chased you guys all the way from Denver firing this thing at anything that moved," Chester said as he gestured toward the suitcase. "It wouldn't be hard to imagine the White House being hit while the President was giving his speech," he added.

"True," Josh began to reply. "That brings me to my next point. It is entirely possible that a jihadist has infiltrated one of two missile defense bases. From there he may attempt to launch a Minuteman III. To what end we are still unsure. If it's a surface detonation... well, we'll be in deep larder depending on where it lands. If it's atmospheric, an EMP will fry electronics and the grid for thousands of miles. Lastly, the countries coming to collect have already started recalling their ambassadors. That, we believe, is a key indicator that the invasion is imminent. President Sarkes," he said as he turned to address the former leader of the free world. "Is there anything I've left out?"

The President was stunned. He just sat there trying to figure out how a farmer in the middle of nowhere Ohio had gotten his hands on so much accurate intel.

"Mr. President?" Josh intoned.

"Uh, allies," Tom blurted out.

"I'm sorry?" Josh asked him to repeat what he said.

"Allies. We have four allies," Tom said with more authority.

"Who are they," Sam asked.

"King George wasn't the only one utilizing emissaries. The current POTUS sent me to The Hague to head off the Brits with one last effort toward détente. It didn't work, obviously. However, I did manage to strike a bargain with Spain, France, the Dutch, and India," Sarkes replied.

"What did that cost us," Dallas asked.

"In exchange for their subversive assistance we agreed to pay them back in full immediately."

"Why didn't we just give the British what we owed them?" Katherine asked.

"It was already too late. The Brits brought everyone to the party. We don't have enough for everyone all at once," Sarkes answered. "It's a dirty little secret that doesn't get much airtime. To use a more current phrase, our country is underwater financially. It's been that way since before Vietnam," he added.

"How much was paid out and where did it come from," Heather wanted to know.

"Spain got ten billion, France and the Netherlands received a fifty billion split, and India took home forty billion. We knew the Brits had deployed assets to watch our facilities so these four countries were willing to take all of our slush funds from around the world."

Stunned silence permeated the room.

"Since no one seems to want to ask this, I will. Just how much is on those trucks?" Dallas asked treading carefully.

"Well, let's see," the President said with a sigh. "There are ten pallets per, times twenty haulers, and each pallet holds eighty-eight bars so that's..." Sarkes said as he started doing the math in his head.

"That's seventeen thousand six hundred bars," Alysin said quickly.

"Sounds about right," Tom replied. "Each bar is worth half a mill so we're looking at," he continued and then stopped to look over at Alysin.

"Eight billion eight hundred million dollars," she replied just as quickly.

"Eight billion! With a 'B'?" James said astounded. "Just how much does that weigh? We can't possibly move that by hand, can we?"

"Each bar weighs four hundred ounces," Ed replied sullenly.

On queue Alysin recited the math, "That's equivalent to twenty-five pounds. Each pallet weighs twenty-two hundred pounds. Each truck is carrying twenty two thousand pounds of gold. The total shipment is four hundred and forty thousand pounds. Four hundred and forty thousand pounds of gold equals eight billion eight hundred million dollars."

"Oh, I like her, Josh. Can we keep her too?" Dallas said jokingly, but thoroughly impressed.

"What's the weight in tonnage," James wanted to know.

"Two hundred tons," Alysin replied with no emotion not realizing the man was just messing with her.

"If you idiots are done with you parlor tricks," Ed interjected. "You'll be happy to know that each truck comes with a material handler apparatus."

"Ed, you're not being very respectful. Perhaps it would best if you stepped outside to check on the men and their progress," the President said gently.

"Fine!" Ed replied in a huff and shoved back his chair. He slammed the door shut on his way out.

Ignoring Agent Monahan's tantrum, James turned to Josh and said, "So what's the plan?"

"I asked Brent to make a call and request some combat engineers with their equipment so we can get this stuff over the creek and into the Moonville Tunnel. I think Fort Campbell is the closest. It's about six or seven hours by car. A military convoy with heavy transports carrying bridging equipment and the assorted personnel in troop movers will probably take ten minimum," Josh answered.

"Those guys aren't there, Josh," Tom said knowingly.

"Oh?" Josh replied.

"Yeah," Brent added. "They're reinforcing the troops at Fort Knox. The next closest unit would be Fort Drum, but they were sent to West Point. My guess is that they'll be coming from Bragg."

"So that's an eight hour drive, but factoring in the mountains and the equipment they'll be hauling, we're looking at twelve to sixteen hours. Do you think they'd realize the urgency and distance and put it all on a plane or two?" Josh questioned optimistically.

There was laughter from Gregg and his former unit.

Realizing the futility of his comment Josh smiled. "I see. So nothing's changed in that department."

"Weren't you guys based out of Bragg?" Emily said.

"Yes, ma'am?" Hoplite answered.

"Don't you SpecOps boys work somewhat outside the regular chain of command?" she added.

"Well..." Gregg provided.

"General, give Carlos your phone," Em ordered.

"It's not as simple as all that, Emily," Josh interjected. "Their commanding officer will need to have received the order from the President or the Secretary of Defense. On top of that, it is entirely possible that the President and his staff don't have a means to communicate given the high degree of probability that they were just hit by a pulse from one of those things."

"The PEOC is probably still functioning," Tom said as an afterthought more to himself than anyone else. "General, gimme that cell," he commanded.

Three minutes later the former President was connected to the hardened SAT phone located in the SecDef's office. When it started ringing, Tom turned on the speaker phone and handed it to Hoplite.

"Mr. President," Secretary Fielding said as he answered.

"No, sir. This is Captain Rayna. Commanding Officer of the Delta One Convoy. We have a situation," he replied in a short clipped tone.

With the group listening in, the heard the Secretary demand, "How did you get this number, Captain! Where in *the* hell are you guys? There are bodies, trucks, and helo's strewn all over the damn place from the Ohio line east. Is the cargo still intact?"

"Yes, sir. The materials and Ironside are in one piece. We've lost our air support and a number of service vehicles."

"What happened? Your comms went silent over sixteen hours ago!" the man thundered.

"All of our communications were fried in the ambush. We've got two Agents KIA, double that wounded, plus two hostile KIA. Ironside called the PEOC when the POTUS broadcast went dark and they connected us to you," Hoplite responded.

The head of the DoD relaxed slightly and replied more calmly, "OK. Gimme a sitrep. Where are you, son? What are your options?"

"We're on a farm about a hundred and twenty clicks southwest of Columbus and we need a favor, sir," the Captain answered.

"Anything! Name it!" the SecDef answered.

Brent leaned into the device being held aloft by Hoplite and interjected, "Hey, Larry. This is Brent Howard."

"General?" the Secretary said astonished. "You old grunt! What the hell are you doing there?"

"It's a long story. Some other time. Listen, the Delta One convoy is a certified 'Charlie Foxtrot'. We've got a plan, but I need the assets ASAFP."

"What do you need?"

"We still got some C-5's down at Pope Field?"

"I think so, why? What's going on?"

"I called my replacement and requested some engineers, their bridging equipment, full combat loads, and some demo charges but they need to get here pronto. Do me a favor and light a fire under the SOCOM (Special Operation Command) down at Bragg. Have a platoon of those 4th Battalion guys and their gear put on a bird and flown up here. Have them land at Rickenbacker. Then I need you to order up some HET's (Heavy Equipment Transports) from Defense Supply Center Columbus (DSCC) and have the trucks meet them at the plane. You got all that?"

"Yeah, I got it. Should be there by nightfall. Do they know where they're going?" he asked.

"Coordinates have already been provided," the former Chairman of the Joint Chiefs said abruptly.

The Secretary sighed mightily then added, "I really don't want to know anything about this, do I?"

"No, you sure don't," Brent answered. "We'll talk later."

"Will do. This number good for call backs?" the SecDef asked.

"Roger that," Brent answered. "Someone will answer 24/7."

"Very good. Talk to ya," the Secretary replied then hung up.

Gregg and his former team stared at the General bugged eyed.

"What?" Brent said. "I got people," he said as he shrugged sheepishly at the collected group. When no one moved or spoke, he said, "What are you looking at?"

"Uh, nothing. Sorry, sir. It's just..." Gregg started to say. "Damn. Wish we knew you when we were deployed is all."

# Chapter 22

The scuttlebutt had been swirling around Minot for days. Friends of Abbas' roommates had been calling and relaying information regarding installation wide inspections at the F.E. Warren airbase. Some said it was a readiness drill, others said it was an inspection. However, the theory that piqued his interest was the far-flung idea that a former Airman and his psychiatrist were looking for someone.

Abbas knew this day would come. He had prepared himself for this eventuality.

Regardless of what the rumor mill churned out, it was widely understood that Minot AFB could expect the same treatment shortly after they finished in Wyoming. By the time whoever arrived, Abbas would be safely hidden away in the L10 launch facility of the 742d Strategic Missile Squadron. It was the furthest missile site from the base and the small North Dakota town. By the time they made it to that silo, his bird would be in the air. No recall, no remote detonation, and no stopping the inevitable.

*Time to tie up loose ends*, he thought as he washed himself and donned the traditional white cotton outfit. He was really going to enjoy this. There wasn't a collection of humanity walking the Earth that he hated more than his three roommates. They were loud, drunken, philandering womanizers who only dreamed of riches. They represented everything about America that he and his brother were trying to obliterate. Sheer decadence on full display all day and only seemed to ramp up each night.

The timing of it all couldn't have been planned any better. Two of his three roommates were passed out in their rooms sleeping off the previous night's excess. The third had ditched the other two at the bar in lieu of female companionship. He would be back shortly in order to shower and change before their shift.

At 3:45 am, Abbas exited his room in his traditional garment as effortlessly as if he were headed to the kitchen for breakfast. He calmly entered the first bedroom he encountered and found his greedy prick of a roommate passed out on his stomach. The stench from the trashcan full of vomit was overwhelming. He pulled his robe up to cover his mouth and nose in an effort to stem the odor.

He stopped and observed the sweaty pockmarked face and then grabbed him by the hair, lifting his head off of the mattress. The man audibly groaned. In one fluid motion, Abbas drew the five-inch carbon steel blade across the exposed throat. The spray of blood painted the sheets, floor, and wall as the carotid artery continuously pumped the man's life force from the gaping wound. The roommate gurgled and reflexively reached for the injury. The cut was so deep that his vocal chords were severed, rendering him speechless. There were no screams for help. In less than a minute, he bled out and died.

Abbas repeated the same sickening act on the second roommate. As he entered the kitchen, he checked the time. *Any minute,* he thought. He retreated momentarily to the missing roommate's bedroom and retrieved the drunken bastard's most prized possession. Securing himself in the shadows near the door to the apartment, he waited patiently for him to arrive. Unfortunately for the remaining airmen, he staggered in the door at 3:55 am. As a defiant symbolic act, Abbas had taken the man's own collectible Samurai sword and attacked him from behind. In one swift stroke, Abbas decapitated him.

Acting as casually as if nothing had actually happened, he re-entered his room and donned his uniform. The man didn't even bother wiping anything down to remove fingerprints or genetic material. At precisely 4:00 am CST, he retrieved a secreted never used burner phone, powered it up, dialed a memorized number, spoke three words, and hung up. As he exited the apartment and headed for his car, he removed the battery and SIM card then snapped the miniature flip-phone in half. Abbas deposited the pieces in separate trash cans on his way through the apartment complex. At 4:05 am, he began the drive toward Minot AFB and his long waited for destiny.

* * *

Prior to all of the commotion on the farm, at 5:00 am EST, before the sun had even started its ascendency, the cell phone in Suhrab's pocket hummed quietly. The man had carried it for weeks, always making sure it was charged and on. He opened the flip-phone and said nothing.

Through the ear piece, he heard his brother's unmistakable voice.

He said, "Twenty-four hours," then the line immediately went dead.

Repeating his brother's actions, Suhrab removed the battery, SIM card, and snapped the phone in half. He quietly stood, briefly stretched, and picked up a small backpack. Excited, he began heading toward his men. Upon seeing the bag on his shoulder, each of the men knew it was time for the ritual Ghusl bathing and prayers.

He surprised them when he said, "Today is the day we've been waiting for."

The three other men smiled broadly.

Sleeping in shifts, each of the four had observed the farm for several hours throughout the night. Suhrab had prepared his men for the eventuality they were now staring in the face. Today was going to be their day of reckoning.

The remaining members of the cell followed their leader further into the darkened forest and down to the spring fed creek. Suhrab threw the pieces of the phone in downstream. The four removed their shoes and all articles of clothing. Once nude, the insurgents retrieved ceremonial cups along with bars of soap from their packs. One by one, they entered the chilly water to begin the ritualistic bath. Now was not the time for banter or joviality. With Suhrab's words ringing in their collective ears, today was about business. Today was a day for extreme focus.

In unison, they rinsed their mouths and nostrils, then proceeded to wash both hands up to the wrists and between the fingers. From there, they cleaned their groins then performed wudu and cleansed the remainder of their bodies. As per the ritual, Suhrab and his remaining followers poured water over their heads three times so it flowed all over the body. Once that step was completed, they poured three cups of water over the right shoulder, then the left.

Shivering, each of the men slowly left the creek and placed the cup and soap back in the packs. From there, they removed a pair of sandals along with a matching set of loose fitting white cotton pants and tunic.

Small ornately woven prayer rugs were unrolled and pointed south-southeast toward Mecca. The men stepped forward until they were just behind their prayer rugs. In muted Arabic, Suhrab led his men in the salat and the standing, bowing, and prostrating movements of rak'a. In unison, the men mutedly stated, 'Allahu Akbar' before each movement.

Once the ritual bathing and prayers were complete, each of them donned their 'street clothes', all except Mahtab. Suhrab had chosen his loyal soldier for martyrdom by suicide. The two men embraced affectionately as brothers then Suhrab handed him an oversized satchel. There was no need to open it. Mahtab knew his mission and how it would end.

While Suhrab's loyal soldier began walking toward the road, the leader of the group looked at the two remaining men, Navid and Adar.

Navid had been a pain in his ass since the day he'd arrived in the caves. As a result, Suhrab took some small inward pleasure in choosing him to wear the other suicide vest. The distinction between Mahtab and Navid was that Navid's vest was to be used as a last resort. Mahtab's sole mission was martyrdom.

"Adar," Suhrab began. "Once we have departed, I want you to continue to watch the farm. Based on what I could hear of their conversations last night, I believe they are headed to an abandoned railroad tunnel. When Navid radios back and confirms their destination, I want you to kill the women... and the injured agents. Anyone still there... the sick, elderly, children... everyone. Then join Navid at the destination."

With a grin, Adar nodded his understanding.

In silence, Navid and Suhrab followed the trail back to the road, just as Mahtab had done minutes earlier.

As they approached their car hidden under a pile of brush, Suhrab only said, "I'll see you after."

Navid didn't acknowledge his leaders words. He didn't have to.

When the last of the brush was removed, the jihadist entered the vehicle and started the engine. He passed Suhrab walking up the road without as much as a wave of acknowledgement. Several hundred yards later, Navid spotted Mahtab standing off the road in some brush just beyond a frequently used clay and gravel driveway. With no love lost between the two men after the death of Mahtab's best friend, Taj, the pair gave each other the finger as Navid drove by.

Once Suhrab arrived, under the cover of darkness, the two men stealthily ascended the gravel and clay driveway toward the old farmhouse. No lights were on inside the home and there were no security lights to speak off. The only light visible was a dimly lit bulb to the side of the front door. It illuminated the house numbers and an old faded wooden sign that read 'Wrigley Family Home - Welcome'.

The pair worked their way around the home checking for unlocked doors and windows. None were open. They checked the old pick-up and the newer sedan too, both were locked as well.

The two men took cover behind a healthy firewood stack and waited. The boredom of waiting, coupled with the hour, allowed them to catch some additional sleep which they greedily accepted. The adrenaline rush from Abbas' phone call was wearing off. They viewed this as a good thing. Each man would need full control of their faculties in order to think straight throughout the course of the day.

The sound of the screen door slamming shut startled them awake. Suhrab checked his watch. It was 7:15 AM. Moments later the screen door slammed shut again. Suhrab and Mahtab peered through the openings between the wood and watched the encounter.

"Well, we sure have enjoyed your visit," the old man said to their visitor.

"It was good to see you too, Pop-Pop. Charlene and I are gonna swing through and say 'hi' to Juan and Josh then head over to Chillicothe to see her family," the young man replied.

Both of the hidden men glanced at the other. Suhrab nodded. With that, they then withdrew suppressed handguns from their bags.

"Oh, that'll be nice. I'm sure they'll appreciate that. I've already called them to tell them the good news and that you'd be visiting soon. Be sure and tell them Martha and I said 'hello'."

The jihadists watched as they placed luggage in the back of the sedan and closed the trunk.

"Now," Suhrab whispered.

The two men went opposite directions and came around the wood pile simultaneously.

"Will you and Charlene be headed back this way soon?" the old man asked as they began heading toward the door.

"Excuse me," a voice called out to them as they neared the side door to the house.

The elderly man turned first and was immediately hit in the chest by a round from Suhrab's suppressed weapon. The muted crack of the shot startled the younger man and he turned quickly. Mahtab's shot caught him in the shoulder as he turned away from him. A second shot, just seconds behind the first, severed his spine.

The sound of dull firecrackers outside drew the attention of the grandmother in the kitchen. As the screen door creaked open, she witnessed Suhrab fire the coup de grâce into the young man's head. She shrieked out in terror.

Shots immediately rang out and bullets began hurtling her direction.

"Run, Charlene!" she screamed out as two bullets tore into her body.

The first round caught her in the leg and hobbled her. The second shot entered her rib cage and exited through her lung and back. Blood smeared across the wall as she slid toward the kitchen.

With the wind knocked out of her and staggering from the leg wound, she dragged herself through the kitchen screaming.

"Charlene get out! They killed Junius and Edward!"

Suhrab and Mahtab hurriedly entered the house and put the old woman out of her misery. Above them, movement could be heard on the second floor.

"I'll handle it," Mahtab said without emotion.

Suhrab stowed his weapon then reviewed his surroundings. By all accounts, it appeared as if the old woman was in the middle of fixing breakfast. As uncompassionate as a sociopath can be, Suhrab casually busied himself by finishing to cook the breakfast Mrs. Wrigley had started. He quickly inspected the pans on the stovetop. Recognizing the bacon frying in the pan, he walked over, opened the window, and threw the bacon, pan and all, outside, then closed the window. As he turned to inspect the eggs, two muted shots rang out upstairs. Just then, the timer on the stove reached zero. He pressed the 'Off' button and thought to look inside the oven. The elderly woman had made fresh biscuits.

As Mahtab entered the kitchen, Suhrab was plating the eggs and biscuits. A half used bottle of honey sat on the counter so they grabbed that as they went to the table.

The pair sat and ate quietly, unaffected by the fact that they were surrounded by death.

As they put the dirty plates in the sink, Mahtab asked, "Think anyone from the farm heard that?"

Suhrab shook his head 'no' and answered, "Too far. The suppressors make it sound like a book slapped shut. Nothing more."

The pair searched the house for the keys to the truck. Finding those hanging on a hook by the back door, they exited the house and searched the young man's pockets for the keys to the sedan. Once inside the vehicles, the jihadists removed the personnel effects from both by simply throwing everything in the driveway.

"Was there a baby upstairs," Suhrab asked.

"I checked all the rooms. I didn't see one. Why?" Mahtab asked as he approached the four-door sedan.

"There was a car seat in this vehicle."

Mahtab shrugged.

"He's in Allah's hands now."

Suhrab went to the wood pile, retrieved their bags, and then began heading toward the side door.

"Come, let's get you ready," he stated.

* * *

"Hey, man," Dallas mumbled quietly to the couple as they stood on the front porch.

"What's up," Josh replied cheerfully as he drew on his pipe and watched the activity surrounding the cargo from a distance.

"We really gonna do this? You think this country is ready for an all-out fight?" Dallas asked.

Before Josh had a second to answer, Dallas began quickly rattling off the issues foremost on his mind. "I mean, there's a lunatic in some bunkered silo trying to send us back to the Stone Age, and as far as we know, there's an armada sitting off of our coast. People are chasing gold like it's the lost city of El Dorado out here. If the townies are making a run at the banks in McArthur, God only knows what they are doing in the cities. Shouldn't we warn some people or something?" Dallas asked in a concerned tone.

Josh paused for a long moment before answering. He was content to stare off into the distance holding his soon to be bride, but his oldest living friend had asked a question that needed to be answered.

"I've given that some thought and I said as much in there earlier. If there are terrorists, jihadist's, Iranians, or whatever you want to call them running around the countryside with these suitcase EMP devices, my guess is they are being coordinated by the Brits. That means they are going to target our coastal bases to make it easier to come ashore. The best possible scenario I can think of is if this Abbas character doesn't get it launched until after the invasion has begun. Then it will render the bulk of their equipment and ours useless at the same time. It'll be a fair fight after that," Josh answered wistfully.

"That nugget notwithstanding, we've got family and friends out there that need to be here, or somewhere safe at a minimum," Dallas said in a concerned tone.

"I know. I'd shelter them all if I could, but at the end of the day I've helped as many as I could. I've tried telling scores more, but no one wants to listen to something they can quickly label as a paranoid delusion until it all goes sideways. If you speak up, they throw you in the psyche ward and forget about you. You should hang out with the Tin Hatters and discuss that topic for a while."

Dallas started to interrupt when Josh said, "Wrap your head around this. Over half of the population of the United States lives within five hundred miles of Columbus, Ohio, and us for that matter. Couple that with the fact that there are a shade over one hundred and forty million people living east of the Mississippi River. Government analysts have estimated that in a scenario like this, only twenty million will survive the first year."

"That's crap. You're making those numbers up," Dallas replied.

"I wish I were. Think about it. If you draw a five hundred mile circle around McArthur, to the north and west you've got St. Louis, Indy, and Chicago. Head east and you have Pittsburgh, Philadelphia, and New York. It doesn't get any better going south. There you have Atlanta, Charlotte, and Charleston... both in West Virginia and in South Carolina. Everything inside of the furthest cities is a threat to us now. Go ask Brent or Sarkes if you don't believe me. They've seen the same reports and projections I have. They probably have more accurate estimates than I do at this point. Think on this before you do though. Do you remember the EPA changing the emissions thresholds for things like wood burning stoves, fireplaces, and what not?"

Dallas suddenly remembered all of the hoops he had to jump through to get *his* cabin built. The building inspectors mandated that if he wanted to burn anything he would need to install air quality scrubbers that easily doubled the cost of the venting and chimney stack. In the end, he had it installed after all the inspections were done. It wasn't hard to find locals that didn't care for D.C. or the fed regulations, plus, money talks.

Dejected, Dallas surmised, "With no power, the fact that the government practically banned the burning of fossil fuels means half the people will probably freeze to death in the first winter."

"Bingo," Josh said. "If Abbas sets this thing off at peak FAA hours, anyone on a plane is a goner. People in surgery die on the table. Patients on life support make it a couple of hours. Dialysis recipients are gone in a few days. Diabetics that are insulin dependent are gone in a few months. Formerly upstanding members of society *will* start resorting to any means necessary to procure what *they* need to survive. I'm talking real depravity. Actions that they considered unfathomable or unconscionable, things they'd never believe they were capable of in a millions years just a few days before. From there, once everyone realizes the power's not coming back, the gang activity starts. Anyone caught in a major city won't be staying downtown in a hotel, I can tell you that much."

"Why do I feel like you're setting me up again?" Dallas asked.

Josh chuckled at the comment. "The ones that do manage to get out are probably headed into the countryside because they *think* that's where they can easily find food. In the cities, every two-bit hood and gang leader will smell the opportunity. Can you imagine what chaos would descend with no law enforcement or National Guard?

"Our existing system of government would be rendered non-existent in the blink of an eye, not that it was functioning all that well to begin with. The small fish get absorbed into the larger gang organizations or they are annihilated for kicks. Whoever takes over in the urban areas will move quickly to enforce their own code of conduct and laws. Whoever doesn't get out is gonna wind up in a brothel, press ganged into the 'organization', or dead. I have absolutely no hope for humanity surviving in these places."

"The planners already calculated this stuff?" Dallas asked then corrected himself. "Never mind, don't answer that." Pausing for moment, he asked for clarification, "So towns like McArthur are a beacon to the wandering masses then, that what you're saying?"

"Maybe not our little slice of Americana per se, but certainly larger ones nearby like Athens and Circleville for sure," Josh answered. "Unfortunately, that also makes these places targets once the gangs have exhausted everything in the major cities. I seriously doubt that the urban dwellers will suddenly start growing their own food or doing something even remotely productive. At best, they'll plant a cash crop like marijuana and then use that as collateral for food, sex, booze, bullets, pretty much anything of value," Josh concluded.

"That's a bleak outlook, hun," Samantha stated.

"Maybe, but that's what the government planners and the military have envisioned in their little 'doomsday playbook'. Ya'll saw the carnage that descended on New Orleans after Katrina. You've heard the stories of kids being raped in the Superdome while their mothers offered themselves for drugs, food, or protection. The only reason they didn't resort to cannibalism was because the troops finally made it into the city. I'm just glad we don't live anywhere near Houston at this point."

"Why? What's there," Sam asked curiously.

"That's where FEMA relocated most of the dealers, savages, rapists, and murderers after the hurricane. The proof is in the numbers. Crime was at a steady rate until those folks got moved in there. After their arrival, violent crimes went through the roof. They are still dealing with the aftermath," Josh explained.

"There's gotta be something we can do for our friends. Type up an email, make a phone call... send 'em a friggin' carrier pigeon, I don't know," Dallas said exacerbated.

Josh straightened ever so slightly at the suggestion. Enough so that the other two noticed.

Dallas cocked a weary eyebrow at his old friend. "Do tell," he said with a smirk.

"Grab Gregg and meet me in my office," Josh said quickly as he stepped off his porch leaving the other two behind.

The pair watched as Josh reflexively looked left and right, slid the barn door open, and then quickly entered and closed it.

"That is one strange duck, but I love him," Dallas added.

"How do you do that?" she asked.

"Do what?" he replied.

"How do you innocently plant barely the whisper of an idea in his head, and then make that man your marionette?"

"Years of practice. We do it to each other actually. He got me with his portable sawmill just the other day. Katherine's the same way."

"What do you mean?"

"She is her father's daughter. I knew as soon as we lit that bonfire she'd get a spark from one of her sisters. It was the fastest exit plan off that freezing mountain," he replied more thoroughly.

"So you guys threw it just to get out of the cold?" Sam responded indignantly.

"Hell no!" Dallas remarked incredulously. "Someone was going to lose that war game, but that little girl out foxed the foxes. I never would have guessed she had night vision goggles in her pack."

"So why didn't you inspect their packs?"

"Arrogance," Dallas replied bluntly.

"Serves you right."

Dallas grunted.

"And just so you know, I gave them those as Christmas presents."

"You *bitch*," Dallas said playfully.

"And don't you forget it," she retorted with wink.

The man ambled off of the porch shaking his head and began heading toward Gregg and the Three Sisters farmhouse. Twenty minutes later the pair entered the office and immediately closed the door behind them. As they approached, Josh was finishing a conversation with someone on the walkie.

"What was that all about?" Dallas asked.

"Oh, I sent Juan and a few of our new residents on some errands. They were reporting in is all," Josh replied breezily.

"Bull," Dallas said to his friend. "Double bull. I've had enough with the compartmentalization, secrets, and clandestine planning. Spill it."

Gregg stood and watched the two men stare each other down. Josh blinked first.

"Damn it. I hate it when you give me the stink eye. Fine," Josh reluctantly said.

Dallas removed the map he swiped off of the dining room table from his back pocket and unfolded it on the workbench. "Where?"

Josh sighed as he explained, "I have Brent and Emily using the quad-copter to survey the washed out trestle and the tunnel. They are here," he said as he pointed. "Don't worry, Gregg. It's an in-and-out deal. Abelardo is providing overwatch as we withdraw from the farm. He's here. Jesus is up the road from the turn out by Lake Hope waiting on us. Their father is sitting on top of the Moonville Tunnel with a three hundred and sixty degree field of view. Happy?"

"And James?" Dallas asked. "I haven't seen him in sometime and the rifle is missing from the barn. I checked."

"Bus-ted," Gregg mumbled under his breath.

"I'm playing a hunch," Josh answered.

"And that has him in the woods playing with the .50? Start talking or so help me..." Dallas threatened.

"Calm down, all right. He's covering the eastern access to the tunnel. Hoplite's comment got me to thinking so I made some calls. The old rail line is now the Moonville Rail Trail. It was turned into a nice wide gravel hiking path a few years ago. If we have to find another way in, that's the only other route."

"Okay, but why?"

"Because I think the Army is going to send us overkill. We asked for two pieces of bridging equipment and a platoon. They'll probably send double because of the players involved... maybe," his friend replied.

"And?" Dallas asked.

Josh groaned at all of his planning being dragged out of him.

"And I believe that whoever trailed this convoy from Denver is still out there. It's weird, I just feel like we are being watched. That's why Abelardo is watching the farm and not spotting with Jesus. Happy?"

"Now I am. Was that so hard?" Dallas said chastising Josh.

"I didn't tell you ya jerk because I was going to surprise you with the gift of finally being able to ride into battle. I swear. You and Amanda always ruined every surprise I ever tried to give you."

"Hey! Don't lump me in with that psychotic witch! I told you there was something off about that girl from the start, remember?"

"Do I need to be here for this?" Gregg chimed in, disrupting the back and forth exchange. The two men stopped their bickering and turned to look at him.

Josh stood up, lifted the roll top on the side desk, and exposed the Ham radio.

"I thought you guys might like to reach out and check on family, start setting up comm times, channels, frequencies, and what not. We've got a few hours to kill. See if you can't find some people willing to help that are near Troy or Boone. Maybe you can get loved ones some sort of warning. If the radio operators you reach are willing to listen, try to get them to understand what's possibly coming. If they want to salvage their equipment, tell them they need to build a Faraday cage to store their gear in. Warn as many people as possible. First though, I'd like Dallas to try and contact some of his duck hunting buddies down in Beaufort, near Lejeune. Maybe they can shed some light on any impending doom from the sea."

"And then?" Gregg asked.

"Then we wait," Josh replied. "We'll wait for the cavalry at the tunnel. Then we'll wait a little more."

"For what?" Gregg asked.

"Hopefully," Josh replied, "We'll receive word that Abbas has taken a bullet and is now a martyr. If he's dead, we all go home."

"And if he's not?" Dallas interjected.

With a sigh Josh answered.

"If he succeeds, we'll sit tight, see what comes apart and where then try to put it all back together again."

"So you're going with the Humpty Dumpty plan of attack then are you?" Dallas deadpanned.

"Best we can do at this point."

# Chapter 23

The last of the cargo-laden trucks in the convoy had barely exited through the pasture gate when the rusty Chevy came out of the hidden hillside farm road. Josh's radio immediately squawked.

"Patrón, you've got a visitor," Abelardo said into the device.

"That was fast. How many?" Josh replied.

"Just the one, Señor."

"Description?"

"It's old man Wrigley's truck... but he's not driving."

"Who is?" Josh asked.

"I have no idea, but he's alone and wearing a white sheet or something," Abelardo provided.

"Stay there for another fifteen minutes then go check on the Wrigley's. Radio in anything you find."

"Roger that."

The fear for what the boy might discover when he got to the worn down farmhouse weighed heavily on him. Josh knew from experience that if these were the same people that had no compunction about bringing down aircraft, there wasn't much hope for his friend Junius Wrigley and his wife. Better he see these monsters for who they really are now instead of in the field when it matters.

Josh turned to Dallas and said, "You ready?"

Dallas gave a quick nod and gripped the Secret Service sniper rifle he'd swiped from the back of their SUV. Josh leaned forward and tore off the one-foot square canvas cutout from the back flap of the deuce and a half.

"What do you see?" Josh asked calmly.

"Nothing so far... oh, wait. He just came around the bend," Dallas replied.

"Is he gaining on us?"

"Nope. He seems content to follow at a safe distance."

"Anything in his hand like a dead man switch? Is he wearing a vest of any kind? Any weapons visible?" Josh wanted to know, trying rule out various scenarios and possibilities. If he didn't know what he was up against then he couldn't adequately plan and execute.

"Can't tell about the vest. If I didn't know any better I'd say he's got a martyrs outfit on though. He probably bathed himself in the stream this morning. If he's a suicide then the truck is most likely rigged too," Dallas answered.

"Can you see his hands yet?" Gregg asked repeating Josh's initial question.

"No joy. They're below the dash," Dallas replied.

"Okay. Hop up. Let Gregg have a look," Josh said as more of a request than a command.

The two men quickly switched places. Gregg adjusted the knobs slightly for his eyes until the driver came into focus. The man in the trailing vehicle kept a healthy distance as the convoy rambled through the winding forest laden road. The constantly changing contour of the road made it impossible for Gregg to get a good look at the driver for several minutes.

At the first opportunity to lay eyes on their pursuer, Gregg immediately recognized the man. "Well what do ya know! It *is* a small world after all. Hello there, Mahtab," Gregg said. "Do we have permission to shoot these guys?"

"You know him?" Dallas asked amazed.

"Ever been boot stomped by a bunch of angry Arabs?" Gregg asked rhetorically.

Dallas chuckled and retorted, "Can't say I've had that pleasure."

Josh could see that he was about to start ribbing the man when Josh raised his shirt, flashed him his own scars, and nodded in the direction of Gregg. Dallas immediately realized his mistake.

"I'm sorry, man. I didn't know. Who is this guy to you? One of the interrogators?" Dallas asked.

"Just a minion," Gregg started to say before the radio squawked and cut him off.

"Patrón! Patrón! Come in Patrón!" Abelardo yelled into the walkie.

"Oh crap," Dallas said under his breath.

"Calm down. Go slow. What did you find?" Josh replied.

"They're all dead, Patrón! They killed old man Wrigley! It's a bloodbath over here!" Abelardo said panicked.

"Breathe, Abelardo. Just breathe. Check the entire house. Look in every room and closet. How many are there?" Josh answered in soothing tone.

"I count four."

"Do you recognize them?"

"Yes," he said through his tears. "It's Mr. and Mrs. Wrigley, their grandson, and his wife."

*They just had a baby!*

"Find the baby, Abelardo! The grandson and his wife just had a baby! They were visiting! Call me back when you find the baby! Go! Now!" Josh commanded.

Dejected, Josh looked down at Gregg who was staring at him. Without warning, Josh stood up and pulled the entire cover out of Gregg's line of sight.

"Stand up!" Josh ordered. "I want that son-of-a-bitch to know who is about to blow his damn head off!"

Gregg smirked and handed the rifle to Dallas. He grabbed the metal tube frame and leaned his upper body out so the driver could get a good look.

Mahtab rounded the bend to see that his distance had not increased. The road began to straighten out and exit the forest. He shifted gears to speed up and keep pace with the convoy as it made its way through the open farm country. When he looked up he saw a man hanging out of the truck waving. He squinted in the sunlight to look more closely.

"By Allah! Mr. Chastain," he said to himself.

Mahtab began grabbing for the walkie, but it slid out of reach on the ever-curving road. He needed to alert Suhrab that the convoy was a trap. When he leaned further, Dallas put a round through his windshield as a warning. The old windscreen crackled and shattered on impact. Thousands of pieces of glass filled the cab of the truck as the window collapsed in on him.

Mahtab down shifted and floored the accelerator. Between shifts of the gear stick, he reached inside his garment and armed his explosives.

"Suicide vest!" Dallas called out as he watched the driver's every move through the rifle's scope.

"Here he comes, Gregg!" Josh yelled over the wind.

Gregg quickly re-entered the cargo hold and retook his prone position. Dallas handed him the rifle even before he was situated.

"I've already chambered the next round!" Dallas informed him.

"One hundred yards," Josh said as he called out the distance.

Gregg took a deep breath and closed his eyes. *Focus, shut out the noise.* His thoughts immediately flashed to the torture. His mind always did. Gregg needed to summon the anger, the hatred. He needed to access all of it.

Gregg began tallying the abuse. *One punch, head shot, kick to the gut.*

"Seventy five yards!"

*Lashings, brandings, tasers, and waterboards.*

"Fifty yards! Any time you're ready, soldier!" Josh barked.

*Chair to the ribs.*

"Thirty yards!"

*Broken fingers and knife wounds. Miscarriage, hysterectomy, and the video. There it is. The video.*

Gregg exhaled and opened his eyes.

"No virgins for you, Mahtab," he said, pulled the trigger, and unleashed hell.

No sooner did Gregg see the leaking brain matter explode from the back of his head through the scope as Mahtab's fresh corpse released the dead man's switch. The truck exploded into a fireball. The hood peeled off from its hinges and flew over the cab.

Josh and the other two men could feel the heat and the shockwave from the blast. The concussion of the explosion turned the wheels of old man Wrigley's truck, sending the vehicle careening headlong into the roadside drainage ditch. They watched as the rolling inferno flipped over several times until it eventually came to rest on its roof.

The smoldering metal frame continued to cook as the ever-progressing convoy put more distance between them. No one bothered to call in on the walkie and ask what happened. Everyone heard the exchange. Josh hadn't realized it, but he had depressed the transmit button during the entire engagement. When he caught the error, he stopped transmitting and stowed the device.

Things just got real.

The men and the convoy lumbered along in silence for some time before someone clicked in to alert Josh to change channels. Slowly and reluctantly he changed the channel.

"Yeah, this is Josh," he said disheartened at losing even a single life, let alone a family of four.

"Thought you'd like to know that 'Red Route One' is open if needed," James replied.

Amazed, Josh said, "The whole thing? The entire way?"

"That's affirmative. It would seem that the forestry service has been busy around these parts," the big man responded.

"Thanks. Switching back," his friend answered.

Josh quickly changed channels and found Abelardo calling in frantically.

"Come in, Señor!" the young man said sounding destitute.

"I'm here," Josh replied.

"I've got the baby!" Abelardo whispered excitedly.

"Excellent! Why are you whispering?"

"He's asleep in his crib. I don't want to wake him up," Abelardo answered again in a hushed voice.

"Find the car seat and take him back to the farmhouse. Have him checked out by your mother," Josh directed.

"I didn't drive. Why do I need that?" he asked.

"It'll make it easier to carry," Josh answered.

Josh was still thinking through alternatives for Abelardo when the young man added, "Shouldn't be hard to find."

"Why's that?" Josh asked inquisitively.

"I'm looking through the bedroom window now. The car seat, diapers, and luggage are lying in the driveway."

Josh's face flashed hot. *That baby didn't get there in a farm truck. Where's the grandson's car?*

"Get that kid to your mother and have it checked out, NOW!" Josh commanded with a sense of urgency. He then barked into the walkie, "Stop the convoy!"

\* \* \*

Jesus was reaching in his bag for the trail mix when a car began approaching the crossroads. He stopped his search for the snack and picked up his binoculars. The car quickly pulled off onto the side of the road, but then sat there. *What's he doing,* he thought.

The older of the two Martinez sons watched as the driver exited the vehicle, popped the trunk, and removed a jack and lug wrench.

*What the hell?*

The man jacked up the car, took a rear tire off, and leaned it against the quarter panel. To anyone passing by, it would just look like another disabled car on the side of the road.

The man looked up and down the roadway for any other cars, but there weren't any. He quickly lifted the half open trunk all the way up and grabbed a bag and a rifle. Jesus watched in disbelief as he slung the pack over his shoulder and darted up the hillside into the woods.

*You've got to be kidding me. I've gotta call this in.*

Jesus clicked in on channel three like Josh had told him and immediately changed channels. He waited the prearranged sixty seconds for a reply. When none came, he switched back and tried again. Still no reply.

He quickly and quietly repacked his bag and started trailing the unknown man through the underbrush of the forest. To Jesus, it wasn't all that dissimilar to tracking game. Whoever he was following though was bounding through the woods without care. In their effort to get wherever he was going quickly, the man was stepping on practically every fallen branch in his path. Whatever wasn't stepped on was broken off the limb.

*A blind man could follow this guy*, Jesus thought.

Just when he was starting to become worried that the trespasser had gotten wise and started taking more care, Jesus would find where he slid down the hillside. He shook his head in disbelief.

*The clumsy idiot took chunks of earth and piles of debris down the hill with him.*

Jesus silently trailed the fool over ridges and through valleys for nearly forty-five minutes. When he belly crawled his way to the latest ridge and peered over with his rifle scope, he spotted the man sitting on a rocky outcropping casually eating a sandwich. Every couple of minutes, he would pick up a handset and stare at it like he was waiting for a call.

"Who or what are you waiting for?" Jesus said to himself as he watched.

\* \* \*

"What the hell is this?"

"Beats me, Lieutenant," the Sergeant yelled over the whine of the Wolverine bridging equipment's engine as its tracks rumbled down the ramp from the plane. "All I know is we got a call from the Secretary of Defense, himself. We were told to have these heavy equipment tractors (HET) delivered by the time your bird touched down."

"And the five-ton? We brought everything we needed from Bragg. What's in that?" Lt. Stokes asked.

"Oh, according to the SecDef, that truck was loaded with gear on special request from a," the man began to answer before reviewing his notes. "Here's it is. That truck is to be delivered to a General Howard USMC, at the coordinates previously provided," the enlisted man replied. The Lieutenant nodded and started to turn away, but the man stopped him. "I need you to sign this requisition, sir."

The Officer, junior as he may be, shot the man a look that told him all he needed to know. "Right," the sergeant said. "Commanding officer was indisposed," he concluded and snapped a quick salute.

The Lieutenant gave a brief return salute and left the man to dismiss himself before barking at his men. "You've got ten minutes to get this bridging equipment loaded and locked down for transport. Move it people!"

* * *

Jesus watched the man for nearly an hour. Whoever he was, he seemed overly preoccupied with the radio and his watch. Just as he was about to try and retrieve some water from his canteen, without warning, his prey leaned over and adjusted the tuning knob on his radio, turned the device on, and spoke.

"This is 'Aalam' calling 'Sentinel'. Come in 'Sentinel'."

He waited fifteen seconds and tried again. Still there was no response given. Jesus heard what he assumed were Arabic curses being muttered and the man tried several more times over the next fifteen minutes. Giving up, the man stowed the radio in his pack, checked his watch again, and sat for another few minutes. A short time later, a small rug was removed from his backpack.

Curious, Jesus pulled back the cuff of his coat to see if he was right. It was approaching five o'clock. It was time for prayers. While the man began his prayer ritual, Jesus took the opportunity to approach the penitent man from behind. The chanting started shortly after the bowing. This afforded Jesus even more opportunity to get closer. When the man came back up from his latest bow, Jesus poked him in the back of his head with the barrel of his Sig Sauer 1911 Scorpion.

As a test of the intelligence Josh and the others had gathered to date, and partly because he was playing a hunch, Jesus said 'don't move' in Spanish.

"No te muevas!"

Not surprisingly, the man understood perfectly what Jesus had just said. Replying in his executioner's native tongue, he answered, "May I finish my prayers before you kill me?"

Jesus circled around in front of him kicking the man's pack and rifle away as he did so.

Continuing in Spanish, Jesus replied, "By all means, continue, but first, what's your name?"

The man half smiled and replied in English, "Suhrab, and yours?"

Switching to English as well, Jesus returned the smile and replied, "Some other time, Señor Esfahani," and gestured to the prayer rug. "Don't let me stop you."

Suhrab's face went ashen, but he didn't react. He simply took a deep breath and resumed his ritual.

In that moment, as he watched the man kneeling and bowing, a thought occurred to him. He stood directly in front of him and he couldn't shake it. As a result, he started laughing uncontrollably while the man continued his prayers.

"What is so funny?" the terrorist asked, annoyed at having his prayers interrupted a second time.

The oldest Martinez son just stood there grinning ear to ear. Once he was able to compose himself, he replied, "Because, Señor, you praying before the feet of Jesus!"

# Chapter 24

Before departing the Wrigley's, Abelardo stripped sheets off of the beds and covered the dead. The man was truly at a loss for what to do. All he could *think* to do was recite the Lord's Prayer and cross himself. Until whatever this day was unfolding to become, the disposition of the Wrigley family would have to wait.

Returning back to the secreted room with the car seat in hand, Abelardo silently watched the baby sleep in his crib. After a few quiet moments of reflection and observation, he checked his watch then gently inspected the infant for any injuries or wounds. To his untrained eye, the baby seemed to be perfectly healthy. His mother, Basilia, would perform a more thorough assessment once he returned to their farmhouse. The only thing of note that he did discover was the hospital bracelet the child wore.

"So, your name's Declan Edward Wrigley," he said to the wrinkled mass in front of him. "I think I'll just call you the 'Baby Deeks'."

Much to Abelardo's dismay, the newborn awoke as he tried to get him into the car seat. The tyke didn't stop crying until he was half way home. Abelardo knew nothing of bottles, diapers, burping, or pacifiers. He had never been as relieved as when the baby eventually relented and fell back asleep. The gentle swinging of the contraption and his constant humming of nursery rhymes soothed him on the walk back. Granted, the songs were all in Spanish, but the kid didn't know that.

He finished the brisk twenty-minute walk and entered his parent's farmhouse to find the structure empty.

*Where's mom? Where are the injured Agents,* he thought to himself as he set the car seat with a mollified Baby Deeks on the floor. So as to not wake the sleeping child, he carefully and quietly removed the binoculars from his neck and backpack from his shoulders. He set both on the table. Peering out through the kitchen window, he noticed that his mother's car was still parked out back.

*Maybe they all walked down to the cabin.*

Abelardo turned the corner to head toward the back door and went to reach for the keys. They weren't there. He turned his head and slowly began surveying the kitchen. Nothing seemed out of place, but something definitely didn't feel right.

Reaching behind his back, Abelardo withdrew the .45 from his waistband. He quietly and deliberately checked and cleared each room of the house. Empty.

*Where are the Agents? Where is everyone? Maybe Josh knows where they went.*

He picked up his walkie to make contact when he heard the distinct sound of multiple shots being fired.

*Mom!*

The fit young man flew through the house and went straight through the kitchen leaving the baby to sleep in his car seat on the floor. With his pistol gripped tightly in his hand, he ran as fast and as hard as he could down the rutted farm road toward Josh's cabin.

The February chill felt like it was burning his lungs with every exerted breath. It seemed as if an eternity passed prior to exiting the worn tractor path just beyond the Three Sisters farmhouse. He rounded the hedgerow, but the tears induced by the cold air blurred his vision. He quickly wiped them with his sleeve and tried to focus on the distant shadows.

Abelardo's eyes began to adjust. In front of him he saw the four Agents lying in a clump on the ground at the side of the house. Josh's daughters, along with Samantha, Emily, and his mother were lined up shoulder to shoulder against the cabin wall. Their hands were bound behind them. Whoever was screaming at them had his back to the hedgerow. He could hear Basilia cursing back at the 'coward' in rapid fire Spanish.

Frustrated by their lack of candor, Adar radioed Navid again. In Arabic, he asked if the convoy had arrived at the tunnel. Again, Navid stated that they should have arrived hours ago but had not.

Adar stowed the radio then began threatening the women again.

"Where are they headed? Where did they go? They are not at the tunnel! Where are they?" he screamed at them.

Abelardo closed the distance between the two as fast as he could before being heard. When he got within thirty yards, he raised his pistol. His mother and the rest of the assembled saw him clear the brush and turn off the road, but purposefully did not acknowledged him. When he brought the weapon level, they instinctively scattered, ducked, and dove to the ground.

The man renewed his demands when Abelardo's first shot rang out and buried itself in the log of the cabin.

*Damn it!*

The assailant quickly spun toward the shot's origin. The young assistant farm manager and mechanic was taking far more careful aim when the second shot discharged the weapon. The round hit Adar in the shoulder and managed to drop him to one knee. *Got 'em!*

As Adar started to get up, Abelardo fired three more rounds hitting him in the torso twice before he crashed into him. The on-rusher's momentum sent the pair sliding into a snow drift that had collected at the base of the cabin's foundation. Landing on top of the shooter, Abelardo began savagely beating the recumbent man.

All of the Abelardo's fears and rage demanded to be unleashed. Not wasting time on rabbit punches to the man's kidneys, Abelardo immediately began pistol whipping the back of Adar's head. Bleeding heavily from the three rounds he'd absorbed, Adar flailed momentarily as he struggled to roll over onto his back and instinctively fight back. The repetitive blows to his head quickly forced him into a state of unconsciousness. The continual trauma to his head, combined with the excessive bleeding from the bullet wounds, eventually expired the man.

"Get his gun!" his mother screamed at him.

His mother's voice can cut through the fog of sheer unadulterated violence. He barely slowed the beating as he reached over and took the weapon from the terrorist's hand and cast it aside. Exhausted and out of breath, Abelardo ultimately relented.

Abelardo had no idea how long he'd punished the man or how many blows he'd delivered, but when he finally stood, his mother and extended family were staring at him aghast. Adar's head had been fractured so many times, it resembled a withering jack-o-lantern rotting on a suburban front porch than a man's developed skull.

Recovering his senses, Abelardo felt a warm liquid heat covering his face so he used his free hand to wipe it off. When he looked at it, the palm of his hand was dripping with blood.

Having never been witness to such savagery, Emily naively asked, "Is he dead?"

The young man turned and looked down at the body. "He damn well better be," was all he said as he pulled a knife from the sheath on his belt and walked toward his mother and the others.

In quick succession he cut each of them free from their bonds.

"How did you know we were down here?" Heather asked.

"I heard the shots from the house," he answered blankly.

"Josh said you were watching the road. What were you doing at the house?" his mother asked.

Abelardo's face contorted and the air was sucked out of him. As he stared at his shuffling feet, he kicked at the snow and replied softly, "Some guy stole old man Wrigley's truck and followed the convoy. Josh had me check on the family."

Basilia stepped toward her youngest child and lifted his chin. His demeanor coupled with a mother's intuition told her he was going to have difficulty explaining what he'd discovered.

"What was at the house, son?" she asked gently.

She could see the tears starting to well up in his eyes. Disregarding the wet blood splatter, she wrapped her arms around her son and held him tightly.

"What did you see at the Wrigley's?" she quietly whispered again and again until he answered.

The dam behind his tear ducts broke and he began sobbing uncontrollably. Burying his face in her shoulder, Abelardo returned the motherly embrace.

"They killed them all, they're all dead!" he wailed. Through the sobs and gasps for air he added, "I saw him pointing his gun at you and I don't know what happened. I'm so sorry, mom!"

"Sh, sh, sh," she said to calm him. "It's okay. Everything's okay. We're all safe."

The pair held each other for some time as the others looked on. With his breathing slowing and the sobbing less intense, Basilia began extricating herself from her sons embrace when she asked, "Can you walk?"

He nodded then sniffed loudly and hocked a giant loogie in the dead terrorists direction.

"There he is," Katherine proclaimed.

"Emily, Sam… help me get him to the house. Katherine, you and your sisters find something to cover the Agents," his mother directed compassionately. "We'll bury them later."

"What do you want us to do with this guy," Layla asked, gesturing toward what was left of the terrorist buried in the snow.

Basilia glanced at her son for a long moment before she replied, "Get some horses out of the barn and drag that piece of shit off into the woods. Let the boars have their way with his rotting corpse."

With Sam and his mother on either side of him, the pair helped steady Abelardo as he was led toward the Martinez farmhouse. Emily remained a respectful distance behind. As they neared the structure, the wailing of an infant could be heard.

"What is that? Did you bring home a baby, Abelardo?" his mother asked astonished.

Sniffling loudly, he replied, "Yeah, that's Baby Deeks. Everyone else was dead but I found him in that panic room we built for old man Wrigley a couple years back."

"Dios mío," his mother proclaimed and quickened their pace.

The foursome entered the house to find a full throated infant wailing in his car seat.

"Aww," Emily declared in a motherly tone. "He's probably hungry," she stated as she began unbuckling him from the contraption.

"Food and diapers are in my pack on the table," Abelardo replied.

"Phew- wee!" the young woman declared. "He's got a stinker!"

As Sam and Emily busied themselves with the process of getting the baby undressed, cleaned, and changed, Basilia performed a basic physical exam on the infant.

"Declan Edward Wrigley," his mother said as she read the hospital bracelet.

"Baby Deeks," her son corrected. "That's what I nicknamed him."

"This is a newborn… no more than a few days old. Did you see any hospital paperwork or discharge orders, anything like that?"

"I don't know," her son replied in a melancholy tone. "Maybe… I wasn't really concerned with documents."

Basilia looked at her son and nodded toward the other room. Reluctantly, he followed her.

"Son," she began. "Son? Look at me."

Eventually he relented and glanced up at her.

"I need you to go back to the Wrigley's and find any paperwork associated with this baby."

Abelardo immediately began shaking his head 'no'.

"I know you don't want to, I know you don't… but we can't very well send Emily. She's been through enough… and so has Layla… and Heather is too green for this. Probably Sam too. Go upstairs and shower, change your clothes. Then find Katherine and my car keys and head back up there. I think the keys are in that bastardos pocket. Take her with you. Do you understand my instructions?"

Grudgingly, he agreed and headed upstairs.

*　*　*

James sat on the edge of the roadway in his ghillie suit and waited. When the Jake-break sounded, he peered over the brush and hoped it was the cavalry. *Thank God.*

He stepped out of the roadside brambles, slung his massive rifle, and raised his hand to the driver of the lead vehicle. *I sure hope this works.*

The processions momentum slowly ground to a halt in front of the large camouflaged man. The passenger quickly exited the lead vehicle with his weapon drawn.

"State your business," the young man bellowed over the rattle of the diesel valves.

"I'm here to lead you boys in," James replied forcefully in order to be heard as well.

"We aren't expecting an assist," the man answered as he started to lift his weapon.

"Whoa, son! There's no need for that," the big man said surprised the soldier was drawing down on him.

"Who are you? Who sent you?" the man demanded.

"My name is Master Sergeant James Rooney. I'm here at the request of President Sarkes. There's been a slight change of plans."

The young engineer relaxed slightly, but didn't holster his weapon.

"Look LT, we don't have a lot of time. You boys need to gear up. What did you bring?"

The officer didn't reply.

"Look, kid, I was standing right next to General Howard when the original request for assistance was made and I was there again when those orders were amended. You and your men were loaded at Bragg and flown to Rickenbacker. So give the über paranoia a rest, will ya."

The man hesitantly holstered his weapon.

"Good. Now, what did you bring?"

"We were told full combat loads," the young man answered.

"And your equipment?" James asked quickly. "We've got a big ass tunnel that needs to be blown at both ends."

The man smiled.

"Got you covered there, Sergeant. We brought everything *and* the kitchen sink."

\* \* \*

Josh ordered the lead driver of the downsized caravan to slow his approach as they rounded the last bend.

"The turnout is just up ahead. You'd never see it if you weren't told where to look," Josh explained.

The driver made the turn at Josh's direction and then pulled the truck off to the side to make room for the bridging equipment when it arrived. The other two trucks followed suit.

Juan and Brent heard the vehicles approaching and left their position atop the tunnel. The General had sent Emily back to the farm while he observed with Juan. The pair worked their way toward Josh in an effort to alert them to the repeated calls from Jesus. Josh and the driver were startled as the men climbed their way up the banks of the creek.

"What are you doing here?" he said as he directed the question to his former CO. "And what are you doing out of position? I needed you covering from above," Josh questioned of Juan.

"I wanted to watch," the retired General said sheepishly as he placed his hands behind his head to try and get more air into his aching lungs.

"Patrón, check your radio. Jesus has been trying to reach you for over an hour," Juan said out of breath.

Josh removed the walkie from his belt. "Damn it," he said as he inspected the device. "The battery's dead. What did he say?"

"He's tracking a man headed this way," Juan answered.

"Anything else? Weapons or explosives?" Josh asked quickly.

"Only that he abandoned a vehicle and is carrying a duffle and a rifle," Juan started to reply when the woods suddenly erupted with gunfire. Josh and the other men ducked behind the haulers for cover.

With the echoes of war erupting around him, Navid Kashani jumped, rolled, and scampered his way down the hillside as quickly as he could until he was lying prone in the ditch. He lay there trying to control his own breathing before arming his vest. He calmly checked his weapon and placed it on his stomach. He then connected the wire to the blasting cap.

Josh listened and waited for the firing to dissipate before peering around the fender. No sooner had his sightline cleared the brush guard as the fusillade erupted anew.

He quickly ducked back behind the steel obstacle and called out above the cacophony, "I count one, maybe two shooters. Can anybody confirm?"

The question was met with grumbles and the vigorous shaking of heads. The men utilized to handle the haulers hadn't seen combat. These were ROTC reserve units or cadets from the Air Force Academy near where the convoy originated. They most definitely were going to need some motivation.

Josh looked over and saw the young man next to him trembling. He held out his Beretta and smiled. "Trade?"

The lad had a 'deer in the headlights' look about him so Josh wrenched the weapon from his hands.

Josh knocked the boot of a now prone Juan and asked, "You see anything?"

"I've got a bead on one… maybe," Juan replied.

"You should pop your head back up there and let 'em open up again," came a snarky reply from the General. "That'll help us locate him, right Juan?"

"Smart ass," Josh responded as he tossed the man's M-16 at his former CO. "Keep an eye on him, Juan." Turning his attention to Brent, he ordered, "Don't let that bastard get the upper hand. Throw a wall of lead at that hillside from the midpoint down."

General Brent Howard hadn't fired a weapon in any form of combat for nearly twenty years. The smile that formed reminded Josh of a child that had been granted to most special of treats. He watched as Brent checked to see if a round was chambered then heard the clicking of the selector switch being moved to full-auto and the safety being switched off. The man was ready to lay down some covering fire.

Josh began to duck and cover his way down the line of heavy haulers while Brent put a spray and pray fusillade into the trees and shrubs. Return fire erupted almost immediately. Brent continued the tit-for-tat trading of rounds as Josh work his way among each of the young soldiers. As he checked on each of the reservists, he offered encouragement and direction. Josh's driver watched as each man checked his weapon and summoned his courage. There was no way they were going to puss out and let a retired General do all of the shooting. When Josh returned to his original position, he kicked Juan's leg.

"You ready?" he asked.

"Whenever you are," he answered.

"Why don't we just frag their ass?" Brent intoned.

"That'd be great if we had any. Agent Monahan and his superior intellect didn't allow for them to be outfitted properly," his friend replied.

Josh was about to pop up and draw fire from the tree line when his weaponless driver grabbed his arm.

"Can I have my weapon back, sir?"

He squatted back down and looked him over. He appeared to have gotten over the initial shock of being shot at.

"Sure thing, kid. The General here was just keeping it warm for ya," Josh replied as Brent threw him the spent weapon and handed it to the soldier.

"Sir?" he asked.

Josh checked for some sort of rank insignia, but didn't see any. He replied, "Yes, Cadet?" all the same.

"What did you say to the other men?"

Josh smiled at the question, "Oh, you know, just the usual rah-rah speech. You ready?"

The boy nodded then quickly swapped out magazines and chambered a round.

"Here we go, Juan. Three… two…"

The low rumble of the wide military tires on pavement could be heard in the distance. Brent grabbed Josh's arm and said, "Wait."

Josh halted his countdown. What little light remained from the setting sun was extinguished when the massive hauler made the turn onto the abandoned rail line.

No sooner had it crossed the threshold of the tree line and entered the clearing as it started taking fire. The driver quickly parked the giant machine and its trailer in front of the three diminutive trucks and jumped from the passenger side door.

Before he even hit the ground, the command Humvee burst through the opening of the wood line. It too began taking immediate fire. Barely a second passed before its turret mounted Browning .50 cal. sparked to life and began mowing down saplings and removing chunks from the old growth forest trees.

Without prompting, the reserve units found their courage, worked their way to the trailer holding the bridging equipment, and opened up with their M-16's. A wall of lead was thrown into the woods and none was returned. Keeping their promise to Sam and Basilia, Josh and Juan stayed safely tucked behind the cargo trucks. Brent was sandwiched between the two.

When the .50 emptied its first belt, the platoon leader yelled, "Cease fire! Cease fire!"

Navid quickly attached the dead man switch to the vest's wiring apparatus and waited for the sound of the gunner reloading before he moved a muscle. When the empty .50 cal ammo can and countless expended magazines began to hit the ground, he sprang up and shouted, "Allahu akbar!"

Before the soldiers realized what was happening, he started firing rounds at the Kevlar protected turret and then threw himself under the HET's enormous diesel cells. When he landed, he released the button.

The explosion from the vest punctured the tanks and ignited the fuel. The secondary detonation from the accelerant rocked the twenty-ton hauler. If it had not been for the enormity of the piece of bridging equipment on the trailer, the entire rig would have been lifted off of the ground. The fireball charred everything within a thirty-foot radius. Men were thrown yards off their feet by the shockwave. The heat from the blast seared the flesh of anyone not behind cover when it erupted. Beneath the mass of twisted metal, only a crater remained. All that was left was the plume of thick black smoke emanating from the burning hulk of steel. The machine was barely recognizable as a piece of military hardware.

Josh, Juan, and Brent immediately exited from behind their hauler and began pulling screaming bodies away from the inferno.

"Where's your med kit!" Josh screamed at one of the survivors as he dragged him from the inferno.

The platoon leader shot from his Humvee and quickly cleared the end of the trailer. He began assisting the pair. "Check the right leg!" the young Lieutenant offered.

"Bingo!" Josh decreed. "Juan, the thigh pocket! Help me drag these guys outta here and wrap the burns!"

Josh stood and grabbed the man by his harness straps. "I got this one! Go get the next one! Radio your medic and tell him to get his ass down here!" he commanded.

The junior officer did as ordered and issued the command to his squad leader. He then sprinted to the next man in the line. One by one, the burning and concussed personnel were dragged away from the smoldering rig and blast site. Uninjured reservists and cadets from the haulers descended on the scene with panicked efficiency and quickly cleared the area. Triage on the wounded began immediately. The combat engineers set up a perimeter around the area given the heightened state of operations.

"Juan!" Josh barked. "Call Basilia and have her bring all of her med gear. Tell her to focus on burn care and blast concussion injuries. That means a lot of ointments, wraps, and material for splints!"

Juan stuck out his hand toward Brent and waited as the man fished in his pocket for his cell. After handing the device off, Brent went back to helping evacuate the wounded.

The medic assigned to the combat engineers did his best to provide aid and comfort to the men caught in Navid's blast radius until Juan's wife arrived. Together, the medic plus Basilia, Sam, Heather, and Layla prepped everyone for airlifting.

When the civilian medevac landed, Josh approached the pilot's door and asked where they'd originated from.

"Pomeroy," the female pilot replied.

"Where's the nearest burn unit?"

The pilot looked at the men being loaded, visually assessing the extent of their burns and assorted injuries, then shook her head.

"The closest burn unit is located ninety miles away at Ohio State."

"Damn it!" Josh exclaimed. "I've got another ten guys down here burned to shit! Are there any other medevac choppers nearby that can assist?"

"Roger that, sir. I'm on it!" she answered and immediately began calling in assistance from cities and towns in neighboring counties. In all, four additional medevac choppers from Chillicothe, Portsmouth, Jeffersonville, and McConnelsville were called into service. Twenty minutes after the initial flight departed, the first of the additional helicopters arrived on scene.

The triaging and staging of the injured saw the most severe cases evac'd in the first two flights. By the time the fourth chopper arrived, they'd received word that two of the soldiers had coded and died in flight.

# Chapter 25

Once the last of the wounded were outbound, the Lieutenant started giving commands to get the bridging equipment unloaded.

Josh headed toward him and said, "That won't be necessary, LT."

With the thumping from the ascending bird subsiding, the young man recognized someone.

"Excuse me, sir. I'll be with you in one moment." The man then turned and approached the person he'd recognized.

"General Howard, sir. I was under the impression that you were retired." Then he recalled his brief conversation at Rickenbacker. "By the way, how did you manage to requisition a five-ton deuce loaded with comm equipment and building materials?"

"I *am* retired, but that truck isn't for me. It's for you," Brent replied jovially.

Unaware how this was supposed to be funny, the Lieutenant answered, "How's that?"

"When you and your men are done here, and before you head back to Bragg, that material is going to be used to set up some OP/LP (observation/listening posts) in a ring around the state park you guys passed getting in here. We also need a couple here at this site," the General stated and then concluded. "We'll get to that later, don't you worry."

The young man nodded. "So who's in charge of this?"

"Well, that depends," he answered. "If you want the man handling the Delta One convoy, that'd be Captain Rayna. He's on the other side overseeing the offload in that tunnel over there," and pointed across the ravine. "The one that cooked up this rope-a-dope is this guy," he concluded and motioned to Josh.

"You mean the cargo isn't on these haulers?" the man asked.

Josh walked over and threw back one of the canvas covers and said, "Nope. The only thing on these trucks is a dozen empty pallets."

The Lieutenant reviewed Josh with a puzzled look.

"Sir, how can that be? This man is a civilian. Why was he put in command of anything?"

"Well, technically, I am too. Meet Lt. Colonel Josiah Simmons, USMC retired."

The junior officer snapped to attention and saluted out of reflex at the mere pronouncement of a superior officer's rank. Realizing his error, his sheepishly brought his hand back down.

"First Lieutenant Eustace Stokes, sir. Sorry about that."

Josh simply held out his hand and chuckled.

"Pleased to meet you, son."

While the two shook hands, a horn blared from across the washed out gorge.

"That's your queue, Lieutenant. Did you guys bring the bang like we asked?" Josh asked.

"And then some. Follow me, sir."

Josh, Brent, and Juan followed the Officer to the back of a deuce and a half. He easily sprang up into the back of the truck and started rattling off the various gear and equipment they'd brought along.

"They didn't tell us what the objective was before we left so we grabbed a whole lot of everything. Let's see, we have a dozen forty pound cratering charges. That should do the trick on that tunnel of yours. Then we've got an equal amount of Bangalore and claymore mines, and the requisite blasting caps, det cord, clackers, and what not for all of that. Umm," he started to say as he looked further.

"We have a couple thousand 5.56x45mm NATO rounds for the M-16's, two mortars and four crates of shells for those, and two crates of hand grenades." He paused and then said, "Huh."

"What?" Josh asked.

"Oh, one of my Sergeant's has an affinity for bazooka's is all. He must have thrown these in here when I wasn't looking," the Lieutenant replied. "I prefer the Javelins."

Josh was grinning from ear to ear.

"Perfect, you and your men start humping those cratering charges over there and get to work. Whoever isn't doing the wiring and rigging is on patrol, understood?"

"Yes, sir," the officer said and exited the truck. As he scampered off to find his squad leaders, Josh climbed up and started unloading the dozen charges.

"Help me with these," Josh said to Brent and Juan.

"What are you doing?" the General asked.

"I'm 'assisting' our young Lieutenant friend. What does it look like I'm doing?" Josh answered and asked.

"If I didn't know better, I'd say it looks like you're in an awful big hurry to push that young man on to the other side of that ravine so you can steal his truck."

"How very perceptive of you, Herr General. I knew a man once that said, and I quote, 'You beg, borrow, and steal until your men have what they need to get the job done'. Now, are you gonna stand there and judge or are you helping me by distracting the LT?"

The old man chuckled at having his motivational speech reiterated back to him and replied enthusiastically, "Well, help of course!"

Josh and Juan continued to unload the munitions needed to seal the tunnel. The two nearly pissed themselves when they heard the former Chairman of the Joint Chiefs say, "Hey Lieutenant, it's getting past my bedtime. We're gonna borrow your rig so I can get some shut eye. Have Captain Rayna and the Delta One boys give you a ride back to the farm."

Once the truck had been emptied of the explosives, only the other munitions remained aboard. As Brent departed with the Lieutenant's truck load of munitions, Josh and the rest of his group followed the engineers across the creek to check on Captain Rayna and collect their other compatriots. As they stood in the tunnel, the assembled men gawked at the vast assembly of gold that was about to be sealed behind a couple thousand tons of rock.

Dallas reached out and picked one up. "Think they'd notice if one was missing?" he said as he surveyed the faces of the others.

No one answered. Josh shrugged at him.

He thought long and hard at the possibilities. Then he shrugged back, and said, "Stuff's probably cursed."

With a clank, he set it back on the stack.

The engineering sapper approached and broke up their mental scheming and said, "Sir's, we're ready to seal the tunnel."

"Okay. Thank you, Sergeant," Hoplite replied.

The man turned to exit and then stopped.

"Sir, what do you want us to do with the prisoner?"

"I thought the only shooter was the suicidal jihadi," Josh answered. "Abelardo took out one at the farm and Gregg took the third. There was a fourth?"

"Yes, sir. We found one hiding in the woods. Well, I shouldn't say we. A civilian just dragged him in... said his name was Jesus."

"Any injuries?" Gregg asked.

"Not a scratch on either of them. We think the captured combatant was only a forward observer. It doesn't appear that he took part in the assault."

*I wonder. Nah, it couldn't be,* Gregg thought.

"Where is he, Sergeant?" Gregg wanted to know. "Maybe he can give us some useful intel."

"He's restrained in the back of that truck over there," the engineer answered as he gestured toward a number of parked vehicles.

Juan sprinted toward the truck ever hopeful that Jesus was alive and well. The father spotted his son and veered toward him immediately. The man grabbed his oldest child and hugged him fiercely.

Josh and the rest of the group made their way to the back of the truck. Gregg latched on to the handle, stepped into the footholds welded onto the dropped tailgate, and easily made his way into the back of the truck in a fluid motion. He was totally unprepared for what he heard next.

"Mr. Chastain. What an absolute pleasure it is to see you again."

"Ho-ly shit," Gregg started to say when Josh entered the rig.

"You know this man?" Josh asked.

"I don't believe it," Gregg responded.

"Who is this?" he was asked again.

Gregg cleared his throat and haltingly said, "Lt. Col. Simmons, I'd like you to meet Suhrab Akhtar Esfahani."

"No way," Josh said in utter surprise.

"Yup. He's got a beard now and he's bit disheveled, but I'd recognize those coal black lifeless eyes anywhere."

"Ho-ly sh—," Josh exclaimed.

Before Josh could get the entire expletive out of his mouth, Gregg hauled off and punched the man right in the face.

"Sorry, sir," Gregg said. "Been waitin' over a year to do that."

Josh was actually envious. He never got to confront the men who tortured him and scarred up his body. He was told months later, as he lay in his hospital bed, that the faction who had abducted him in Bosnia all those years ago was killed in a firefight during the rescue mission.

"What do you think we should do with him?" Josh asked.

"For starters, I think we should drag his demented ass back to old man Wrigley's and turn that place into his own personal house of fuckin' horrors. This guy's full of intel," Gregg responded forcefully.

"And Sheriff Watson? We have to tell him something. There are four dead bodies and an orphaned child. As far as I'm concerned, they represent the first casualties of this war. Plus, jail sucks and I'm not going back for this idiot," Josh replied with a smile.

Gregg paused for a few reflective moments and then sighed.

"Yeah, you're probably right. Grab someone's phone and give him a call. Have him meet us at the Wrigley's. We'll probably need to provide a full briefing, not the partial ones he's received so far. While you're doing that, I'll link-up with Hoplite and have him call up the chain and see what they want us to do."

Suhrab guffawed under his breath.

"What are you laughing at?" Josh asked. "You aren't headed for a picnic, that I can guarantee you."

"You Americans and your morality. If you think about it, and reflect on your Christian teachings, it's actually the vehicle that has led to this. To your undoing," the man answered.

Josh smirked at the comment. "Actually, it was greed and our unabated federal spending that has led to this, but you've made me curious. This little adventure of yours, the portable EMP devices, what was the point of that? A terror campaign designed to start a revolution? An Islamic version of the Crusades?"

"Absolutely!" he responded.

"My, my, Gregg. You neglected to mention just how militant this guy was," Josh intoned.

Gregg just shrugged in reply.

"Well, Suhrab, I think you should have studied your history a little more closely," Josh retorted. "Those didn't end well for Christianity. I imagine you'll have the same result."

"There's a difference you are not accounting for, I think, Col. Simmons," Suhrab responded coolly. "We Muslims have something that you Christians have never had."

"Oh? Do tell?"

"Resolve. That is the thing that most separates us."

"So you actually believe that out of the nearly eight billion people on this planet that aren't Muslim, compared to the two billion that are, they would all willingly be subjected to humiliation, convert to Islam, or die?"

Suhrab smiled. "You know the Koran?"

"Not as well as I should, but I know enough," Josh replied. "You've made some major assumptions in your equation though, *Mr. Esfahani*," Josh replied with emphasis.

"Oh? Do tell?" the man answered, imitating Josh.

"It just seems to me that the morality that is so intrinsic and ingrained in Christianity is exactly what has allowed your faith to prosper."

"You can't be serious. Allah has never needed assistance from the Jews or the Christians," the man replied in a tone that was dripping with anti-Semitism.

"Mr. Esfahani, we are just talking here. However, if you are incapable of having a civil conversation about religion in general, I will find a Rabbi to come to your cell and read the Torah in Hebrew to you just to piss you off. Am I clear?" Josh asked and paused.

"Ooo, I vote for that!" Gregg inserted quickly. "He busted me in the ribs with a chair just for uttering Yiddish words. I gotta see that! Please!" he begged. "Please! Dear God! Let's do that!"

Josh had to chuckle at Gregg's giddiness.

"Or, I could just walk away and let Mr. Chastain here have his way with you. I have a feeling that my presence is the only thing keeping his emotions relatively in check and not beating you to death. Are we understood?"

The tables had most definitely turned on Suhrab. Six months ago he would have been the one calmly chastising his prisoner. Now he was the one receiving the warning. After reviewing his predicament and recognizing the wanton abandon in Gregg's eye, he opted to nod his understanding.

"Good. Now, your issues with the Jewish faith notwithstanding, yes, I am serious. Think about it. If we hadn't stepped in and held the Israeli's back during that little nuke-fest in your country, there'd be far fewer cities in your native land to call home. Maybe if we just kept on going after we re-took Fallujah, your cities wouldn't have burned to begin with and this might all be moot. Did our morality get in the way in 1990 and 1991? I think not. Personally, I think it was a different trait there. In that case, I'd say it was our humanity that muddied the waters there more than anything else.

"Aside from that, you have to consider a great deal of 'maybe's' as well. There were a number of times throughout the course of history, where, if had it played out differently, the Islamic faith would still be a culture of Bedouins, if it existed at all."

Suhrab cocked an eyebrow at Josh so he just kept on going.

"For example, what if we had aided the Russians in Afghanistan instead of supplying arms to al-Qaeda? Then we might have averted Bin Laden and 9/11. Or even further back, if we had sided with the Shah more forcefully in 1978-79, then we would not have had to deal with jihad's and the Ayatollah, because that's really where Islamic fanaticism was truly born. Better yet, if Stalin and Roosevelt had done a better job of carving up the Middle East with their little National Geographic map, then the world quite possibly would have never heard of any of this and the British might not have gone exploring for oil in the region. However, this is all alternate universe type stuff. Regardless, you and I will have many discussions concerning faith in the coming days... Provided you can keep a civil tongue."

"Excellent!" Suhrab replied emphatically. "Finally, I have found an intellectual equal! A versed and learned academic!"

"You're not seriously going to engage in theological debates with this ass-clown, are you?" Gregg questioned openly.

"Oh, I wouldn't call them debates. At this point, I think it's safe to say that neither of us will be successful in converting the other. If I'm being honest, I don't really have an issue with the Islamic faith. I honestly believe they aren't all bad people, just like Christians aren't all snake handlers and picketing abortion clinics. Most Muslims just haven't read their own book, but I think it's been intentionally left that way. It's a far cry from a religion of peace, if their text is any indication. For me, I'd say it's just bad ideology. Christians today don't observe most of Leviticus simply because the human mindset, society at large, and scientific understanding have progressed, evolved even. We've learned more about our body and mind in the two centuries since that text was written. A similar argument could be made for the Koran, minus the learning part."

Then Josh paused and surveyed the bound man.

"I'm not sure he and I will ever have a conversation anyway."

"Why's that?" Gregg asked.

"Because, the minute Em finds out he's here and alive, she'll probably want to put a bullet in his head."

"Ah, Emily... the good doctor. She has forgiven the wayward soldier and his lies, yes? Please, give *Em* my best... will you," Suhrab intoned cruelly.

Gregg abruptly turned and slammed several well placed fists into the side of the man's head again.

"Don't you ever say her name! The only words that better come out of your filthy fucking sewer better be the answers to my questions! You got that!"

\* \* \*

Sheriff Watson met Josh, Gregg, and Brent at old man Wrigley's as requested and received a full briefing about all of the activity at the farm.

It took a while.

First, given their current location, they had to explain how and why the Wrigley family met their fate. This in turn led to the topic of the tunnel and the arrival of the Combat Engineers, Hoplite, and President Sarkes. Finally, Gregg concluded with the reason behind his presence and that of Suhrab and the three dead jihadi's. Josh added the Tin Hatter's, which Jim had already met, and the portable EMP devices.

Jim look like he was having an information overload and was about to have a serious conniption fit. Needless to say, it took him some time to process all of the information he'd just be inundated with.

For several minutes, he asked for clarification on certain fact oriented subjects. Then he asked for Gregg and Brent to leave the room so he could have a word with Josh in private.

Once the pair were alone, he said, "I got a call from Emily and Sam."

"Oh shit," Josh replied.

Jim smirked.

"I've already been by the farm. By the time I got there, Basilia was back and the three of them did their utmost to convince me that there was a couple willing to adopt the boy. I'm mentioning this to you now privately as I've promised Emily that she and Gregg could hold onto the baby instead of putting it in the system while we track down the next of kin. Given the revelations of this little briefing of yours, I feel content in waiting a week before calling Social Services. If Abbas is thwarted, then the Chastain's will have to go through the regular process just like everyone else. Understood?"

Josh nodded.

"If not, and Abbas does what he's planning on doing, keeping that baby so close to his roots is the best option available."

\* \* \*

With the tunnel blown, Hoplite and the Engineers withdrew from the location and returned to the farm. The Captain confirmed Rayburn's wishes via the SecDef. He in turn briefed Agent Monahan, Josh, Brent, and the assorted farm contingent.

"Per the SecDef's orders, the twenty seven men comprising the survivors of the convoy security team, along with the Combat Engineering platoon will be staying in McArthur for the foreseeable future. The ROTC convoy drivers that aren't in the hospital are to head to Rickenbacker and catch the next transport back to Colorado and their collegiate life. Starting tomorrow, my men and engineers will begin the process of setting up defensive perimeters and fortifications around the collapsed tunnel, as well as LP/OP construction, spider holes, and sniper nests near the park and the gold laden cache."

Turning to Josh, he asked, "Sir, may we continue to use your barn to billet the men? I'd prefer not to draw attention to our presence or mission here."

"Mi casa es tu casa," Josh replied.

\* \* \*

Once Capt. Rayna's briefing was complete, Gregg, Josh, and Brent returned to the Wrigley home and got Suhrab started on his first regimen of sleep deprivation. Endless re-runs of the 700 Club played at full volume TV 24/7 on some innocuous channel they'd found while channel surfing. Once that task was complete, the three returned to the farm just after midnight. The 'borrowed' vehicle that they'd absconded with from Lt. Stokes was reluctantly returned given Rayburn's declaration to remain in place.

Everyone was exhausted physically and mentally. This included the Tin Hatters who had spent the day cowering in Josh's basement theorizing about the world around them while completely oblivious to the happenings right outside of Josh's cabin. Juan and Jesus had returned earlier than the others and relieved everyone in the Martinez farmhouse of their worry. This included updating the man's daughters and fiancé. As a result, Josh's cabin and the Three Sisters farmhouse were dark upon their arrival.

Gregg made his way to through the hedgerow toward Emily at Three Sisters while Josh and Brent headed for the darkened cabin. All any of them wanted to do was shower, have a quick bite to eat, crawl into bed, and sleep for days.

As Gregg was about to enter their room, he saw the shadow of light escaping from underneath the door. He smiled at the thought of Emily falling asleep with a book on her chest. The man decided right then and there that he was going to do everything in his power to become the husband that Em deserved from the outset of the marriage. No more half-truths. No more feigning interest in whatever she was saying or doing. She was now his one and only priority.

He slowly turned the handle and opened the door so as to not awaken his sleeping wife. In a barely perceptible whisper, he heard her say, "Before you come in, you have to promise not to freak out. I've got a surprise for you."

Gregg stopped and listened to her words. "Yeah well, I have one too."

*She needs to know about Suhrab,* he thought.

"Let me go first," she answered, continuing her hushed tone.

When Gregg didn't answer she said, "Okay?"

Gregg lifted his head up toward the ceiling and exhaled. "All right, you go first."

"Come in and find out, but keep your eyes closed until I say," she replied.

Gregg quietly entered the room and turned to close the door, not seeing Emily. When he heard it click shut, he shifted to face toward her approximate location.

"What's your news?" he said.

"You promise you won't freak out?"

Greg sighed and nodded. "I promise."

"All right, you can open them," she instructed.

Gregg did so and what he saw shocked his system like nothing had done ever before.

There was his wife, sitting in a rocking chair, feeding… a baby.

Gregg dropped to his knees and started weeping. He'd never seen anything so beautiful.

"I'd like you to meet our son, Declan."

# Epilogue

Three hours after the White House was incapacitated, President Rayburn and his contingent of Secret Service personnel stepped off of the K12 bus at the entrance to Andrews AFB. Many an odd look was flashed their way on the Metro's Green line out of DC. The glances were still present on the faces of the men standing guard at the main gate as his protection detail requested a vehicle to drive the POTUS the rest of the way in to Air Force One.

Upon arrival at the bunker located on site, Rayburn attempted to receive updates to no avail. There were surprisingly few details available as most of the White House had been hit by the EMP. He was even less pleased when he was told he had to wait in the command bunker until the cover of night.

"Has anyone been in touch with Sarkes? Do we know where he is yet?" Rayburn asked the assembled staff. The members looked around the room bewildered. The President sighed and said, "How about the SecDef?"

"Here, sir," the man said as he entered the bunker.

"Finally! Fielding!" the POTUS exclaimed. "What is going on? For a command post, we seem to be devoid of knowledge."

"Sorry I'm late, Mr. President. If you'd follow me, sir, I need to bring you up to speed," the Secretary of Defense replied.

The pair withdrew to a separate anti room and the SecDef placed a hard metal briefcase on a table. Once the door was shut, he entered the combination and opened it. Inside the hardened case sat a laptop. Once the device was opened, Fielding entered his twelve-digit password. Now unlocked, the screen contained a dozen thumbnail sized images.

Rayburn sat in the chair while Secretary Fielding stood behind him and narrated as the man pulled up each image.

"Going left to right and top to bottom, these high reconnaissance and satellite images you are about to see were current as of thirty minutes ago. Please select the first image," the SecDef ordered.

Rayburn tapped his finger on the screen and the icon expanded to cover the entire screen. In front of him was an image of the Atlantic Ocean. Embedded within were tiny red dots.

"Sir, if you look from the southern tip of Greenland and go southeast toward the U.K., you'll notice that just about every one of our SOSUS sonar arrays has seen a flurry of activity. Similar sensors have been tripped in the Pacific. Please close the photo and select the next."

"I thought those were decommissioned in the 90's?" Rayburn asked.

Fielding didn't answer. He just cocked a knowing eyebrow at the man. The President understood and turned back toward the monitor.

As the next image appeared full screen, again the Atlantic was displayed.

"See those islands about a thousand miles west of Portugal? Tap on them to zoom in, sir," Fielding instructed.

Jim Rayburn did and what he saw made him shiver. "How many ships have the analysts counted?"

"At present there are over two hundred. Unfortunately, more are on the way."

"From where?"

"Northern and Western Africa and the Mediterranean. What you're looking at represents the bulk of the British Isles and the Soviet Northern Fleet. The Dutch, French, and Spanish are en route so we should have some idea what their plan is as soon as they can get word out. There's another mass assembling in the Sea of Okhotsk just north of Japan. Once the Indian Fleet arrives, we'll know more there as well."

"How many ships do we have?"

"The U.S. Navy currently has three hundred ships at its disposal, give or take. Add in our allies' vessels and we are nearly seven. Almost a one-to-one ratio," the SecDef responded.

The pair worked their way through image after image until only one remained. It depicted the Gulf of St. Lawrence down to Quebec.

"What the hell are those!" Rayburn demanded.

"Sir, that's an amphibious assault ship and transport dock. The *HMS Ocean* and the *HMS Albion*. The *Ocean* is carrying a full complement of eight hundred Royal Marines, forty vehicles, and eighteen helos."

"Where are they going?"

The Secretary of Defense sighed and took a seat across the table from the President. He slowly closed the lid of the laptop as he contemplated his response. Fielding removed his glasses and cleaned them with his tie.

As he put them back on he answered. "Sir, they are headed to Cleveland."

"What about the Canadians? Can't we call the Canadian Prime Minister? Tell them to stop opening the locks and letting those ships through!"

"The PM reports to the crown, sir. They're in it whether they like it or not. Ohio just became a battleground state... in every sense of the word."

Thank you for reading *Foreign & Domestic, Part II – Hannibal is at the Gates*. I hope you will consider visiting the Amazon website to leave a review so others may know what you thought of the book and/or the series and to purchase the remaining installments in the series.

Other books by David J. Kershner:

*Foreign & Domestic, Part I – When Rome Stumbles*
*Foreign & Domestic, Part III – By the Dawn's Early Light*
*Foreign & Domestic, Part IV – Colder Weather*
*Foreign & Domestic, Part V – A Time for Reckoning*
*Just a Small Gathering*

Coming Soon:

*Home Remedies, Poultices, Salves, & Tinctures*
*Preparing to Prepare: A General Guide to Self-Sufficiency & Preparedness*